Bookworm II
The Very Ugly Duckling

ALSO BY CHRISTOPHER G. NUTTALL

Bookworm series
Bookworm

DIZZY SPELLS SERIES
A LIFE LESS ORDINARY

Royal Sorceress series
The Royal Sorceress
The Great Game

Inverse Shadows Universe
Sufficiently Advanced Technology

Bookworm II
The Very Ugly Duckling

Christopher G. Nuttall

Elsewhen Press

Bookworm II: The Very Ugly Duckling
First published in Great Britain by Elsewhen Press, 2014
An imprint of Alnpete Limited

Elsewhen Press, PO Box 757, Dartford, Kent DA2 7TQ
www.elsewhen.press

British Library Cataloguing in Publication Data.
A catalogue record for this book is available from the British Library.

ISBN 978-1-908168-28-3 Print edition
ISBN 978-1-908168-38-2 eBook edition

This book is a work of fiction. All names, characters, places, libraries, and events are either a product of the author's fertile imagination or are used fictitiously. Any resemblance to actual events, repositories, places or people (living, dead or undead) is purely coincidental.

To Peter, Laura and Faith Nuttall

Chapter One

The Witch-King, Elaine thought, *must have been out of his mind.*

She lifted her eyes from the small book on the table, resisting the urge to rub them in the hopes that certain memories would fade from her mind. She'd always had a good memory, even before the entire contents of the Great Library had been dumped into her head, but the Witch-King's spellbook was too horrifying to remember. Somehow, reading it naturally – rather than having the knowledge stored in her mind – made it worse. It was far too easy to see just how twisted he'd become by necromancy.

There were *laws* against reading such books, unless one happened to be the Grand Sorcerer. Elaine knew that many young magicians had chafed against such restrictions, assuming that the Grand Sorcerers had wanted to keep certain types of knowledge to themselves, but *she* understood perfectly. There were spells and forms of magic that were inherently corrupting, so much so that even using one of them *once* would taint a person for the rest of his or her life. If Elaine had had the power to make some of them work, she had a feeling that Lady Light Spinner would, with the greatest of regret, have ordered her execution. Even so, she was effectively a prisoner in the Great Library.

It wasn't something she resented, most of the time. She was, after all, one of the most important people in the Empire – and she had a seat on the Privy Council, which *controlled* the Empire. And she had the ear of the Grand Sorceress. But there were times when it gnawed at her, such as when she'd been asked to read the Witch-King's book and see if there were any hints as to his current location. Somehow, against all logic and common sense, the Witch-King was still alive. The gods alone knew where he might be hiding.

Elaine shivered, remembering the brief moment of mental

contact when she'd been trying to stop the maddened Kane from destroying the Golden City. In that instant, she had realised that the Witch-King was still alive, trapped as a lich – and quite insane. He was effectively immortal; he'd had literally hundreds of years to prepare his plans, while remaining hidden from even the most intensive probes. If he couldn't be found, Elaine suspected, he would simply start another plan that would take generations to come to fruition. How did one fight an enemy who could take so long to prepare his offensive? They might well miss the clues until it was far too late.

She looked back at the book and scowled. All magicians of real power – Elaine had very little, despite the knowledge in her head – kept a private spellbook, a tradition the Witch-King had honoured. Unsurprisingly, the spells had grown darker and darker the more she'd read, showing her how to control an army with her mind, corrupt a child or even create a horde of monsters from dead human flesh. She couldn't imagine why *anyone* would dare risk using any of those spells, but not everyone had her unique insight into how magic worked. Besides, corruption rarely set in immediately. Someone might use a mildly dark spell, then a slightly darker spell ... and, before they knew it, they were corrupted, thinking nothing of using the darkest of spells.

The book should be destroyed, she thought, although training and inclination mediated against it. The Black Vault existed for books that were judged too dangerous to be allowed to be copied and shared everywhere; surely, she had been told, the book would be safe there. But Elaine's very existence proved otherwise. If the Witch-King's book had been in the Black Vault, its knowledge would have been dumped into her head along with the rest of the Great Library.

She closed the book, placed it back in the box and concentrated for a long moment, muttering bespoke charms under her breath. Standard lock spells were one thing, but the spells she had devised herself were almost impossible to detect – or to open, without the right code. Even the most powerful of magicians should have had problems opening the box – and if they managed to crack through one spell by brute force, the second would incinerate the book. It was better that the book be reduced to ash, Elaine had told herself, than risk it falling into enemy hands. She hadn't told either Lady Light Spinner, the Grand Sorceress, or Inquisitor Dread about the precaution. It would only have upset them.

Standing, she picked up the box and placed it within a stack of others, each one completely indistinguishable from the rest. Only the Head Librarian could find anything within the Black Vault; even the most powerful magician in the world would have had problems, at least until he managed to bend the magic shaping and maintaining the pocket dimension to his will. *Elaine* could have done it, she thought, but few others could have managed such a feat. They would always be tempted to use raw power rather than subtle magic.

Shaking her head, she took a long look around the compartment. Massive bookshelves, bursting with books, ran for as far as the eye could see, each tome forbidden to the vast majority of the population. There were chests of papers belonging to the Grand Sorcerers, sealed away too so that their heirs could keep their knowledge to themselves, as well as books and artefacts that had been offered to the Grand Sorcerer by other magicians. The magic that shaped the Black Vault would keep everything preserved, Elaine knew. Generations could pass outside and the books would remain undamaged.

And hopefully unread, she told herself, as she stepped through the mirror and out into the unrestricted stacks. Mirrors served as gateways between the normal world and the pocket dimensions used to store the library's vast collection of books, but only one person could use them to access the Black Vault. Elaine smiled to herself as she felt the library's magic pulsing around her, closing the gateway, then started to walk towards her office. Moments later, she realised that she had a visitor. Inquisitor Dread.

"Inquisitor," she said, as she stepped into her office. "Make yourself at home."

She had to smile as she sat down facing the hooded man. There had been a time when she wouldn't have dared joke with an Inquisitor, when she wouldn't have wanted to face one ... but Dread was a friend, of sorts. And one of the very few who knew what had happened during the selection process for the Grand Sorcerer. Most of the world believed that the battle between contenders got out of control, wrecking large parts of the city. Elaine knew better.

"Elaine," Dread said. As always, his voice was near toneless. "I trust that you are prepared?"

Elaine blinked in surprise ... and then remembered. They had been scheduled to run a specific security check on the Great Library. And she'd almost been late! No one could have contacted her in the Black Vault, save for the Grand Sorceress.

"I think so," Elaine said. "Are *you* ready?"

Dread shrugged, one hand touching the burns on his face. "It wouldn't matter if I was bleeding out and dying," he said, flatly. "I'd still have a job to do."

Elaine nodded, closed her eyes and reached out with her mind. As always, the wards of the Great Library answered her, recognising their mistress. Elaine found the experience slightly disturbing; the Great Library's wards were old enough to have developed a certain intelligence of their own, something that gave them an odd sense of humour. Anyone who linked into the wards felt as if they were becoming part of the building itself.

No wonder Miss Prim fled the moment she could, Elaine thought, ruefully. *She must have hated being convinced that she had birds nesting in her hair.*

Pushing the disconcerting sensations aside, Elaine studied the wards carefully. Hundreds of sorcerers had created them, piece by piece; few of them had really understood what they were creating. The Witch-King, before his fall from grace, had been one of them. No wonder he had been able to slip a booby trap through the wards – and no wonder no one had expected anything of the sort! They'd thought that all the magicians who might have built themselves a secret password to get through the wards were dead.

Elaine shivered at the memory. Barely six months ago, she had been a normal librarian, one of many who worked in the Great Library. And then she'd picked up the book that had been carefully steered to her, the book that had been primed to channel all of the knowledge in the library into her mind.

And then things had *really* become complicated.

She smiled to herself as the wards flickered and danced around her. One thing the spell *had* done – something she doubted the Witch-King had meant it to do – was show her precisely how spells *really* worked. Most magicians used their raw power to cover up the gaps in their knowledge, doing it so naturally that they never really realised what they were doing. Elaine, on the other hand, had little power, but by disassembling spells and putting them back together again she was able to do much more than she *should* have been.

Carefully, she began to study how the Great Library's wards went together ... and swallowed a curse as she realised that there were more holes in the library's security than anyone had ever discovered. Most of them were countered by other wards, but someone with *real* knowledge might have been able to exploit them. She couldn't help wondering if there had been more thefts from the library than had ever been officially acknowledged. The librarians would be reluctant to admit failure when every ambitious magician would try to take advantage of the library's weakness.

All right, she told herself. *Here we go.*

Piece by piece, she shaped tiny spells in her mind and uploaded them into the library's wards, mapping them out *thoroughly*. By now, it would be impossible to disassemble the wards and recast them, no matter how much better they could have become with some careful fiddling and other improvements. They had simply become *part* of the library. But she could still make some improvements ...

She pulled herself out of the wards and opened her eyes, feeling drained. Unlike Miss Prim, her inherent magic wasn't strong enough to sustain the contact indefinitely, not when the wards drew on her as savagely as any other spell she knew. Dread would probably have been able to hold the contact for hours – the Inquisitors were chosen for magical strength as well as skill and bloody-mindedness – but the wards would have rejected him. The only other person who could have manipulated them was the Grand Sorceress.

"Ready," she said, as she sagged. Sweat was pouring down her back, despite the cool air. "The spell can be triggered at any time."

Dread nodded, one hand on his staff. "Do you want to do it now or wait until later?"

Elaine hesitated. On the one hand, she *was* exhausted – and really needed to get some sleep in her office to allow her magic to recharge. But on the other hand, she didn't want to have to do the whole process over again – and she would have to, if they delayed too long. The new spells she'd added to the wards wouldn't last indefinitely.

"I think so," she said. "Ready?"

Dread bowed his head in acknowledgement.

Elaine allowed herself a tired smile, then linked with the wards again, sending a final command into the network. She felt the wards shift as she fell out of the connection, her magic depleted so badly that she wouldn't have been able to light a candle, even with the newer lighting spells she'd developed personally. Not that it mattered; now that she'd given the order, the wards could do the rest on their own, sweeping the entire library for signs of unwanted dark magic – or other surprises. Light magic was associated with goodness, naturally, but there were plenty of ways light spells could be used to cause trouble.

"It's done," she said, as she collapsed into her seat. "The spells are searching now."

Dread put out a hand and squeezed hers, an odd gesture of affection from the Inquisitor. "I thank you," he said. "Now ... relax."

Elaine nodded, torn between watching as the wards searched the library and closing her eyes and trying to sleep. Standard search spells could locate an object within range very quickly, assuming they knew what they were actually looking *for*. The task she'd assigned to the library's wards was far harder. They were to locate and catalogue any magic that wasn't actually part of the library's protections and filing system, then report back to Elaine. There would probably be plenty of reports of various cheating spells used by students desperate to pass their exams, but she wasn't too worried about those. The real danger came from darker magic.

She had almost dozed off completely when the wards twitched against her mind. A moment later, a glowing image of the library appeared in front of them, showing the location of every spell and magical artefact that hadn't been cleared to enter the library. Elaine sucked in her breath when she saw the vast number of cheating spells and charmed note-takers. The Peerless School had always encouraged creative thinking and rule-bending, but surely there were limits.

"I shouldn't worry about it," Dread said. "Magic is all about looking for ways to cheat."

Elaine blinked in surprise. "You're advocating *cheating*?"

"Drawing information out of a book isn't cheating," Dread pointed out, dryly. "Neither is the use of memory potions to enhance one's recall. They are taught, after all, because someone might want to use them. Cheating is getting someone else to do the work and most of those spells won't help with that."

"I suppose," Elaine muttered, remembering her own schooling. There had been times when she'd been tempted to cheat, if it had been possible to cheat her way into a greater level of inherent magic. But that had been impossible – then. Now, she knew a thousand ways to boost her power ... and the terrible price they demanded. Sanity, for starters. "And that ...?"

Dread followed her pointing finger. "*That* isn't a standard method of cheating at all," he said. "That's a damned *compulsion* spell."

Elaine pressed her hands against the glowing image, trying to get it to focus in on the user. It turned out to be a seventeen-year-old girl preparing for her exams. Charity Conidian, Elaine recalled; one of the daughters of a Privy Councillor. Why would *she* want to cheat when it would reflect badly on her father? But the charm might not be her work at all.

"I'll ask Vane to bring her into my office," Elaine said, as she staggered to her feet. "You can interview her there without disturbing the other students."

Vane obeyed without question. Elaine's deputy wasn't a good librarian – she certainly lacked the obsession with books that had driven Elaine when she was younger – but she was good at dealing with people, a quality that Elaine lacked. Her smile, undoubted power and family connections allowed her to handle the library's staff and visitors, leaving Elaine to work on managing the library's collection and writing her own spellbook.

"Draw some energy from the wards," Dread advised, as Elaine yawned. "You might need it."

Elaine shook her head. The library's wards simply didn't work that way.

Charity Conidian proved to be the sort of girl that Elaine had hated, back when she'd been in school. Beautiful, rich, well-connected ... and actually good at her studies. Long blonde hair framed a heart-shaped face that was probably the result of endless cosmetic charms – or so Elaine told herself. Charity reminded her of Millicent, before Kane had almost destroyed her mind. Six months later, Millicent still hadn't recovered completely.

"Good afternoon," Dread said, lifting his wand. The girl's eyes went wide, but he had the compulsion spell off her before it could force her to do anything drastic. "Who put that spell on you?"

"My father," Charity said. Very few people would be stupid enough to lie to an Inquisitor. "I asked him to do it."

Elaine stared at her. Compulsion spells were not exactly illegal, but using one on someone without a very good reason was likely to get the magician in hot water. And using one on one's own daughter? The books in Elaine's head told her that it had happened before, in far more detail than she'd ever wanted to know. *None* of the reasons were very good.

"Your father, the Conidian, put a basic compulsion spell on you," Dread said. He didn't sound as if he believed her either. "Why?"

Charity sagged. "I was having problems keeping up with my studies," she admitted, "and father promised me an establishment of my own if I graduated in the top ten. But I just couldn't concentrate! So I went to him and asked him for the charm."

Elaine and Dread shared a glance. As far as she knew – and thanks to the Witch-King her memory went back as far as the foundation of the Empire itself – that was unprecedented.

She found herself giving the girl a look of mild respect. Actually *going* to someone and asking them to use such a charm, just to help them study? Elaine couldn't decide if it was a stroke of genius or absolute madness.

"Compulsion charms can be dangerous," Dread said, "*particularly* if someone accepted them voluntarily. I suggest that you learn to master the art of studying *without* such help."

He scowled at her. "And your father will hear from me about it," he added. "He should know better than to use such charms on his daughter."

Charity bowed her head, then retreated from the office.

"Well," Dread said, once the door was closed. "*That* was a fine waste of time."

"Maybe," Elaine said. The Conidian served on the Privy Council, after all. She had a feeling that she hadn't heard the last of the whole affair. "But at least we know the monitoring system works now."

"Yes," Dread said. "Until someone else finds a new way to break in."

Chapter Two

"Well?"

Johan Conidian winced at his father's tone as he eyed the druid. He'd faced his father furious about something Johan had done, but the note of pleading – desperate pleading – in his voice was worse. His father was a powerful magician, with enough political power to earn himself a seat on the Privy Council; he shouldn't have to beg or plead for good news. And yet there was no mistaking the plea in his voice.

The druid eyed Johan sadly, then turned his attention to Johan's father. "I'm afraid that there is still no trace of magic in his body," he said, flatly. "Nor are there any signs that he will develop it later in life."

Johan couldn't help a wince. He came from a family that had magic running through its veins, one where his siblings had started developing their powers before they even reached their teens. But he had no magic at all ... and, it seemed, no hope of developing it. In a world where magical power meant political power, he was a cripple. If he'd been born into a mundane family, he would never have known what he was missing. But he was part of the Conidian family ...

The sight of his father made him wince again. The Conidian was as tall as his son, but he looked tough, the sort of man who would never back down from a challenge, while Johan had inherited a slimmer build from his mother. His father's hair was turning grey; Johan's was still brown. And his father wore the fine robes of a Privy Councillor while Johan wore nothing but a drab black suit. A reminder, if any were needed, that he would never be more than a mundane freak who just happened to have magical relatives.

Most of his family pitied magical children who were born to mundane families. How awful it must be for them, his aunts and uncles had tittered, to know that they were far above their parents, let alone their non-magical siblings. But the jokes had long since stopped being funny, not to Johan. It was far worse to be the sole mundane in a family of magicians.

"I have run extensive tests," the druid said, pointing to the array of devices he'd brought with him. Hiring the services of such a capable and well-known druid had cost the Conidian a pretty penny. "There is simply no trace of independent magic within Johan's body. He doesn't even seem to absorb background magic, despite living in a highly-magical environment. I'm afraid, sir, that you're just raising false hopes and wasting money."

Johan clenched his fists at the pity in the man's tone. But the druid was right; if he'd had the slightest trace of magic in his blood, the background magic of the wards protecting House Conidian should have been drawn to him. Instead, being in the colossal house was almost like being in prison. He could not leave the building or do any one of a multitude of other tasks without asking one of his parents or siblings to do it for him. His parents did it, reluctantly. But his brothers and sisters were far more unpleasant about it.

"It isn't unknown for people to develop magic comparatively late in life," the druid continued. "However, in most such cases, the *potential* for magic already exists, waiting to be triggered."

The Conidian leaned forward. "Is there *nothing* that can help him?"

Johan felt a stab of pain through his heart. He *was* a cripple – and his father was growing desperate to have him develop magic, any magic. Once, he'd read a handful of the darker tomes in his father's private library, searching for something that would help him. But all he had learned was just how dangerous some magical rituals could be. And, for that matter, just how angry his father could become. Magical tomes were not to be shared with non-magicians.

"There are rituals that can enhance one's magic," the druid admitted, reluctantly. "However, in all known cases, they require a spark of magic to work. Johan could not perform even the first set of spells. And, even if he could, he would be risking insanity. Those rituals are immensely dangerous."

His eyes seemed to narrow for a long chilling moment.

"And research into what separates a magician from a mundane has long been banned," he added. "I would not advise you to start asking too many questions."

Johan turned away, unable to bear the pity in the man's eyes. Everyone knew that magic was the gift of the gods, everyone knew that those who had magic were favoured by the gods ... which didn't, in his view, explain why so many magicians were bullies or patronising assholes. To be born without magic was to be automatically lower on the social scale, no matter one's birthright. He could be related to the long-gone Imperial Family and his lack of magic would still drag him down.

It's not fair, he thought, bitterly. *They have all the power and I have none.*

No one knew quite how magic worked. Some magicians were born of magical family lines, others – for no apparent reason – appeared among mundane families. The priests claimed that the former were from divinely-blessed families and the latter were saints in the making, but Johan had his suspicions about those claims. His father donated a great deal of money to several of the larger temples and he knew that other magical families did the same. Why would the priests offend their paymasters by *not* promoting their interests?

And, just as no one knew why magic sometimes appeared in non-magical bloodlines, no one knew why magic had skipped Johan.

Johan had heard too many theories as he grew older and it became apparent that he would never be able to cast a single spell. His father and mother had argued long into the night about his parentage before certain spells had been cast, proving that the Conidian was indeed his father. Some of his siblings had suggested that Johan had been really rude to the gods in a past life ... or that he was just a freak, a monster in human form. A Powerless ...

And he *was* powerless.

He watched as the druid packed up his tools, slotting them all into a tiny bag he wore at his belt. Once, the sight would have fascinated him; the bag was tiny, yet it was large enough on the inside to take all the equipment that a druid might need at any moment. Now, it was just depressing. He could use such artefacts, but he would never be able to make them for himself or even modify the ones he bought. Nor, for that matter, would he ever be a druid. Who would want a mundane doctor when a druid could heal most wounds in a matter of minutes?

"My Lord," the druid said, once he had finished packing. "I do offer my sympathies."

The Conidian rose and escorted the druid out of his study, leaving Johan behind. It was rare for any of his children to be left alone in their father's workspace – he normally kept it locked and sealed with powerful wards – and Johan couldn't help finding it ominous. Sure, he couldn't open any of the sealed chests to read his father's private papers, but it was still worrying. It suggested that his father wanted to have a few words with him after the druid was safely out of the house.

Muttering curses under his breath, Johan rose to his feet and looked around. His father had only bought the house after the disastrous events of six months ago – Johan had never been given a clear explanation of why the investiture of the Grand Sorceress had gone so badly wrong, with hundreds of magicians killed – but he had already managed to make the room seem his own. A handful of portraits of his children dotted one wall, a set of awards given to him by various sycophants were pinned to another; the final two walls were covered in bookshelves, protected by additional wards. Johan reached out and felt his fingers skittering across the wards, gently repelled from touching the books. His father had said, back when they were moving in, that the books were off-limits to everyone, even his eldest son. Trying to break into his father's study was a guaranteed thrashing.

Not that it matters to me, Johan thought, feeling the bitterness growing stronger. *I couldn't even begin to take down the wards.*

He heard his father's measured tread and hastily sat back down. The Conidian was normally a very controlled man, but Johan knew that he was growing increasingly frustrated – and desperate – by his son's condition. Johan knew that he couldn't help it, but who else was there for his father to blame? The gods knew that his mother was not only innocent of adultery, she was a powerful magician in her own right. But Johan ...? Johan was defenceless.

The door opened and his father stepped in, closing the door firmly behind him. Johan shivered, despite himself. The last time his father had been so ... *controlled* had been just after a practical joke had gone spectacularly wrong, landing all of his sons in hot water. It had been a painful evening for them all. But now ... Johan didn't *think* that he'd done anything bad, yet he still shivered. He knew just how disappointed his father was with his son's lack of magic.

"I'm sorry," he said, quickly. "I wish ..."

"So do I," the Conidian admitted. For a moment, his control slipped. "So do I."

Johan took a breath. "Father ... I would like to apply for a position in the Civil Service," he said, hoping that his father would be sympathetic. "I'm sixteen, old enough to take up an apprenticeship or strike out on my own. There are jobs there that I could do, after all the tutoring you gave me ..."

It had been impossible, of course, for Johan to go to the Peerless School. That school was for magicians only – and, according to Johan's brother, weak magicians had a hellish time of it while they were trying to study. The strong preyed on the weak; Johan had listened in horror as Jamal had laughed about turning weaker students into frogs, or casting compulsion charms on them and embarrassing them in front of the whole school. He and his cronies even joked about tricking girls into using stripping spells on themselves. If a weak magician found it hard, he knew that a mundane would find it impossible to survive ... and no mundane could pass any of the magical exams.

The Conidian had been sympathetic to his son's desire for education, but he had flatly refused to send Johan to any of the mundane schools. Instead, he had hired mundane tutors, who had given Johan lessons in everything from reading and writing to history and politics. Johan had learned more than he wanted to know about how the Empire worked ... and about how those without magic were often denied a chance to reach the very highest levels. But there *were* plenty of jobs for mundanes, particularly in the Civil Service. If he had been able to travel, he might have found his existence more bearable.

"I'm afraid that is out of the question," the Conidian said. There was a certain amount of understanding in his tone, but also a great deal of inflexibility. "You are a scion of the Conidian Family and you should not be ..."

"Doing what?" Johan snapped, interrupting his father as his temper flared. He could count on the fingers of one hand the number of times he had dared be disrespectful of his father, let alone talk over him, but he was too angry to care. "Which part of the family business can I run?"

His father's eyes darkened with rage, although he held himself under tight control. But Johan knew, whatever his father might say, that there was no way he could take over part of the family business. The magicians who had allied themselves with his father would not respect a powerless mundane, no matter his lineage. And the agreements that bound them all together wouldn't respond to Johan at all. In some ways, he had freedoms that none of his siblings would ever know. But the price was really too high.

"You would not be ill-treated," the Conidian said, finally. "But I cannot allow you to leave the family."

Johan winced. Powerless – children born to magical families without magic of their own – were vanishingly rare; indeed, their existence had been considered rumour until Johan himself had been born. He suspected, given how many problems his existence had caused his family, that other powerless had simply been killed or abandoned as soon as it became clear that they weren't going to develop magic. There were times when Johan wished that he'd been given up for adoption as a child. He would quickly have forgotten his roots, leaving him *happy*.

"Father," he said, knowing that he was pleading, "I want to do something *useful*."

"I cannot allow you to strike out on your own," his father said, flatly. He held up a hand before Johan could say a word. "I do understand how you feel, but there are obligations that come from being part of House Conidian and you must respect them."

Johan felt tears of anger and frustration forming at the

corner of his eyes. "What do I get from being part of the family?" He demanded. "I am constantly reminded of my own weakness, my own *failure*! There hasn't been a week when my *powerful* brothers and sisters don't play jokes on their powerless wreck of a brother. I can't even leave the house without permission!"

He stood up and started to pace, fighting the urge to flee before he started crying openly. "What sort of life do I have when even the maids and cooks have more power than I?"

"Go to your room," his father said, softly. "We can talk about finding you another tutor ..."

Johan spun around to face his father. "What good does it do to study when I will never be able to *use* that knowledge?"

"There are people who say that learning is its own reward," his father pointed out.

"*That* is not part of the family heritage," Johan snapped. Part of his mind realised that he was being incredibly rude to his father, but he was too far gone to care. "We have spent the last five generations building up wealth, building up a patronage network that has ensured us the support of hundreds of weaker magicians and given us the chance to establish ourselves firmly among the elite of the Empire. Ambition runs in our blood. Everything we learn is put to use, not hoarded away ..."

His father sighed. "Johan ..."

"But I will remain here for the rest of my life," Johan thundered. "A prisoner ... no, a *pet*. I won't be able to find a wife; will you buy one for me? And if we have mundane *powerless* children, what will you do with them? Will you keep us all as one happy family of prisoners?"

His father lifted a hand in a spell-casting pose, then dropped it back to his knee. "Out," he ordered. He had never used magic to discipline his children, but there was always a first time. "Now."

Johan turned and stormed out, slamming the door behind him.

***

Duncan Conidian watched his son leave, feeling his anger drain away into pity ... and sadness. He wasn't good with showing love and affection; the endless lust for power and position that ran through the blood – as Johan had correctly identified – made it harder for him to spend time with his children. Indeed, he'd relied on his wife to bear and raise them while he concentrated on the family's ambitions. It had ensured that his relationship with his children wasn't as strong as it should have been.

But how could he have developed a strong relationship with Johan? His son was right; he *was*, to all intents and purposes, a prisoner in House Conidian. Duncan did understand why Johan wanted to be something else, something *significant* ... and there *were* positions for talented young men, even if they were powerless. And if Johan had been born to a mundane family, Duncan had no doubt that he would have risen high in the ranks, even earning the respect of magicians.

"But he's my son," he muttered, remembering with shame his reaction when he first realised that he'd sired a Powerless. He'd accused his wife of adultery, a row that had turned into a blazing magical duel that could easily have killed both of them. Even now, their relationship was fragile. "He would still have our blood."

It was blood that tied families together; Johan, powerless though he was, still shared the same blood as the rest of his family. If he were to be captured by a magician, that magician would be able to use his blood against House Conidian ... and, as Johan had no defences, there would be no way for him to save himself. Johan had to be protected because he couldn't protect himself, which meant that he couldn't be allowed to go far from the house. It was unfortunate, but there was no choice.

Johan hated it when his older brother made him humiliate himself, or when his younger sister turned him into a doll. And how could anyone blame him for such hatred? But such tricks, cruel as they were, paled in comparison to what a genuinely evil magician could do. Johan was sheltered, too sheltered. He had no idea what dangers might be lurking outside, beyond the wards.

I'm sorry, Duncan thought, *but there is no choice.*

There was a tap at the door. "My Lord," a maid said,

"there is an Inquisitor at the door."

Duncan sighed. Inquisitors were always bad news.

"I'm coming," he said. There was no way he was going to show an Inquisitor his study. "Show him into the Reception Room to wait."

The maid bowed her head, then left the room.

Chapter Three

After Dread had left, Elaine walked back through the Great Library to her own quarters and passed through the wards with a sigh of relief. Miss Prim had left so quickly that she'd abandoned almost all of her possessions; Elaine had had most of them stored, but she hadn't had the heart to remove a handful of paintings of the countryside hundreds of miles from the Golden City. It had taken her some time to realise just how trapped Miss Prim had felt in the Great Library; the paintings had been all she'd had to remind her of the open world outside its walls.

Shaking her head, she sealed the wards behind her and walked over to the large mirror. It had been a gift from Daria, who had told her that she should *try* to develop a little vanity now that she was not only a mature woman, but one of the most politically powerful magicians in the Empire. She stood in front of the mirror and eyed herself, noting the long brown hair that framed a mousy face – cute was the best she could hope for, rather than beautiful. Her soft brown eyes looked almost sad ...

Irritated, Elaine waved a hand in front of her face, cancelling the glamour. The brown eyes vanished, replaced by bright red orbs that looked utterly inhuman. There was no trace of anything but red light, no matter how closely she looked. The strange sense of ... *taint* that hung over her magic like an oil slick returned at the same moment, as if it wasn't there until she looked for it. It bothered her more than she wanted to admit, she knew; if she'd been a more powerful magician, she had the feeling that the taint would do more than give her headaches and strange burning sensations on a regular basis.

Touched by uncontrolled magic, she thought, as she replaced the glamour. It was hardly uncommon for magicians – male or female – to use glamours to conceal unwanted warts or acne, but she knew just how badly others would respond to bright red eyes. Back at the Peerless School, removing glamours had been a common practical joke. Her glamour was much stronger than anything a teenage magician should be able to produce and it still bothered her when she was out in public. Anyone who had been touched so badly by uncontrolled magic tended to be suspected of everything from dark rituals to demon-summoning.

She would have liked to stay in the library for the rest of the day, but she knew that she had to go to the Imperial Palace. Besides, she wasn't too sure if the impulse to remain where she was came from her own mind or from her bond to the library. The Great Library was old enough for the wards to mutate and develop quirks of their own, just like most of the other ancient buildings in the Golden City. Many of them, however, had been destroyed during Kane's rampage. The city was still rebuilding, six months later.

And some of the scars will never heal, she thought, as she pulled on her cloak and left her quarters, walking up through the library to the sole exit. Her staff nodded politely to her as she passed; most of them, thankfully, were newcomers, rather than men and women who remembered her as the mere assistant she'd been before Miss Prim's departure. But then, so many magicians had been killed that the former staff had had a chance to get better jobs elsewhere in the Golden City. It still amused her to think that she might have been promoted anyway ...

No, she knew that was nonsense. Without her, Kane – and through him the Witch-King – would have taken the Empire for himself. No matter how much she tried to hide from it, she was no longer a non-entity. She was the Bookworm, the Head Librarian and a member of the Privy Council ... and she still wanted to run and hide whenever the great and good turned their attention in her direction.

Outside, the air was cool, reminding her that winter was drawing near. There had already been snowfalls to the north, she knew; this winter was going to be harder than any other in living memory. The Golden City had once been protected from the worst of the weather by powerful spells, embedded into the buildings over countless generations. Kane had destroyed them, accidentally or otherwise, and no one – not even Elaine – had been able to find a way to replace them quickly. The Grand Sorceress was already making preparations for the coming winter, but few others took the threat seriously. How could they when everyone knew that it was always summer in the Golden City?

The weather should tell them, Elaine thought, sourly. The young men and women on the streets had taken to wearing longer robes and dresses, rather than the scandalously short outfits they'd been wearing only five months ago. No one outside the Privy Council *really* knew what had happened during the contest to select the next Grand Sorcerer, but the devastation had loosened the bonds of society. Elaine honestly couldn't decide if that was a good or bad thing.

She hesitated as she turned the corner and approached the Imperial Palace. It was easily the largest – on the outside – building in the Golden City, surrounded by gardens that called attention to the Emperor's wealth and power. Living space was at a premium in the city hemmed in as it was by mountain ranges. To have a private garden – and a building that didn't make use of transdimensional magical engineering to be bigger on the inside than the outside – was conspicuous consumption on a grand scale. Almost everyone else, no matter how wealthy and powerful they were, had to make do with tiny patches of land, if that.

The Palace was surrounded by a handful of young men and women, yelling slogans as they marched to and fro under the watchful eyes of the guards. Levellers, Elaine realised; mundanes who wished a greater share in government. Kane's attack hadn't just loosened the social bonds; he'd also weakened the faith in the system that kept it going. Right now, mundanes were asking if they could really trust the Grand Sorceress to keep the rest of the magicians in line. Elaine honestly wasn't sure what to make of that either.

It was hard for her to walk forward and up to the gates. She had never liked company, and the pressure of the crowd, even composed of non-magicians, pushed at her composure. By the time she stepped through the wards and started to walk up to the palace, she was trembling, even though she knew that there was no reason to fear. She might have been a weak magician, but she had been able to protect herself even before she'd become a Bookworm and started to unlock some of the true secrets of magic.

She missed Daria dreadfully, she realised, as she stepped through the doors and into the palace. Her friend had always boosted her confidence, telling her to keep chugging on despite her fears and near-panics. And now Daria was off on a mission that even Elaine knew little about, leaving Elaine all alone. She knew she could talk to Dread – the Inquisitor always had time for her, despite the pressures of his job – but there were few other friends in her life. Most of the people who had introduced themselves to her after she'd been raised to the Privy Council had clearly wanted to use her, rather than know her.

The Imperial Palace felt ... *strange*. It was a magical building, yet the magic was blurred with the mundane to a degree that would have puzzled her, if she hadn't known more about its history than anyone else. There had been plenty of non-magicians in the long-gone Imperial Line; hell, the last Emperor hadn't been a magician, which explained what had happened to him during the Necromantic Wars. Unlike the Great Library or any of the Aristocratic Houses, it wasn't designed to bond with just one person, but with an entire family line. And that family line was gone.

There were always rumours of heirs, Elaine knew. But none of them had ever proven real.

No guards blocked her path as she made her way down the corridor and into the Reception Room. Lady Light Spinner, Grand Sorceress and unquestioned ruler of the Empire, was her own best protection. Elaine knew, without a shadow of a doubt, that Light Spinner could have beaten the old Elaine without raising a sweat ... and maybe even the new Elaine, if she had no time to prepare. The magic crackling around her figure was a warning to would-be challengers. This was the magician who was considered the most powerful in the world.

She was taller than Elaine, her features hidden behind a black veil that concealed everything apart from her eyes. Elaine was one of the very few people who knew what lurked behind the veil – and of the terrible price Light Spinner had paid for her mastery of magic. If others knew ... some would be impressed, Elaine suspected, and others would call for her immediate execution. Elaine had a feeling that Light Spinner's own experience had helped her acceptance of Elaine's warped eyes.

"You missed the meeting," Light Spinner said, as she waved a hand in the air. A comfortable chair materialised in front of the Grand Sorceress's desk, waiting for Elaine. "I could have done with another voice."

Elaine felt herself flush, even though there was droll amusement rather than condemnation in Light Spinner's voice. No matter how important or powerful she had become, she would *never* feel at ease addressing the great and powerful. There were times when she found it hard to talk to Dread, even though they were friends ... or as close as an Inquisitor could become to being friends with anyone.

"I'm sorry," she said, bowing her head. "I ..."

Light Spinner snorted. "I shouldn't worry too much about it," she said. "There were complaints about the Levellers and complaints about Hawthorne. I found the latter to be far more serious."

"I know," Elaine said. "Is there still no trace of him?"

Light Spinner's head moved, slightly. "The Inquisitors are still searching for him," she said. "They have found nothing."

Elaine wasn't surprised. Hawthorne was a Dark Wizard, a rogue who had set himself up as the ruler of a handful of villages nearly a thousand miles from the Golden City. The Inquisitors had captured him and liberated his territory, dragging him back in chains to face the previous Grand Sorcerer, but he had died before Hawthorne could stand trial. And then, in the chaos caused by Kane's offensive, Hawthorne had managed to escape and flee into the countryside. There were rumours of his presence everywhere, but no hard information.

It only added to the unease spreading through the Empire, she knew. No one apart from Light Spinner knew just how many Inquisitors there were, but everyone knew that the Inquisitors had taken heavy losses in the battle with Kane.

Right now, there were a hundred problem cases that had to be stamped on before they got out of hand, but Light Spinner barely had the manpower to deal with half of them. And the longer they were allowed to fester, the harder it would be to deal with them.

"I've had to pull the Inquisitors out of Ida," Light Spinner added. "They found nothing there too."

Elaine hesitated, trying to think of the words that would convince Light Spinner to change her mind. But she knew that it would be futile. Unravelling the mysteries surrounding Ida was important – it might lead them to the Witch-King – yet keeping the Empire intact was also important. Chaos would provide an opportunity for him to keep manipulating events until the entire web simply fell apart.

She gritted her teeth in frustration. Just *how* did one fight an opponent like that?

"I did send Princess Sacharissa back to take the throne," Light Spinner reminded her. "With her father in chains, I'm sure we can rely on her to obey."

"Out of gratitude, not fear," Elaine commented. Princess Sacharissa had been her father's tool rather than his daughter, destined to be married off to enhance her father's status among the other kings and princes of the realm. There had been no love lost between father and daughter, Elaine knew, even before it had become clear that the girl's brother and half-brother were part of the Witch-King's web. "But I think she will miss Dread."

"I have no doubt of it," Light Spinner said, bluntly. "But the needs of the Empire come first."

Elaine nodded, feeling a twinge of sympathy for the older woman. Light Spinner had worked to gain power – and, as the Empire's structure dictated, responsibility. Right now, *she* was the law of the land; if she chose to alter the Empire's laws, there were few who would dare to say no. Elaine would never have sought such a position, even assuming that she could have held a lower position against ambitious subordinates long enough to climb higher. It would have kept her firmly in the public eye.

"I saw the Levellers outside," she said, changing the

subject. "Are you going to do anything about them?"

Light Spinner shrugged. "There's no point in doing *anything* about them," she said, snidely. "What can they do to us?"

Elaine had to smile, although she managed to conceal it a moment later. Light Spinner was Millicent's aunt – and Millicent had never been very good at handling critical remarks from those she considered beneath her. She would *never* have ignored the Levellers, even if they were powerless mundanes. It was far more likely that she would have sent out the City Guard to arrest and enslave them.

But Elaine knew that Light Spinner was right. It was true that mundanes couldn't pose much of a threat to magicians, yet harsh action might well rebound on her. Mundanes who happened to hold important posts might take offence, while the more forward-thinking magicians in the city might start worrying about who she would lash out at next. Elaine had never considered that the Grand Sorcerer was constrained, not until she'd been invited to join the Privy Council. Building the Empire had taken centuries; destroying it would take mere years, if the Grand Sorcerer became a tyrant.

Light Spinner looked up at her, suddenly. The magic field shifted, drawing Elaine's attention towards her. *This* was the meat of the matter, she realised; *this* was why she'd been summoned. Fighting the compulsion to pay attention was difficult, almost impossible. But somehow she held her own.

"We are critically short of magicians in all categories," Light Spinner said, bluntly. "Quite apart from Inquisitors, we need warders, enchanters, curse-breakers and alchemists. We may have to start widening our net when it comes to recruiting new magicians."

Elaine swallowed, knowing just how much tradition Light Spinner was talking about throwing away. Unless they were powerful or wealthy, common-born magicians often received very limited training rather than attending the Peerless School. Elaine herself wouldn't have been able to attend without someone paying her fees. The gods knew that her Guardian hadn't been willing to pay more than the bare minimum for her.

"We may also need to teach them some of *your* magic

tricks," Light Spinner added. "Do you think that you could teach a class?"

"I'm not sure," Elaine confessed, finally. "It might be possible."

She *had* worked on improving the basic spells, but actually explaining how magic spells actually went together? Writing her own spellbook would be the work of years, even with her new and unique insights. But she could understand why Light Spinner wanted the information. Many of the new magicians would be on the same level as herself, at least when it came to raw magic.

But she didn't want to face a class. She had enough problems facing two or three people at once.

"I can try to work out a basic syllabus," she said, wincing at the thought of how the Spell Masters at the Peerless School would respond to her work. One of those who had tried to hammer spellwork into her head had been given, she saw now, to pushing too much power into his spells. They had worked, but they lacked the elegance that allowed her to save power. "But I don't know how well they will work for new students."

She'd tried to teach Dread a few spells, knowing that the Inquisitor was used to controlling himself. But even *he* had been unable to master the modified spell.

"I may have you try to teach one or two new students," Light Spinner mused. "Because we *are* critically short of personnel."

Elaine scowled at the reminder. It was her duty to try, even if she didn't know if she would succeed. But then, that was true of just about everyone these days.

"I'll do my best," she promised. "When do you want me to start?"

"We are currently combing the countryside for new recruits," Light Spinner said. "But many of the more promising ones will have a great deal to unlearn."

Elaine nodded, then stopped as she sensed a sudden change in the magic field. For a moment, she thought that Light Spinner was calling on her magic, before she realised that the source was outside the Palace's wards. A second later, there was a sudden pulse of magic ...

... And then nothing. The field just seemed to snap back to normal.

She found her voice. "What ... what was *that*?"

"I don't know," Light Spinner said. She sounded as disturbed as Elaine felt. "But I think we had better find out."

Chapter Four

"I think I'd better run," Charity said. "That Inquisitor is here because of me."

Johan blinked. He could easily imagine an Inquisitor coming for Jamal – his older brother was an asshole, plain and simple – but Charity? His sister was sweet, innocent and determined to do well at her studies. And, unlike most of his other siblings, she hardly ever played magical pranks on her powerless brother.

"You?"

"Father gave me a spell to help me study," Charity said, as she stood up and headed towards the door. "But I think I want to give father time to cool down before I face him."

"I'll come with you," Johan said, picking up his coat. He'd hoped to talk to Charity, even if she didn't really understand what he went through on a daily basis. But now ... maybe he could spend some time away from home too. "Where are we going?"

"I thought I'd go see my boyfriend," Charity said. She gave him an understanding look as he flushed, brightly. "But I'll help you get out of the house."

Johan scowled inwardly as they walked downstairs and stopped in front of the door, just long enough for Charity to cast the charm that unlocked it and allowed them to leave the house. A mundane – or a powerless – would be trapped without a magician to open the door; Johan knew, no matter what his father said, that he was effectively a prisoner. Outside, hardly anyone knew of his existence. The family rarely mentioned him to any of their friends, even their closest allies. It would be an admission of weakness in the family bloodline that they could ill afford.

Outside, it was chillier than he had expected, but he couldn't help feeling a sensation of freedom that more than compensated for the cold. Away from the house, he told himself, he could just blend into the mundane population. They would never know that he was a Conidian – and neither would anyone else. He would just be another teenage boy wandering the streets.

"Here," Charity said. She passed him a handful of silver coins. "I'll be expecting them repaid, sooner or later."

"Thank you," Johan said, genuinely touched. He was given an allowance by his father, but – unlike the rest of his siblings – he was unable to look after it for himself. The one time he had, it had been stolen by Jamal and spent on sweets. "I'll pay you back tonight."

Charity waved as she walked off in one direction; Johan hesitated, then walked in the opposite direction, heading away from her. If their father decided to use tracking spells to find them, at least they wouldn't be together. And it was more likely that he would go after Charity first. Johan had no idea what spell their father might have given her, but if an Inquisitor had turned up it had to be bad.

The sense of freedom grew stronger as he turned into a shopping alley and walked down, passing countless people as they thronged through the city. Despite the weather, many of them wore traditional clothes from their part of the Empire, some of them completely covered and others barely wearing anything at all. Johan had to remind himself not to stare; unlike his other brothers, he had few opportunities to meet girls. Who would want to marry a powerless?

He bought himself a sweet treat from a vendor and walked onwards, nibbling at it and trying to make it last. Charity had given him a surprising amount of money, but he would still need to eat dinner ... unless he went home early. But his father would be raging and Johan didn't want to face him any sooner than strictly necessary. Instead, he found himself walking towards the Imperial Palace, feeling a flicker of bitter envy. If he'd been born a magician, like the rest of his family, he might have one day risen to be Grand Sorcerer. But instead, he would always be below the rest of them – and everyone else who had magic. The thought tormented him as he turned to look at the gates. There was a small crowd gathered outside, shouting slogans and trying to pull onlookers into their protest.

Puzzled, Johan stepped closer. His father had muttered things about protest movements and other insecurities in the wake of ... whatever had happened to reduce part of the city to rubble, but he hadn't gone into detail. Jamal had been sneering, of course, and Johan had long since learned not to pay attention to Jamal's sneering. It inevitably turned into an attack on his younger and powerless brother. Johan found it hard to understand why Jamal, who would inherit their father's position even if his brother hadn't been powerless, was such an asshole, but maybe it came from his sense of entitlement. Whatever Jamal wanted, Jamal got. Even the occasional thrashing from their father hadn't been enough to cure him of his tendency to bully.

"Hey," a young voice said. "You want one of these?"

Johan turned to see a young lady, wearing a green dress that exposed the tops of her breasts. He found himself tongue-tied as she smiled at him, then pressed a piece of paper into his hand. Johan took it automatically, then watched as she twirled away and headed towards the next curious onlooker. Someone must have charmed her dress, he realised; it clung to her in all the right places, but hinted at her curves rather than revealed. Charity had had something similar until their mother had seen her and thrown a fit.

He tore his gaze away from the girl and looked down at the piece of paper. It was surprisingly simple – and seditious. It asked, openly, why rule by magicians was the natural order; why should those without magic be governed by those with magic? Where was the justice, it asked, in granting one group of people power over others? After all, the writer went on to say, a strong man was not automatically considered superior to all other men.

Johan knew what his father would say if he read the paper. He would be openly sarcastic, mocking the writer for daydreaming of a world without magic. What was the old joke? The human race was improved when a swordsman took up arms against a magician, no matter the outcome. A swordsman would be quickly killed by any capable magician ... and if the magician was killed himself, he was clearly too stupid or weak to use magic. It would be a very poor magician who lost to a swordsman.

"There is no magic in the Iron Dragons that take people from kingdom to kingdom," a voice thundered. Johan turned to see a blonde-haired man, standing on a box and addressing the crowd. "There is no magic in the aqueducts that supply the Empire with water. There is no magic in the printing presses that provide us with our reading material. There is no magic ..."

Johan listened, feeling oddly hopeful. It was true; magic was powerful, but it was not the be-all and end-all of existence. The gods knew that he had tried to find out how one worked on the Iron Dragons, although his father had dismissed the possibility the one time he'd brought it up. He was simply too blue-blooded to work on the lines, his father had said, years ago. It wasn't until he'd grown older that he'd realised that his father wouldn't allow him to work anywhere.

"They call us *mundane*," the man thundered. "They call us *powerless*! They call us *nothing*! And yet it is us who run the Empire. The Grand Sorceress could not control her realm without the mundanes who work for her and her council. Why, then, are we powerless?"

His voice lowered. "Because they have *power*," he said. "But we are far from powerless.

"We trusted in the Grand Sorcerers to protect us from the dark magicians, those who would abuse their powers. But they have *failed*. Only six months ago, countless people – magicians and so-called mundanes – were slaughtered at what should have been the investiture of the new Grand Sorcerer. What happened on that day? We do not know! All we know is that thousands of people died!"

Johan nodded. His father had never been able to get a clear answer as to what had happened in the Golden City, nor – to the best of his knowledge – had anybody else. Jamal had snidely remarked that the contest had clearly gotten out of hand and, for once, Johan was inclined to agree with his elder brother. But if the contest had been so dangerous, why not hold it somewhere well away from innocent civilians? Even if the powerless were dismissed, the gods alone knew how many magicians had died.

"And we don't even know why," the speaker hissed.

"Why, then, should we trust them?"

A very good question, Johan thought. He knew a whole family of magicians – and most of them delighted in tormenting the sole powerless among them. Charity wasn't too bad; Jamal was a nightmare ... even eleven-year-old Chime was a holy terror. It didn't bode well for the conduct of superior sorcerers. Their father was a good man, in his way, but he didn't hesitate to trample over anyone who got in his way.

A hand fell on his shoulder.

"Well," a familiar – far too familiar – voice said. "I should have known that you would be here, weakling."

Johan gritted his teeth as he turned to face his elder brother. Jamal was taller than Johan, wearing the multicoloured robes that identified him as a recent graduate from the Peerless School; his face, thinner than Johan's face, seemed twisted into a permanent sneer. Most of his other siblings had become unbearable after they realised that Johan was largely unable to fight back; Jamal had been thoroughly unpleasant even before Johan's lack of magic was discovered. There were times when Johan wondered just why Jamal was such a bully, when he had so much to look forward to, and times when he felt that his brother just liked feeling superior to people.

"You found me," he said, fighting down the urge to cringe. "Did father send you?"

Jamal looked surprised – and a little disappointed. "I'm afraid not," he sneered, as he pulled Johan back from the crowd. "*Should* father be sending me after you?"

It was a little unlikely, Johan had to admit. Jamal and their father had had an argument over something and he'd moved out, setting up his own establishment on the other side of the Golden City. It clearly hadn't been *that* bad an argument, not if they were still talking, but it gave Jamal a freedom that Johan couldn't help envying. Even if he'd been older, his father wouldn't allow him to leave the house permanently. It had been one of the reasons why he wanted to find a job that didn't require magic.

"...No," he said, finally.

"Glad to hear it," his brother said. His eyes narrowed as

they reached the corner. "But I do have a bone to pick with you."

Johan swallowed. Jamal blamed Johan for everything that went wrong in his life, quite unfairly. Well, largely unfairly. Johan might not have been able to brew a potion to save his life, but he *had* managed to sneak a few herbs into Jamal's drink after one particularly bad bullying session and give his brother a few very uncomfortable nights.

"I was talking to Marina, of House Clyburn," Jamal said. "Father and I were closing the deal for the marriage contract. I would have been her husband."

"Oh," Johan said. He had an awful feeling that he knew where this was going. House Clyburn was poor in wealth, but rich in blood and connections. An alliance between them and House Conidian, sealed by the marriage of two of their children, would bring money to one and connections to the other. "And?"

Jamal leaned forward. "And they insisted on hearing about our entire family," he hissed. "When they found out about you, they cancelled the negotiations and tore up the contract."

"I'm sorry," Johan said, weakly. "I ..."

For a moment, he almost felt sorry for his brother. Alliances between strongly-magical families were meant to blend the best of their lines together to produce children that were vastly more powerful than their parents. But the merest suspicion of weakness in the family line could destroy an alliance. A weak magician alone would have been bad, but a powerless ... that was even worse. His mere existence had destroyed the planned contract. No *wonder* his father had been so desperate to find even the merest hint of magic.

"And *look* at them," Jamal added, waving towards the speaker, who was still pontificating. "They are *powerless*, just like you! And we are not going to stand for it!"

Johan looked at his brother ... and, in a sudden flash of insight, understood. Jamal had been raised to be the Heir to House Conidian, to take over the family magic and patronage network when their father died. No *wonder* he was such an asshole; their father pressured him constantly, trying to shape him into a worthy heir. Johan's complete lack of power should have reassured his brother, but it also undermined him too.

He looked up as he saw a handful of other magicians wearing graduate robes. "What are you going to do ...?"

"Hush," Jamal said. He waved a hand and Johan found himself frozen, utterly unable to move or look away from the speaker and his audience. "I just want you to watch and learn."

"That's your brother," one of the other magicians said. "Why isn't he joining us?"

"He's too soft," Jamal said, quickly. "Father wants him to watch to toughen him up."

Johan would have laughed if he could have moved a muscle. Jamal wouldn't want to advertise his powerless brother, even – perhaps particularly – to his closest friends. It was a good excuse, he had to admit ... and it made it unlikely that any of the others would help him, if they were so inclined. Besides, they'd probably mistaken him for Jay. If they'd realised that Johan existed, they might have started to wonder why he hadn't attended the Peerless School.

"Stay here," Jamal said, with an oddly-nervous laugh. "And watch carefully as we teach these upstarts a lesson."

The other magicians laughed, then started to march towards the crowd, lifting their wands into ready position. Some of the protesters saw them coming and started to scatter, but others were trapped by the sheer press of the crowd, unable to escape. A hail of rocks and stones flew towards the magicians, only to be stopped easily by shield charms. Johan watched, literally unable to tear his eyes away, as Jamal cast the first spell.

He felt his body try to shiver. The nightmare spell was a child's prank ... which didn't stop it being thoroughly unpleasant if the victim had no magic to defend himself. A dozen protesters started to scream in horror as they saw their worst nightmares coming to life, their screams echoing over the square. Other spells were being cast; Johan watched, helplessly, as a handful of protesters became frogs, or were frozen in place, or were compelled into attacking their fellows. He felt absolute mind-numbing horror as he saw a man attacking the girl next to him with his fists, tears running down his cheeks as his hands moved of their own accord.

Another girl was compelled to tear off her shirt and display her charms for all to see; a third was forced to wet herself, then kneel down in her own filth.

The crowd came apart into screaming panic. A man ran, fists raised, at Jamal who eyed him quizzically. He slammed right into the shield charm and fell to the ground, blood pouring from his nose. Jamal laughed out loud – his laughter somehow echoed over the screams – and kicked the man in the face. The man sank into merciful unconsciousness. Johan watched in absolute horror as Jamal targeted the speaker directly. Someone must have trapped him on his soapbox, Johan realised. The speaker should have tried to run.

Jamal played with him. One spell gave him boils, another moved him like a puppet, a third left him howling gibberish at the gates. Johan watched as his brother allowed one of his friends to take over, casting his own spells towards the speaker. It was unlikely that he would survive, Johan realised. The spells might be intended as pranks, but the speaker was completely defenceless.

Pure rage boiled through Johan as he watched the crowd fleeing, save only for the frozen, the compelled and the transfigured. They'd been broken, knocked down so far that they might not be able to recover ... Johan had been transfigured so many times that he was used to it, but mundanes who rarely dealt with even a single magician would find it a new and terrifying experience. Jamal walked onwards, laughing at the City Guardsmen as they shrank back into the gates. It would be a brave or stupid City Guardsman who tried to stand up to a magician on the rampage. That was a job for the Inquisitors. Where *were* they?

He cursed, mentally. Could it be that Jamal's actions had actually been *approved* by the Grand Sorceress? She couldn't find the Levellers – or so the paper had named them – very amusing. Indeed, they were a challenge to her prestige, even if they were no threat to her position. Someone like Jamal would make a perfect – and deniable – tool to use against them.

Johan struggled, throwing himself against the spell ... but

nothing happened. Rage met frustration ... and something broke free inside his mind. For a long chilling moment, the entire world dimmed, as if he were about to take a sneeze ... and then *something* blasted through his mind. He was vaguely aware of someone – Jamal? – yelling in shock, then the spell holding him snapped. He tumbled ...

And then he fell down into absolute blackness.

Chapter Five

Elaine felt Light Spinner's magic billowing through the air as she ran to a window and leapt out, floating on the air and heading towards the riot. For a moment, Elaine wanted to follow her, but sanity reasserted itself before she could jump out of the window herself. She simply didn't have the power to fly – or levitate – herself for longer than a few seconds, no matter how tightly she finessed the spells. Instead, she ran to the door – passing a handful of servants, who looked thoroughly terrified – and out into the gardens.

She was greeted by absolute chaos. On the other side of the railing, people were running in all directions, while the City Guardsmen were hanging back, desperately trying to pretend that they weren't there. Shouts and screams echoed over the palace as Light Spinner swooped down, her raw power scattering the remaining protesters. There was so much magic crawling through the air that Elaine found herself wondering if the whole affair was a trap for the Grand Sorceress, before deciding that any such trap would be unnecessary. Someone with the power to create the magic pulse wouldn't need such tricks. They could just walk into the palace and challenge her directly.

Elaine reached the gates and stared in horror at the scene before her. Countless people were scattered on the ground, some bleeding badly after being trampled by their fellows. Others were held in place by magic, or transfigured into animals or inanimate objects; a dozen had warts and boils burned into their faces through various prank curses and hexes. The Levellers had been thoroughly hammered by person or persons unknown, she thought, feeling sick. *This* was the sort of abuse of magic the Grand Sorceress was supposed to prevent ... and it had happened right in front of her residence.

Light Spinner dropped to the ground, robes billowing

around her, as a pair of Inquisitors arrived. Elaine heard her snapping at them – where had they been when all seven hells were breaking loose? – but tuned her out, searching instead for the source of the magical pulse. It was easy to tell that the magical field had been badly disturbed, as if someone had rung a colossal bell and the echoes were still audible. She might not have been the most sensitive magician in the world, but it was easy to trace the pulse back to its source.

A young man lay on the ground, completely stunned. Elaine knelt down beside him and took his pulse, then drew her wand and started casting diagnostic charms. The results shimmered up in front of her; a moment later, she felt her eyes narrow in puzzlement. None of the charms seemed able to decide if she were dealing with a magician or a mundane. There was magic in him, definitely, yet it was concentrated in his brain. But a normal magician would have magic flowing through his body.

She looked up as more Inquisitors and a string of druids finally arrived, followed by a small army of City Guardsmen, who had been emboldened by the appearance of their ultimate superior and her Inquisitors. Elaine couldn't blame them for keeping back; City Guardsmen weren't meant to take on magicians, no matter the situation. It was rare to have any Guardsman with magic of his own; the ones who did tended to be transferred to the Inquisition.

"Find out what happened," Light Spinner ordered, her voice somehow effortlessly ringing out above the throng. "And get these people some medical attention!"

Elaine scowled inwardly as Light Spinner, followed by a worried-looking Dread, came over to where she was waiting. It was impossible to read her expression behind the veil, but Elaine knew her well enough to know that she was deeply annoyed; someone, for whatever reason, had seen fit to challenge her authority right in front of her palace. And she'd also heard the Leveller attack on her person ...

Light Spinner stopped, peering down at the young man. "Is that ... is that the source of the pulse?"

"I think so," Elaine admitted. "Who is he?"

She studied the young man for a long moment, feeling an odd sense that she'd seen someone like him before. He was handsome enough, with short brown hair and flawless face, but there were odd lines carved into his skin that suggested age or bitter experience. His clothing, however, suggested the aristocracy; bland his outfit might have been, but the tailoring was superb. Elaine could never have afforded such clothes, at least until she had been promoted. And she would have considered it a waste of money in any case.

"He reminds me of Duncan or Jamal Conidian," Dread said, slowly. "What happened to him?"

"I'm not sure," Elaine confessed. Dread was right; there was something about the stunned youth that reminded her of Charity Conidian. She cast the charms again, allowing him to see the results as they appeared in front of them. "But he was the source of the magic pulse."

Light Spinner shook her head. "Take him to the hospital," she ordered, as she stepped backwards. "You can run tests on him there."

Elaine nodded. There was something ... *odd* about the way the magic field was responding to the boy. No, she corrected herself, the young man. She cast a second charm over him and discovered that he was a mere sixteen years old, even though he *looked* older. A moment later, Dread bent down and searched the man with practiced ease, turning up nothing apart from a medallion hanging around his neck. There were a handful of tracking charms placed on it, all seemingly inactive.

"No wand," Dread said. "And he isn't wearing school robes."

Elaine heard the puzzlement in his voice and frowned. Most magicians owned and used a wand, but there were quite a few who didn't. Their magic worked better without one; Light Spinner, like most of the other Senior Magicians, wouldn't use a wand at all unless she required absolute precision. A reputation for wand dependency would suggest to her enemies that removing her wand would render her helpless.

But it was rare for a school-age youth *not* to own a wand. He would carry it everywhere, even if he didn't use it regularly. Unless, of course, he had no magic.

She raised her own wand and cast a levitation charm. "I'll

take him to the hospital," she said, as she floated the stunned man into the air. Thankfully, it was easier to levitate someone else than herself. "Can you find out who he is and why he was here?"

"I can try," Dread said, with droll amusement.

Elaine felt herself flushing. The only person who had any right to issue orders to the Inquisitors was Light Spinner, who also seemed rather amused at Elaine's presumption. Irked at herself, Elaine manipulated her wand, sending the floating body drifting ahead of her as she walked away from the crowd. The hospital wasn't far from the palace, thankfully. Levitation charms didn't require much power, but maintaining them for long was incredibly draining.

The hospital seemed to be in chaos as she entered, she discovered. Druids and healers were running everywhere, while a handful of City Guardsmen were bringing in wounded from the riot outside the palace. Elaine hesitated then, as she wasn't wearing her purple robes, lifted her Privy Council ring and showed it to one of the druids, who blanched. Everyone knew that the Privy Councillors had almost unlimited authority, even though Elaine rarely used it. She just didn't have the mindset for going into a building and barking orders.

But she had to right now.

"I want a private room," she said, sharply. "And a druid to attend me as soon as possible."

She thought better of that a moment later. "No, I want the druid once everyone else is dealt with," she added. There was no reason to believe that her charge was in immediate danger; if she took a druid away from emergency medical care, it was likely that someone innocent would die. "Until then, find me a room."

The druid showed her to a small room, bringing back unhappy memories of the day she'd been turned into a Bookworm. Elaine levitated her charge inside and gently put him down on the bed, then collapsed into a chair in sudden exhaustion. It didn't seem fair, somehow, that she knew so much, yet she didn't have the power to make half of the spells she knew work. But she knew, better than anyone, that life wasn't fair. Sweat prickled her back as she sagged, then forced herself to stand upright and take some water from the sink. She needed a drink desperately.

Outside, she could hear the chaos growing louder as more and more patients were brought into the hospital. Elaine hoped that most of them could be healed quickly, but the druids were likely to be overworked and understaffed, particularly after a number of the most powerful druids had been killed by Kane. Taking another sip of water, she stepped over to the young man and started to cast another series of charms. The results seemed thoroughly unique.

There was magic, but it was definitely concentrated in his brain. No matter how she fine-tuned the scans, it was definitely isolated ... she even ran a scan of herself, just to make sure that the charms were working properly. It wasn't the only oddity. Unconscious magic helped children to heal quickly, even without immediate medical care, but there were definite signs that her charge *hadn't* healed quickly. She scowled, feeling knowledge from a thousand medical textbooks spinning through her head; there were signs that magic *had* been used to treat him, but it was external magic. A mundane who had been treated by the druids would have shown the same results.

And his body showed the faint disturbance caused by one too many transfigurations. The spells used weren't *dangerous*, not in the sense that they could accidentally *kill*, but so many transfigurations had to have inflicted *some* damage. Elaine shivered, remembering the day Millicent had turned her into a frog for a week, back at the Peerless School. If her readings were accurate, this young man had gone through much worse ...

"But if you're related to Duncan Conidian," Elaine said, out loud, "why didn't you defend yourself?"

Maybe he couldn't, her own thoughts answered her. *No wand, no school robes ... and you never saw him in the Great Library. What does that suggest?*

She shivered. Not seeing him in the library proved nothing; she wasn't sociable enough to wander the halls and reading rooms, chatting to students. That was *Vane's* job. Added together, however, it was starting to suggest a very disturbing picture. Absently, she tried to find out why the young man was still asleep and found nothing. She couldn't help remembering the days after she'd been turned into a Bookworm. She'd been stunned for several days too.

There was a knock at the door, which opened to reveal Dread. The Inquisitor looked as stony-faced as ever, but Elaine knew him well enough to realise that he was tired and not entirely happy with the world. Elaine cancelled her charms and looked over at him, wondering what he'd found out. And, for that matter, just what had happened outside the palace.

"His name is Johan, Johan Conidian," Dread said. His voice was almost devoid of emotion, another sure sign that he was more tired than he wanted to let on. "And he's a Powerless."

Elaine shook her head. "There's magic in there," she said. "Very odd magic, but it is there."

She scowled as Dread started to cast his own charms, feeling a moment of pity for the young man. The Conidian Family was powerfully magical; if Johan was genuinely powerless, his life must have been hellish. Elaine might have been a low-power magician, but she was still a magician. A Powerless wouldn't be *any* sort of magician ... and, born to a magical family, would get absolutely no respect. No *wonder* he'd been transfigured so often. His brothers and sisters must have thought of him as a permanent target for their pranks.

The Peerless School encouraged a limited amount of pranks – Elaine thought of it as bullying – in the hopes it would provide incentive for the prank victims to study and develop their magic. But all such pranks were supposed to be carried out *in* the school ... and targeted on other student magicians. Targeting a Powerless, one who couldn't defend himself at all, was just *evil*. But it seemed that the Conidian had allowed it to happen. Had he thought, Elaine asked himself, that repeated pranks would encourage his son to develop magic? Or had he merely hated the living evidence of weakness in his bloodline?

Dread finished casting charms and stepped backwards. "Wonderful," he said, sardonically. "The last time I saw anything like this was when I first met you."

Elaine remembered. "But he wasn't in the Great Library

when it happened," she pointed out, keeping her voice calm. Magical accidents that boosted – or weakened – someone's power were rarely good news. There were times when she still marvelled that she had been allowed to wake up, after becoming a Bookworm. "I don't think that any such spell could have affected him."

"I do not know if that would make a difference," Dread countered. "And what has happened to him now?"

"Unknown," Elaine said, tersely. All the knowledge in her head seemed useless. There were plenty of cases where trauma affected a person's magic, but they had all required the victim to be a magician. Johan ... had *never* been a magician. He hadn't even had the signs that Elaine had shown, back in the orphanage. "He had no magic. Now ... he has magic inside him."

Dread lifted his staff, then tapped its iron tip on the floor. "What is he going to become?"

"I don't think that you should kill him now," Elaine said, quickly. "This is utterly unprecedented."

"So is what happened to you," Dread reminded her, "and you know who was behind it."

Elaine shivered. The Witch-King ... did *he* have something to do with Johan's accident? But there was no way to be *sure*, one way or the other. For all they knew, it was Johan's grandchildren who would be the essential part of the Witch-King's plot.

"I think that the Grand Sorceress should make that decision," Elaine said. She knew that Dread had the authority to kill, if he believed that the Empire's security was at risk, but she didn't want to see Johan dead. If nothing else, what had happened to him might revolutionise the study of magic. He had been Powerless ... and if he'd developed magic, it would change the world. "What happened outside?"

Dread's face twisted into a grim scowl. "A bunch of magicians, mainly students, attacked the Leveller rally," he said. "So far, we have nineteen dead, thirty-seven injured, twelve forced transfigurations and thirteen people suffering the after-effects of various compulsion charms."

Elaine shuddered. She knew, all too well, just how

vulnerable non-magicians were to magic, even if they had purchased protective amulets and spells from magicians. Even student magicians could have inflicted considerable harm on the protesters ... and they had, it seemed. By the time Light Spinner had intervened, they'd killed nineteen mundanes.

She gritted her teeth. "Who did it?"

"We're still putting together a case," Dread said. "The Grand Sorceress is not happy. No matter what the Levellers were doing – or saying – such attacks cannot be tolerated. However, we don't have any real idea just *who* carried out the attack. The witnesses all agree that they used disguise charms to obscure their faces. They didn't even bother to come up with actual *faces*; they just ensured that no one could see their features."

Elaine rubbed her eyes, suddenly feeling very tired. She knew what would happen now; if they hadn't been caught in the act, the perpetrators would swear blind that they were innocent ... and, as they probably had magical relatives, they would bring colossal pressure to bear on Light Spinner to let them off with a slap on the wrist. If, of course, there was enough proof to bring them to face her in the first place. Few magical families would care if their children killed – directly or indirectly – a handful of mundanes. What were *they* going to do about it?

"The last thing we need is another challenge to the Grand Sorceress's authority," Dread added. "We may wind up quietly ignoring the whole affair."

"I know," Elaine said.

She'd thought that the Grand Sorcerer was all-powerful. It hadn't been until she'd joined the Privy Council that she'd realised that there were limits, particularly when other powerful magicians – or magical families – were involved. Even the most powerful magician in the world would have hesitated to confront several families acting in concert ... and they *would*, if they believed that their children were in danger. Light Spinner might be unable to get anything done if the families chose to challenge her openly.

And, with the Empire already weakened by Kane, the last thing they needed was the suggestion that the Grand

Sorceress couldn't keep order. It would undermine the Empire's stability further ... she scowled as she remembered her last letter from Bee. He'd told her that his mistress, the Empress of the South, had been asking him for his impressions of the Grand Sorceress and openly questioning her ability to handle the task of running the Empire.

"I'll concentrate on Johan," she said, finally. "Can you interview his family? See what they make of the whole affair?"

"Once I get some free time," Dread said. He turned and started to walk towards the door. "If we can catch the perpetrators red-handed, it might be harder for them to hide behind their families."

Elaine nodded, then turned back to Johan as Dread left the room.

"What are you?" she asked. There was no reply, apart from the steady rise and fall of his chest. "And what are you becoming?"

Chapter Six

Johan felt ... *weird*.

It was an odd sensation, one that seemed to twist and turn through his head, making it impossible for him to even get a grip on what it actually *was*. He thought he had a headache, save that there was no pain; it was almost as if he were *dreaming* that he had a headache. But there was something very wrong in his head ...

Johan had nightmares regularly, but this was different. There was a sense of reality that was lacking in his other nightmares, a sense that he couldn't escape no matter what he did. In a way, he was almost *aware* that he was dreaming ... and, at the same time, he was convinced that he *wasn't* dreaming. There was a sudden stab of pain, so painful that he screamed ...

... And then he snapped awake.

His head suddenly hurt as light blazed down from high overhead. Stunned, he squeezed his eyes shut as daggers seemed to plunge through his eyeballs and into his skull. He tried to recall what had happened, but nothing came to mind. Had one of his siblings played a trick on him ... or had something else happened? His memory seemed to have failed him, although it was hard to concentrate. Pain ... and something *else* ... seemed to be coiling in his mind, burning through his thoughts. He just wanted to roll over and die.

"Johan," a voice said. It was soft, female ... and completely unfamiliar. "Can you hear me?"

Johan felt his entire body twisting in pain. He opened his mouth to speak, then closed it again as his stomach heaved violently. By all the gods! It was worse than when he'd caught that bug as a young man and spent two weeks in bed with cramps ... his siblings, of course, had escaped entirely, thanks to their magic. Had he been ill? Or had something else happened, something his mind refused to remember?

"Yes," he managed, finally. The urge to retch was growing stronger and stronger. "I ... sick ..."

He opened his eyes. The light had dimmed, thankfully, but he could still see two anxious faces peering down at him. One wore the white robes of a druid, complete with golden sickle on his belt; the other wore the purple robes of a Privy Councillor. Johan found himself coughing instead of laughing, even though seeing her was funny. What sort of Privy Councillor would come to investigate a mere Powerless? A moment later, he retched violently, but there was nothing in his stomach to throw up. It was no relief.

"You've had a bit of a nasty blow, young man," the druid said. His voice made him sound ancient, but that was rather reassuring. Incompetent magicians didn't last long. "How are you feeling?"

"Head hurts," Johan managed. His chest hurt too. "Throat dry. I ..."

"Here," the druid said, passing him a flask of clear liquid. Johan sipped it gratefully, recognising the taste of purified water. The water made his head feel better, although *something* was still pounding away inside his skull. It was funny; he almost felt as though he were outside his body, looking in. "How much do you remember ...?"

As if the question had unlocked memories he'd pushed aside, Johan suddenly remembered *everything*. The Levellers, the rally, Jamal ... and something that had unlocked itself inside his skull. He reached up to touch his head, feeling it throbbing lightly, as a desperate hope suddenly blossomed to life inside his mind. What if ... what if he'd developed *magic*? No matter how much he'd fought before, he had never broken out of any of Jamal's spells. Even the weakest compulsion had held him in thrall until the spell was lifted.

But it seemed too good to be true.

"Jamal," he said, suddenly. "He was at the rally and ..."

The Privy Councillor leaned forward. "Your brother was one of those who attacked the rally?"

Johan found himself staring at her. She was young – he doubted that she was much older than Jamal – yet there were lines on her mousy face that suggested that she was older than her years. It was hard to credit the fact that she was a Privy Councillor, but who else would dare wear purple outside the house? There were *laws* against wearing robes if there was no claim to them.

"Yes," he said, sourly. Memories of horror rose up in front of his eyes, mocking him. Jamal wouldn't be punished, of course. He was *never* punished when he was cruel to outsiders, or even to his siblings. "He and his friends attacked the rally."

The druid waved his wand at Johan. "And what happened to you?"

"I don't know," Johan admitted. He described what had happened as best as he could, ending with the sudden collapse of Jamal's spell. "What do *you* think happened to me?"

"I wish I knew," the druid said. He looked at the Privy Councillor. "Medically, he's fine, although I would suggest two more days in bed for observation. I don't know enough about his ... *other* condition to comment. This is completely unprecedented."

The Privy Councillor didn't seem surprised. "I'll see to him," she said, as the druid started to walk towards the door. "Do you have any other advice?"

"Get a witness statement from him," the druid said.

Johan watched him leave the room, then turned his head so he could look at the Privy Councillor. "My Lady," he said, carefully, "what happened to me?"

The Privy Councillor seemed oddly bothered by the formality. Johan felt a moment of panic – his father had drilled etiquette into him, but he hadn't really expected his powerless son ever to have to meet a Privy Councillor – and wondered if he had gotten it wrong, before pushing the thought aside. No doubt it was about to be explained to him in great detail just *where* he had gone wrong.

"My name is Elaine," the Privy Councillor said. Now the druid was gone, her voice seemed to relax slightly. "I don't really need such formality."

Johan studied her for a long moment. There was none of the style his mother affected, none of the confidence that Charity strove to project at all times ... and there was no family name. That meant ... what? No family? But any family would be proud to have a Privy Councillor in the family. They were always powerful magicians as well as the trusted friends and confidants of the Grand Sorcerer. Or at least everyone took them to be the Grand Sorcerer's friends. He had his doubts about how close his father was to the Grand Sorceress.

But the name was oddly familiar ...

Of course, he thought, remembering one of his father's rants. *The Head Librarian.*

"My name is Johan," he said, finally. "What did he mean about my condition?"

Elaine looked down at the floor, then back up at him. "There is magic in you," she said, flatly. "But it is very odd magic indeed. You were tested before, I understand?"

Johan found himself unable to speak. Magic! It was like a dream come true ... and that made him suspicious. One of his father's more useful pieces of advice had been a warning that anything that sounded too good to be true probably was. He'd tried to send away for a potion that claimed to bring power to the powerless, only to have his father point out that it was utterly useless. And he had been tested extensively, every year. They'd never found a trace of magic.

"I was," he said, suddenly despondent. It was better than hope. "They found nothing."

"We found something," Elaine assured him. "But like I said, it's odd."

She gave him a long considering look. "Do you know any spells?"

"Charity tried to teach me a few," Johan said, before he could stop himself. If she chose to take that to the Inquisition ... teaching magic to mundanes was strictly forbidden, even though there was nothing they could do with it. "But they never worked."

The memory was a bitter one. His sweet sister had sat down with him and talked him through a series of spells, spells so basic that even his younger siblings could cast them at a very early age. He'd mastered the words and hand gestures that should have cast the spells, but nothing had ever happened. Of course not, Jamal had sneered. The Powerless had no magic to make the spells work.

And then he'd blackmailed Charity by threatening to tell their father.

"I had to struggle to make my spells work too," Elaine admitted. "I was fourteen when I cast my first successful spell."

Johan gave her an appraising look. He was old enough to remember both Chanel and Chime developing magic and casting spells with apparent confidence by the time they were seven years old. Even Jamal, according to their father, had developed later than that. It was that sort of access to magic that marked someone who could become a Privy Councillor, not a late developer. Everyone knew that the later magic appeared, the weaker the magician. Their magic clearly didn't want to get free.

But clearly what everyone knew wasn't enough.

Elaine motioned for him to sit upright. "Cast a spell," she ordered. "Any spell."

Johan hesitated. Part of him wanted to test it at once, part of him was scared that it would fail and that he would go back to being powerless. Maybe it was just a freak response to the spells, he told himself, or maybe Jamal had created something to give the illusion of magical powers where none existed. Was his brother really *that* good at magic? Whatever else could be said about Jamal, he *was* a skilled magician.

But, in the end, the desire to test it won out.

Charity had explained, back during the first lesson, that creating light was one of the easiest spells in the spellbooks. Almost every magician worth his salt could cast it, which hadn't made him feel better when it had failed time and time again. He'd never told anyone that he had spent time practicing after she'd stopped trying to teach him, but nothing had happened, not even a single spark.

Carefully, he ran through the words and gestures ... and nothing happened.

The sense of disappointment was crushing. He sagged, almost slipping and falling off the bed. Elaine reached out, put a hand on his shoulder, then started to cast new charms over him. Johan closed his eyes, angrily blinking away tears.

He might as well reconcile himself to being a prisoner for the rest of his life, he told himself, and serving as the target for his nephews and nieces as they came into their magic.

"The magic twitched," Elaine informed him. "Try again."

Johan stared at her, wanting to push her away, but not quite daring. "There's no point," he said, bitterly. "What's the use of *trying*?"

"I felt the same way too," Elaine said. There was so much bitterness in her voice that he found himself believing her. "But try again."

Johan sat upright and cast the spell again. Nothing happened.

"Again," Elaine ordered, watching the results from her wand. "And again."

Johan gritted his teeth, hating her in that moment ... and cast the spell one final time. There was a sudden ... *surge* within his head and brilliant white light blossomed into existence, right in front of him. It was far brighter than anything Charity had produced to show him how she did it, bright enough to blind ... Elaine let out a cry and covered her eyes, just as a wave of heat struck them both. But Charity's spell hadn't produced any *heat* ...

"Cancel it," Elaine ordered.

"I don't know *how*," Johan protested, feeling panic bubbling through his mind. Charity hadn't taught him how to cancel spells. The light was growing brighter, so bright that he could see it through his closed eyelids. "How?"

"Draw in your magic," Elaine ordered. "Focus your mind and concentrate on bringing it back into yourself."

Johan tried, but nothing happened. The light was still growing brighter and the room was growing uncomfortably warm. Panicking, he wished it gone ... and the light snapped out of existence. The room seemed a great deal dimmer now the light had faded away.

"Interesting," Elaine said. Her face seemed soaked in sweat. There was a nasty red mark on the side of her face that had been facing the light. "But you definitely have magic."

"I have magic," Johan said, dazed. It couldn't be true ... and yet it was. He *knew*, deep inside, that he had cast his first spell. The light spell was merely the beginning. "I have magic!"

"You do," Elaine confirmed, dryly.

She didn't understand. Even if she had come into her magic at fourteen, she would still have been a known magician. Her magic would have been detectable, even if she had been unable to access it. No one would have teased and tormented her like Johan had been treated by his family. Her family would have respected her even if she wasn't a strong magician. And if she hadn't been born to a magical family, her magic would have been a sign of favour from the gods. But Johan ... he'd been completely powerless, without even a hint of magic ...

Until now.

A sense of exultation ran through him. He wanted to jump to his feet and scream for joy, he wanted to run home and make his father proud of him, he wanted to find Jamal and teach his older brother a lesson ... there were so many things he wanted to do. His father couldn't keep him a prisoner now, could he? How could he when all of his children were now magicians? Johan could take magical lessons, he could master magic ... he could become powerful. He could rise ...

... And yet he was no longer sure if he wanted to make his family proud. What had they done for him?

He'd hoped to go into the Civil Service and just leave them behind. He would have missed Charity, but the others ... none of them had really cared for their powerless brother. Even Charity had played pranks on him from time to time. And his father's disappointment was worse than his rages. Even now ... did he really want to seek their approval?

"I want to do it again," he said, quickly. "Can I? Please."

Elaine frowned. "I think I should teach you how to cancel spells first," she said, firmly. "And I also need to talk to you about what happened two days ago."

Johan gaped at her. "Two *days*?"

"You were asleep for two days," Elaine confirmed. "Since then ... investigations have been proceeding. But we will want a witness statement from you."

"I understand," Johan said, reluctantly. He wanted to try more magic, but he had a feeling that she would want him to take it slowly. The gods knew that his father had closely supervised his children as their magic started to blossom into life. "What do you want to know?"

"Who carried out the attack," Elaine said. "And why."

Johan hesitated. Did he really want to land Jamal in serious trouble? Now that Johan had magic too, maybe they could patch up their relationship ... he dismissed the thought, angrily. No matter the pressures piled on Jamal, there was no escaping the fact that his brother was a nasty bastard ... and that he'd tortured dozens of people two days ago. Johan had been powerless, he knew what it must have felt like to be at Jamal's mercy. How could he defend his brother, even if he now shared the same magic? Besides, it wasn't as if Jamal had shown him any kindness since it had become clear that he had no magic.

"My brother," he admitted, reluctantly. His father would be furious, but Johan found it hard to care. A thrashing would be better than the sense of disappointment that radiated from his father every time he came face to face with his powerless son. "And he thought that they were getting uppity."

Elaine's face twisted. "I have no doubt he did," she said. "Do you know who *else* was involved?"

"Some of his friends," Johan said. "I don't know their names. We were never introduced. He was so scared of having them think that he had weak blood that he never introduced me to any of his friends. But you can get it out of him ..."

"The Inquisitors probably can," Elaine agreed. "Do you know the name of the druids who tested you for magic?"

Johan frowned, surprised by the sudden question. "No," he admitted. "But wouldn't there be records?"

"Depends how much your father paid out in bribes," Elaine said. Her lips turned downwards, briefly. "I'll check the records here, then find out from your father if necessary."

Johan yawned suddenly. "Sorry," he apologised. "Why am I tired?"

"You haven't eaten for two days," Elaine pointed out, dryly. "I'll order you some food, then you can rest before we start carrying out more tests. There are quite a few oddities about your magic."

"*My* magic," Johan said, with heavy satisfaction. "Are you going to teach me how to use it?"

"I don't know yet," Elaine told him. "But I do know that the Grand Sorceress is very interested in your progress."

Johan looked at her, thoughtfully. Once, having wealthy and powerful people paying attention to him would have seemed welcome. Now, it was downright terrifying.

And yet he was a magician!

"I should ask you," he said. "Has this ever happened before?"

"A mundane developing magic?" Elaine asked. There was an odd note to her voice, a suggestion that she wasn't quite sure she was answering the right question. "No, it hasn't. And that's why it bothers us."

Johan nodded in understanding. If *anyone* could develop magic, the Empire's social structure would be up-ended and destroyed. He could understand, now, why the Grand Sorceress was so interested in him ...

He'd been right. It was *definitely* terrifying.

Chapter Seven

More disturbed than she wanted to admit, Elaine ordered dinner for both of them and then concentrated on analysing the wards surrounding the chamber. They were some of the most complex wards outside the truly ancient buildings, constructed by some of the best ward masters in the Empire. Among other things, they monitored the condition of patients within the hospital, alerted the staff if anything went wrong and prevented self-harm or suicide. And Johan's magic, whatever it was, had damaged them.

The wards tracked and nullified bursts of uncontrolled magic. It wasn't uncommon for magicians to lose control of their magic when they were ill or badly injured; the wards should have tapered any burst of magic down and redirected it somewhere harmless, if they hadn't managed to simply absorb it. But Johan's magic had burned through them as easily as fire burned paper. The wards had been badly damaged, rendered utterly useless.

And it happened so quickly, Elaine thought, *that no one managed to sound the alert.*

She looked back at Johan as a nurse entered the room, wheeling a trolley of food ahead of her. It smelt better than she recalled, the last time she'd been in hospital, but then she'd been so desperately worried about her new talents that she hadn't really been able to enjoy a few days of rest. And besides, Johan *did* come from a powerful family. The hospital administrator was probably trying to butter his father up ...

But *that* wouldn't go very well, Elaine knew. Lady Light Spinner had issued orders that no one, apart from Elaine and Dread, were to see Johan. If his father turned up and demanded entry – he hadn't, as far as Elaine knew – he would be denied. The administrator's hopes of a new hospital wing, donated by a grateful and wealthy father, might be thoroughly dashed.

"There are nutrient potions in the soup," the nurse said, addressing Johan. "You're to drink all of it, as you haven't eaten in two days. Then – and only then – you can eat the rest of your food."

Johan looked mutinous. Elaine wasn't surprised. The soup might have tasted nice before the potions had been added, but few potions really tasted good. Her tutor had used to say that potions were addictive and anything that discouraged people from taking them was a good idea. It made sense ... and besides, nicer-tasting potions required more expensive ingredients.

"Drink it," she urged. "You need energy more than anything else right now."

To set a good example, she took her own bowl and began to sip it, while quietly continuing to examine the wards. Johan hadn't even been *breathing* hard when his spell had finally been cancelled, suggesting vast magical power. He'd been tired, sure, but how much of that had been the magic and how much his general lack of food? And the spell had clearly gone out of control. *That* was unusual. One of the reasons the light spell was used as a teaching tool was because it was very hard to lose control of it. Even the rawest student should have been able to do it.

But Johan's spell had produced heat as well as a blinding light.

She raised a hand and touched her cheek, wincing slightly at the pain. It must be what sunburn felt like, she told herself grimly; if she'd been looking right at it, she might well have been seriously hurt, despite her protections. A quick check revealed that some of her protections had been damaged too, accidentally. If Johan had meant her harm, he might have been able to burn right through her protections, no matter how subtle they were. The results would have been disastrous.

"I'm sorry," Johan said, meekly. His eyes were watching her. "I didn't mean to hurt you."

That was a good sign, Elaine told herself. The more powerful the magician, the harder it was for them to care about the lesser magicians, let alone the mundanes. Millicent had been completely heartless until Kane had broken her mind; the gods alone knew if she would ever recover completely. She seemed normal, until she broke down and started crying for no apparent reason. Even the most advanced medical magic couldn't heal a damaged mind.

"Accidents happen," Elaine said. "We're just going to have to work on how much power you put into your spells."

She finished her soup and started on the main meal, a serving of chicken and rice in a spicy sauce. Johan hesitated, then joined her, eating with more enthusiasm as he realised that the meal was actually very good. Elaine watched him eat, wondering just how much magic he had. There had been more than one odd thing about the spell he'd cast.

"Tell me about your family," she said, as she finished her dish. "What are they like?"

Johan made a face. "My father is strict; my mother is more concerned with being a social climber than with her family," he admitted. "My siblings are horrors – apart from Charity, I think, and even she can be a horror at times. The cooks and maids pitied me or looked down on me. Is it any wonder I wanted to leave?"

Elaine nodded in sympathy. She'd grown up at the orphanage – her guardian would hardly have taken her into his home – and had never known her family. Discovering who her father had actually *been* had convinced her that there were worse things than growing up without a mother or father. But it was clear that Johan's parents hadn't done anything about the abuse their son was frequently subjected to by his siblings.

The thought made her twist up her face in frustration. There were so many different cultures within the Empire that there were no laws that dictated how one should bring up a child. It was disconcerting to realise that her upbringing hadn't been the worst in the Empire, not when there were places where men were brought up in military camps and others where women were taught to be submissive, slaves in all but name. By the Empire's standards, Johan's father could raise his children however he wished and no one could object, no matter how despicable he became.

She shivered. Millicent had talked, late at night in the

dorms, about how she'd had her first lessons beaten into her. It hadn't been until much later that Elaine had realised that she'd been telling the truth.

"I don't blame you," Elaine said. She hesitated, then pressed on. "If you don't want to go back, you don't *have* to go back."

Johan's face twisted. He was too young to hide his inner conflict, not from her.

"I don't know," he admitted, finally. "I just don't know."

Elaine could understand that. The desire to prove himself, combined with a desire to reject everything his family stood for. She'd spent too long trying to prove herself to her Guardian before deciding that it was better not to try to amuse such an uncaring audience. And then he'd sold her out to Kane. The man had long since fled the Golden City ahead of a baying horde of creditors who wanted his blood.

She finished her dinner and put the plate to one side. "I want you to get some rest," she ordered, firmly. "You need to sleep properly before you start drawing on your magic."

Johan scowled at her. "I want to try something else," he said. "She taught me a few more spells ..."

"You could drain yourself too deeply," Elaine warned. It was true, but only one of her concerns. If a light spell could damage the wards around the room, she needed to carry out further tests in a much more heavily warded chamber. She might even need to borrow a compartment in the Inquisitor Training Centre. "Get some proper sleep, then we can carry out more tests in the morning. I can find you a sleeping potion if you would like ..."

"Please," Johan said, as he finished his own dinner. "But I really hate their taste."

Elaine took his plate, then cast a summoning spell in the air. A moment later, a small potions bottle drifted out of a cupboard and floated over to them. Elaine picked it out of the air and passed it to him. Johan took it and drank, complaining that it was disgusting. A moment later, he yawned violently and slumped over in bed. Elaine gently tucked him in, then stepped backwards and cast another series of diagnostic charms. Once again, the results were unique; the magic flowing through Johan's brain didn't seem to have changed, even though he'd drawn on his new power to cast the light spell.

Odd, Elaine thought. *Very odd.*

Everyone knew that magic was a muscle, one that had to be flexed carefully as a magician grew up, developing the channels in his or her mind for the magic to flow freely out into the world. Elaine well remembered exhausting herself after casting one or two spells, despite the best efforts of the Peerless School. Even now, there were limitations to her abilities, no matter how much she knew. But a powerful magician, like Light Spinner, wouldn't have drained their magic at all to cast the light spell.

And Johan didn't seem drained either.

It makes no sense, Elaine told herself, in frustration. If he'd had so much power, it should have burst out much sooner – and he wouldn't have had to grow up as a Powerless. But if he hadn't had power until a freak accident had given him power, surely he should have started off with a low level of magic until he'd learned to grow and develop his power? On the face of it, he seemed to have been gifted with power to match the Grand Sorceress, *without* having to go through all the training and development Light Spinner had endured. And it *still* didn't make sense.

Shaking her head, she stepped well clear of the bed and started to add her own wards to the room. If one good thing had come out of the crisis, it saved her the job of dismantling the hospital's wards and then rebuilding them with her own additions. Instead, she added a simple watch-ward – parents used it to ensure that their children were safe in bed – and a security ward. One would inform her if Johan awoke, although as he'd drunk the whole bottle of potion he should remain asleep until the following morning. The other would alert her if someone tried to enter the room without her permission.

And someone *would*, Elaine was sure. If word got out, if people realised the truth, they would want to get their hands on him. Either out of hope that the freak accident could be duplicated ... or out of determination to ensure that it *couldn't* be duplicated. If one could turn a mundane – or a Powerless – into a magician to rival the Grand Sorceress, it would turn the world upside down. Elaine honestly wasn't sure which way *she* would jump. If Light Spinner had been determined to keep *Elaine* where she could be watched, what would she make of *Johan*?

She was still musing when she reached the receptionist, who looked harassed after two days without proper sleep. The hospital had been besieged by the friends and relatives of those who had been caught up in the rally, which had apparently included a number of innocent bystanders. Elaine had been busy, but she had heard that none of the perpetrators had been caught and the entire city was on edge. Bullying by magicians was nothing new, yet this was on a terrifying scale.

"I need the name of the druid who attended the Conidian Family, two days ago," Elaine said. The bureaucrats who ran the hospital had a mania for keeping records that impressed even Elaine, who had trained as a librarian as well as a magician. Even if the files were sealed, they would be available to a Privy Councillor. "Please can you find it for me?"

The receptionist nodded and turned away, busying herself with the files. "Druid Zacharias," she said, after a long moment. "He didn't file anything other than a note he visited at the Conidian's request."

Elaine took the file, and directions to the druid's office, then left the receptionist behind and walked down the long corridor. By tradition, every druid was supposed to live in the hospital, but some of the richer and older ones scorned that rule, choosing to live out in the city. Thankfully, Zacharias seemed to be one of the more traditional ones. A quick glimpse at the file noted that he was particularly focused on helping young children to develop their magic. That made a certain kind of sense.

She tapped on his door, unable to fight down a hint of *déjà vu*. It hadn't been *that* long since she'd been here herself, taking her first steps towards becoming a magician. Part of her wondered what would have happened if her magic had developed earlier, part of her knew better than to think it would have made any difference. Or perhaps it would have, if she'd still been young enough to adopt. There were plenty of magical bloodlines that would have adopted a magical child, even one of unknown origin.

"Good afternoon," she said, as she saw the druid behind his desk. He looked younger than she had expected, younger and hungry for success. No doubt the Conidian had offered him a substantial sum if Johan should happen to develop magic, enough to set him up in a private practice. Had something he'd tried actually *worked*? "I need to talk to you about Johan Conidian."

Zacharias frowned. "I'm afraid I can't tell you anything without the permission of his father," he started. "I ..."

Elaine sighed and tapped her robes meaningfully.

"A tragic tale, simply tragic," Zacharias said, switching tune without missing a beat. "His father and mother both powerful, their son as powerless as any mundane. I tested him over the last three years and found nothing, not even a *trace* of magic. His siblings were all astonishingly powerful for their age; him? Absolutely nothing at all. His father was always pushing at me to invent new tests, or to try new treatments, but it was hopeless. I only did it to humour him."

"I see," Elaine said, disapprovingly. "Precisely what treatments did you try?"

"Magic exposure, forced transfiguration, charged potions, even hypnotic spells," Zacharias admitted. "I could use all of them to help a spark of magic become a flame, but there was absolutely no result."

Elaine sighed. At least he hadn't tried anything truly dangerous – or illegal – but it was still pointless. The treatments would have not only been futile, but humiliating. And as he said, without a spark of magic they wouldn't have worked at all. If his client hadn't insisted so strongly, Zacharias wouldn't have tried them in the first place. It was just a waste of time and expensive potions.

"But you found nothing," she mused. A thought struck her and she leaned forward. "I suppose there's no chance he's a bastard?"

"His father ran all sorts of tests, apparently," Zacharias said. He grinned, rather unpleasantly. "Johan is very definitely Duncan's son, My Lady. Even a blood-rite adoption would leave *some* trace, some clue that Johan wasn't his natural son. Everything came up white."

"And a blood-rite couldn't be carried out without the full knowledge and agreement of the parents," Elaine said. She'd looked them up, back when she'd dared hope that a kindly couple would take her from the orphanage. Giving up her vanished father's blood would have been a small price to pay for actual *parents*. "Was there anything else *odd* about him? Or the conditions of his birth?"

"Nothing that I was able to trace," Zacharias said, after a long moment. "Madame Conidian was never a dueller, or anything other than a society butterfly. If she was ever cursed, there was never any trace of it in her body – and I ran the most extensive tests possible. *And* all of her other children are strongly magical. The Conidian has a more ... dubious medical history, but nothing that should have caused one of his children to be born a Powerless."

He looked up from the stack of paperwork in front of him. "Is there a reason behind these questions?"

"Johan was at the rally two days ago," Elaine said, which was technically accurate. Few had known that House Conidian had birthed a Powerless; Elaine certainly hadn't known, which would – she hoped – account for her interests. The druid's oaths should keep him from telling the world. "The druids ended up taking a look at him."

She shook her head. The rest of the story was better kept a secret, for the moment. Light Spinner would decide who was to be told – and when. And Dread would have to interview Johan just to get evidence against his brother. That wouldn't be easy for the young man, but Jamal Conidian needed to be brought to justice. The city was on a knife-edge and would remain that way as long as the perpetrators remained unidentified.

"I need your file on him," she said, shortly. He rustled through his filing cabinet, then produced a large file which he passed to her reluctantly. Elaine took it, glanced at the cover, then filled out a formal receipt. The bureaucrats wouldn't be pleased with either of them if the file went missing. "And thank you."

Leaving the office, she dashed out a quick note to Lady Light Spinner, explaining what had happened, and then a second one to Dread asking him to interview Johan as quickly as possible. And then she headed back to his room, where she would rest until he woke up. No doubt he would be eager to test his new magic ...

And, Elaine realised, so was she. This was something *new*, something she hadn't had crammed into her mind. There was a chance to perform genuinely original research ...

She just hoped it didn't end up coming back to haunt them.

Chapter Eight

When Johan opened his eyes, he thought that it had just been a dream. He'd dreamed of having magic so often that it hurt when he returned to the real world and discovered that he was still a Powerless. But this time, he found himself still in the hospital room with a grim-faced Inquisitor sitting next to him, studying him through cold dispassionate eyes. It was real!

"I need to take your statement about your brother's involvement in the recent affray," the Inquisitor said, without introducing himself. It was difficult to be sure, but it looked as though he had not slept in days. "Starting with ... what exactly happened that day?"

Johan hesitated. Betraying his brother so casually caused him a pang, but his brother had been thoroughly horrible to him for all of his life ... and he had caused at least nineteen deaths. He couldn't remember the rest of the figures that Elaine had quoted at him, yet it had been far worse than any of his other pranks and carried out on helpless victims. He took a breath and started to explain what had happened.

It took longer than he had assumed, for the Inquisitor was a skilful interrogator. Whenever something wasn't entirely clear, he went over it again and again until he had drawn every last detail out of Johan's mouth. The experience left him with a pounding headache by the time the Inquisitor stood up, revealing Elaine standing by the door with a worried expression on her face. Johan could have kicked himself. He'd been so focused on the Inquisitor's inquisition that he hadn't even noticed that she was there.

"Thank you for your cooperation," the Inquisitor said, tightly. His stony expression didn't change as he headed towards the door. "You will be informed if more testimony is required."

Elaine shut the door behind the Inquisitor, then walked

over to the bed. "I'm sorry about that," she said, as she sat down facing him. "But your testimony was required urgently."

Johan scowled. "Why?"

"None of the other witnesses saw anything," Elaine said. She paused, then continued. "Nothing useful, at any rate. The attackers disguised their faces; you were the only one to see them properly and only then because Jamal identified himself to you. Glamours don't usually stand up to such exposure. Without you, proving that Jamal was there would have been tricky."

"Good thing I was there," Johan said, although he wasn't so sure if telling them everything had been a good idea. Part of him was still scared of his brother, the brother who had once openly threatened to kill him on the grounds his mere existence brought shame to the family. But, for once in his life, Jamal wasn't going to get away with something. It was worth the headache to see him face justice. "What are we going to do today?"

"Experiment with your magic," Elaine said, standing up. "We're not going to do it here, though."

She walked over to a cabinet and pulled out a set of clothes. Johan blinked in surprise as he realised that they were apprentice robes, normally only issued to magicians who apprenticed themselves to an older magician for individual tutoring. Unlike the drab robes worn by students, they were bright blue with a dark sash running around the waist. He took them when she handed them to him and examined them carefully. There was even a holster for his wand! But he had none ...

"These robes," he said, remembering his father's cautionary tales. "If I wear them, do I commit myself to anything?"

Elaine smiled. It transformed her face, Johan realised, turning her from a slightly mousy girl to someone who was genuinely beautiful. Still not as pretty as Charity, even without the glamours, but genuinely stunning in her own right.

"You're wise to be careful," Elaine said, "but there are no binding contracts woven into the robes. We thought that it might give you a legal status, if necessary."

Johan nodded in understanding. Magically-binding agreements and contracts could be sealed by accident, particularly when weak or unskilled magicians were involved. A strong magician wouldn't be in any danger, but if Elaine had had bad intentions she could have constructed a spell that made him her apprentice in truth, if he donned the robes without asking first. It didn't seem logical, yet his father was fond of telling his children that the older forms of magic were rarely logical.

He sat upright, then flushed as he realised that Elaine was still in the room. She flushed too, then turned her back, allowing him enough privacy to remove the hospital nightshirt and pull the robes over his head. It felt surprisingly rough against his skin, something that puzzled him until he realised that he wasn't accepting a *real* apprenticeship. Ancient customs, woven into the magic surrounding the city, disapproved of him wearing the robes. But at least they weren't the black robes worn by full sorcerers ...

"You can turn around now," he said, once he'd finished dressing. "How do I look?"

Elaine eyed him critically. "It's obvious that you're unused to wearing such robes," she said, dryly. "But that isn't uncommon in the Golden City."

She took a look around the room, then headed towards the door. "I've taken the liberty of assigning you quarters in the Great Library," she added. "For the moment, you'll be sleeping and studying there. We'll discuss other rules later tonight."

Johan stared at her. "I thought I wasn't allowed to go to the Great Library ..."

His voice trailed off. Mundanes – and Powerless – were not allowed to enter the Great Library. He'd found that out when he'd tried to visit during one of his infrequent excursions outside the house. There were wards around the building to prevent anyone without magic from walking in ... and anyone who tried to help one enter the building would be in deep trouble. Or so Charity had said, when he'd begged her to take him with her one day.

But he had magic now ...

He kept his thoughts to himself as they walked through the hospital and out onto the streets, turning southwards to head towards the Great Library. Johan was not as familiar with the mood of the streets as he would have liked, but it seemed clear to him that there were fewer people around than there should have been. Even after the disaster six months ago, the city's position at the heart of the Empire had ensured that it would recover quickly, yet now ... there were only a handful of people on the streets.

"Your idiot brother scared a lot of people," Elaine said, when he commented on it. "And the fact that we haven't brought him to justice yet has only made matters worse."

Johan scowled as they turned and approached the Great Library. The wards had prevented him from entering last time, but now ... he found that he could walk up to the doors without impediment. He was aware of Elaine watching him closely as he stepped through the doors and into the lobby, her eyes missing nothing. It was another test, he realised, but a test of what? Did she doubt that he had magic? Or was she looking for something else?

The interior of the Great Library was just as Charity had described it. Winding corridors, often lined with books; large and small reading rooms ... and mirrors everywhere. He noticed several students giving him sharp glances, as if they weren't quite sure who he was or what he was doing with the Head Librarian. The robes, he realised, had convinced them that he was an apprentice ... and that was rare in the Golden City, rare enough to suggest that there was something significant about him. Most magical students went to the Peerless School, after all.

"Once upon a time, professors would come and stay here for a few weeks while they researched," Elaine commented, as they reached a long corridor lined with doors. "As they were often powerful sorcerers too, the librarians ensured that they had individual rooms that were crafted to suit their requirements. The custom declined in later years, but the rooms are still available. One suite will be yours as long as you wish it."

She led him into a large workspace and grinned at him.

"We will be carrying out our experiments here."

Johan looked around. The room was almost completely empty, apart from a workbench in the far corner. Odd runes had been carved into the stone walls ... designed, he suspected, to channel rogue magic out of the room. There were a set of circles carved into the floor, lined with other runes ... he wished, suddenly, that he'd actually taken Charity up on her offer of loaning him a rune dictionary. He might have understood just what the runes meant.

Elaine gave him an odd look. "What do you sense about the room?"

"It's big," Johan said. He knew that wasn't the right answer, but nothing else came to mind. "I don't know. What should I be sensing?"

"Later," Elaine said, shortly. She led him around the room – being careful not to cross into the circles on the floor – and up to the workbench. "What can you tell me about these items?"

Johan frowned. There were five books; two of them clearly ancient, three of them produced by a new-fangled printing press. Beside them, there was a cup, a dagger and a sharp sword ... and a tiny statuette of a man in sorcerer's robes. He reached out and picked up one of the older books, opening its covers to discover that it was written in the Old Tongue. His tutors had taught him how to read it, but the handwriting style was so old that he could barely make out one word in four.

"Nothing," he said, reluctantly. "The two older books are clearly magic; the newer books are just ... common." He blinked in surprise as he realised that one of the newer books was actually one of the romance novels Charity and his younger sisters devoured whenever their father wasn't around to express his disapproval. "And everything else is just what it seems."

Elaine picked up the statuette, held it lightly in her hand for a long moment, then passed it to Johan. "What can you tell me about that?"

Johan frowned, staring down at the statuette. It was perfect, every detail crafted out by a master craftsman, right down to the warts on the sorcerer's nose. The material was probably silver, he decided after a long moment, although he'd never seen anything so detailed before in silver. His father would have loved it. It would be expensive ... but, apart from that, there was nothing special about it at all.

"It's silver," he said, convinced that he was failing a test. But he didn't even know what he was supposed to be looking for. "What else is there?"

"Interesting," Elaine said, out loud. "You don't sense *anything* from the statuette?"

Johan closed his eyes, concentrating on the feel of the silver against his fingertips. It felt ... cold and hard and metallic, nothing else. Frustrated, he put the silver statuette down on the table and looked up at her. Her face was twisted into a puzzled expression that worried him. What could puzzle an experienced magician?

"Nothing," he said, shortly. "What *is* it?"

"There was a sorcerer who wished to contemplate the meaning of life, the universe and everything .... or something to that effect," Elaine said, a hint of disapproval echoing through her voice. "In order to divorce himself completely from the concerns of the outside world, he had himself turned into a silver statuette and placed in the Great Library. That was two hundred years ago, more or less. He's still contemplating."

Johan blanched. He'd been transformed into all kinds of inanimate objects by his siblings and it had always been a terrifying experience, even if they used spells that ensured that no permanent harm could come to the victim. The thought of spending decades – no, centuries – as an object was horrifying. Who in their right mind would consider it practical research?

"It isn't practical research," Elaine explained, when he asked. "He's delving into the ultimate connections that bind the universe together."

"Oh," Johan said. He looked back at the statuette, remembering some of the horror stories his father used as cautionary tales. "How do you know he hasn't gone mad – or lost cohesion altogether? And what's to stop someone melting him down for the silver?"

"The spells should prevent it," Elaine said. She knelt down

and retrieved a notebook from under the workbench. "And a magician should be able to sense that there was something ... *alive* about the statuette."

Johan froze. He hadn't sensed *anything*.

It had always been one of his nightmares, back when Jamal had transformed him into something, that the maids would throw him out of the house without ever realising what they were doing. The wards should have prevented it, but he'd never been *sure*. Now, he realised just how easy it would have been for that to happen. Part of him just wanted to throw up; he forced himself to swallow hard, unwilling to show weakness in front of anyone. But he knew that he wouldn't sleep well when bedtime rolled around.

"I meant to ask you," Elaine said, her voice distracting him from his fears. "What sort of procedures did the druid try on you?"

The memories made Johan wince. "All sorts of spells," he said. "He gave me various potions to drink, then put a wand in my hand and told me to use it. Nothing happened."

He scowled at the thought. "Then he hypnotised me and told me to use magic," he added. "It was like being under a compulsion charm, but ... different, almost pleasurable. I tried to use magic, I was *sure* I could use magic, yet nothing happened. Why didn't it work?"

"Some magicians have problems with their confidence," Elaine explained. Johan leaned forward, interested. The druid had never offered any explanation, even when Johan had threatened to refuse to cooperate any further. "They have low self-esteem or their families keep putting them down ... hypnosis relieves them of their feelings, allowing them to believe that they can succeed."

She shook her head. "But the process wouldn't do anything if the magic wasn't there," she mused. "Did he try anything involving blood?"

Johan shook his head.

"Good," Elaine said, without elaboration.

Johan suspected that he understood. His father's books on magic were supposed to be completely off-limits to him, but Jamal had borrowed a couple and Johan had taken advantage of the opportunity to peek into some of them. They *had* talked about potential magic-enhancing rituals, all of which were dangerous and some of which were thoroughly illegal. The druid had never gone that far ...

... But would he have, if his father had insisted?

"Time to try a different test," Elaine said., drawing him out of his thoughts. She stepped over the circle and sat down in the centre, then beckoned for him to follow her. Johan expected a tingle as he crossed the line, but felt nothing. "I want you to cast this spell."

Johan took the notebook and scanned the page quickly. It was nothing more than a set of words and gestures; thankfully, as far as he could tell, he didn't need a wand. But there was nothing to say what the spell actually *did*.

He looked up. His father had told his children *never* to perform a spell unless they knew what it did – or at least what it was *meant* to do.

"It's harmless," Elaine assured him. She must have known what he was thinking, but then it *was* a standard safety precaution. "You can cast it without needing to worry."

Johan hesitated, then muttered the words and performed the gestures. Nothing happened.

"Maybe I need a wand," he said, despondently. His second try was no more successful than his first. If he had true magic, why didn't it work properly? Surely none of his siblings had had so many problems. "Can I get one?"

Elaine snickered, although Johan didn't see the joke. "I'll let you in on a dirty little secret," she said, dryly. "You *don't* need a wand to perform magic."

"I know that," Johan snapped, feeling a flicker of anger. "But all my family have wands ..."

"They're nothing more than focusing devices," Elaine said. "I know, I know, the wand-makers tell you that you need a specific wand. But it's just a trick to convince people to buy the most expensive wand they can afford. You could cast a spell using a pencil if you tried."

Johan couldn't help himself. He started to laugh. Jamal had been *delighted* with his wand, which had gold and silver worked into the wood; he'd boasted endlessly for *months* after he'd bought it. The thought of using a pencil as a wand ... it was hilarious. Jamal might as well have saved the fifty gold he'd spent on it.

"It's a con," he said. "Why do they ...?"

"Money," Elaine said, dryly. "Why would anyone spend twenty gold on a wand when they could take a stick off a tree and use that instead? As long as there isn't any iron in the wand, anything would do."

She leaned forward. "The spell is designed to cool the air," she said, shortly. "I want you to cast it again."

Johan looked down at the instructions, trying to see how they actually worked. But it seemed impossible. Spell-crafting, according to his father, was immensely complicated and difficult. Very few people had the mindset to create truly new spells ...

Shaking his head, he raised his hands and cast the spell for the third time.

The temperature plunged rapidly.

Chapter Nine

Elaine cursed her own mistake as she felt the protective wards *scream* in her head. She'd assumed that Johan's problems with the light spell had stemmed from inexperience, not something inherent to his newfound powers. The fact he hadn't been able to cast the spell without knowing what it did should have warned her. Most magicians could cast a spell without understanding it – that was why they were cautioned not to cast spells without knowing what they actually were – but Johan was clearly an exception to the rule.

She cast a warming charm as her teeth began to chatter, silently grateful that the library's wards were designed to minimise the effects of rogue magic. They were also far more powerful than the ones protecting the hospital. If they hadn't been, a simple cooling charm would have frozen them both to death. A spell designed for a homemaker would have killed them ... the irony would have amused her, if she'd had a chance to meditate on it. Instead, she had to deal with the results of her experiment ...

"Cancel the spell," she ordered, sharply. The spell shouldn't have lasted long, but Johan's magic might keep it going. She'd written restrictions into the spell that Johan might have left out, quite by accident. "Tell it to fade away!"

Johan stared at her, clearly unsure of what to do. Elaine held his eyes, silently willing him to concentrate and, a moment later, the temperature began to rise. She cancelled her own charm and smiled weakly at Johan, who seemed equally stunned. In hindsight, perhaps they should have looked at cancelling charms first.

You wanted to experiment, she told herself. *Idiot.*

"That ... was interesting," she said, out loud. She concentrated, sending out a specific request to the library's wards. "You seem to break some of the known laws of spell-casting."

She looked up as a pair of mugs floated into the room. "Take this," she ordered, picking one of them out of the air and passing it to Johan. "You need something to warm you up."

It wasn't uncommon for magicians to hurt themselves, but none of the books in her head suggested that a magician had managed it with such a simple charm. She took her own mug and sipped the hot chocolate gratefully, wondering if they would ever be able to control Johan's magic. The wards around the compartment hadn't been damaged as badly as the ones in the hospital, but it was clear that there *had* been some damage. Luckily, the library was already regenerating the wards.

"Thank you," Johan said. The gratitude in his voice bothered her. Hadn't anyone been nice to him in the past? "What happened?"

"I think that your problem isn't too much power," Elaine said, carefully. "I think your magic is ... different."

There were legends, the books had told her, of magicians who seemed to break all known laws of magic. The seventh son of a seventh son, a magician with multiple lives, a dark wizard who split his soul into seven separate pieces, an enchanter who aged backwards, growing younger as he grew older ... but none of them had ever been substantiated. Large magical families were the norm, yet the seventh-born had never seemed to have any real advantage over his siblings ... and Johan was the third-born, not the seventh.

And he'd seemed powerless. Until now.

Johan looked both delighted and terrified. "What ... what does that mean?"

"It means that you need to be tested," Elaine said. Logically, Johan's gift couldn't be *too* different from hers ... could it? "And that we need to figure out how to train you to control your magic."

She finished her hot chocolate, thinking hard. "Time for another test," she said, once he had put his mug aside. She took the notebook back, turned a couple of pages, then passed it to him. "Cast *that* spell."

Johan muttered the words, but – as Elaine had expected –

nothing happened.

"It looks as though you need to know what you're trying to do to actually make it work," Elaine said, as Johan looked disappointed. "I want you to try something else."

That was ... *odd*, but it could have been worse. She'd feared that his magic would be driven by emotion ... and *that* was the short route to madness and dark wizardry. Sure, emotion could power spells, but the price for that was becoming far too attached to that emotion, which might be anger or hatred. Madness would beckon and the magician would be too far gone to notice.

Some trainee magicians were allowed to practice on each other, but Elaine had a feeling that would be very dangerous, at least until they had a better handle on how Johan's powers actually *worked*. If a lighting charm and a cooling charm had produced near-lethal results, what would a levitation charm do, let alone a transfiguration spell? She had a mental vision of the unhappy student being slammed into the ceiling at terrifying speed, and shuddered. Most of the transfiguration spells would be worse than lethal ...

She crossed her legs and sat, as comfortably as she could. "Sit in a manner you find comfortable," she ordered. Surprisingly, he knelt back on his haunches. Elaine frowned, wondering if he'd been treated like a servant – or a slave – and then remembered that his family worshipped a god that demanded kneeling as part of the rites. "I want you to close your eyes and listen for your heartbeat."

The comforting sound of her own heartbeat echoed in her ears as she cleared her mind. It was a basic exercise, one she'd been taught in her first year at the Peerless School ... and one of the few exercises that she'd mastered before Millicent and her cronies. It didn't require magical strength; rather, it required an awareness of one's own mind and how best to calm it down.

"Focus on your heartbeat," she ordered, trying to split her attention between her own mind and issuing instructions to him. She honestly had no idea how her tutor had managed to teach an entire class when sinking into her own mind had to be a colossal temptation. "Listen to it pounding inside your chest. And then see if you can touch your magic."

It was there, shimmering throughout her body. Elaine felt ... *aware* of it, aware of the raw power ... and the faint, almost imperceptible dark sheen that hung over her magic like a cloud. Heat seemed to stab through her eyes, only to vanish moments later, leaving her grimly aware that it was still there. No matter how often she washed, she knew, part of her would always feel unclean.

"Focus," she said, forcing herself to remain awake. She'd often slipped fully into the trance in the past, using the exercise to merge fully with her magic. "Concentrate on your magic."

"I *can't*," Johan said. The frustration in his voice was enough to bring him out of the trance, if he'd ever been in it. Boys tended to have a harder time picking up the skill than girls, which often led them to underestimate the value of the exercise. But without it, their magic would be dangerously crippled. "What am I supposed to do?"

Elaine opened her eyes. Johan's eyes were squeezed shut.

"You're trying too hard," she said, reaching out to take his hands. He jumped at her touch, his eyelids flying open. Had no one touched him before? How many people, Elaine thought, had refused to even *talk* to a Powerless, for fear that it might prove contagious? It might have been kinder to send Johan to an orphanage. "Relax."

She talked him through it again, careful not to close her own eyes. Johan relaxed slightly, although it was clear that he still had his doubts. Elaine wasn't too surprised. She was so practiced that it was hard for her to remember just how difficult it had been at the start.

"I can hear my heartbeat," Johan whispered. "But I can't feel anything else."

His magic is all in his mind, Elaine thought. The standard exercises were focused on the heartbeat because magic ran through the entire body, but Johan's magic was concentrated in his mind. For once, she found herself at a complete loss. All of the exercises she had been taught assumed that the magician was ... normal. Johan very definitely was *not*.

The exercises wouldn't hurt, she knew. Mundanes used them too, even if they didn't have magic. But they probably wouldn't *help*.

"Open your eyes," she ordered. "Unless you actually *want* to sleep."

Johan grinned, embarrassed. "How often do people drop off while they're practicing?"

Elaine grinned back. "It's the one class in the Peerless School where you can fall asleep and not be punished for it," she said. One of her tutors had had the nasty habit of firing hexes at any student foolish enough to fall asleep in her class. The others had normally just sent the offending student to the Administrator for punishment. "But you are expected to master the art before moving up to the next level."

"Maybe you should tell me what the exercise is supposed to *do*," Johan said. "If I need to actually *know* ..."

Elaine felt a hint of pride. Her student had figured something out for himself, despite an almost-complete lack of magical education.

"Magic flows through our bloodstream," she said, then hesitated. "Well, a normal magician's magic flows through her bloodstream. It's why magicians heal so quickly from injuries and rarely catch diseases, among other things. The exercise is designed to allow you to make contact with your magic on a conscious level and direct it, both inside and outside your body. You could, for instance, tell it to heal you quicker – or channel it out deliberately."

Johan hesitated, then scowled in understanding. "Jamal is never ..."

He broke off and started again. "But I couldn't feel my magic," he said, carefully. "What does *that* mean?"

"Your magic is concentrated in your brain, as far as I can tell," Elaine said. She cast another diagnostic charm and studied the results. There didn't seem to be any major change since the last time she'd checked him. "Nor does it seem to be spreading out through your blood. I may have to speak with some of my old tutors and ask for advice."

"I see," Johan said. Elaine rather suspected that he didn't. Magical control was largely instinctive for young magicians. His siblings had probably had a great deal to unlearn when they'd gone to the Peerless School. "So what do I do with it?"

"I'm not sure," Elaine admitted. She looked down at her

hands for a long moment. "I would like to take a blood sample, for tests. Would you allow that?"

She saw the conflict on Johan's face and felt a stab of guilt. Giving a blood sample away was dangerous for *anyone*, but it was hellishly dangerous for a magician, particularly an untrained one. Blood rites were either strongly controlled or very definitely illegal, with very good reason, yet dark wizards weren't known for caring about the law. Even though he'd been a Powerless, access to Johan's blood could have been used by a dark wizard to endanger his entire family.

"I want your sworn word that you will not let the sample be taken or used by anyone else," Johan said, after a long moment. "As a magician, you can swear such an oath."

"I would have to run the tests myself," Elaine hedged. Johan had been told to be careful with oaths ... as had she, with far more reason. An oath sworn on her magic would have disastrous consequences if she broke it deliberately. But part of her didn't want to share her experiments with anyone else. "Very well. I will swear."

She made the oath, then used her wand to draw a small blood sample out of Johan's arm. It was clear that he *didn't* heal quickly, she realised, as she bottled the sample and stowed it away in her personal pocket dimension. Even Dread or Light Spinner would have had problems breaking in and, if they did, a second spell would destroy the interior, reducing the blood sample to worthless ash.

"It didn't hurt," Johan marvelled. "Why did it always hurt before?"

Elaine made a mental note to have a few words with the hospital's administrators. Casting a numbing spell was hardly *difficult*. Zacharias had taken out his frustration at wasting time on the Powerless boy, not his far too powerful and well-connected father. Elaine could understand the irritation, but there were definite limits.

"The druid who attended you was an asshole," Elaine said. She kept her eyes on the tiny cut, noting that it wasn't even clotting over. It would have been simple to tell him to try to heal himself, but she doubted that he could do it safely. Druids had extensive training to ensure that they didn't accidentally make the patient's condition worse.   "Don't worry about it."

She cast a healing spell and watched as the wound sealed itself up. "Time to try something else," she said, standing up. "Have you ever tried to cook?"

"The cooks used to let me help in the kitchen, before my mother told me that I couldn't go bother them," Johan said, morosely. He seemed rather puzzled by the question. "But I don't know how good I was at it."

Elaine smiled, leading him over to the workbench. She opened the compartment underneath the wooden top and produced a cauldron, several bags of ingredients, a bottle of water and a spelled heater, ready to warm up the liquid. Potions could be fun, if one had the patience to do more than memorise a handful of recipes. It still surprised her just how few students failed to work out how to proceed beyond rote learning, even though she now knew more potion recipes than all of the tutors in the Peerless School.

"On the face of it," she lectured, "a potion could be made by anyone, mundane or magical. But potions, certainly anything involving magical ingredients, require a magician to make them. Why would that be the case?"

Johan thought about it, furrowing his brow. "Because magic is needed to work with magic?"

"Close enough," Elaine said. "The art to potions isn't just brewing, but mixing together the intrinsic magic in the ingredients. *That* requires the power of a magician to manipulate the potion while it is being prepared. A skilled brewer will eventually gain a *feel* for how potions work that will allow them to develop newer and better potions."

She set up the cauldron with practiced ease, then poured in the water. "I took the liberty of preparing the ingredients earlier, she said, as she stepped aside to allow Johan to stand in front of it. "I'm going to issue instructions and you are going to brew."

Johan nodded, looking surprisingly interested. *That* would probably change, Elaine suspected, no matter the outcome of *this* experiment. Few students had the patience to do more than memorise the simpler formulas. Johan didn't strike her as having the determination to study and brew until he was an expert.

"Right," she said. "Start by adding the shredded root weed ..."

Seven minutes later, it was clear that everything was *not* going according to plan. Johan could follow instructions, but his potion refused to blend together into the bright orange liquid Elaine remembered from her studies. The Numbing Potion was a firm favourite among her fellow classmates – she hadn't realised until midway through her first year precisely why it was taught to them – and it was considered simple to brew. But Johan's potion was nothing more than muddy water and wasted ingredients.

Elaine wasn't too surprised. Johan wasn't in touch with his magic at all, despite being born to a magical family. He didn't know how to extend his magic outside his body, let alone into the potion. All he could do was cast spells ... it would be enough for him, she was sure, but she knew that they had to unlock the mystery behind his power. Why did he have such odd limits?

"It hasn't worked," she said, shaking her head. Johan stirred it frantically, but nothing happened. "We'll have to figure out a way for you to get in touch with your magic before returning to potions."

"Charity always made it seem so easy," Johan muttered, crossly. "Why can't *I* do it?"

"Because your magic isn't manipulating the potion," Elaine said. A thought struck her and she picked up the grimoire from where it lay on the bench. "Put this on your head and see what happens."

Johan gave her a look that suggested he thought she had gone insane, but obeyed.

"Nothing," he said, after a long moment. "It's just a heavy book."

Elaine took the book back, thinking hard. Even mundanes could sense the wards surrounding the Great Library, but Johan hadn't noticed a thing. Nor had he sensed the almost stifling presence of the wards in the chamber, or the magic surrounding some of the artefacts on the table, where even an untrained magician should have been able to sense them. His vast power in one field seemed to be matched by almost complete helplessness in others. It just didn't make sense.

Johan leaned forward. "Are you all right?"

"I need to think of better tests," Elaine said. She considered, then pushed the thought aside for later contemplation. There were other issues that needed to be addressed. "And I need to teach you how to cancel your spells properly. In fact, we'll do that now."

She couldn't help smiling at his relief, which covered her concern. Johan's case was completely unprecedented, unlike hers. But there were enough similarities to worry her, starting with the fact that someone seemingly powerless had developed remarkable abilities that might be very dangerous.

Could this be the work of the Witch-King?

Chapter Ten

Where in the name of all of the gods was Johan?

Duncan Conidian tossed the question over and over in his mind, trying to think of a proper answer. There had been tracking spells attached to Johan, but none of them seemed to be working any longer. That was ... *worrying*. Jamal and Charity had both mastered the art of removing such spells, yet Jamal would hardly do anything for Johan and he'd threatened Charity with an awful fate if she even *thought* about removing the spells. As humiliating as it was for Johan to know that his father was watching him, it was far safer for him than letting him wander the streets without some protection. After all, he had none of his own.

But it was three days after he'd vanished and there had been nothing, nothing at all. Duncan couldn't help imagining his body being found as the Inquisitors and City Guardsmen cleaned up after the riot, but surely someone would have notified him? Or perhaps not; Johan's mere *existence* was a closely-guarded secret. The family would be shunned if the world knew that they had produced a Powerless. Johan might be dead and no one would ever know.

He'd made very quiet inquiries, but there had been no positive results and he didn't dare push too hard. Even the people who were completely dependent on his patronage might turn against him if they knew about Johan, or start using the information for blackmail purposes. The family couldn't take the risk, not when they had a chance to rise to the very highest levels of society. But where was Johan?

Jamal had come home, smirking from one side of his face to the other – and Duncan had interrogated him, wondering if Johan had been transfigured and abandoned somewhere. But Jamal had sworn blind that he'd had nothing to do with Johan's disappearance and Duncan had been forced to believe him. Asking his eldest son and heir to swear on his magic would have been a grave insult, after all. And besides, whatever cruel tricks Jamal had played in the past, he had never really risked Johan's life.

Not that you did much to stop it, he told himself, angrily. Once, he'd thought that Jamal's bullying would bring out the magic he was so sure lurked inside Johan. And then he'd stopped thinking about his second son altogether. It had been easier to turn a blind eye than face the fact that his bloodline had produced a Powerless. Jamal had been right, all those years ago. Johan should have had his memory modified and been sent to an orphanage. Cruel, but kinder than endless taunting from his siblings.

There was a tap on the door.

"Come in," he snapped. The hesitant sound told him that it was almost certainly one of the maids. "And it had better be important!"

May stepped into the room, her eyes downcast. Jamal had hired her purely because of her looks, Duncan knew – and she *was* a looker. Duncan didn't care – his son should learn to be a man in all ways and experimenting with a maid was far less dangerous than flirting with the daughter of another magical family – but Jamal had moved on after a few months of having May in his bed. She'd since tried to seduce Duncan himself, fearful for her position in the household. Duncan's reaction had taught her never to try that again.

"The Druid Zacharias is at the door," May whispered. Her voice was barely loud enough to be heard, unsurprisingly. She was absolutely terrified of him. "He wishes to speak with you urgently."

Duncan's eyes narrowed. The *druid?* He'd called Zacharias three days ago for yet another series of tests on Johan; he certainly hadn't expected to see him again for another year, where they might run yet more tests. Zacharias was lean and hungry, ready to do anything for gold coins, something that made him more than a little untrustworthy. No one knew better than Duncan just how easily oaths could be subverted by a devious magician.

"Send him in," he ordered. "And then wait outside."

May bowed and retreated. Duncan cast a handful of concealing charms over his desk – he didn't want Zacharias to see anything he didn't have to – and then waited for May to show the druid back into his office. Zacharias looked ... *keen*. That bothered Duncan more than he wanted to admit. The druid definitely knew something ... and wanted something else in exchange.

"There have been developments," Zacharias said. "Are you aware that your son Johan was taken to the hospital?"

Duncan stared at him, his feelings torn between relief and fear. Johan was safe ... but if they'd tested him, they'd know he was Powerless. And if they'd actually identified him ...

"... No," he said, finally. "But it is a relief to hear that he is safe."

Zacharias smiled. "He may also have developed magic," he said.

It took Duncan several seconds to understand what the druid had said. "Magic?"

"Magic," Zacharias repeated.

Duncan swallowed, feeling hope swelling inside his heart. "If this is a joke, or a hoax," he said, "I swear to you that you will regret it."

"He was apparently caught up in the riot three days ago," Zacharias explained, pretending to ignore the threat. "For some reason, he was out of it for two days, during which time he was cared for by the Head Librarian and an Inquisitor. As he was one of my patients, I managed to take a look at his record. The tests definitely detected magic."

His smile grew wider. "And they did some experiments when he awoke," he added. "One of them apparently damaged the wards in the hospital room."

Duncan pushed his emotions aside and thought fast. They hadn't told him, which meant ... what? If they'd tested his blood, they might well have realised that Johan was a Conidian, even if he hadn't been formally registered. They should have contacted him at once, no matter what had happened, unless ... Lady Light Spinner had ordered otherwise. Just what had happened at the riot? Every magician in the city – and considerably further away – had sensed that pulse.

And Johan apparently had magic. What did *that* have to do with the pulse?

"You said that the Head Librarian was taking care of him," he said. "Why?"

"I do not know," Zacharias admitted. "She is no druid."

Duncan nodded. He'd met the Head Librarian at a couple of Privy Council meetings, but she tended to skip them. And she'd never struck him as a formidable personality, rarely speaking up or doing more than casting a vote when the time came. He'd always assumed that Light Spinner had deliberately appointed a non-entity to the post. Off-hand, he couldn't recall her ever voting against the Grand Sorceress.

But if she had taken over ... something very odd was happening.

"Thank you," he said. Zacharias hadn't *quite* betrayed his oaths by coming to him, but it still suggested that the druid was desperate for money and connections. "You will be rewarded."

"Thank you, My Lord," Zacharias said.

Duncan called for May. "Show the druid to the door, then fetch me my finest robes," he ordered, when she appeared. He disliked wearing his Privy Councillor robes inside the house, even though they were charmed to be comfortable. Jamal, on the other hand, wore his finest robes everywhere. "And then I want you to tell my driver that I wish to go out."

He watched them go, then picked up his wand and badge of office. If his son was in the hospital, he had every right to see him ... even if it would draw attention to Johan. And if Zacharias was wrong ...

If this is a trick of some kind, he thought, *everyone will know I sired a Powerless ...*

His thoughts were interrupted by a thunderous knocking that seemed to resonate through the house. Cursing under his breath, Duncan strode out into the hallway, careful to keep one hand on his wand. He saw Charity appear at the top of the stairs and shot her an angry glare, telling her to remain where she was. He'd grounded her after she'd confessed to letting Johan leave the house without a proper escort. *That* sort of carelessness required harsh punishment, no matter how Johan had talked her into it.

"Open that door," he ordered, silently cursing inwardly when he realised that Zacharias had yet to leave the house.

The druid would probably start talking about the newcomers as soon as he got back to the hospital. "Now!"

May obeyed; three Inquisitors strode in to the house, their faces half-hidden behind grey hoods that hung down over their eyes. Duncan stared, unable to quite hide his dismay; even as a Privy Councillor, he had few dealings with the Inquisition. They reported to the Grand Sorceress and the Grand Sorceress alone.

"I am Inquisitor Dread," the leader said. His jaw, what little of it could be seen, suggested that he wasn't a man who would give up easily. It seemed to be made of solid granite. "I have here a warrant for the arrest of Jamal Conidian. You will present him to us at once."

Duncan hesitated – why would they have a warrant for his eldest son? – and then stepped forward, remembering himself. The Inquisition could scare magicians who had no connections, but *he* was the head of House Conidian, with a patronage network that gave him influence and power beyond their wildest dreams. He was not going to let them intimidate him.

"I would like to see the warrant," he said. Only one person could issue such a warrant; the Grand Sorceress herself. "And I would like to know on what charges my son is being investigated."

Dread pulled a parchment scroll from his robe and handed it over. Duncan unwrapped it, careful to test the sigil at the bottom to ensure that it actually *was* signed by Lady Light Spinner. A mere touch revealed that it was genuine. Cursing under his breath, Duncan skimmed through the list of charges. Attacking mundanes, forced transfiguration, use of compulsion spells, accessory to murder (or at least manslaughter) ... it looked as though the Inquisition had dragged up at least twenty different charges in the hopes that one of them would stick. The paragraph at the bottom, placing everything in context, was remarkably illuminative. He hadn't known that Jamal had been at the riot, let alone that he'd been the ringleader who had triggered it!

"Summon your son," Dread said. His voice was toneless, but there was a hint that he was looking forward to some violence. The house was heavily warded, yet they were already inside the main defences and all three of the Inquisitors would be skilled warriors. "Now."

Duncan hesitated, then nodded. "JAMAL," he bellowed. Had he ever been so furious with his eldest son before? There were ways to act that didn't involve bullying others ... particularly people who couldn't fight back. In hindsight, letting him pick on Johan so much had been a mistake. "GET DOWN HERE, NOW!"

Jamal appeared at the top of the stairs, then stopped, staring at the Inquisitors.

"Jamal of House Conidian," Dread said, into the silence. "I arrest you on the charges" – he listed them, reciting the entire series of charges from memory – "and whatever else may develop after a careful review of all the evidence. It is my duty to warn you that you have no right to remain silent, having threatened the peace of the realm. Anything you wish to say in your own defence may be presented to the Grand Sorceress and the Privy Council when they judge your case.

"It is also my duty to inform you that if you refuse to come quietly, we are authorised to use all necessary force to bring you with us to the Watchtower," he continued. "I spent part of the last three days clearing up the mess you caused and cancelling the spells you inflicted on your victims. *Please*; resist."

Jamal's hand twitched towards his wand. For a nightmarish moment, Duncan was *sure* that his impulsive and arrogant elder son *would* try to fight. But there were three Inquisitors, all experienced ... and Jamal was nowhere near as good as he liked to think. A fight would probably end with House Conidian being depopulated and destroyed. And, if by some dark miracle Jamal won, the Grand Sorceress would have his head even if she had to send a small army after him to get it.

"Don't," Duncan ordered, quietly. He turned to face Dread. "I will, of course, be sending a lawyer to attend to him."

"Of course," Dread agreed. If he was disappointed at the thought of avoiding violence, his voice didn't show it. "He will be held at the Watchtower until the day of his trial."

He looked up at Jamal. "Come here," he ordered. "Now."

Slowly, unwillingly, Jamal advanced down the stairs until he was on the lower floor. Dread waved his wand at Jamal and a handful of items, including Jamal's wand, sprang out of Jamal's robes and flew into a bag one of the other Inquisitors held out for them. A moment later, Jamal's body jerked violently and then started to inch towards the door, as if he wasn't quite in control of himself. Dread was manipulating him like a puppet, Duncan realised, feeling cold rage push aside his other feelings. How *dare* the Inquisitor treat his son as a common criminal?

"You will be permitted to visit his cell by prior arrangement," Dread informed him, ignoring the simmering rage that had to be visible on Duncan's face. "However, you will be expected to abide by the prison guidelines. Failure to do so will have unfortunate consequences."

He followed Jamal's body as it moved out of the door, leaving Duncan staring at his retreating back.

"You will not say a *word* about this to anyone," Duncan snapped, rounding on the druid. Zacharias seemed surprised by his intensity, but nodded quickly. A few words from Duncan in the right set of ears and the druid would never work again. "And get *out*."

May closed the door behind the druid as Duncan glared up the stairwell. "Charity, get down here," he snapped. Unsurprisingly, his eldest daughter had hidden herself past the top of the stairs, even if she was meant to stay in her room. "I need you!"

Charity looked nervous as she made her way down the stairs. "Yes, father?"

"I want you to go to the hospital," Duncan ordered. "Your brother was admitted there three days ago – and no one told us anything until now. Not that it would have been easy for them to identify him, but never mind ... I want you to go see him, to find out how he is. If they refuse to tell you anything, remember how your mother acts in shops and act like that."

Charity's face twisted. She'd been the target of her mother's attempts to turn her into a proper young lady, which seemed to include screaming at shopkeepers and dressmakers if their products weren't *exactly* what she wanted. Being both a great lady and a magician, her screaming fits were terrifying. Charity had complained often enough about having to go with her to convince Duncan to relent and forbid further unwanted trips.

"You're his elder sister," he reassured her. The lines of blood responsibility made her superior to Johan, although Johan's nature didn't make him superior to *his* younger siblings. "You have every right to know how he is."

He took a breath. "Once you get into his room, ask him ... ask him if the story is true," he added. "He'll know what I mean, if it is actually true. And if he's not injured, have him discharged and brought home. You should have the authority to make that happen."

Charity's eyes narrowed. "If *what* story is true?"

"Wait and see," he snapped. "Go there, now."

"I thought I was supposed to be grounded," Charity pointed out, snidely. "You told me that I wasn't to leave ..."

"I will send you there with a painful bottom if you don't go now," Duncan snapped. He couldn't blame his daughter for feeling irked, but there was no time to waste. "*I* have to go to the Palace and see the Grand Sorceress."

He scowled. It was not going to be a pleasant interview. If Jamal was responsible for the riot, it would be hard to convince the Grand Sorceress to mitigate his punishment. The gods knew that House Conidian had plenty of enemies, including several on the Privy Council. He could easily see them trying to convince Light Spinner not to let Jamal off lightly. Mundane deaths were less important than magical deaths, but they wouldn't care.

The thought made him scowl. At worst, Jamal would be executed ... which would leave him without a proper Heir. Charity had been groomed for marriage, not leadership of the house; Johan, naturally, had been incapable of handling the family magic. Unless, of course, the rumour was actually true ...

But if it wasn't, House Conidian would be badly weakened until Jay or Jolie grew into young men. And that would take years.

Charity picked up her coat and pulled it on, covering her robes, then headed out of the door. Duncan watched her go, then followed her down to where his driver was waiting with the carriage. Using a carriage in the Golden City was a sign of wealth and power – and he would need both in the days to come.

Oh, Jamal, he thought, *what were you thinking?*

He would ask, of course, when he visited his son in the Watchtower. It would be interesting to see what Jamal had to say for himself.

But he had an awful feeling that he already knew the *real* answer.

Chapter Eleven

"I'm going to cast a spell," Elaine said. "I want you to cancel it."

Johan nodded. Elaine had taught him several cancelling spells, each one more complex than the last, and he was looking forward to trying them. If his magic couldn't be cancelled as easily as a normal magician's magic, he might be in some trouble when it came to actually *using* his gift. As it was, he seemed almost ridiculously powerful. But would that be any good if he couldn't be an effective magician?

Elaine waved her wand in the air, creating a glowing ball of light that cast an eerie radiance over the compartment. Johan watched her precision with some envy; he hadn't dared try the light spell again after the first result, but Elaine was clearly a skilled and practiced magician – and probably very powerful. She would have to be to serve on the Privy Council, he knew, either in magical or political terms. His father had once noted that the whole system was designed to ensure that sorcerers who might try to unseat the Grand Sorceress were given a stake in the system.

"I meant to ask," he said. "Why do *you* use a wand?"

"I need it for precise spellwork," Elaine said, a hint of embarrassment in her tone. "And much of my spellwork *depends* on precision."

Johan frowned. "And would you be helpless if you lost your wand?"

Elaine shook her head. "I'd just have problems casting the more complex spells," she admitted. "But then, as *anything* can be used as a wand as long as there is no iron in it, I can always use something as a replacement."

She smirked. "Magicians who talk about the wands all the time are clearly overcompensating for something," she added, then nodded towards the glowing ball of light.

"Cancel it."

Johan had to smirk too, remembering Jamal's boasts – and then he cast the spell. The ball of light blinked out ... and Elaine stumbled backwards, staggering slightly. Johan stared in alarm, wondering what had happened ... and trying to decide what to do. Surely, he told himself, he couldn't have *hurt* her. Could he?

"Sorry," Elaine mumbled. "That was a bit of a shock."

"I didn't mean to do anything," Johan said, frantically. Panic threatened to bubble up inside his mind, overpowering common sense. Elaine's condition reminded him all too strongly of how he'd felt after his first unwanted transfiguration. "What did I do?"

Elaine pulled herself together with an effort. "Your spell was, as always, too powerful," she said. "You not only cancelled my light spell, you also cancelled most of the protections I cast on myself."

Johan stared at her. He was the first to admit that he knew little about such spells – Charity had never taught him anything about them – but surely they couldn't be *that* easy to defeat.

"They can't be," Elaine said. "Under normal circumstances, you would have to break them down or overpower them ... which, I suppose, is what you did. But a normal cancelling spell shouldn't have done anything to my protections. I wrote countermeasures into them just to ensure that no one could do that."

Johan nodded, unsure what to think. Protections would be useless, he assumed, if a simple cancelling spell could destroy them. So would the wards his father controlled, the ones that protected the house. Breaking them down, according to his father, would require both power and skill. But if his spell could just burn through them ...

"I'm sorry," he said, and meant it. He *liked* Elaine. She was the first person he'd met who had never talked down to him. "I don't know what I did."

"I'm not sure either," Elaine admitted. She knelt down, composing herself, then looked up at Johan. "How are you feeling? Any tiredness?"

"No," Johan said. He felt as if he could go on for hours.

"Is that normal?"

"... No," Elaine said. She stood upright, frowning. "The level of power you use even in a single spell should have exhausted you. You're very new to magic, yet you seem to have vast reserves of power. I'm not quite sure what that will do to you."

She smiled, rather wanly. Johan realised, with a flash of bitter guilt, that having her protections stripped away had *hurt*, even if she seemed normal now. He hadn't meant to hurt her ... he considered, briefly, abandoning magic altogether, before dismissing the thought. This was his one chance to prove himself in a world that sneered at those without magic. He couldn't abandon it, no matter the danger.

"I want to try something else," Elaine said. She picked up the notepad and wrote down the details of another spell, then passed it to Johan. "How does that sound?"

Johan glanced at it. "It looks simple enough," he said, slowly. "What does it do?"

"Levitates objects," Elaine said. She walked over to the workbench and removed the cauldron, placing it and its useless contents on the floor. The books floated up into the air and headed out of the room, presumably to somewhere where the other librarians would pick them up and return them to the shelves. "I want you to try to make the table float into the air."

She walked back to stand behind Johan as he stared at it. The workbench was heavy, made of solid wood; it seemed impossible for a single man to lift, even with magic. But he'd seen Jamal levitating heavier things – and Johan himself, more than once. Maybe if he tried ...

He said the words, his tongue stumbling slightly over the longer ones, and made the gestures. The workbench shivered, then launched itself into the air and smashed against the ceiling with terrifying force. It shattered, sending pieces of wood flying everywhere; Elaine raised her wand and hastily cast a protective ward in front of them. Johan watched in horror as the remains of the table glanced off the ward and crashed down on the floor. Splinters, sawdust and even pieces of stone drifted through the air, slowly settling down.

Johan looked up. The ceiling was cracked and broken, tiny lines radiating outwards from where the table had struck the stone. A sudden horrified image of doing that to a *person* ran through his mind; they'd be smashed into a bloody pulp, rendered utterly unidentifiable. If Jamal had been able to put him in danger with lighter spells, the gods only knew what *Johan* could do now.

"I ..." His voice sounded shaky, even to himself. "I didn't mean to do that."

"You shouldn't have been *able* to do that," Elaine commented. She took the notepad, ripped out the page she'd written on and stuffed the paper into her robes. "You see, that spell was a fake. A normal magician could cast it all day and the workbench wouldn't even have moved a millimetre. But you made it work."

Johan scowled. "I thought it was illegal to write down fake spells," he said. "Or isn't that a rule that applies to Privy Councillors?"

Elaine didn't seem to take his jibe personally. "That law has never been honoured," she answered, instead. "Every sorcerer who comes up with his own spells does *something* to them to make it difficult for others to work out how to cast them. Quite a few fledging magicians have run into trouble trying to cast such altered spells, particularly ones designed to rebound on the caster if the spell isn't fixed first. But this ..."

She tapped her pocket meaningfully. "A real magician would have *known* that it wasn't a real spell," she explained. "He would probably have reported me to the Inquisition. But you ... you managed to cast it."

Johan felt himself torn between indignation and exhilaration. On one hand, he was insulted at the trick she'd played; on the other hand, he knew more about his abilities now than he'd known before she'd given him the fake spell.

"Thank you, I suppose," he said, grudgingly. "What do we do now?"

"I think you're going to have to work on control," Elaine said, "which isn't going to be simple because your magic is different from everyone else's magic. Most of the exercises I was taught aren't likely to be helpful for you. What do you actually *feel* when you cast a spell?"

Johan frowned, trying to put his feelings into words. "It ... it just *happens*," he said, softly. "I cast the spell ... and it works."

Elaine's frown matched his. "You don't feel any *effort*?" She asked. "No *strain*. No sense of actually having to *work*?"

"No," Johan said. "It just *happens*."

"Strange," Elaine said.

Johan could understand. Jamal had pretended that his magic came to him effortlessly, but Johan had seen him staggering home after a particularly gruelling session at the Peerless School, so drained that he'd almost forgotten to be unpleasant to his powerless brother. His younger siblings had cast their first spells ... and then collapsed into sleep, unable to even keep their eyes open a moment longer. For Johan to do it so effortlessly ...

A thought struck him. "Could I have been doing magic all along without noticing?"

"I don't see how," Elaine said, after a moment's thought. "There are some magicians who wind up so badly wounded that all of their magic is diverted to heal them, leaving none for them to use to cast spells, but they were still *magicians*. You were never a magician until suddenly you were."

Her eyes narrowed. "Why *then*?"

"I don't know," Johan said. "If all I wanted was to be free of Jamal's spell, wouldn't it have happened a great deal earlier?"

"Precisely what I was wondering, particularly given the damage to your body caused by repeated transfigurations," Elaine said. "If you had something in you that lashed out, why did it wait so long to work?"

She reached out and squeezed his hand. "What else did he do to you?"

Johan didn't really want to talk about it, even to her. And he wasn't really sure that he wanted the mystery solved either.

"I need to know," Elaine said. Johan gave her a sharp glance. Had she read his mind? He'd heard that there were magicians who could do that, although he'd never met one.

Jamal certainly couldn't, or he would have used the ability to torment Johan all the more. "It will be painful, but it has to be discussed."

"Once, then," Johan said, feeling the age-old bitterness welling up inside him. Was he *never* to be free of Jamal's torments? "He turned me into frogs, snakes, rats and all kinds of objects. He cast compulsion charms on me and forced me to steal food from the pantry or humiliate myself in front of the maids. He hung me upside down with levitation charms and floated me up and over the city."

Elaine blanched. Johan could practically read *her* mind. The other charms, as unpleasant as they were, could be countered, but if Jamal had lost control of the levitation charm Johan would have plunged to certain death.

"If you had magic, such experiences should have brought it out of you," Elaine said. There was a low note of pure anger in her tone. "But floating you into the air ... that could have been really dangerous. Your magic might have disrupted his, sending you plunging down towards the ground. Didn't your father have anything to say about it?"

Johan shook his head. "I used to think that he would tell Jamal off after I got my magic," he said. "And then ... and then he didn't seem to care."

"It isn't uncommon to use pressure to try to get magic to develop early," Elaine said. "But doing it like that ... your success could have killed you."

She shook her head. "And as to why you developed magic now ... we'll just have to keep working on it."

Johan nodded, reluctantly. In truth, he didn't really want to question the miracle.

"I think," Elaine started, and then stopped. "Wait a moment ..."

She cocked her head, clearly listening to a message from the library's wards. "That's interesting," she said, after a moment. "Your sister is here, asking for you."

"*Charity*," Johan said. "Why ...?"

"The more pertinent question is how she knew to come here," Elaine commented. "Vane is speaking to her now, but she's being quite insistent. Do you want to see her?"

Johan hesitated. "I don't know," he admitted. His father

had political power ... did he have enough to force his way into the Great Library against the wishes of the Head Librarian? Or could he bring pressure to bear on Elaine? "What would happen if I said no?"

"Vane would tell her to go away," Elaine said. "There's no pressure to talk to her if you don't want to talk to her."

"You have sisters?" Johan asked.

"No," Elaine said. "Just powers of observation."

Johan scowled down at his hands. Charity was almost tolerable ... and he wanted to show off a little, to gloat to the family that had mistreated him for so long. But at the same time he wasn't sure he wanted to see *any* of them again. He didn't *have* to be part of the family, not when he could cut all ties and vanish. They couldn't keep him prisoner now.

"I don't know," Elaine said, into the silence. "But I do think that we need to find out just what they know."

"I'll talk to her," Johan decided. "Can you ask her to join us here?"

"She can meet us in one of the study rooms," Elaine said, standing up and walking towards the door. "I don't want her to see this room."

Johan followed her through another series of winding corridors – the Great Library was a maze, designed to make it harder for intruders to find the books they wanted – and into a small room designed for students. There was a table, a handful of chairs and a bookshelf with a handful of well-known reference textbooks chained to the shelf. Johan grinned as he realised that the users would be able to put them on the table, but not take them out of the room.

"People keep trying to take them out of the room and it's too much hassle to spell them to remain here," Elaine said, when she saw him looking at the books. "I can stop people taking them out of the library, but not moving them from room to room. And we *still* have problems with students hiding books behind the shelves or charming them to be impossible to find without the right counter-charm."

"Particularly before exams," Johan guessed. "Can't you do something to stop them?"

"We try," Elaine said. "Anything unique can be charmed to remain in one place, but newer books are often harder to protect ...”

She looked up as the door opened again. “And here is your sister,” she said. “Do you want me to stay here?”

Johan found himself torn. Part of him wanted Elaine to stay, part of him wanted to talk to Charity in private ... if there *was* such a thing in the Great Library. It was one of the most heavily warded buildings in the Golden City. In the end, he shook his head. Elaine nodded in agreement and walked past Charity, out into the corridor. The young girl who had shown Charity into the room smiled brightly at Johan and then followed Elaine, leaving Charity and Johan alone.

Charity looked ... *worried*, Johan realised. She’d been sweating over her exams, but this was worse ... worse than she’d been when she’d feared that her last boyfriend wouldn’t be good enough for her father. Johan felt a cold shiver running through his body; what, he wondered, had scared her so badly. And how much did she *know*?

“Johan,” she said. Surprisingly, she enveloped him in a hug. “I’ve been so worried. And it was all my fault!”

“I don’t see how,” Johan said. “What happened to you?”

“Jamal’s been arrested,” Charity said. She sounded too shocked for it to be a joke. “The Inquisitors came and took him away!”

“And not before time,” Johan said, unable to hide his amusement. His brother had worked hard to kill all sibling loyalty he might have otherwise felt. “I’m sure father is really annoyed about it.”

“He is,” Charity said. “And he was worried about you too.”

“I doubt it,” Johan muttered. His father had never expressed any worry about Johan personally, only the family name. If a dark wizard *had* captured him, his father would have been more concerned about the threat to the *powerful* members of the family. As if there *was* any threat. Away from his family, Johan would have been just another mundane. “How long is Jamal going to remain in jail?”

“No, don’t tell me,” he added. “Father’s going to go to the Grand Sorceress, spin some sob story about Jamal having been overworked and convince her to let him go free, no doubt with an apology for wasting his time. Who *cares* about some mundanes when *Jamal* is the one at risk?"

"He's your brother," Charity pointed out. "And this could really upset the family's position ..."

Johan fought down the urge to sneer, despite his growing anger. "And why should I care?"

"The family gave you a life," Charity said. "You owe father respect, if nothing else, and you should not undermine his position."

"How *can* you take his side?" Johan demanded. "You know what he did to me, what Jamal did to me ... you *rat*, you ..."

Charity shrank. She shrank so rapidly that her clothes fell down around her, hitting the ground where she'd been. Johan stumbled back in shock, staring at where his sister had been standing. A moment later, a rat nosed its way out from under the robes and stared up at him.

He found his voice, somehow. "Charity?"

Chapter Twelve

"She was prepared to offer me quite a high bribe," Vane said. "I don't know what I would have done if you hadn't agreed to let her see him."

Elaine scowled. Bribes were an accepted part of public life, but *she* didn't like them, if only because she had never been wealthy enough to bribe anyone. And she would not have been forgiving if any of her subordinates had accepted a bribe. Vane, at least, was smart enough to realise it.

Her scowl deepened as she puzzled over a different question. How had Charity known where to find Johan? The hospital hadn't alerted his father, even after he'd finally been identified; Elaine had issued orders to keep all information related to Johan under tight control. And much of it was in her skull anyway. The hospital staff were all bound by their oaths ... she muttered a curse under her breath as she realised the answer. Zacharias could have told Johan's father about him, without breaking his oaths. After all, Johan was still technically a minor and thus his father had the right to be informed about his condition ...

Bastard, she thought, although she wasn't sure what she could do in response. The druid hadn't technically violated his oaths, so the hospital would be reluctant to punish him — and besides, Johan *was* a minor. Old enough to be declared an adult, but his father would have been unlikely to make the declaration, not when Johan had once been largely helpless in the magical world. Far better to keep him as a permanent and powerless dependent.

She was still thinking dark thoughts when the wards sounded the alert. *Something* had happened inside the study room. Elaine turned and ran towards the door; Vane followed her, clearly worried. *She* might not be as closely tied to the wards as Elaine herself, but she had enough access to know that something was wrong.

Elaine gripped her wand as she pushed open the door ... then stopped as she saw a rat on the floor, with Johan cowering back in shock. The rat had to be Charity, she realised in horror; whatever they'd said to one another, it had provoked an angry reaction from Johan. And probably an unexpected one, considering his condition. At least he hadn't *intended* to turn his sister into a rat. But that would be small consolation for his victim.

"I didn't mean to do it," Johan stammered, when she touched his shoulder. "It just ... *happened.*"

Like everything else, Elaine thought. She reached out and touched the rat with her wand, casting an analysis charm. It had seemed too dangerous to let Johan play around with transfiguration spells, but seeing that it had happened by accident ... well, she might as well take advantage of it. The results seemed odd; the rat seemed to be a *real* rat, but there were still human mental patterns in the rat's brain.

Elaine let out a sigh of relief. The spells used for prank transfigurations protected their victim from losing their minds, but uncontrolled magic was far harder to predict. Charity might have become a real rat, complete with a ratty brain that was unable to remember that she had once been human. It had happened, more than once, as a form of punishment. And, when done without permission, it was effectively considered murder.

"I understand," she said, as soothingly as she could. "I'm going to cast the reversal charm now."

Charity looked up hopefully, her ratty eyes seeming to plead with Elaine. She wouldn't have been able to counter the spell herself, even if it had been normal. It had clearly burned through whatever protections she had, just as easily as Johan had destroyed Elaine's protections earlier. Elaine tapped Charity's head with the wand, muttering the spell under her breath. Nothing happened.

Johan's eyes were wide with panic. "You can't undo it?"

"I need to try a more complex spell," Elaine said. Casting a transfiguration that could only be undone by the caster was frowned upon, although it was not – technically – illegal. Besides, Johan wouldn't have known how to do it ... if that would have mattered. "Give me a moment."

She raised her wand, chanting the most powerful reversal spell she had crafted herself. It should have undone even a locked spell as it undid the tiny glitches in reality caused by the magic, rather than attacking the spell directly. Nothing happened.

"That's bad," Vane said. Elaine's subordinate gave her a worried look. "Do you want me to try?"

Elaine shook her head. Vane might have more raw power, but raw power was unlikely to be helpful in this situation. She needed ... something else.

"No," she said, out loud. "Go to the main desk and get back to work – and don't say anything to anyone. I'll deal with this."

Vane bowed and retreated, closing the door as she left.

"Johan," Elaine said, turning to the younger man, "I know it's hard, but you need to focus right now."

Johan stared at her, blankly. "I've killed her," he said. "I ..."

"No, you haven't," Elaine said. "A real rat would be running around, trying to escape or hunting for cheese. Charity is waiting for you to undo the spell. Now ... I want you to cast the cancelling charm again. Focus your mind and take off the spell."

"I don't know *how*," Johan said. The fear in his voice was clearly making it harder for him to think clearly. "*How*?"

"The cancelling charm will undo the spell," Elaine said. It wouldn't have been true of a normal transfiguration spell, but *Johan* didn't know that. "Cast it now."

Johan lifted his hand and muttered the spell. There was a brilliant flash of light; when it faded, Charity was lying on the floor, completely naked. She let out a gasp of shock, then realised that she was unclothed and tried desperately to cover herself. Elaine sighed, tried to avoid noticing that Charity was physically perfect, and used her wand to direct her clothes into her arms.

"I'm sorry," Johan said, as he turned his back. He sounded thoroughly miserable. "I never meant that to happen."

"Don't worry about it," Charity said, although her tone suggested that she was more shaken up than she wanted to admit. "You have *magic*!"

"Yeah," Johan said. He seemed a little more cheerful by her nonchalant response. "How about *that*?"

Elaine tuned them out and started casting diagnostic charms. As far as she could tell, none of the after-effects of transfiguration were present in Charity's body. There wasn't even a *hint* that she had been a rat only moments ago. Her magical field was strong, if nowhere near as developed as Light Spinner or Dread's. Elaine couldn't help another flicker of envy, even though she didn't envy either of them their upbringings. Having siblings was no pleasure if they were merciless bullies.

"This is *wonderful*," Charity said. "Father is going to be *so* thrilled!"

"I don't want to go back," Johan said, firmly. "Father can do without me. He has Jamal, after all."

"Jamal is in jail," Charity said. She hesitated, clearly worried about being turned back into a rat – or something worse – and then pressed on. "Johan, if you have magic, you could become the Prime Heir."

Elaine found herself, for the first time, wishing that she'd paid more attention to what was going on outside the library. If Jamal was in jail, his father would be trying to bring as much pressure as he could to bear against the Grand Sorcerer, trying to ensure that he was let off with a slap on the wrist. Light Spinner might insist on the Privy Council serving as his judges, providing some political cover, but which way would they jump?

Vane would probably be able to guess, Elaine thought, sourly. *She* was no expert at reading people. Elaine herself would vote to convict, but the others? Some of them might join her purely to take a shot at Jamal's father, rather than Jamal himself. Others would support Jamal's attack on the Levellers and refuse to convict. And then Light Spinner would have to uphold or veto the verdict.

"I don't *want* to be the Heir," Johan insisted. "And it isn't as if Jamal is going to be executed for this, is it?"

He looked over at Elaine. "Is it?"

"I don't know," Elaine admitted, reluctantly. "It depends which way the Privy Council jumps."

"You'll *see*," Johan predicted. "Jamal will get away with

it. He always does."

The pain in his voice made Elaine wince. She could understand *precisely* why Johan didn't want to go back to his family, even though he was still a declared minor. Legally, however, they would have every right to claim him ... unless Light Spinner agreed that Johan should stay in the Great Library.

It might be dangerous if they did try to claim him, Elaine thought, with a hint of rueful amusement. Most people would be careful around magicians, even low-power ones like herself, but Johan's family had thought of him as powerless for so long that they might not realise that everything had changed. *I wonder what he would do to them.*

Charity leaned forward, reaching out to take Johan's hand. "And if he doesn't?"

"Father will bribe or threaten whoever it takes to free Jamal," Johan said, pulling his hand away from her. "I think he'll be out of jail by the end of the week."

He stood up and stepped away from his sister. "Tell father that I have no interest in returning to the family," he added. "If he didn't want me when I had no magic, he won't get me when I do have magic."

"Wait," Charity said. "Please ..."

"I didn't notice you insisting that I should be treated better," Johan snapped. "I remember you laughing at some of Jamal's *games*. But they weren't games to me, were they?"

He headed for the door. Elaine hesitated, then nodded slightly. "Wait in the next room," she said, hoping that he would obey orders. She wasn't sure what she could do if he refused, short of trying to force him to obey. "I need a few words with Charity."

Charity started to speak as soon as Johan had slammed the door behind him. "I apologise for my brother," she said, softly. "He's not had an easy life."

"No," Elaine agreed. The orphanage had been bad, but growing up a Powerless among magicians had been worse. Much worse. "He hasn't."

"I am not sure why *you* are dealing with this," Charity said, clearly digging for information. "But I do know that it involves my family."

"Yes," Elaine agreed.

Charity's eyes narrowed. "My father would insist that you immediately send Johan home," she said. Her voice was calm, but there was a deadly glint in her eyes. "And my father does have the influence to bring pressure to bear on you ..."

"Yes," Elaine said, again.

"I really don't understand why this is your problem," Charity said, having decided that threats weren't likely to work. "My father ..."

Elaine scowled at her, remembering Millicent and her cronies, boys and girls who had had the Empire presented to them on a silver platter. Charity was just like them; young, beautiful, wealthy and powerful. She had never realised just how unfair the world could be.

"Your father has other problems at the moment," she said, wondering if Charity would pick up on the subtext. Elaine would be one of Jamal's judges. "I suggest that you tell him to respect Johan's wishes and leave this affair strictly alone."

Charity looked oddly despondent. "And if he wishes to see his son?"

"He can send along a visiting card, like everyone else," Elaine said, fighting down the urge to yawn. It had been a long day and it was far from over. "And Johan will decide if he wants to see him, like everyone else."

She headed to the door. "The library will show you out," she said, as she paused in the doorway. "I would advise you not to forget what happened today. Your brother is not what he used to be."

Elaine stopped outside the door and made contact with the wards, altering the interior of the library to steer Charity to the main entrance without allowing her to go anywhere else. It was impolite, to say the least, but she doubted that Charity would want to stay in the library in any case. Besides, it would demonstrate her power for the younger – but far more arrogant – girl.

Bracing herself, she turned and marched into the room Johan occupied. He was sitting in one of the seats, staring down at his hands and trying, desperately, not to cry. Elaine couldn't really blame him; no matter his feelings towards his family, cutting ties with them was a hard decision at the best of times. And *these* were far from the best of times. She still couldn't believe that Charity had attempted to guilt him into coming home.

"I ... my father only wants me back because I have magic," Johan said. His voice dripped of bitterness – and helpless rage. "Now I have magic, I'm *useful*."

"It has happened before," Elaine said, knowing that it would be no consolation. "And you can give your brother a nasty surprise if you ever meet him again."

Johan looked up at her. "Do you think that father knows I was the one who identified Jamal?"

"The Inquisitors wouldn't have mentioned names," Elaine said. "Too many witnesses got pressured into changing their stories. I think your father probably doesn't know who told them about his son."

"I should tell him," Johan said. He laughed, rather weakly. "He wouldn't want me home *then*."

Elaine scowled. The Patriarch of a magical family had wide authority to bring up his children – and discipline them – as he saw fit. He might just declare that Johan was no longer part of his family, disinheriting him completely ... or he might try to assert his authority to punish his rebellious son. Legally speaking, the law would be on his side. Johan wasn't an apprentice or an Inquisitor ...

"It might not be a good idea," she cautioned. She reached out and touched his shoulder, lightly. "What happened between you and Charity?"

"I called her a rat," Johan said. "And ... and she *became* one."

He looked up at her, eyes bright with unshed tears. "Is that always going to happen to me now? My magic sparking off by accident and ... *things* happening?"

"I think you just have to learn how to control it," Elaine said. Magicians knew that they were using magic, even when stress or panic caused them to lose control. Johan, it seemed, didn't even have *that* level of awareness. "There are some spells we might be able to use, but ..."

She shook her head. "I will need to do some research," she

admitted. "And maybe consult with a few other experts."

"Please," Johan said. "I could have really hurt her."

"Charity didn't panic," Elaine reminded him. "She knew what to do if transfigured. All you have to do is keep your magic under control in future."

Johan grimaced. "Easier said than done."

Elaine cleared her throat. "I will have to attend a meeting at the palace tonight," she added, reluctantly. "Do you want me to find someone to stay with you in your rooms?"

"No," Johan said, quickly. "I'm not a baby!"

Elaine nodded, regretting Daria's absence. *She* would have made an ideal supervisor, unlike most of her other friends and acquaintances. Daria had a gift for making friends; Elaine often found herself tongue-tied when meeting new people. It had turned her into a social recluse even before she'd become a Bookworm.

Johan met her eyes. "What do you think I could *do* with my magic?"

"Once you learn to control it," Elaine said, after a moment, "you could do almost anything with it. There are no shortage of jobs for skilled magicians. Or you could help us study your gift, let us see how it works ..."

"I want to be *someone*," Johan said. "I always wanted to travel, to see the world ... and my father would have left me shut up in my house."

Elaine frowned. Ambition was something she understood, but it wasn't really something she *shared*. She had been happy enough as a library assistant, then as the Head Librarian. Being a Privy Councillor, even one who rarely attended meetings, was somewhat beyond the limit of her ambition. But Johan had been born to a powerful family, often overshadowed by his relatives. Why would he *not* be ambitious?

And he wants to get away from his family, Elaine thought. She could certainly understand *that*.

"I rarely travel," she admitted. "But there are places we could go, if you wish. How much of the city have you actually *seen*?"

"Very little," Johan said. The way he said it made Elaine's heart go out to him. "I was rarely allowed to leave the house.”

“I'll take you somewhere tomorrow,” Elaine promised. She reached out mentally and touched the library wards. “Your room will have a few books for you to study, along with some food. If you feel hungry, eat; if you feel tired, sleep. The meeting ... could take a while.”

Johan frowned. “You're going to be discussing *me*?”

“I'm afraid so,” Elaine said. “And your brother.”

“Tell them to hang him,” Johan said, darkly. “I saw what he did to those helpless people.”

That was a good sign, Elaine told herself. Johan had magic now, but he hadn't forgotten what it was like to be powerless. But it still didn't answer the real question nagging at her mind. What, really, was the source of his strange powers?

“I'll pass on your words,” she said, “but it may be a long hard fight before sentence is passed.”

“Why,” Johan asked sardonically, “am I not surprised?”

Chapter Thirteen

There were additional guards on the streets, Elaine noticed as she walked towards the Imperial Palace, backed up by a handful of Inquisitors. None of them looked happy; there just weren't enough Inquisitors to waste on patrolling the city, even when there was a strong possibility that another riot might break out. Elaine nodded to a couple she knew as she passed through the gates and walked up to the palace, praying that Light Spinner hadn't called a full meeting of the Privy Council. She *hated* sitting at the table and hated speaking still more.

Thankfully, the only other person in the room was Dread, looking tired and cross as he stood to attention, clearly having declined the offer of a seat. The Grand Sorceress wasn't a monarch from the ancient times; there was no rule that dictated that everyone else had to remain standing in her presence, let alone prostrate themselves in front of her. Elaine bowed quickly as she entered the room, then took one of the comfortable seats. Light Spinner's eyes glinted tired amusement at her.

"I have just been speaking with the Conidian," Light Spinner said. There was no trace of amusement in her voice, merely a bone-weariness that matched Elaine's own feelings. "He wishes his son to be freed from the Watchtower."

Elaine rubbed her eyes. "I thought that there was a case against him," she said, crossly. "We *know* he was there."

"Several aristocratic brats have sworn blind that he was gambling with them until the wee small hours that day," Dread said. "We don't believe them, of course, but as they are not suspects in a crime we cannot use truth spells to ensure that they are telling the truth."

"They might well be the others," Elaine said. Johan had been unable to identify the others, but somehow she doubted that Jamal Conidian would associate himself with lower-class magicians, even if they had magic. "We could arrest them on suspicion."

"And then have half the establishment up in arms," Light Spinner said, coldly. "But we will also have riots if someone *isn't* brought to justice for the crime."

"Right now, they are waiting to see if someone is hauled in front of the authorities," Dread added. "If we fail to do so ..."

"Jamal Conidian is not suited to be the Head of a Great House," Elaine said, flatly. "If half the stories his brother tells are true, he is a bully, a cad, a liar, a philanderer ..."

"We get the idea," Dread said, hastily. "But we have to work within the boundaries of the politically possible."

Elaine scowled. Convict Jamal; have the Conidian Family as enemies, perhaps joined by several of the other Great Houses. Don't convict Jamal; have riots, perhaps even an uprising, by the non-magical community. Light Spinner was caught between the demons of all seven hells and the great blue sea. It was hard to escape the thought that she might choose to free Jamal, believing that the Levellers posed the lesser threat. Elaine knew that it would be hard to blame her.

"But that is a secondary matter right now," Light Spinner said. Her dark eyes met Elaine's and held them. "What progress have you made with Johan Conidian?"

Elaine took a moment to gather her thoughts. "He has definitely developed magic," she said, "of a very strange nature. As far as I know" – and thanks to the Witch-King her knowledge was extensive – "his existence is utterly unprecedented."

She took a breath, then continued. "The average magician requires both knowledge and power to work magic reliably," she explained. Both of them knew it already – it was common knowledge – but it had to be said again, just to make sure they understood. "They are taught the words and gestures required to cast spells, yet the more power they have, the more steps they can skip or simply overpower to cast the spell. Their magic is strong enough to overcome failings in technique."

The words brought back bitter memories. Millicent had been casting spells effortlessly, while Elaine had had to cast them over and over again before she got everything right and the spell condescended to work. Now, she understood magic intimately, she understood just how much Millicent had been skipping over and how much more she could have done ... but it was still humiliating. It had taken her nearly a year to learn how to start protecting herself against some of Millicent's tricks.

"But even a normal magician requires *some* technique," she said, pushing her thoughts aside. "At the very least, he or she requires a close connection to his magic. Johan, on the other hand, seems to be all power and no technique. He can make things happen without, I suspect, ever needing an understanding of *why* certain things work and others don't."

She met Light Spinner's eyes, willing her to understand. "He *cannot* cast spells without being able to visualise the effects," she said. "If he doesn't know what a spell is meant to do, he can't cast it. On the other hand, upon being given a fake spell, he managed to make it do what I said it should be able to do. And when he does cast spells, the results are always squinty. The only spell that could be said to have worked properly was one he cast *without* any of the standard spells."

Dread leaned forward. "What did he do?"

"Turned his sister into a rat," Elaine said. The memory made her want to shiver. Too much could have gone wrong, crippling or killing Charity outright. "No wand, no words, no gestures ... he just did it."

"Maybe trying to teach him standard spells is a mistake," Light Spinner mused. "Maybe you should concentrate on the effects you want instead."

Elaine nodded. It *was* a good thought. Most practical magical training revolved around proper spellcasting; intent, vocalisation and gestures. The wand served to help students focus their minds, channelling their power out of their body. But perhaps if they concentrated on intent alone ...

"That leads to a different question," Dread said, bluntly. "Is Johan a danger to anyone else?"

"... Perhaps," Elaine said. She had never thought that she would be *grateful* that forced transfiguration was regarded as nothing more than a prank, at least as long as it was inflicted on another magician. "The blunt truth is, Inquisitor, he doesn't have any real control over his magic ... and what spells he casts are often far too overpowered. His attempt to learn how to cancel his magic accidentally destroyed my protections too."

Dread gave her a considering look. "*That* must have been terrifying."

It had been, Elaine knew, but she wasn't going to tell him that. Not yet and perhaps not ever.

"I do not believe that he intended to turn his sister into a rat," she said, instead. "It would probably be best if he continued to receive private training, rather than being allowed to enrol at the Peerless School. And, ideally, he should be kept away from his family."

"The Conidian has not mentioned Johan to me," Light Spinner said. "But he does have a legal claim on his son."

Elaine blinked in surprise, then realised that Charity probably hadn't had a chance to mention Johan's determination to stay at the Great Library before the Conidian had gone to speak with Light Spinner. Once he found out, Elaine had no doubt that he would be on his way back to the Imperial Palace. Charity's story, if she told him everything, would whet his appetite for drawing his newly-empowered son back into the fold.

"Not if you choose to assert the Security of the Realm," Elaine pointed out. "You could block the Conidian's attempts to regain control of his son."

"True," Light Spinner agreed.

Dread had a more practical concern. "I dislike the thought of a magician with unpredictable powers," he said, "but we are ignoring the real problem in the room. Is Johan connected to the Witch-King?"

Light Spinner turned to look at Elaine, expectantly.

"It may be impossible to give any *certain* answer," Elaine said, carefully. "We know so little about how the Witch-King works his manipulations that it is difficult to say anything for certain. However, I do not believe that this is necessarily his work."

"Are you *sure*?" Dread asked. "Do you have any reason not to be suspicious?"

He leaned forward. "The last freak magical accident we

had was yours," he said. "The Witch-King used you to steal all the knowledge in the Great Library. You were not evil, you were not deliberately involved, but you were still his tool. Johan may not be evil, yet he could still be being manipulated by an unseen foe with incredible patience and knowledge at his disposal."

The hell of it, Elaine knew, was that he was right. It was impossible to prove that the Witch-King was involved ... or that he wasn't involved. The handful of people who knew that the Witch-King had somehow survived the Second Necromantic War had been digging through the files, trying to see his fingerprints, but it was like chasing ghosts. Two items, separated by a century, might be part of his plan. Or they might just be imagining a connection where none existed.

We need to find him, she thought. *But where the hell* is *he?*

"We cannot just kill people on suspicion," she argued, remembering her first real conversation with Dread, back in Ida. Then, Dread had worried that she might have had her own magic boosted – and people who had their magic boosted often went insane. It had been an uncomfortable conversation, not least because she had been trying to hide her new status as a Bookworm from him. "Johan might become a threat ... or a powerful ally."

She looked over at Light Spinner, who was regarding them both calmly. "And he represents a window into a whole new area of research," she added. "Everything I have seen insists that he was a Powerless, that he had no magic at all. Now, he has formidable magic of a type unseen in history. We cannot let this opportunity go to waste."

"It also makes him a target," Dread observed. "There will be those who believe that studying his magic is the key to bestowing magical abilities. The Levellers will want him; others, such as his own brother, will want him dead. We may not be able to protect him."

Elaine winced. Dread was right. If magic was the key to social superiority – and it was – the mundanes would want it. And those who already had power would want to safeguard their positions by *preventing* it from being studied. It was yet another reason for Johan never to go home.

"You can assign an Inquisitor to him to serve as a bodyguard," Elaine said, remembering that two had been assigned to her. "Who would pick a fight with them?"

"There aren't enough Inquisitors in the city to spare one for more than a few hours at best," Dread said. "As it is, we're all getting by on less sleep and more bad-temper than ever before."

I wonder how anyone tells the difference, Elaine thought, although she wasn't brave or stupid enough to say it out loud. There were potions that could keep people going for days or even weeks without sleep, but after a week or two the side effects started to become increasingly noticeable. Inquisitors might be able to take it; students were warned that staying awake for more than two days, no matter how frantic they were to complete an essay before the deadline, would have unfortunate effects on their grades.

"We'll see what can be organised," Light Spinner said. "Thankfully, rumours haven't started to spread throughout the city, but the Privy Council will have to be briefed."

Elaine nodded, reluctantly. Some of them would probably agree with her, but others - Vlad Deferens in particular – would want Johan dead before the research wizards could start unlocking the secret of his powers. Quite why Light Spinner had asked Deferens to join her Privy Council – and, for that matter, why he'd accepted – was a mystery to her. Even if she had been unable to forget the fact the man was a woman-hater, one with a very good reason to hate Elaine in particular, it was hard to avoid realising that he was also a complete bastard.

Maybe she wanted him where she could see him, Elaine thought. Everyone knew that Deferens had wanted to be Grand Sorcerer ... and everyone knew that he had been forced out of the contest early, after humiliating himself in public. If there was a true challenger to Light Spinner, it was the man who had never had the chance to face her in the final contest ... which had been lucky for Deferens. Light Spinner had been the sole survivor among the other contestants, winning almost by default.

She pushed the thought aside and looked up at Light Spinner. "Perhaps we could come to an arrangement with the

Conidian," she said. "He has a strong interest in keeping his son's powers a secret."

"No he doesn't," Dread grunted. "Johan's nature blocked Jamal's plans to get married. The Conidian has every reason to shout the news from the rooftops."

Elaine swore under her breath. He was right.

"Then we need some other form of protection for him," Elaine said. "He could live here ..."

"Out of the question," Dread snapped. "The Grand Sorceress *also* lives here."

"Maybe he could become your formal apprentice," Light Spinner suggested, calmly. "As such, he would be effectively independent from his father as long as the apprenticeship lasts."

"But his father would be required to give consent," Elaine pointed out. The whole idea of taking on an apprentice was terrifying, but it might have been a workable solution ... if the Conidian agreed. But it was unlikely that he would. "I don't think he would agree quickly, if at all."

"I can order you to take him on," Light Spinner said. "That would effectively block his objections, particularly as it would *also* announce that Johan is *indeed* a magician. The rumours that suggest he *isn't* would be answered."

"The Conidian might go along with that," Elaine mused. "But would Johan?"

She considered it, quickly. The basic idea was that a junior magician was apprenticed to a stronger senior magician, someone who could teach them – and shut them down, if necessary. But if her darker thoughts about Johan's true nature were accurate, it was unlikely that they would find *anyone* stronger than him. Light Spinner, perhaps, or Dread ... neither of whom could take on an apprentice.

"It would provide the most protection for him," Light Spinner assured her. "And it is clear that he doesn't want to leave you."

Her eyes glinted. "I could probably turn Howarth Hall over to you," she added. "If you want it, of course."

Elaine had to smile. Lord Howarth, her Guardian, had vanished from the city. His ancestral home had been ransacked by his creditors, who'd taken everything apart from the building itself. She was marginally surprised that it hadn't been sold – land was *very* profitable in the Golden City, particularly if there were gardens attached – but there were legal issues surrounding the Hall that would take years for the lawyers to sort out. Or a word from Light Spinner, if she felt disposed to settle the matter.

"No, thank you," she said. Howarth Hall had never been her home. She'd often wondered quite why Lord Howarth had served as her Guardian, at least in name; now, she knew that it was one of the Witch-King's manipulations. Nothing else could have kept him carrying out a role that distracted him from gambling and running up debts. "Burn it to the ground or sell it to the next set of immigrants from far away. I don't care."

Light Spinner chuckled, rather unkindly. "You do realise that having land in the city could set you up for life? You would automatically be considered part of the highest nobility in the Empire."

Elaine shook her head, firmly. Howarth Hall had been stripped, after all. She would have to bring in everything from beds to bookshelves – and a kitchen, and hire staff ... no, taking the hall would mean spending most of her savings on renovating it. Selling the land was a more attractive thought, but she didn't want anything from Lord Howarth. The gods knew he'd never done anything for her.

"Suit yourself," Light Spinner said. Droll amusement ran through her voice. "But you may have to find yourself a house if you're taking on an apprentice. You can't keep him locked up in the library indefinitely."

"I know," Elaine said. She closed her eyes, wondering just what Johan would make of the offer. Student magicians wanted to be apprenticed to great and powerful sorcerers, not librarians. "I'll ask him, either tonight or tomorrow. And then I'll let you know."

She bowed to Light Spinner and Dread, then returned to the library, unable to avoid feeling cold as she walked through the darkening streets. Once, the Golden City had never slept; now, the streets were almost deserted, apart from a handful of beggars and the ever-present City Guardsmen, who eyed her nervously as she walked home. Magic or no magic, Elaine still found them a little intimidating. She had never been a strong woman ...

Back at the library, she checked on Johan and was amused to discover that he'd gone to sleep in a chair, with a book on his lap. Shaking her head, she ordered dinner for herself, checked the wards, then climbed into her own bed without bothering to undress. There would be time enough for a proper wash in the morning, she told herself. Closing her eyes, she meditated for a few moments, then went to sleep.

That night, she dreamt of the Witch-King ...

... And woke up screaming.

Chapter Fourteen

"He turned you into a *rat*?"

Charity nodded, refusing to meet his eyes. Duncan would have wondered if she had been lying to him, if she hadn't been trembling like a leaf. Whatever had happened in the Great Library had scared her badly and, as soon as she was safe, she had collapsed. No normal transfiguration could have had such an effect. Charity had been Jamal's victim more than once until she'd learned to defend herself.

But it was great news, wasn't it? His second son had finally come into his magic!

"So," he said, carefully. "When is Johan coming home?"

"He said he wouldn't be coming home," Charity said. "He said if you didn't want him without magic, you couldn't have him *with* magic."

Duncan could have kicked himself. He'd allowed his disappointment to show far too much – and Johan had now rejected him. And, now that he had magic, it would be hard to claim that Johan would be in danger if he went out of the house. Maybe there was still time to train Johan to take over as Prime Heir – if Jamal were to be executed – but if Johan didn't want to learn ...

Charity had wanted to learn so badly that she'd asked for a spell that *compelled* her to learn, even when she wanted to slack off. Johan had no such motivation.

And, his thoughts mocked him, *why should he*?

Everyone knew that mundanes – and Powerless – were crippled. They couldn't enter into binding agreements, for the very simple reason that they had no magic to uphold the agreements. Nor could a Powerless hope to control even the simplest set of wards, let alone the ancient wards built into the family's ancestral home. Johan was far from stupid, but he couldn't have served as Prime Heir. And nor could Charity. As the daughter of a proven breeder – particularly now that Johan had finally developed magic – she would serve far better as a marriage partner for another magician than as Prime Heir.

But if Johan *could* serve as Prime Heir, wasn't it his duty to the family?

"I don't think he sees it that way," Charity said, when Duncan said that out loud. There was an expression on her face that reminded him of the day he'd discovered the identity of her first boyfriend, a grim assertion that she would not allow groundings, thrashings or even punishment hexes to dissuade her from her chosen course. She was as stubborn as Duncan himself. "You allowed him to be treated like ... well, badly ... and now he doesn't want anything to do with you."

Duncan fought down the anger that demanded that he lash out at her. Charity was right – and nothing would change that, no matter how mad he got at her. Instead, he tried to think. He had to lure Johan back, deal with Jamal's situation – and then somehow turn the whole affair to the family's advantage. If it got out that his second son no longer wanted anything to do with them ... the family's enemies would scent weakness. And then they would attack.

"Tell me what he said," he ordered. "Everything."

Charity looked mutinous, but obeyed. Duncan listened with growing concern as she explained what had happened, including the minor detail that the Head Librarian had been unable to break the transfiguration spell. *That* was more than a little worrying; Duncan was practiced enough to know that most accidental magic was easy to undo, as long as it didn't actually kill the target. Casting a spell that could only be undone by the caster required a great deal more practice, far too much for Johan to master in three days.

He closed his eyes as Charity finally came to a halt, swaying unsteadily on her feet.

"Thank you," he said, without opening his eyes. "You can go – and there will be a reward for this."

"Thank you," Charity said. She didn't sound too pleased with his promise of a reward. No doubt she'd felt as if she were betraying her brother, even though their father had every right to know what was happening to him. "What will happen to Jamal?"

"We don't know yet," Duncan said. "Go."

He opened his eyes long enough to see Charity flouncing out of the room, swinging her hips in a manner calculated to annoy her father, then looked down at the notes on his desk. Jamal was in deep trouble – and there would almost certainly have to be a trial. Light Spinner had pointed out, a smile no doubt hidden behind her veil, that Jamal was responsible for at least nineteen deaths and countless injuries. Mundanes or not, someone was going to have to answer for those deaths.

The Inquisitors hadn't allowed him to speak to his son, which had been lucky for him. Duncan had intended to force Jamal to give up the names of his allies, names that might have bought him a lighter sentence ... but instead all he'd been able to do was send his son a note, a note that would no doubt be read by every Inquisitor in the Watchtower before Jamal received it. And his son might conclude that it had been *written* by the Inquisitors.

Shaking his head, he reached for another sheet of paper and started to write a formal letter to Johan. He could go in person, but if his second son was as hostile as Charity claimed ... he wrote out a formal note, then tore it up in disgust. Charity had been right; it was far too late to brush aside Johan's treatment as he grew up. The pranks that had helped Charity and her younger siblings tap into their powers had turned into a never-ending torment for Johan. But what choice had they had?

Magic was the source of power, everyone knew that. And the younger one's powers developed, the greater their powers would be in adulthood. Everyone knew that too. But if it had taken sixteen years for Johan's powers to emerge ...

"By the gods," Duncan muttered to himself. "What have I done?"

Cursing, he started to rewrite the letter. There was so much he wanted to say, but he didn't quite dare, not when he had a feeling that another Privy Councillor would be reading the letter. Light Spinner had been smart, assigning the Head Librarian to Johan's case. Her fellow Privy Councillors didn't take her seriously, not when she was nothing more than a quiet little mouse. But it was clearly time to find out more about her. Even if she was just Light Spinner's crony, seats on the Privy Council didn't go to just *anyone*.

Finishing the letter, he called for a maid. When May appeared, he passed the sheet of paper to her and told her to take it to the Great Library. It was late at night, but she would be safe on the streets. There were enough City Guardsmen on patrol to keep thugs and other criminals well away from the centre of the city.

And then he headed to bed.

***

Elaine sat upright, sweat pouring down her face as the nightmare shimmered back into the realms of unreality. Dreams were important, everyone agreed, but they were also the random products of a person's mind. There were times, Elaine thought, when having so much information in her head was a definite disadvantage. None of the theories had ever been proven, despite countless books having been written to support one side of the argument and discredit the other.

It was hot, too hot. She glanced around, half-expecting to see a fire, before her mind cleared enough to remind her that she was still wearing her full robes. Muttering curses under her breath, she swung her legs out of bed and stood upright, wincing slightly at the feel of the sweaty material against her skin. Her hands refused to cooperate at first; she almost panicked before realising that she'd been dreaming so vividly that the dream-pain had left lingering shadows in her mind. As if the thought were enough, her hands started to work properly, but she still fumbled as she undid her robes and allowed them to fall to the floor.

Some of her fellow students at the Peerless School had worn nothing under their robes, but Elaine had never had that sort of confidence – and besides, making robes jump off a person's body was a well-known trick. She wore a set of underclothes underneath her robes that hadn't made her sleep any better; it took her two tries before she managed to pull them off and stand naked in the centre of the room. A simple spell would lower the temperature, but she didn't dare cast any magic. Her mind was in no state to shape the required spells.

Picking up her robes and underclothes, she carried them over to the basket and dumped them inside for the maids. Maid service was not something she was used to, but she had to admit that it came in handy. The robes she'd worn as a simple library assistant had been easy to wash – or clean with magic – when Daria and she had been living together, but the Privy Council robes required special treatment. She'd actually contemplated suggesting to Light Spinner that they change the heavy robes for something more practical, but the purple robes were traditional and some traditions couldn't be gainsaid, even by the Grand Sorceress. They represented continuity even when the autocrat's face changed.

It was useless to go back to sleep, she decided. Instead, she turned and walked into the bathroom, marvelling again at the luxury someone had decided the Head Librarian needed to do the job. Elaine had tried to look it up in the records, but there was apparently no paper that stated just *who* had made that decision, although she would have bet half of her salary that it had been the first Head Librarian. Maybe he or she had been as bound to the library as Miss Prim had been, before the last Grand Sorcerer had died. Or maybe, like Elaine, the first librarian couldn't be bothered buying a house to suit his dignity.

She snorted at the thought as she twisted the tap, filling the bathtub with water. It would have only cost her a month's salary to buy a house on the other side of the Four Peaks, but High Society would have sneered, no matter how grand the house. Everyone who was anyone had a residence inside the Golden City, where space was constrained and only the very wealthy could afford anything bigger than a tiny apartment. And where they could reach anyone else of wealth and power, just by taking a short walk.

The Golden City is a microcosm of the Empire, she thought. *But now the bonds holding the Empire together have frayed.*

She climbed into the bath and let out a sigh of pure pleasure as she sat down, the water coming up to her neck. Hot baths had been an impossible luxury while she'd been living with Daria; their apartment had had no bath and she had never been able to work up the nerve to go to the public baths, even during the women-only hours. Daria had, of course, and she'd filled Elaine's ears with tales of all she'd seen and heard while bathing. None of them had managed to convince Elaine to overcome her fear of crowds. But now ... now she could soak as long as she wanted.

Closing her eyes, she started to meditate.

The nightmare had been intense, but little more than a cluster of jumbled images that didn't seem to make sense, no matter how hard she tried to concentrate on them. She knew too much about history – even the history that had been carefully removed from the official textbooks – to separate out the past from what might be the future. It was hard to realise that the Witch-King had once been a great hero, that the man who'd won the First Necromantic War had gone on to be the leader of the enemy in the Second Necromantic War. As far as she knew, Elaine was the only living person who had access to that knowledge. Light Spinner could delve into the Black Vault at any time, but she'd never done so. There was just too much else for the Grand Sorceress to do.

Images flickered in front of her mind as she posed questions to herself, feeling the answers popping up inside her skull. But none of them answered the *real* question. Where was the Witch-King now? And how had he managed to remain alive – or undead – for so long?

There were rituals in the Black Vault that extended one's lifespan, provided that one was willing to sacrifice other lives and make bargains with dark creatures. Elaine had been tempted until she'd realised that granting herself an additional hundred years would have required her to sacrifice someone she actually *liked*. And there were probably other dangers; the writers of the ritual hadn't been too clear about the costs, but there were other books that added stern warnings of the dangers of dealing with demons. It could cost someone their life, or their soul, or even their sanity. Had the Witch-King made such a bargain?

It was a possibility, she had to admit. His conduct as a hero had been very different from his conduct as a villain. Had he surrendered his soul and, as a soulless monster, lost the ability to tell the difference between right and wrong? Had *that* allowed him to tap into magic that other magicians knew to leave well alone? Or was she following the wrong path?

It doesn't matter, she told herself. *All that matters is that we have to find him.*

She pulled herself out of the bath, despite part of her mind suggesting that she could sleep in the water. She'd done it once, back when she'd first moved into the Great Library, and it had been embarrassing, even though no one knew apart from her. The wards would have prevented her from actually *drowning*; they were configured to protect the books and their mistress, in that order. But what protection would they offer against another of Johan's overpowered spells?

It was not a pleasant thought. Johan had damaged the wards in both the hospital and the library – and he'd destroyed her protections. Elaine knew that it had been an accident, that he hadn't meant to do it, but it suggested that he might manage to do *real* damage. It might be a good idea to find somewhere else to continue his training, even if she would have to build up more analysis wards ... or find someone else to do it for her.

Maybe we should use Howarth Hall, she thought, as she used a spell to dry herself. *I wouldn't care in the slightest if the building were to be burned to the ground – and his creditors would be delighted. The empty ground would be worth far more than a stripped building.*

She smiled at the thought, then walked over to stand in front of the mirror. Her body looked normal, if slightly thin; Daria had always nagged her to eat, but Daria was away on a mission for the Inquisitors. And there were her red eyes ... somehow, in the night, the glamour had come undone. Bee had taken one look and fled from her, unable to meet their stare. Elaine still felt a little hurt whenever she remembered that, although it was hard to blame him. Any sort of permanent change to a person's body could indicate that person had been playing with dangerous magic.

And it was strange to realise that she had actually been quite lucky. And so had Light Spinner.

She rebuilt the glamour, then walked naked back into the

living room and sat down on the carpet, focusing her mind. Her protections had taken weeks of effort to put in place – and Johan had destroyed them in a split-second. A more powerful magician could have built them quicker, but no magician would ever truly trust another to protect him. Closing her eyes, Elaine started to cast the first protective spell, followed rapidly by the second. They were of her own design, capable of warding off threats from many more powerful magicians ... but she doubted they could stand up to Johan. Even the analysis charms woven into the library's wards hadn't been able to provide a clear explanation of what he'd done.

"Better not let *that* get out," she muttered to herself as the third protection spell fell into place. "There will be panic in the streets."

Light Spinner was the most powerful magician known to exist, although that didn't automatically mean that she *was* the most powerful magician. But she wasn't all-powerful; several lesser magicians, working in concert, could probably bring her down. Johan, on the other hand, seemed ... *different*. If he could break Elaine's protections, what could he do to another magician? The irony would have made her giggle, if it hadn't been so serious. If the Empire accepted the concept of might making right – and it did – it would have to accept that Johan might be the mightiest of them all.

She cursed Zacharias under her breath, then focused on the fourth spell. If he'd kept his mouth shut, they might have had more time to examine Johan before his father started demanding to see his son. But he hadn't ... and who could blame him? He had close links to Johan's family, after all. His oaths had not been violated by going to the father, even if his motives had been less than pure.

A fifth ward fell into place, then a sixth ... Elaine stopped, gasping for breath. Even her own spells required magic to work and she was draining her reserves. Concentrating, she checked that all six protective spells were working properly, then stood upright. The remainder would have to be done once she had recovered.

She felt a quiver running through the wards and smiled.

Johan had awakened.

Chapter Fifteen

Johan felt oddly relaxed as he opened his eyes, although he wasn't sure why. He was in an unfamiliar room ... and then it struck him. Jamal couldn't slip into this room and hide an unpleasant surprise among his possessions. He was safe. And the room had a selection of *interesting* books on the shelves.

There was a quiet tap on the door, barely loud enough to be heard. Johan checked that he was decent – Elaine's maids had provided him with a selection of nightclothes, allowing him to choose the most suitable – and called for the visitor to come in. It was a young girl, barely older than Johan himself, wearing the grey robes worn by most of the library's staff. He couldn't help a flicker of envy as he saw the wand at her belt, despite what Elaine had told him.

The girl bowed. "Master Johan, the Head Librarian would like the pleasure of your company in her quarters," she said. "If you wish, I will escort you there."

"I wish," Johan said. He swung his legs out of bed and stood upright. "Or should I dress first?"

"I think that would be a good idea," the girl said, with a smile that made Johan's heart flip-flop. "She won't mind waiting if you dress quickly."

She turned her back, revealing that her robes were designed to be tighter around her buttocks than strictly necessary. Johan stared, then forced himself to look away as he felt a stirring in his loins. He'd ogled the maids, of course – Jamal had done a great deal more than ogle – but they'd never condescended to share his bed. What favours could *he* do them? But, even now, this girl was a magician. Staring at her might have unpleasant consequences. Charity still boasted of the day she'd hit an unwanted admirer with a hex far beyond her tender years.

Cursing himself, Johan found a pair of clean trousers and a

shirt in the wardrobe and hastily pulled them on. Glancing at himself in the mirror, he had to admit that he looked very different. They weren't magician's robes, but they suited him. He coughed, then indicated to the girl that she could lead him to Elaine. Somehow, he managed to keep his eyes on the back of her head, despite the seductive rhythm of her hips.

"In here," the girl said. "And good luck."

"Thank you," Johan said. He hesitated, then worked up the nerve to ask. "What is your name?"

"Jayne," the girl said. "Jayne of House Rendang."

Johan nodded, thinking hard. House Rendang was one of the minor houses, if he recalled correctly; he'd never paid close attention to his father's lectures on who was who. It wasn't as if the other Great Houses would ever want to know that he existed. But now ... he found himself staring after Jayne as she walked away, then forced himself to turn and enter Elaine's quarters. Elaine herself was sitting at a table, reading a broadsheet.

"Come in," she called, lowering the sheet so that he could see her face. "How did you sleep?"

"Very well, thank you," Johan said, as he sat down facing her. "It was a safe place to sleep."

"Back at the Peerless School, there were rules that stipulated that no pranks were to be played in a person's dorm or bedroom," Elaine said. "I assume your father didn't make such rules?"

Johan shook his head, mutely.

"You may stay here for as long as you like," Elaine said. She passed him a menu. "Choose what you want, then I'll order it for you."

"Thank you," Johan said, scanning the list of food. It wasn't very long, but it all looked good. "I'll have the steak sandwich with eggs."

Elaine cocked her head slightly, communing with the wards, then nodded. "Done," she said. "It will take some time, though."

Johan nodded, unsurprised. "Why does the Great Library have a kitchen anyway?"

"There are plenty of students who come here for the entire

day," Elaine said. "So they go to the canteen to eat when they're feeling hungry, then go back to their studies. I have to watch them carefully to ensure that no food is consumed within the library itself. That would earn them a public whipping."

There was something in her voice that told Johan she wasn't joking. Charity had said that the Peerless School had firm ideas on discipline, but she hadn't gone into details. It sounded worse than their father's strict ideas on how to bring up children. But then, no matter how dire the punishments, they hadn't done much for Jamal. He had graduated as annoying and obnoxious a bully as he'd started.

He changed the subject. "What's going to happen to me now?"

"That will require a long discussion," Elaine said. She stood up, picked up a jug of something hot and black from a side table, and poured two mugs with practiced skill. "Would you prefer to wait until after breakfast?"

"I would just like to get it over with," Johan admitted. He took the mug she passed him and sipped it, grimacing slightly at the taste. "What *is* this stuff?"

"Students call it Study Muck," Elaine said. "It helps them wake up in the morning after a hard night spent partying."

Johan took another sip. "I suppose the shock value would help," he muttered. "It tastes foul."

"I can order something else if you'd prefer," Elaine said. "But most students do drink that, although they often add milk to soften the taste."

"Oh," Johan said. He closed his eyes for a long moment, then opened them and stared at her. "What happened last night?"

Elaine took a breath. "There was some debate over the precise way to handle your case," she said. "You may never be able to go to the Peerless School."

Johan felt a strange mixture of relief and disappointment. Most magicians went to the Peerless School – it allowed them a chance to make contacts as well as develop their magic – but from Charity's descriptions he wasn't so sure that he wanted to go. Jamal was bad enough; having hundreds of students practicing their hexes on him would be far worse. But at the same time, it *was* where future careers were made.

And Jayne went to the Peerless School, he was sure ...

Stop it, he told himself, savagely. *You barely know the girl!*

"Your powers are just too different," Elaine admitted. She placed her fingertips together, contemplatively. "On one hand, they might be able to hurt you; on the other hand, your odd spells might be able to hurt *them*. It isn't something that the new Administrator could tolerate. Even with the new ideas I have for teaching you control, you don't have the right level of skill to be allowed to join classes."

She took a breath. "And I don't think that you will ever be able to master potions or several other magical arts," she added. "Your powers are ..."

"Different," Johan interrupted. "So ... what *was* decided?"

"There's also a legal issue," Elaine added. "Your father has a claim on you, a claim he has yet to renounce. You would find yourself bound to him unless that claim was superseded."

She leaned forward. "I would like to offer you an apprenticeship, with me," she said. "It would solve many of our problems."

"It would," Johan agreed. From what little he knew, parents surrendered custody of their children to their new master, who would serve in their place until the apprenticeship was finished. "I will ..."

Elaine held up a hand. "You need to enter this with full awareness of what you're getting into," she warned. "Your case is far from normal."

Before she could continue, two plates drifted into the room and landed on the table in front of them. Johan's sandwich looked good, but Elaine's plate was piled high with bacon, eggs and potatoes. It seemed a lot for such a slight girl, Johan thought, before realising that she probably needed to consume plenty of calories to power her magic. Charity had been much the same as she grew into maturity.

Johan hesitated, then muttered the traditional blessing – old habits die hard – before picking up the sandwich and biting into it. The steak had been cooked to perfection, he realised in delight; they'd even cut off the fat, leaving it pure meat. It was so close to how he liked it that he couldn't help wondering if someone had contacted the family's cooks and asked about his favourite foods. Or it might have been a coincidence.

"Tasty," he said, though a mouthful of steak, bread and raw tomato. "Thank you."

Elaine shuddered. "Eat with your mouth closed," she said, dryly. "It isn't a pleasant sight."

Johan flushed, but obeyed. *Jamal* had been given rigorous etiquette lessons for the past eleven years; he might be a bully, yet none of his social equals had ever sneered at how he carried himself. But Johan had been allowed to skip those lessons as it had become clear that he would never play a role in society. He'd forgotten most of them as he'd grown older.

He watched with some amazement as Elaine put away most of her food, wondering just where she put it. Her robes were nowhere near as tight as Jayne's, but it was clear that she was almost painfully thin. Charity had been like that after her first term at the Peerless School, when she hadn't eaten enough to power her spells. The cooks had fed her up remorselessly until she'd put on plenty of weight.

"The normal rules of an apprenticeship are that the apprentice serves the master in exchange for tuition," Elaine said. "You have nothing to offer me – and I don't really need an assistant – so we will have to skip that requirement. A more serious concern is that your magic might not respond well to the oaths of apprenticeship. You might not be bound by the rights and duties of other apprentices."

Johan struggled to recall what they were. "Obedience, loyalty, secrecy ..."

"And dedication to your studies," Elaine said. "If you served under a druid, you would be expected to master healing magic in four years – unless, for some reason, you proved utterly incapable and had to be released from your oaths. The point is that you would be agreeing to make a magically-binding oath that would make you follow *all* of those duties ... and, given the odd nature of your magic, the oaths might not take."

"I don't understand," Johan admitted. His studies had

never been too detailed, not when he'd never expected a magical apprenticeship. "I thought that anyone could swear an oath."

Elaine smiled, but it didn't quite touch her eyes. "Only magicians can willingly enter a magically-binding oath," she explained. "You would swear to uphold the duties of an apprentice; I would swear to uphold the duties of a master. But your magic might not be capable of binding you to me. And, if so, it would be very dangerous for me to bind myself to you."

"Because you would be compelled to carry out your side of the oath even if I wasn't," Johan guessed. Elaine nodded. "Do we actually *need* the oath?"

"It would make it harder for your father to demand that you go back to his house," Elaine said, flatly. She held up her hand. "There's a book on apprenticeships I want you to read, although much of the information is generalised. You don't have to make your decision immediately. However ..."

She took another sip from her mug. "You and I will be experimenting with your powers, trying to teach you how to control them," she explained. "Normally, a master would know much more than an apprentice. But in this case, I would be guessing at where to go ... as would you. The apprenticeship might turn into a joke.

"Your magic might add other complications," she added. "You would be swearing to obey me, but you might well be more powerful than I. That may warp the bond in odd ways. Assuming it forms at all, of course."

"My head hurts," Johan complained, making a show of rubbing his temples. "Can we just tell everyone that I'm your apprentice?"

"They'll want to see proof," Elaine pointed out. "And without a working bond, we couldn't present them with anything."

"I'll think about it," Johan promised. He looked down at the table, then up at Elaine. "What are we going to do today?"

"There are some ideas I wish to try," Elaine said. "But we can deal with them after breakfast."

Johan nodded. "Can I look at the broadsheet?" He asked.

"I want to know if there's anything about me in it."

Elaine shrugged. Johan took the broadsheet and frowned as he saw a drawing of Jamal glaring up at him. The artist had managed to make him seem mad, bad and dangerous to know, something that made Johan smile. It *was* a perfectly accurate rendition, at least in his opinion. The text beside it noted that Jamal had been arrested by the Inquisition and was currently being held in the Watchtower, but very little else. His father's lawyers had probably had a few words with the editor, Johan decided. If they printed anything they couldn't prove, they'd be sued until they didn't even have clothes to wear while begging on the streets.

"I thought they would have kept it a secret," he muttered. "But the whole city knows he's under arrest."

"Someone in the Watchtower probably leaked it," Elaine said, sourly. "Or one of the Privy Councillors, taking an opportunity to embarrass your father. There's no way to know for sure."

"Nothing about me," Johan said, unsure if he should be relieved or annoyed. "How many people *know*?"

"Your family, the Grand Sorceress, the Inquisitors and myself," Elaine said. "And that wretched druid."

Johan nodded and went to the second page. This story mentioned that the Dark Wizard Hawthorne had been sighted near a city in the Western Hills, where several children had been reported missing. The writer stated that a number of Inquisitors were already in the area and expected an arrest soon. Johan suspected that the writer didn't really know what he was talking about. If the Inquisitors were really closing in on the Dark Wizard, they wouldn't want a broadsheet story to scare the bastard off before they caught him.

"That's the problem with the broadsheets," Elaine commented, wryly. "They either print nonsense or they print the truth in embarrassing detail."

"Maybe I should go after him," Johan said, seeing a line that claimed that there was a ten thousand gold bounty for Hawthorn's head, preferably detached from his body. "I could get the gold and ..."

"Get killed," Elaine snapped. "You are nowhere near

ready to face a hostile magician, let alone one so touched by darkness."

Johan winced at her tone, but had to admit that she had a point.

A letter floated into the room and landed on the table in front of them. Johan took one look and felt his heart sink. His father's handwriting was distinctive, particularly when he was annoyed. He'd seen enough notes his father had sent to various tutors to recognise the signs of irritation. It was a droll reminder that, no matter how hard he studied, he could never please his father.

"I don't want to read it," he muttered. "Can you destroy it?"

"I could," Elaine said. "But I think you should read it."

Johan sighed. "Is it even safe to touch?"

Elaine waved her wand over the envelope, casting a simple charm. "There's a spell to ensure that only you can open it," she said, "but nothing else. It should be fine."

Swallowing, Johan picked up the letter and tore it open. His father had written a note on his finest paper, paper that cost one gold per sheet. If nothing else, it was a way of telling him just how much his father cared. But it was really too late for that.

Son,

I have heard the news from your sister that you are now a magician. This is good news, particularly in light of other recent developments. I believe that you should come home, where you and I can sit down and discuss the family's response to these new challenges. You would be welcome. Charity has forgiven you your little mistake.

My treatment of you in the past has been far from ideal. I am truly sorry for the suffering you have undergone on your path towards magic. Now, I believe that we can rebuild our relationship and work together to ensure that the family's position is solid. Towards this, I would be willing to sponsor you to enter the Peerless School ...

Johan felt the letter grow suddenly warm and dropped it, a half-second before it burst into flame. How *could* his father so casually claim to accept him, now that he was a magician? The message was arrogant and condescending and ... he gritted his teeth, willing his rage to abate. His father didn't even realise that he *couldn't* enter the Peerless School ...

"That's a *no*," he said, addressing the pile of ashes. Surprisingly, the fire hadn't spread to the table, despite the heat. "I am *not* going home."

"You may wish to write and tell him that," Elaine said. "He *did* send you a formal letter."

"Fine," Johan sneered. "Can you pass me a sheet of the cheapest paper you have?"

Elaine sighed, but walked over to a drawer and produced a cheap notepad. Johan took it and glared down at the blank sheet, trying to decide what to write. He didn't know any words unpleasant enough to get the full depth of his feelings across to his father ...

... And to think that he would once have done anything for his father's approval.

"I've made up my mind," he said, firmly. "I wish to be your apprentice."

"Then read the book," Elaine said. "I'll give you an hour."

Chapter Sixteen

True to her word, Elaine gave Johan an hour to read the book. It shouldn't really have taken that long – it was a short book – but it would give them both time to think. Johan should not enter into an apprenticeship without knowing the possible dangers, while *she* needed to think about his latest display of accidental magic. It was more interesting, she knew, to note what *hadn't* happened as well as what *had*.

He hadn't damaged the wards, or the table, or anything else. The only thing that had been destroyed had been the letter, while the rest of the room had been completely unharmed. It suggested that he was definitely better off visualising the outcome of what he wanted, rather than trying to guide his magic through the words and gestures used by other magicians. But what did it really *mean*?

Taking a breath, she tapped on the door and waited for him to call her inside. When he did, she was surprised to see Jayne there too, unloading a trolley of books. They were all on apprenticeships, she noted, as Jayne saw her and gave a hasty bow. Evidently, Johan had worked out how to request books and other materials from the library staff.

"Thank you, Jayne," Johan said, flushing slightly. "I'll call you when the books need to be returned."

Elaine watched the younger girl go, then looked at Johan. He was clearly attracted to Jayne, unsurprisingly. She *was* attractive ... and she wasn't as much of a brat as many of the other girls from various Great Houses. And she had something apart from fluff between her ears.

"The staff aren't there for you to bother," she said in mild reproof. She smiled as he blushed bright red. "If you want to flirt with her, you can do it when she's off-duty."

Johan's face turned even redder. "I'm sorry," he said. "I just ..."

Elaine understood. He wouldn't have met many girls,

given his effective imprisonment, and those he had met would have shunned him; Jayne might have been the first girl who had responded to him as a *person*, rather than a horror to be ignored or even killed for daring to exist. She couldn't blame him for wanting to try his luck ... after all, magicians had a degree of sexual freedom unthinkable to mundanes.

"Flirt with her when she's off-duty, or even invite her here," Elaine said, remembering days when she'd thought that she would go through life alone. She still did, even though she was no longer a maiden. "But for the moment ..."

She settled back on a comfortable chair and met his eyes. "Did you read the book?"

"I did," Johan said. He frowned, breaking eye contact. "It wasn't always pleasant reading."

Elaine nodded. One advantage of the Peerless School was that it was hard for tutors to take advantage of their pupils. An apprenticeship bond, on the other hand, allowed an unscrupulous teacher to take merciless advantage of his apprentice. The apprentice could become an unpaid servant, a criminal accomplice or even a sexual partner, and it would be completely legal. She couldn't blame Johan for hesitating. There was a good reason why apprenticeship bonds were rare.

"The choice is yours," she said, flatly. "I won't force it on you."

"My father might," Johan said. "Did you read the letter?"

Elaine quirked her eyebrows. "And how was I supposed to read the letter?"

Johan nodded, ruefully.

"My father said that he wanted me home because of my magic," he said. "And that Charity forgave me. And that we could work together to save the family. And that he would sponsor me to enter the Peerless School ..."

"So he doesn't know everything," Elaine said, thoughtfully. Light Spinner and Dread wouldn't have said a word to anyone, but she knew just how easy it was for rumours to spread. Clearly, Charity's report of her accidental transformation hadn't allowed her father to deduce that there was something weird about Johan's magic. But it should have done. "Or maybe he's hoping that you don't know everything."

Johan slapped the table. "Will I *ever* be free of him?"

"*My* father is dead," Elaine said, although she understood what he meant. Whatever his faults, Johan's father hadn't knocked up a random woman just to ensure that his abandoned daughter eventually became a Bookworm. "As you grow older, he will have less and less influence over you."

"I can't enter the Peerless School," Johan protested. "Doesn't he know that?"

"Not yet," Elaine said. It *was* a problem. Any normal magician would jump at the chance to enter the Peerless School. It would puzzle anyone who realised that Johan *wasn't* going to go there. Combined with what had happened to Charity, she knew, it would be far too informative. "But you couldn't go there until the start of next term anyway, which is four months off. There will be time enough for us to work out a solution by then."

She smiled, then stood up. "I have some other experiments I would like to try," she said. "Coming?"

Johan stood up, eying her nervously. "Do you have any ... advice to offer about Jayne?"

Elaine almost giggled. What sort of person would view *her* as an expert on relationships? The sole relationship she'd had had been destroyed by a pair of bright red eyes ... and besides, she knew almost nothing about Jayne. She was just a student who was looking for extra money by working in the library when she wasn't in classes.

"Just be careful," she said, finally. "Men and women often see things differently. She may not realise that you're interested in her; she might even have a boyfriend already. And she might be put off if you come on too hard. So be careful."

She turned away so he wouldn't see her smile, then led the way back to the experimental chamber. The wards Johan had damaged had regenerated themselves completely, she was relieved to discover; rebuilding them would have been a nightmarish task if they'd been shattered beyond hope of repair. In the long run, they would *definitely* have to move out of the Great Library. An accident here could have disastrous consequences for the entire Empire.

"The first piece of magic you did was to break your brother's spell," she said, once the door was shut and the analysis spells were running properly. "What did you do to do it?"

"I don't know," Johan admitted. He sounded rather frustrated by the question. "I just *did* it."

"Two-thirds of the entire magical population of the world would be *unable* to do it," Elaine said, calmly. "Cancelling spells can require gestures ... and it's hard to move if one is frozen in place. Even *I* would have great difficulty in breaking free. But enough magicians can do it to convince duellists that the only way to win is to kill their opponents while frozen, before they can break free."

She shivered as memories ran through her head, memories that weren't really hers. Duelling as practiced today was a pale shadow of the past, when magicians had fought at the drop of a hat and done truly terrifying things to their enemies. A magician who froze his opponent could do *anything* to him ... and many had, while their enemies were helpless.

Johan's voice penetrated her thoughts. "Are you all right?"

Elaine nodded, pulling herself back to the present. "I think so," she said, numbly. "I want to cast another such spell on you and see if you can break free."

***

Johan swallowed, hard. His mouth felt so dry it hurt.

He trusted Elaine, insofar as he trusted anyone. She certainly didn't have the malice that Jamal and the rest of his siblings, even Charity, had shown from time to time. And she talked to him as though he were an equal. But the thought of being helpless again scared him so deeply he could hardly speak.

"All right," he managed, finally. He tried to stop his body shaking, but it only made it worse. "Do it."

Elaine frowned, then waved her wand. Johan felt his body simply ... *stop*. The spell prevented all voluntary movement; indeed, he wasn't even sure if he was still *breathing*. He could hear his heartbeat pounding inside his chest, hammering faster and faster as panic threatened to set in and

... he wanted to be free, he needed to be free, he ...

He fell towards the floor, landing in a heap. The pain helped focus his mind, but his head was still spinning madly as he fought to control himself. He felt a hand touch his shoulder and looked up to see Elaine's concerned eyes staring down at him. But there was something wrong with her eyes ...

"What ..." He stopped, swallowed, and tried again. "What's wrong with your eyes?"

"Long story," Elaine said. She held out a hand, helping him to his feet. As his thoughts settled, the strange blur he'd seen over Elaine's eyes faded away. Soft brown eyes held his, looking sad and guilty. "I'm sorry. I didn't mean to panic you."

Johan grinned, pushing the mystery of her eyes to one side. "I broke the spell, didn't I?"

"You did," Elaine confirmed. "Well done."

"Jamal is in for one hell of a surprise," Johan said, fighting down the urge to start laughing hysterically. Who would have thought that the way to deal with his brother's torments was to tell them to *stop*. "Do it again!"

Elaine's eyes narrowed. "I don't think that would be a good idea," she said. "You're clearly not in a good state."

"Please," Johan begged. The sheer absurdity of the scene struck him and he started to giggle helplessly. He was *begging* for a spell he'd always considered a tool Jamal used to torment him. "Do it, please!"

"Fine," Elaine said. She waved her wand. Johan froze. "Break free, now."

Johan staggered as the spell snapped. This time, he had balanced himself before Elaine used the spell, ensuring that he wouldn't fall over. But there was still *some* effect when the spell snapped ...

"Tell me," Elaine said, as Johan sat down on the cold floor. "Did you feel anything when the spell struck you?"

"I froze," Johan said, dryly. But he thought he knew what she meant. "I didn't sense any magic before then."

"Interesting," Elaine said. "A normal magician would have sensed me casting the charm, giving him a chance to block it. You ... do not."

She frowned, stroking her chin. "I want you to try to block the charm this time," she said, as she motioned him back to his feet. "Start walking, but concentrate on wanting to *keep* walking."

Johan started to pace around the room. Twelve seconds later, the spell struck him and he froze. He broke out a moment later and started to walk again; the next time, he froze again.

"Interesting," Elaine said, again. "You have to actually be affected by the spell to counter it."

"Not good," Johan said. If it took him a few seconds to break the spell every time it caught him, it gave his enemy a chance to hit him with something more lethal. "Do I have to think about a defence all the time?"

"Maybe," Elaine said. "This time, I want you to imagine that there is a shield protecting you from all attacks. It protects you completely – you have to keep that in mind."

"While walking," Johan commented. "Do I have to keep both things in my mind at the same time?"

"Yes," Elaine said. "Or else it may not work."

Concentrating, imagining a protective bubble centred on him, Johan started to walk.

***

Elaine had been told, once, that when a student *wanted* to learn it was a bad idea to discourage them. It was the principle the Peerless School followed, although half the time the students wanted to learn magic they could use on their fellow classmates rather than anything useful. But she was deeply worried about Johan. No matter what sort of brave face he tried to project, it was far too clear that the paralysis spell brought back bad memories, if not outright trauma. Traumatising a magician was far from a good idea even at the best of times.

"Last time," she said, and raised her wand. "Here we go."

She cast the spell. Magic flared around Johan – for a moment, she *saw* a translucent bubble protecting him – and then it flashed back at her. There was no time to react before it caught her and her entire body locked solid, caught in a ridiculous pose. She'd been trapped by her own spell.

It shouldn't have done that, she thought, trying to summon the discipline to cancel the spell without needing to move her hands. *The spell shouldn't have had the energy to reflect all the way back to me ...*

Johan turned and stared. His face was etched with horror, much to Elaine's relief. He'd shown similar horror when he'd accidentally turned Charity into a rat. At least he wasn't likely to go seek revenge on everyone who had abused him, even if he *was* turning his back on his family.

"I didn't mean to," he protested, as he stepped towards her. "I ..."

Elaine would have smiled as reassuringly as she could if she had been able to move a muscle. Instead, she concentrated ... but nothing happened. Had Johan's bubble altered the spell or was she too agitated to think properly? It was hard to be sure. She tried again, and again, yet her body refused to move. Johan touched her, lightly, as if he wasn't quite sure what had happened.

"Move again," he said, desperately. "Please ..."

Elaine toppled forward. She would have hit the ground if Johan hadn't caught her and broken her fall. Carefully, she returned her wand to her belt and stood upright, leaning on him for a long moment. The attempts to free herself had failed, but they had still cost her a great deal of energy. She really needed a rest and some time to think.

"I didn't mean to do that to you," Johan said. "I just imagined a mirror."

"I know," Elaine said, unable to keep an edge out of her voice. "Be careful what you imagine in future."

"That can't be the answer," Johan said. "If that were true ..."

His voice trailed off. Elaine could guess what he was thinking. If that were true, wouldn't poor Jayne have been stripped naked as soon as he looked at her? There were no shortage of spells that did just that, spells that were often used in the Peerless School as *pranks*. But Johan hadn't stripped anyone naked.

"I think you probably have to actually *want* something to happen," Elaine said. It might explain his poor results with actual spellwork. He wanted the spell to work so desperately that it was colossally overpowered. "I think you really wanted to destroy your father's letter."

Johan nodded. "I did," he said.

He reached into his pocket and produced a sheet of paper. "That's the reply I wrote," he explained. "If you're going to take me on as an apprentice, you might as well read it."

Elaine skimmed it. Johan didn't mince words; after giving his father a piece of his mind, he told him in no uncertain terms that he would not be coming home. The letter fairly dripped with anger and hatred. Elaine barely knew Johan's father, but she would have bet good money that he would lose control of his own magic after reading the letter.

"I think you shouldn't be so rude," she said, softly. She disliked confrontation, as a rule, and pointlessly irritating Johan's father would do no good for future relationships between them. "He is still your father."

Johan glared at her, his face twisted into a stubborn pose. "And I don't want anything to do with him, ever again," he said. "I'd sooner be a Nancy-Boy in Red Street than speak to him again."

Elaine lifted her eyebrows. "Where did you hear of them?"

"Jamal mentioned them once," Johan admitted. He frowned, curiosity winning over anger. "What do they actually do?"

"You don't want to know," Elaine said, reluctant to allow him to change the subject. "But you shouldn't send this to your father. He could make life very difficult for you."

Johan's glare returned. "How?"

"He is the head of a magical house and master of a patronage network that stretches over the entire Empire," Elaine pointed out, ruthlessly. "Even if he doesn't try to have you brought home as a runaway child, he can still ensure that you have no hope of getting a job. Your magic might be new and interesting, but not many people will gamble on taking you on when your father is badmouthing you to everyone."

Johan scowled, then bowed his head.

"I won't let him think that I am going back to him," he said, firmly.

"Then don't," Elaine said. "But think carefully about what you want to say."

"He'll think I'm showing weakness," Johan muttered. "I *know* him."

Elaine smiled. "Write it out, then we will have lunch and go to the zoo," she said. "It's been too long since I've been there and you might like it."

"No one ever took me," Johan said, softly. Elaine felt a matching wince as she remembered how few outings she'd been able to take from the orphanage. Only a handful of wealthy benefactors had paid for them ... and they had never met the hidden costs. "Thank you."

He looked up at her, suddenly. "Do I scare you?"

The sudden change in subject surprised Elaine, as – she realised – it had been meant to do.

"No," she said, after a long moment. "Not you personally. But the potential you represent worries me greatly. It could turn the world upside down."

Chapter Seventeen

Johan mulled over what she'd said as they shared a dinner of roast beef, potatoes and several different kinds of vegetables, unable to come to any firm conclusion. If he represented previously undiscovered potential ... what did it *mean*?

Power always comes with a price, his father had been fond of saying, but Johan had never really seen it. Jamal certainly hadn't paid a price for having his power, while Johan had paid too much for not having *any* power. Even now, he couldn't help thinking that he was still paying. The closest thing he had to a friend was scared of his potential. What did that mean for the future?

"If this happened to me," he asked, "what's to stop it happening to someone else?"

"Nothing," Elaine said, simply. "But then, we don't know if you unlocked some hidden power within your blood or if you somehow gained powers in a freak accident."

Johan scowled. "I'm always going to be alone, aren't I?"

"Everyone is alone," Elaine said. The bitterness in her voice surprised him, reminding him that he knew almost nothing about her. Someone who held such a high position should be firmly in the public eye, but Elaine had shunned it to the point that he hadn't known who she was until she introduced herself. "Even the most outgoing person in the world has secrets they don't dare share with their closest friends."

She finished her plate and stood up. "I'm going to change," she said. "I suggest that you do the same. Just wear something suitable for a walk out in the city."

"Father would say I should wear a fine suit if I didn't want to wear robes," Johan pointed out. "Can I just wear plain clothes?"

"If you want," Elaine said. "Just remember you have to walk in whatever you wear."

Johan watched her go, then stood up himself and walked over to the wardrobe. Whoever had filled it had done an excellent job, he had to admit; they'd given him several sets of robes, but also trousers, shirts, waistcoats and underclothes. Pulling out a pair of simple, but elegantly tailored trousers, he undressed quickly and started to pull on the new outfit. A quick glance in the mirror confirmed that he looked different enough that the handful of people who knew him would probably fail to recognise him.

I should start working on glamours, he thought, sourly. His father had a network of friends and clients, all of whom might start looking for him. Johan had no official portrait, as part of his family's attempts to pretend that he didn't exist, but he had the distinctive features of his family. They would probably start by looking at Jamal's portrait, then try to imagine someone younger and a little softer. God knew Jamal had remarked, more than once, that Johan had a weak chin.

He pulled his shirt on hastily as there was another knock at the door, then called to invite the knocker into the room. Elaine stepped inside, wearing a simple pair of trousers and shirt herself, her hair braided into a ponytail and allowed to hang down her back. She looked nothing like the Head Librarian. If she hadn't had a wand at her belt, she wouldn't have even passed for a magician.

She wasn't beautiful, not conventionally beautiful. Certainly nothing like Jayne or Charity, both of whom were stunningly gorgeous. But there was something about her that Johan found oddly compelling.

"I meant to ask," Johan said, trying to cover his embarrassment at staring at her. "Why is there a rule that only magicians can carry wands if wands are useless?"

Elaine gave him an odd look, then nodded. "It's considered rude to brush your magical field up against another magician's field," she said. "If you carry a wand, on the other hand, it's a simple way to identify yourself as a magician. But if you *pretended* to be a magician ... well, you might run into some trouble."

Johan could understand it. Jamal was always picking fights with his fellow magicians, constantly testing himself against them. If he happened to pick on a mundane *pretending* to be a magician ... it would be a one-sided slaughter. And besides, magicians had higher social status than mundanes. If people started pretending to be magicians, the social scale would be upended.

"You may not want to announce yourself," Elaine added, breaking into his thoughts. "Your magic is odd enough that I'd prefer not to see you get into a duel."

"Even with Jamal?" Johan asked. "I could surprise him ..."

Elaine gave him an icy look. "Your brother may be an ass," she said, "but if he'd been a weak magician or a coward it would have been discovered long ago. Magicians constantly jostle for status, after all. And while your powers are odd, you are not all-powerful. Jamal might beat you through experience alone."

Johan scowled. He'd always assumed that his brother was just bragging about how great a duellist he was, showing off to his powerless sibling just how much he could do. But he'd never heard anything to suggest that Jamal genuinely *did* have a reputation outside the house, one held by magicians who had no reason to be nice to him. Maybe Jamal hadn't been boasting after all.

No, he was boasting, Johan told himself. *He might just have had something real to boast about.*

"I understand," he said, out loud. At least Jamal was in jail ... or was he? "How long will Jamal stay in jail?"

"It depends on the Grand Sorceress," Elaine admitted, as she headed towards the door. "And how much political support your father manages to round up."

Johan picked up the letter he'd written and passed it to her. Elaine skimmed it quickly, nodded in approval and stuffed it into an envelope. It drifted away a moment later, heading towards the library's mail room, where it would be handed over to the postmen. Johan, who had once been told that he would never have any other career, had researched them and discovered that a letter could reach its destination in the Golden City within hours. It had seemed like a fun job from the outside ...

... But his father would never have agreed to let him go.

Outside, it was cooler than he remembered as winter came on. The crowds seemed to have largely abandoned their more ... *interesting* outfits, choosing instead to wrap themselves in fur coats or heavy robes. Most of the students seemed to be running to and from the Great Library, studying desperately for the exams at the end of the month. Practical magic, Johan had once been told, could be practiced anywhere, but students who wanted good jobs had to study magical theory, law and many other topics. It still galled him to know that he could have found a good job, even without magic. And now that he did have magic ...

He gritted his teeth. If his father only wanted him with magic, he told himself again, he was damned if he was going to give the old man anything.

Elaine seemed to be picking a rather roundabout route to the zoo, he realised, but it took him several minutes of observation to realise that she was deliberately avoiding the crowds as much as possible. Johan could understand that, even though he had never found the streets too disconcerting. But then, he'd only been able to slip out occasionally and he wouldn't have allowed fear of crowds to keep him from the streets. Taking his eyes off Elaine, he looked around, drinking in his newfound freedom.

Shoppers thronged the streets, looking for bargains, while roadside stalls tried to sell them food and drink. A variety of smells met his nostrils as he saw food from all over the Empire, from plates of hot and spicy curry to boiled fish and stringy vegetables. One stall was offering frozen cream – the seller was bawling loudly that it actually helped cool the blood – while another was offering bowls of hot soup. Johan remembered, with a sudden pang, the day he'd sneaked out of the house and bought himself a meal at one of the stalls. It had tasted good, all the more so because he'd been free ... if only for a few short hours.

It was almost a disappointment when he reached the zoo. On the outside, it was just a long low building, barely larger than his family's house. Elaine led him inside ... and his whole world seemed to shift on its axis. The interior of the building was not only far bigger than the outside, it was spelled to give each animal a proper habitat. All around him, children were marvelling at a strange creature that looked like an oversized spider. The creature seemed to be eying them back with murderous intent.

"A Dark Wizard produced that creature using magic," Elaine commented. "It couldn't have existed otherwise. He was planning to produce a small army of them to terrorise the region, but the Inquisitors stopped him before he got much further. As it is, the eggs the creature produces can be used in a number of interesting and complicated potions."

Johan eyed the spider, feeling oddly reluctant to turn his back on it. The children might be awed, but just looking at it brought out a fear of insects he hadn't known he had. On eight legs, he asked himself, just how fast could it move? He didn't think he really wanted to know the answer.

Elaine seemed more relaxed as they made their way through the zoo, pausing to look at each and every strange creature. Johan found himself relaxing too, wondering why his father had never brought him to the complex, even when he had been young enough to hope that his magic simply hadn't developed yet. He glanced at Elaine, wondering just how old she really was. Glamours could hide signs of ageing, but he had a feeling that she wasn't much older than Charity or Jamal. But if she was on the Privy Council ...

There's no requirement to sit on the council, he reminded himself, *apart from magical power and political power. She could have that at sixteen years old, if her parents were dead ...*

"Thank you for bringing me here," he said, and meant it. "This is fantastic."

Elaine smiled back at him, then walked onwards. There was a giant scorpion, a creature that resembled a cross between a lion and a bear, a massive snake with something firmly fixed over its eyes, a small army of ants that seemed intent on building a colossal anthill in the centre of the zoo ... he found himself starting to grow tired, without even having seen everything in the complex. Five giant monkeys swung over his head, then made rude gestures towards the visitors. The kids laughed and ate it up. Their parents seemed much less amused.

"It's not as if they can punish the monkeys," Elaine

commented, dryly.

Johan laughed.

An hour later, they left the zoo and headed towards a small café. Johan smiled openly as they stepped inside, remembering Charity's tales of how she'd met new friends in similar places, places Johan had never been allowed to visit. Now ... he was almost disappointed. There was no magic in the darkened room, nothing special at all. But then, the café was some distance from the Peerless School. It was quite possible that few magicians came to drink there.

Elaine ordered for them both, then settled back to relax. Johan smiled at her, wondering if he dared ask if he could take Jayne next time. But she'd warned him that Jayne might not be interested ... his head hurt as he contemplated all the possibilities. Jamal, the lucky bastard, had been able to have his fun with the maids. Johan had known that none of them would have let him touch ...

There was a sudden loud noise from outside, followed by screaming. Johan saw Elaine jerk upright, drawing her wand from her belt. Brilliant light seemed to flare through the café's windows as the screaming grew louder. Elaine moved her wand in a complicated pattern – summoning help, Johan assumed - then stood up and headed for the door. Johan hesitated, then followed her. Behind them, the handful of other people in the café were hiding under the tables. He found it hard to blame them.

Outside, all hell seemed to have broken loose. A handful of masked magicians were standing in the middle of the street, casting spells in all directions. Johan saw, to his horror, a pair of small children struck by an odd spell, their forms blurred together into a frozen nightmare. A woman was attacking her husband, several children were attacking their parents ... and others had been turned into frogs or inanimate objects. He froze, remembering what Jamal had done ...

... But Jamal was in jail. He had to be in jail. He couldn't be one of the masked magicians, could he? Johan knew that Jamal was good at getting out of trouble, but surely he wouldn't be stupid enough to worm his way out and then do the same crime *again*? No, this had to be his friends ...

"Power to the powerful," one of the magicians called, amplifying his voice so that it could be heard all over the city. "Power to those who can take it ..."

His voice cut off as Elaine hit him with a stunning spell. He crumpled to the ground, his mask falling to reveal patrician features and long white hair. His comrades turned to stare at Elaine, then started hurling spells in her direction. Eldritch fire crackled around her as she used her wand to deflect the spells; Johan stared in horror, unable to quite comprehend the magnitude of their transgression. They weren't just fighting with another magician, they were fighting with a *Privy Councillor*! There was no way that the Grand Sorceress would let *that* pass.

But they don't know she's a Privy Councillor, he thought, numbly. *She isn't wearing the robes.*

Elaine stumbled backwards as curses and hexes crashed into her protections. Johan hesitated, unsure of what to do, then started to cast the first spell Charity had shown him. One of the magicians snickered out loud – the gestures were recognisable, even if Johan hadn't been wearing magician's robes or carrying a wand – clearly convinced that a light spell couldn't even begin to hurt him. And then he jumped backwards as blinding white light blazed into existence, followed rapidly by a wave of heat.

Johan half-covered his eyes, trying to see past the blaze. It sounded as though the ringleader's robes had caught on fire, but it was impossible to be sure. They were definitely retreating though ... he had to stop them! He cancelled his own spell and smiled as he realised that he'd been right. Several of them were desperately trying to stamp out their burning robes.

He snickered. After having spent nearly sixteen years being tormented by his siblings, it felt *good* to win a fight.

A moment later, he cursed his own stupidity as the ringleader pointed a wand at him and chanted a curse in a language he didn't recognise. He hadn't won *yet*! There was no way to know which spell was going to be used, so he concentrated on forming a protective bubble around his body. Balefire flared through the air and flared around the bubble, but he was utterly unhurt. The ringleader's face was still hidden behind his mask, yet somehow Johan was sure that he was flabbergasted by Johan's new protection. *That* ... was far from normal.

The ringleader's wand slipped. For a moment, Johan thought that he was going to surrender – casting away one's wand was a standard sign – and then he heard a scream beside him. He looked ... and saw Elaine's face contorted in agony. Why wasn't she defending herself? Or why hadn't she run?

Because she was there for you, his own thoughts answered him. *She was trying to protect you.*

Pure rage blazed through his mind, but he forced himself to concentrate on the effects he wanted. The ringleader's wand shattered – he stared at it in disbelief – and then his entire body turned to stone. Behind him, his retreating fellows also turned to granite. Johan looked around, staring in horror at the innocent victims of compulsion charms, then *willed* them all to freeze. He didn't know what would happen if he tried to remove the charms, but if they were frozen they couldn't hurt themselves any further. Or so he hoped.

Silence fell, broken only by gasps of pain from the victims.

It was a scene out of nightmare. Countless bodies lay on the ground, blood pooling below them and drifting towards the gutters. Tiny objects lay everywhere; small animals were hopping around, trying to convince someone to break the spell and free them from their forced transfigurations. Men, women and children had been victimised alike, tortured and humiliated for nothing more than being mundanes ...

Johan turned to Elaine ... and cursed himself for not looking at her sooner. She was lying on the ground in a crumpled heap, sweat running down her forehead. He took her into his arms, shocked by how light she felt, and tried to help her upright. She seemed to be running on willpower alone. What else could keep her going?

"Water," she breathed, as he lowered her into a sitting position. "Get some from the café."

Johan hastened to obey. The patrons were still cowering under the tables, but it was easy enough to get some water from the tap. He poured a glass and took it back outside, holding it in front of her eyes. For a terrible moment, he

thought that she was too far gone to drink ...
And then the Inquisitors arrived.

Chapter Eighteen

It was hard, so hard, to focus her mind, but Elaine knew that she didn't dare collapse. Fighting so many trained magicians at once had been foolish, particularly as she had had no time to rig the field to her advantage, yet she couldn't have stood by and done nothing. If someone had resisted, she'd hoped, the attackers would have panicked and fled rather than fight and perhaps be caught by the Inquisitors.

But she'd drained herself badly even before one of them had hit her with a pain curse. Johan had stood up to them too, but despite his strange powers he was badly unprepared for close-quarter fighting. Thankfully, he'd survived ... and managed to fetch her water. She sipped gratefully at the glass, trying hard to regain her strength. But the only *real* thing she could do to help herself was food and sleep.

"Elaine," a familiar voice said. She looked up into Dread's cold grey eyes. "Are you all right?"

"Drained," Elaine muttered. Her vision seemed to fade out for a long moment before she recovered herself. "Do you have nutrient potion?"

Dread pulled a gourd off his belt and passed it to her. Elaine's fingers fumbled over the lid; he took it back, opened it for her and then held it to her mouth. The potion tasted foul, as always, but she felt a sudden surge of energy as she drank. Forcing herself to stand upright made her feel a little better. Dread reached out a hand to steady her, then let go as it became clear that she could stand on her own two feet.

"I need to know what happened," he said. "And if we should be arresting your friend."

Elaine stared at him, then looked around her. The masked magicians were standing in front of her, trapped in stone. Behind them, several Inquisitors and druids were doing what they could for their victims, although most of them would never truly heal from the scars the rogue magicians had inflicted on them. And Johan ... Johan was sitting on the pavement, watching the Inquisitors with a strange, almost unreadable expression on his face. He looked, Elaine realised suddenly, as if he expected to be blamed for the whole affair.

"I think you owe him a big favour," Elaine said, shaking her head. "He caught most of the bastards."

Dread nodded. "So it would seem," he said. It was impossible to tell if he was serious about threatening to arrest Johan or if he'd merely been trying to galvanise Elaine into recovering faster. "I also need a statement."

"One moment," Elaine promised. She motioned for him to wait and walked over to kneel down next to Johan. "How are you feeling?"

"Strange," Johan admitted. "I stopped them. I *really* stopped them!"

"And let's hope that you got all of them," Elaine said. She'd counted six masked magicians – and there were six statues in front of them, utterly unable to move. But there might well be others. "I'm afraid we have to give statements to the Inquisitors."

Johan made a face. "I don't think they like me," he said. "They keep glancing at me when they think I'm not looking."

"They don't like anyone," Elaine said. She and Dread were friends, of a sort, but there was always a distance between them. At base, Dread was bound by powerful oaths that guided his actions. If he'd thought Elaine was a criminal, their friendship would have meant nothing to him. He would have arrested her without a second thought. "But they're decent people, all the same."

She couldn't really blame Johan for his reaction. Most people found Inquisitors a little worrying, if not outright terrifying. They were very powerful magicians with a wide range of legal powers for dealing with magical crime. And the fact that they hadn't been able to stop Kane, even though few people knew *everything* that had happened six months ago, only made people wonder if it was worth putting up with their existence.

Dread came over at her wave, then stayed with Johan while Elaine went to speak to another Inquisitor. Inquisitor Cass looked sweet and innocent, as if she wouldn't hurt a fly, but she was one of the most formidable magicians Elaine had ever encountered, with specific talents in mental magic. Piece by piece, Cass drew out everything Elaine had seen since the first scream, until she felt as though she'd been wrung out and left to dry. But it was definitely necessary to collect as many witness statements as possible.

Because mundane testimony is automatically downgraded, Elaine thought, sourly. *But they can't argue with mine on those grounds.*

"You shouldn't have fought them like that," Cass said, when she'd finished. "If that was an assessment, you would have failed."

She was right, Elaine knew. Despite all the information on duelling in her head, courtesy of the Witch-King, she had very little practice in fighting. Millicent and her cronies had beaten any duelling ambitions out of her before she'd finished her first year at the Peerless School. Just by standing still, she'd made a very tempting target. And the attackers hadn't hesitated to take advantage of her carelessness.

"Get some proper training," Cass suggested, firmly. "And make sure that your friend gets some too."

She headed over to the statues, beckoning Elaine to follow her. "Whatever he did sure was powerful," Cass added, as she tapped one of the statues with her wand. "Nothing we do seems to be able to break the spell. I don't even know if they are aware in there."

Elaine drew her wand and cast a diagnostic charm, but the results were inconclusive. There was a taint of magic hanging over the statues, enough to interfere with her readings, yet ... she gritted her teeth, puzzled. Had Johan actually *killed* them? If he had, it might cause a blood feud ...

"It might be hard to tell just who he killed," Cass pointed out, rather snidely. "The masks might as well be nailed to their heads."

She was right, Elaine realised. Johan's spell had turned everything from their bodies to their clothes to stone. She tugged at the shape of the mask, but it refused to come free. If they *were* dead, it would be impossible to say for sure who the statue had once been ...

Or maybe not, she thought. *They'll just have to see who doesn't come home tonight.*

"Good work," Dread's voice said. Elaine turned to see him and Johan approaching, having finished their own debriefing. "The Grand Sorceress will be pleased, even though this isn't *all* of them."

Elaine gave him a sharp look. "What do you mean?"

"The witnesses at the first attack claimed that there were ten attackers in all," Dread explained, as he tapped one of the statues with his wand. "One's in the Watchtower, six more are here ... that leaves three unaccounted for."

He looked over at Johan, who seemed to have been cheered up by whatever Dread had said to him. "Can you undo the spell?"

Johan looked at Elaine. "*Should* I undo the spell?"

Elaine hesitated. Given what they'd done to their victims, there *would* be a certain natural justice in leaving them trapped in stone forever. But it wouldn't allow them to be interrogated, nor would it help the Grand Sorceress to make a statement about such behaviour being unacceptable ... she scowled as she realised that Light Spinner might *prefer* to leave them as statues. It would save her from having to make a decision that, no matter the outcome, would make her more enemies.

But it wouldn't be *just*.

"I think so," she said. She glanced at the six statues and frowned. There were seven Inquisitors in the area, but there was no point in taking chances. "Try to do them one at a time."

Johan nodded and closed his eyes, concentrating. For a long moment, nothing happened ... enough to make Elaine worry that he *had* killed them. Killing stained the soul, even if it were done by accident ... and, more importantly, once someone had killed it was easier to kill again and again. And some of the darkest magic spells could only be worked through sacrificing a human in cold blood.

The statue seemed to shimmer, then return to flesh and blood. Dread lifted a hand and cast a stunning spell, blasting the attacker into unconsciousness. Elaine felt a flicker of envy at how casually he'd cast the spell without a wand, then pushed the thought to one side as they moved on to the next statue. The other Inquisitors grabbed the former statue, rolled him over and slapped on the cuffs, then tore off the mask and took a long look.

"Gavin, of House Arndell," Dread observed. The young man was completely unfamiliar to Elaine, but Dread seemed to know everyone who was anyone. "Fourth son of Lord Arndell. Flunked the Peerless School in his second year, two years ago. Since then, he seemed to spend most of his time trying to drink himself to death."

Elaine made a face. *That*, at least, explained why she didn't know him. His time at the Peerless School didn't intersect with her schooling or her post at the Great Library. But flunking out in second year ...? Offhand, she could only recall a handful of such cases, almost all of which had been resolved by private tuition and heavy payments to the Administrator. But someone having left completely?

He was a fourth son, she thought, grimly. *No doubt his father gave up after having three qualified magicians in the family.*

One by one, the other spells were released and their victims stunned. Dread identified them all, allowing Elaine to see a pattern developing. All of them were young – and had little to cling to, apart from their magic. Unless their elder siblings died, they would stand to inherit very little apart from their name. Indeed, *Jamal* was the only one who broke the pattern; he *was* the first son and, as such, his father's Prime Heir.

"Jamal is just nasty," Johan said, when Elaine pointed out that he was the exception. "The others ... just need someone to pick on to feel superior."

Elaine suspected that he was right. A magician in the Golden City – and in the Empire, even more so – was *important*. People would defer to his judgement, for fear that he would turn them into frogs; in a dispute between a magician and a mundane, the magician would almost always win. The masked magicians had nothing to cling to, nothing to make them feel superior, apart from their magic. And the Levellers threatened to take even *that* away from them.

"They could have found work, even if they hadn't passed all their exams," she muttered, tired "Instead, they just wasted their lives."

Shaking her head, she watched as the Inquisitors bundled the captured magicians away. By the time they awoke, they would be in the Watchtower, locked up in separate cells. She found herself hoping that they confessed before their parents were informed that they'd been captured, although it was probably too late. There had been plenty of people who had seen the unmasking and were now heading to the broadsheet reporters. The news would be all over the city by sunset.

"If you need us, we can stay and help with the wounded," she said to Dread. "Or we can go back to the library."

"Help if you can," Dread said. "Some of these people may die if they can't be properly treated."

Elaine nodded and led Johan towards the first gathering of bewitched frogs. Thankfully, the attackers had used prank spells rather than anything more powerful, allowing her to break them one by one without spending too much of her own power.   Johan watched, his face grim, as the frogs became human again, many of them crying out in shock at how they'd been treated. It was impossible to escape the feeling that the attackers, whatever they'd had in mind, were damaging the trust that held society together.   After this, people would be *far* more scared of magicians.

And scared people do stupid things, Elaine thought, as she snapped another spell. A young boy – he couldn't have been more than seven – appeared in front of her. Thankfully, he didn't seem too worried by the experience and even laughed as she pointed him towards the druids for a quick check before they let him go home. The next spell proved to have been cast on his mother, who seemed to be in shock. Elaine motioned for Johan to help her over to the druids and moved on to the next one.

What *had* they been thinking? The thought kept running through her brain as she broke spell after spell, often using her knowledge to dislodge the spell without pushing herself too far and draining her power. Their first attack had been targeted on the Leveller meeting, but this had been random terrorism.   Had they intended to scare the mundane population by proving that they were utterly defenceless? Or had they had something else in mind? But what?

She wondered, briefly, if they'd been after Johan. But they clearly hadn't expected him ... nor had they started the attack inside the café. On the face of it, it looked like everyone had had bad luck; Elaine had been unlucky to be so close to the attack, the terrorists had been unlucky to run into Johan, someone they could hardly have prepared for. But then, no one knew everything about Johan's powers ... and Elaine had kept most of what she *did* know to herself.

The next victim was utterly heartbreaking. Two children, a boy and a girl, seemed to have been turned into glass and melted together. Elaine recognised the spell as one used by construction sorcerers, men who melded bricks and stone into one solid mass; she'd never seen it used on humans before, certainly not *children*. They were alive, according to her diagnostic spell, but suffering horrific agony. Their thoughts were being jammed together ...

She lifted her wand ... and then stopped, unsure of how to proceed. A single mistake would kill them, simply by shattering their minds. Or it might leave them mentally disabled ... she wanted to call a druid, but she knew from the knowledge in her head that a druid couldn't do anything more than herself. The only thing they could do was slice them apart and hope like hell that the shock of separation didn't kill them.

And would someone thank you, part of her mind whispered, *if you separated a couple having sexual relations by slicing a knife between them? You don't know what you might cut off.*

Angrily, she pushed the thought aside. Despite the potion, everything she'd done was starting to catch up with her again. Silly thoughts were only the start of it, she knew. It wouldn't be long before she collapsed.

"Johan," she said, deciding to gamble, "I want you to try to separate them."

Johan came over to her, his face half-averted from the conjoined children. "What ... how?"

"Imagine them separating into two whole beings," Elaine said. All the magic she knew wouldn't be able to guarantee that they'd be completely separated, let alone alive and sane.

But Johan ... might be able to do it, particularly if he believed that it was possible. "Close your eyes and *will* it to happen."

Johan obeyed. The kids seemed to blur, their forms melting back into plastic ... and then they separated, tossed away from each other by a powerful force. They both opened their mouths and started screaming at the exact same moment, the sound blurring together into one note that echoed on the air. It sounded like the end of the world.

"What did I do?" Johan shouted. He had to shout to be heard over the screams. "I didn't mean to hurt them!"

"They've been traumatised," Elaine said, covering her ears. A druid came running up and hit both children with tranquilising spells. Their screams came to an end, but her ears rang for long moments afterwards. "You saved their lives."

"I certainly hope so," the druid said, casting charm after charm. "Their brain patterns are more than a little disrupted."

"But they're separate," Elaine said. She didn't want Johan to get the idea that he'd killed them. "Take them to the hospital and keep me apprised on their progress."

She started to walk towards where the remaining Inquisitors had gathered, beckoning to Johan to follow her. Every footstep felt like she was lifting a leaden weight, forcing her to slow down as she reached Dread. She really was coming to the end of her endurance.

"I'll get you a carriage back to the library," Dread said, as soon as he saw her. "And thank you for your help."

"Keep me updated," Elaine said. "I need to know what will happen to the attackers."

"I will," Dread promised. He looked over at Johan. "And thank you too. Without you, we might never have been able to catch them."

Elaine smiled, despite the tiredness that seemed to be slowly shutting her down. If the attackers hadn't been caught in the act, *proving* their guilt might be impossible. As it was, there would be testimonial from Johan, Elaine and several Inquisitors, all of whom had seen the attack or the stone attackers. There would be far fewer grounds for a lawyer to claim that mundanes were lying ... because, as every magician knew, mundanes always lied.

But the attack still seemed pointless. The first attack had had a point, brutal as it was; the second just seemed like random terrorism. But even terrorists had an end in mind, didn't they? Or did they just want some fun and games with unwilling victims?

She shook her head. No doubt the answer would reveal itself in time.

Chapter Nineteen

It was extremely difficult to get information out of the Watchtower.

Everyone knew that Inquisitors didn't talk. Nor could they be bribed. The only person they talked to openly was the Grand Sorceress, who already had everything she could possibly want. But they did have to work with the City Guard and many of the guards were not averse to taking money – or covert political support – from a wealthy aristocrat. It had taken Duncan a day and a large expenditure of gold, but he'd finally managed to get a copy of Jamal's file.

The report of his crimes had been bad enough – Duncan firmly believed that the mundanes should stay in their place, but torturing them was just bad form – but the *real* shock had been the report of just who had testified against Jamal in the first place. Johan, his *brother*, had given the testimony that had allowed the Inquisitors to arrest him. It was a breach of family loyalty ...

"Really, father," Charity said, when he summoned her and explained what he'd discovered. "What exactly do you expect?"

Duncan eyed his daughter suspiciously. He'd rescinded her grounding after she'd come back from the Great Library, but he knew for a fact that she hadn't left the house since then. And she had barely even left her suite; the maids had been ordered to bring her lunch and dinner so that she didn't have to eat with the rest of the family. He'd allowed it to happen ... which, in hindsight, might have been another mistake.

"Explain," he ordered.

"Jamal has treated him badly ever since it became clear that Johan would never develop powers," Charity pointed out. "He was awful to all of us, but we could defend ourselves, even fight back. Johan could never do that, could he? And, instead of giving him a chance to prove himself in a different field, we even insisted that he stay inside the house as much as possible."

"It was for his own protection," Duncan protested, biting down on his anger. Yelling at Charity – even thrashing her – wouldn't make the situation any better, even if she was speaking to him as though he were an idiot. "If he'd been captured by one of our enemies ..."

"There were precautions you could have taken," Charity snapped. "But your real reason for not letting him out the house was because you were *ashamed*. Ashamed of having a Powerless for a son."

"His mere existence threatened the family," Duncan said, weakly. She was right; whatever he'd told himself, he *had* been ashamed of having a powerless son. He would have been far less concerned if Johan had turned out to prefer boys over girls; the gods knew that there were plenty of ways for him to have children, then live a separate life from his wife. "If they knew that Johan was powerless, they might refuse to let you marry into their families ..."

"And did it occur to you to ask," Charity said, not altering her tone in the slightest, "if I *wanted* to marry into those families?"

She met her father's eyes. "You have shown Johan absolutely no love or acceptance, nor have you given him any reason to consider himself part of the family," she added, before Duncan could explode at her for being an ungrateful daughter. "Every time he manages to slip out, I wonder why he bothers to come back."

Duncan knew the answer to *that*. One of the charms he'd placed on his son, without his knowledge, would eventually tug him back home. It was gentle – a more overt pressure would be noticed, even by a mundane – but impossible to resist in the long run. But now that charm had to be gone too, or Johan would have come home by now. Instead ...

The letter on the desk was surprisingly polite, given what Charity had said. But it was also clear; Johan no longer considered himself part of the family. Instead, he would find his own path. And then he said goodbye.

"But you've done the same to all of us," Charity said, interrupting his thoughts. "You groomed Jamal to take your place, turning him into a spoilt and arrogant brat. You tried to prime me for a good marriage, you told Jay and Jolie what they should be studying when they reach their third year at the Peerless School, just so they could go into careers you would find *useful*. I imagine that you told my sisters the same, didn't you? You try to steer our lives ... but you didn't even do *that* to Johan. I'm surprised you didn't kill him if he brought so much shame to the family."

Duncan started to his feet, his hands gripping the desk tightly.

"Go ahead," Charity said, her voice wavering. Her fingers dug into the hem of her dress, as if she were about to raise it to expose her rear. "Beat me. Thrash me. Turn me into something for a week or even a month. Marry me off to an ugly old warlock with smelly breath. It won't make any difference to the truth!"

Duncan stared at her. She was right.

"Out," he growled.

Charity fled, the door banging closed behind her.

Sighing, feeling his rage abate, Duncan settled back into his chair. Charity had been right; he *had* spoilt his children, in the truest possible sense of the word. But what could he do about it? No wonder Johan didn't consider himself part of the family ...

... And no wonder that he had testified against his brother.

But everything he'd done had seemed so logical, at the time.

He picked up a sheet of notepaper and started to compose a letter to Johan. And another to Jamal, telling him that he was immensely disappointed in his eldest son. Maybe it was too late to turn Jamal into an upright human being, but he owed it to his family to try.

And he knew what Johan wanted, he told himself. Perhaps they could make an agreement.

***

Johan eyed Elaine nervously as the carriage rattled its way towards the Great Library. She was half-lying against him, like a puppet whose strings had been cut. Every few minutes, she would jerk awake and look around, then collapse back against him. He was too worried even to enjoy the sensation of having a girl lying against him ... by the time the carriage reached the library, he was genuinely convinced that she was dying.

The Inquisitor driving the carriage jumped out and opened the door, then levitated Elaine out into the street. Johan found himself envying the man's easy precision as he steered the weightless Elaine into the Great Library and down into the private section, where their quarters were situated. The Inquisitor seemed to have been there before, Johan decided, or maybe he was taking advice and directions from the wards. Once they reached Elaine's rooms, he opened the door and gently lowered her onto the bed.

"Just leave her to sleep it off," he ordered, marching out of the room and waiting impatiently for Johan to follow him. "And stop looking at all the books."

Johan flushed – he'd been more interested in what Elaine's room said about her character – but followed the Inquisitor outside. There, he watched as the man cast a locking charm on her door, then headed back out of the library. Johan watched him go, then headed towards his quarters. It was a surprise to see Jayne standing outside, waiting for him. But it wasn't a bad surprise ...

"Hi," he said, and hoped his voice didn't shake too much. "How are you?"

"What happened?" Jayne asked, urgently. "There are all sorts of rumours flying around ..."

Johan opened his door and led the way inside, wondering if she would follow. He found himself caught between joy and terror as she did; what did one *say* to a girl, particularly a magician, if one wanted to court her? Jamal had probably offered the maids money – or simply threatened them – but the wand at Jayne's belt suggested that would be a dangerous tactic to try. Maybe one should just try to be friendly and build up a rapport. Or ...

"There was another attack," he said, wondering just how much he should say. He *wanted* to show off in front of her, but at the same time he was aware that it would draw too much attention. "Elaine ... ah, the Head Librarian ... tried to stop them. They hurt her and so I stopped them."

Jayne looked doubtful. It dawned on Johan that she didn't have any good reason to believe that he *was* a magician. He had no wand, nor was he even wearing robes! Somehow, he doubted that Elaine had told her staff *everything*. In fact, for all he knew, she'd told them that he was a visiting relative. Technically, that would be an abuse of her position, but everyone knew that everyone did it.

"I did," he insisted. "And then we worked to help the wounded."

He shuddered as he remembered the conjoined children. He'd *willed* them to separate into two people, but he honestly didn't know how well it had worked. If only his magic was more reliable, or at least understood. But it wasn't ...

"Well done," Jayne said. Her face suddenly seemed to light up like the sun as she smiled. "And thank you for saving our boss."

Johan smiled. "It was my pleasure," he assured her, as he sat down. "Wouldn't you like to have a seat?"

Jayne gave him an oddly regretful look. "I'm supposed to be on duty," she admitted, reluctantly. "Madame Vane would be mad if I didn't complete my shift."

"Wait," Johan said, as she started to walk towards the door. "What ... what are you doing this evening?"

"I get off-shift in a couple of hours," Jayne said. "I was planning to eat in the canteen, then go back to my apartment to study."

Johan swallowed, nervously. "Do you want to eat here?"

Jayne lifted her eyebrows. "In the *library*?"

"There's food sent to this room," Johan said, although he understood her surprise. But he didn't have the money to go elsewhere. Somehow he doubted he could afford a fancy meal with the remainder of what Charity had given him. And Elaine was asleep. Waking her just to ask for money probably wouldn't get him anything other than a forced transformation into a toad. "I can order for you too."

"Maybe later," Jayne said. "If Madame Vane caught me eating in the library, even here, I'd be kicked out onto the streets at once."

She smiled, brightly. "But I can eat outside with you, if you'd like ..."

Johan hesitated. He *would* like ... but how could he eat with her when he had no money?

"Soon," he promised, wondering if he could *keep* that promise. "I have to stay close to her tonight."

Jayne nodded in understanding. "See you," she said. "Bye."

She winked at him, then left the room, pulling the door firmly shut behind her. Johan sighed as soon as the door was shut, wondering just how he was meant to get the money to take her out. *Jamal* wouldn't have had a problem, he thought, resentfully; even if his father had refused to give him the cash, shopkeepers would be willing to extend credit based on his status as Prime Heir. But Johan ... hardly anyone knew that he existed. They wouldn't believe that he was related to his father ...

He was still thinking about it when a letter drifted into the room and dropped down into his lap. The envelope was made of the finest paper, which was enough to tell him that it was from his father. He briefly considered incinerating it like the last one, this time without looking at it, but morbid curiosity led him to open it and pull out the paper. It was written in his father's neat precise hand. No secretary for *this* letter.

> *Son*
>
> *I have been informed by your sister that you have good reason to be angry at me and, by extension, the rest of the family. The fault is mine and I do not attempt to deny it. However, we cannot escape the fact that we are related in blood. We share more than just a name, but a bloodline that carries weaknesses as well as strengths.*

Johan gritted his teeth as he read the last line. Weaknesses as well as strengths? Did he mean Johan's apparent powerlessness or something altogether different? Jamal's sense of entitlement, that the world owed him everything and that he could get away with anything, no matter how vile?

Or was he referring to something that had never been shared with the poor little Powerless?

I do not deny, also, that the news of your magic is a great relief to me, as indeed it must be to yourself. Please do not hold the actions I was compelled to take to keep you safe against me; I feared for your safety as well as that of our family, no matter how harsh and unfair I must have seemed at the time. Now, we can rebuild our relationship and add your magic to the family.

Johan growled incoherently. How was it, he asked himself, that his father, even when trying to apologise, sounded like an arrogant asshole? And he was *still* trying to get Johan to return home. Hadn't he *read* the letter Johan had sent? He should have sent the first one, despite Elaine's veto. It would have made his feelings quite clear.

Towards this end, I wish to invite you to dine with us in two days. Your elder brother will not, I am afraid, be able to attend, but the remainder of the family should be present. I offer the word of Lord Duncan Conidian, Patriarch of House Conidian, that you will be free to return to the Great Library after the dinner, should you wish it. And I also pledge before the gods that our efforts to change your mind will be purely verbal, with not a hint of any form of coercion.

Johan had to smile. Did his father think that he didn't *know* Jamal was in prison? Or was he trying to hide it from everyone else? But the only other person who might see the letter was Elaine and she already knew the truth.

And he'd offered his word that Johan would be free to go. *That* was interesting. It suggested that he was serious. And the pledge to avoid coercion ... any attempt to invoke family rights would break that pledge outright, with disastrous consequences. Out of habit, he checked his father's signature. It was genuine.

As a gesture of good faith, I have instructed the bank to provide you with a trust vault comparable to the vaults I opened for Jamal and Charity. The key should be provided to you, along with a draft book, within the next day or two. Whatever decision you make, that money will be yours permanently. You may wish to speak with the bankers to consider investment opportunities.

I await your reply, as does the rest of the family. Whatever you may think of us, I know that Charity, at least, misses you – and was prepared to put herself on the line to explain to me just how badly I have acted.

Yours

Lord Duncan Conidian, Patriarch of House Conidian.

Johan stared down at the letter with mixed feelings. He knew just how much money Jamal had been given, enough to ensure that he wouldn't have to work for the rest of his life, if he was careful. Charity would also have had the same amount, although some of it would have been part of her dowry. But *he* had never been given a vault. How could he even have accessed it without another magician?

The money would be useful, he knew. He could take Jayne out, shower her with presents, treat her like a queen ... or pay Elaine for his apprenticeship. But he didn't want to take *anything* from his father, not now. No matter what his father said, the money came with strings attached. His gratitude would lead him to pay attention to his father's attitudes in future, if not honour his requests. And there *would* be requests. Even when his father was trying to be nice, there was manipulation involved.

And he had already asked for something in return.

Johan *hated* dinner parties, the few he'd been allowed to attend. Mostly, he'd been told to stay in his suite and the door had been charmed to prevent him from leaving. It wouldn't do to let the guests see that House Conidian had produced a Powerless. He'd told himself that he preferred being alone to watching everyone fawn over Jamal, but the truth was that he'd resented his exclusion bitterly.

He could attend one now ...

Everyone would fawn on him, he knew. There were two days in children's lives that were celebrated: their birthdays and their sparks, when they came into their magic. But he had never had a spark, not until now. There would be the best food and drink, expensive presents, perhaps even entertainment and ... the thought made him sick. If they hadn't considered him worthy until now, why should he consider *them* worthy of him?

Shaking his head, he folded the letter and put it in his pocket. Elaine would have to see it; she could tell him if he should go, or if he should refuse the invitation – and the money. But what would he do for money if his father took it back, no matter what he'd said?

Apprentices are supposed to be given an allowance, he thought. The book had told him that much, although there was no fixed scale. *How much would Elaine give me?*

He would have to ask, he knew. And then make up his mind.

Chapter Twenty

Elaine felt somewhat refreshed as she stumbled out of bed in the morning, although the combination of sweaty clothes and lying in a bad position didn't help. She undressed, ran a hot bath and enjoyed a soak, then dressed in new clothes and sent a message to Johan to join her for breakfast. When he entered, he was carrying another creamy-white envelope in his hand.

"Another letter from my father," he said, as Elaine scanned it quickly. "Should I go?"

Elaine scowled. She wanted to take it easy for the day, not grapple with complex political and personal problems. "Do you *want* to go?"

"No," Johan said. "But if he's offering to actually *talk* ... and not try to hold me there ..."

"He has given his word," Elaine agreed, neutrally. There were hidden implications here, she was sure, but she'd never been raised as a member of the Great Houses. "And he's giving you a great deal of money. Maybe he's sincere about wanting to rebuild connections between you and him."

"*Build* them, more like," Johan muttered. Dishes of food appeared in front of them and they started to eat. "Do you think I should go?"

"I don't know," Elaine admitted. Clearly, she would never cure Johan of his habit of talking while eating. "I think that he could make life difficult for you, particularly now that your secret is out and spreading. What you did yesterday will be all over the city by now and ... and people will be asking questions. Something will leak, sooner rather than later."

"Because my father will *want* it to leak," Johan agreed. "And he'd want to dispel any rumours about my status as a Powerless."

Elaine rubbed her forehead, wishing that she could see all

the implications. "Work out what you want to say to him, then go," she advised. "With Jamal currently in jail, you might not have a better chance to talk to him as an equal."

"He won't be alone," Johan objected. "Inviting me to a full dinner party means that the entire family – well, everyone who can make it – will be there. But I can talk to him alone afterwards."

He was interrupted by a purple-edged envelope that flew into the room and landed in front of Elaine. She swore under her breath and opened it, finding a card and a single note written on fine notepaper. The card informed her that a full meeting of the Privy Council would commence in precisely two hours; the note, written in Light Spinner's own hand, told her to attend. Elaine, who would have preferred to avoid the meeting, scowled. She was in no fit state to listen to the various councillors arguing about the current situation.

"I have to attend a meeting at the palace," she said, crossly. "What are your plans for the day?"

Johan hesitated. "Read more books?"

Elaine smiled. It would have been *her* ideal day as a child, although somehow she doubted that Johan felt the same way. "There are quite a few you should read," she said, "although I made a deliberate decision not to give you the standard spell and textbooks provided to new students. Given the nature of your powers, they would probably only confuse you."

"I suppose," Johan said. He didn't sound happy, which made Elaine smile. If he thought she was keeping the books from him, he would look them up for himself. "Can I ask a cheeky question?"

"You may," Elaine said.

"I ... I would like to take Jayne out for a meal," Johan admitted. "But I don't have any money."

Elaine frowned, inwardly. Was *that* why Johan hadn't dismissed his father's offer of a bank vault out of hand? But she could understand him wanting a social life, even if it wasn't a desire she shared. Daria had always been the one dragging her out of the apartment to go places, mostly places where she'd been nothing more than a wallflower. And yet she'd met Bee at one such place.

She stood up, walked over to a chest of drawers and waved

her hand over it, muttering unlocking incantations. Once it opened, she reached inside and produced a small bag and a handful of gold coins. Daria had always taught her to keep some cash on hand, although that hadn't normally been a problem. It was only recently that she'd earned enough money to open a vault at the bank.

"There should be enough money here to go just about anywhere," she said, as she dropped the coins into the bag. "I would suggest" – she allowed her voice to harden – "that you do a little research before picking a place to go. Most of the fancier places are often far more expensive than they deserve. Vane would be able to offer advice, if you asked her."

Johan took the bag, staring at it as if he'd never seen so much money in his life. The chances were, Elaine knew, he hadn't. As a Powerless, he would have been vulnerable to both magical and mundane thieves. His father would probably not even have given him an allowance to spend on sweets or whatever else took his fancy.

"I will have to get dressed and go," Elaine said, feeling tired again. If she tried to stay at the Great Library, Light Spinner would probably send the Inquisitors out to drag Elaine back to the palace. "You have the books in your room?"

"Yes," Johan said. "What are you going to tell them about me?"

"As little as possible," Elaine said. "Or at least as little as I can get away with telling them."

She found herself mulling the letter over as she dressed in her finest robes, then started to walk towards the Imperial Palace. Was Johan's father serious about trying to rebuild connections with his son or was he hoping to take advantage of Johan's new powers for his own purposes? Or was he merely hoping to ensure that the entire world knew that he hadn't birthed a Powerless after all? There was no way to know.

For once, the interior of the Imperial Palace was buzzing with life. Servants moved from room to room, carrying out the orders of the Privy Councillors; outside, guards thronged the grounds, looking for potential threats. Elaine wondered, as she made her way through wards that provided more protection than a whole army of guardsmen, if Light Spinner was making a point. Whatever the Privy Council might think, most of the regime's instruments of compulsion were firmly in her hands.

There were twelve Privy Councillors, all politically and magically powerful – and wealthy, of course. To some extent, Elaine knew, *she* was the sole exception to that rule; her magic was subtle, rather than powerful. If it came down to a duel, she would be beaten by any of the other Privy Councillors, although the unwritten rules of the chamber insisted that Privy Councillors could not fight each other, no matter how strongly they disagreed. The knowledge in Elaine's head whispered that the original Grand Sorcerer had wanted to ensure that some of the most powerful magicians in the world didn't start fighting – and, while trying to kill each other, damage his city.

Elaine took her seat at the stone table and watched as the others sat down. Deferens gave her a twisted smile that told her that, despite serving under a Grand Sorceress, his views on women had never really changed. As always, he wore a bright red outfit under his purple robes, having altered them to show off his clothes. Elaine had often wondered if his hyper-masculinity was actually an act that compensated for something, but from what little she knew of his homeland she suspected that it was actually the standard behaviour for men there. And women, there, were expected to be obedient and silent. Any female magician born there would be lucky to reach five years old before being killed.

Two seats away, Lord Duncan Conidian sat down. Elaine eyed him with some interest, uncomfortably aware that he was studying her too. He looked like an older version of Johan, with lines on his face that suggested a man under heavy stress. Not too surprising, Elaine knew, with one son in jail and another estranged from the family. There was a faint hint of a glamour surrounding him, probably hiding the true state of his hair. At his age, it should have started to turn white.

Elaine sighed, fighting the impulse to shrink back into her seat and hide. She didn't belong here and she knew it, no matter what Light Spinner said. The others in the room had grown up wielding power; they could snap their fingers and expect obedience from just about everyone. But she ... she'd been an orphan, then a mediocre student and then a librarian. All she'd done to earn respect was drain the Blight and save the city from Kane - and only a handful of people knew the full story.

As soon as the final Councillor sat down, Light Spinner entered and took her own seat. The Privy Council didn't stand on formality, not when they were alone. Light Spinner held her hand in the air, casting the first privacy ward; one by one, the other members added their own wards to the mix. No spying magic, as far as Elaine knew, could penetrate such a powerful set of wards. Picking one's way through thirteen wards with thirteen different signatures and styles would take hours, at the very least. It made the room the most secure place in the Empire.

"There is much to discuss," Light Spinner said. She spoke quietly, but the magic of the room projected her voice for all to hear. "Yesterday, terrorists attacked innocent people in the Golden City. They were taken into custody and interrogated by the Inquisitors. We now know that their aim is to ensure that the mundanes remain firmly in their place."

She clicked her fingers. Paper scrolls appeared in front of them. "In the two attacks they launched, nineteen people died and over a hundred were injured, directly or indirectly," she added. "That includes people hurt by friends and family who were under the influence of compulsion spells. This behaviour is completely unacceptable. Unfortunately, as they have taken Oaths of Secrecy, they have been unable to divulge the names of their comrades who remain at large."

Elaine scowled. An Oath of Secrecy literally prevented the oath keeper from giving up any information covered by the oath, no matter what their interrogators tried. Mind-raping spells, simple physical torture, even psychological trickery ... none of them would produce a morsel of information from the prisoners. Indeed, there were legal precedents that agreed that trying to force someone to break such an oath was thoroughly illegal.

Deferens leaned forward. "How many of them *are* there?"

Light Spinner's face was hidden, but Elaine would have bet good money that she was sneering. "The largest group observed was ten," she said. "If we assume that is all of them, there are three more to find. But we don't dare make any such assumption."

She placed her gloved fingertips together, looking directly at Duncan Conidian. "As you can see from the scrolls," she continued, "all of them are scions of the aristocracy. And one of them is a Prime Heir."

Heads turned to look at the Conidian, who looked uncomfortable.

"My son has clearly been misled," the Conidian said, finally. "His conduct has not been in line with what I brought him up to consider acceptable. Should he be released to my custody, I will work to teach him better."

"But you have already failed to teach him better," Lady Lakeside said. Elaine barely knew her, although they sat on the same council. She had no idea which way Lady Lakeside would jump. "And his crimes are hardly *minor*."

She turned to look at Light Spinner. "Grand Sorceress, this young man committed terrorist acts against citizens of the Empire," she said. "He merits the strongest punishment."

"They were committed against mundanes," Deferens pointed out, sweetly. "The strong may do as they wish to the weak."

"He also used a torture curse on the Lady Elaine," Lady Lakeside pointed out, nodding towards Elaine. "*She* is a Privy Councillor."

Elaine had to fight to remain seated upright as the rest of the table stared at her. "That is true," she said, quietly. "I tried to stop them and they attacked me."

"You weren't wearing your robes," Deferens said. "It is arguable that they didn't *know* that they were attacking a Privy Councillor."

Elaine kept her face as expressionless as possible, thinking hard. Deferens knew that she hadn't been wearing her robes ... that probably meant that he had interrogated the eyewitnesses or, more likely, sent someone else to do it for him. And that meant ...

"There is a more important issue here," Deferens said,

confirming her worst fears. *"How* were they stopped?"

He knows about Johan, Elaine thought, as Light Spinner quickly explained. She looked up and met the Conidian's eyes, seeing a strange combination of relief, pride and fear. *What else does he know?*

"You should know the full story," Light Spinner said. "Lady Elaine, if you would ...?"

It's just like writing an essay, Elaine told herself, frantically. "Until recently, Johan Conidian was believed to be a Powerless," she said, out loud. There were a handful of gasps as several councillors realised that the rumours were true. "During the first attack, outside the palace, there was a stunningly powerful magic pulse that was sensed thousands of miles away from the city, centred on Johan. Since then, he has developed magic of a rather curious nature."

She outlined the rest of the story, keeping the details to herself. If they didn't pry too deeply, they would just see Johan as a normal magician, if one with significant power reserves. But she knew that the Privy Councillors were all experienced, with considerable knowledge about their powers. Johan, no matter how they looked at it, had become fantastically powerful in a very short space of time.

Lady Lakeside looked over at the Conidian. "It must be a relief to know that your son is not powerless," she said. "However ... was he *truly* powerless?"

The Conidian gave Elaine a look that suggested that he wanted her dead. "My son was tested yearly by the druids," he admitted, reluctantly. "Until now, they didn't even find a *spark* of magic. He seemed to be a Powerless."

"And to think that there were only ever rumours of his existence," Deferens mused, mockingly. "How *could* you hide him from us?"

The Conidian swung round to glare at the younger man. "You know as well as I do that the life of a Powerless can be hellish," he snapped. "I took steps to keep him safe."

Elaine scowled. On the face of it, the Conidian had a point. Most families would have quietly arranged for a Powerless child to die in an 'accident;' perhaps, if the child was lucky, sending him or her to an orphanage once the child was legally dead. And, with the Conidian Family having only recently moved to the Golden City, it wouldn't have been hard for them to conceal Johan's existence completely.

"That's as may be," Deferens said. "However, if he really *was* Powerless ... we are looking at something that can give power to the powerless. Aren't we?"

He swung round to look at Elaine. "*Aren't* we?"

"Perhaps," Elaine said, reluctantly.

"But my son comes from a strongly magical bloodline," the Conidian protested. "He might just have sparked very late in life."

"There is something very odd about his magic," Deferens said. His gaze never left Elaine's face, watching for the merest twitch that might help answer his questions. "No matter how strongly magical his bloodline, he represents a very odd puzzle. And something that can turn the world upside down."

He looked over at Light Spinner. "Grand Sorceress," he said, "I propose that this young man be put to death."

Elaine had expected it. But it was still a shock.

"That young man is my son," the Conidian said, through gritted teeth. "You cannot just execute him because you find his existence inconvenient."

"We might just be executing another of your sons for his crimes," Deferens pointed out, rudely.

"I will fight tooth and nail to prevent that from happening," the Conidian snapped.

Light Spinner held up a hand and they fell silent. "Johan Conidian represents a fascinating puzzle," she said. "It may even be a gift from the gods."

"Or the demons," Deferens said. "What happens when a magician gets a sudden boost in power?"

Elaine shivered, remembering a conversation she'd had with Dread in Ida. He'd assumed that *she'd* had a power boost and, fearing that it might have driven her mad, had probed gently to determine the truth. The hell of it was that Deferens was right. A sudden power boost tended to drive magicians insane, turning them into deadly threats to everyone else. It was all too easy to imagine Johan, mistreated and abused from a very young age, going that way.

But he has a good heart, Elaine thought, grimly.

"We have moved away from the question at hand," Light Spinner said. "How do we deal with these terrorists?"

"Try them," Lady Lakeside said. "They can state their case in front of us; we will judge them."

Elaine sighed and settled back to listen as the arguments started to rage. The Conidian wouldn't want to sit in judgement of his eldest son; others, his political enemies, were only too keen to force him to serve as a judge. Whichever way he voted, they would find an excuse to condemn him. Elaine felt a moment of pity, which faded away as she remembered just how badly he had treated both of his eldest sons. One was a spoilt brat and a bully, the other had no interest in returning home.

She sighed inwardly, feeling her temples already starting to throb. It was going to be a long day.

Chapter Twenty-One

"I really don't want to do this," Johan muttered, as the carriage came to a stop outside the family home. "I really don't want to ..."

He cursed his own cowardliness as he hopped down and looked up at the house. He'd never really had a chance to take a proper look at it from the outside, not when he'd had to sneak in or out whenever he'd wanted to escape his prison. It was solid stone, but ivy and other plants had grown up around the house, giving it a slightly wild appearance. The windows, he knew, were effectively illusions. Inside, the house was far bigger than it seemed on the outside.

I could walk away, he told himself. *Go back to the library ... Elaine would understand.*

But her report of the meeting two days ago had made it clear that powerful factions within the Privy Council wanted him dead. If a Powerless could be turned into a magician, what would happen if someone discovered how to reproduce the technique upon demand? The very essence of the Empire's society might be upended. Who knew what would happen if the Levellers actually acquired magic powers?

Bracing himself, he walked up to the door and knocked.

It should have opened as I passed through the wards, he thought, resentfully. The door certainly *would* have opened for Jamal or Charity or any of his other siblings, but not for him. Clearly, the wards hadn't been altered, no matter what his father said. He couldn't blame him, not really, but it still rankled. A moment later, May opened the door and bowed low, exposing her impressive cleavage. She'd never done *that* for him before.

"Your family are waiting in the dining room, Sir Magician," she said. "If you will come with me ..."

Sir Magician, Johan thought, sourly. It *was* the standard title for an unattached magician, but not for a child of the household. Was his father making a subtle ploy or was he trying to be flattering? There was no way to tell, short of asking ... and that would have revealed far too much of his inner insecurities. Johan might not have had all the lessons Jamal had been given, but he'd heard enough to know how his father manipulated people, even his friends and allies, just to ensure that the family's position was rock solid.

The dining room was brightly lit, revealing a single heavy wooden table surrounded by chairs. His father sat at the head of the table, as was his right; his mother sat facing him, her face dull and bored. Whatever interest his mother had once had in her children had faded over the years, unsurprisingly. Johan had heard enough arguments between his parents to understand that his powerlessness had damaged their relationship beyond repair.

Charity, flanked by her sisters, sat on one side of the table. Johan flashed her a genuine smile and was surprised by the oddly timid response. Charity had stood up to Jamal more than once, even though she'd never been his match in spell-casting. Had being transformed by him *damaged* her in some way? The gods knew that she'd been transfigured before and survived with nary a hint of damage.

Jay and Jolie sat facing Charity, with an empty seat between them. Johan suspected that *he* was meant to sit there, something that annoyed him; his younger brothers had never been quite as unpleasant as Jamal, but they'd certainly played enough tricks on him to earn his dislike, if not outright hatred. Normally, too, that would have been Jamal's seat. The symbolism was obvious; the youngest in the family supported the eldest without reservation.

But he had never *felt* part of the family ...

His father rose to his feet. "Johan," he said, gravely. "Welcome back."

Traditionally, Johan knew, he was supposed to kneel to receive his father's blessing. But he was damned if he was going to surrender *that* much. If his father wanted his forgiveness, if nothing else, he was going to have to work for it.

"Father," he said, instead. "Thank you for the invitation."

His father's face flickered, just for a second, then returned to its normally expressionless mask. "Please, be seated," he said. He waved to May to pull out Johan's seat, as if he couldn't have done it for himself. "The cooks have produced an excellent meal."

They had, Johan admitted, as the first dishes were brought into the room and placed on the table. He'd always been fond of goulash, crammed with meat, potatoes and spices, although Jamal had disagreed ... and, as always, what Jamal wanted, Jamal got. Or didn't get, in this case. Johan had had to beg the cooks for his favourite meals sometimes, or bribe Charity to do it for him. He hadn't had to beg this time.

He couldn't help feeling uncomfortable as they ate, despite the superb food. He'd spent most of his life being ignored, but that was better than having everyone staring at him as though he had suddenly become famous. His two brothers were glancing at him when they thought he wasn't looking, his younger sisters were staring openly. Only Charity was refusing to even *look* at him, keeping her eyes on her food. It was really an astonishing change in her behaviour, one that worried him more than he wanted to admit. After all, Charity *hadn't* been a total bitch to him.

"Tell me," his father said, as the maids cleared away the dishes, "what you intend to do with your life."

He was *trying* to be nice, Johan decided, but too much of his usual tone had slipped into his voice. "I intend to learn how to use my magic, then work as a magician," he said. He had had other ambitions – he wanted to travel the world – but he didn't want to mention that to his father. "And I want to prove myself."

"You could prove yourself with your family's assistance," his father said, quietly. "We could offer you a great deal you could never obtain for yourself."

He folded his hands together, suggesting that he was about to conclude the deal. "We have a marriage arrangement with House Clyburn," he explained. "You could marry Marina Clyburn."

Johan couldn't help a harsh bark of laughter that burst out of his throat. "I thought she was intended to marry *Jamal*!"

"Jamal ... has disgraced himself," his father admitted. He sounded as though he would have preferred not to say anything of the sort, but he said it. Johan silently gave him points for honesty. "You would be the next in line, binding our houses together."

"She's very pretty," Charity said, suddenly. "You'll like her."

"I saw her portrait," Johan said. "And she *is* pretty."

Marina *was* stunning, he had to admit; tall and slim, with brown-black hair and firm breasts ... she was every man's dream. The question of who would marry her had occupied High Society for years, because she brought far more than just a pretty face to a marriage contract. She brought connections to the aristocracy that stretched all the way back to the foundation of the Empire. But she was three years older than him ...

... And she wouldn't have even *considered* him as a potential suitor while he'd been powerless.

He scowled down at the table. "And what does *she* think about this?"

"She knows that it is her duty to enter into a marriage contract for the good of House Clyburn," his father said. "She will not object to receiving you instead of Jamal."

"She might consider you preferable," Charity said, snidely.

Their father glared at her, then looked at Johan.

Johan thought about it, refusing to meet his father's eyes. Marriage contracts were rarely about love, particularly not in High Society. If his father and her father agreed, they would be pushed together even if they hated each other. Indeed, as long as they produced at least two children to carry on the family name, they could have as little to do with one another as they liked. There would be nothing stopping them from having lovers, even living apart, as long as they remained married in name.

But it was just another form of treating Johan – and Marina, and even Jamal – as an *object*, as something that could not think for itself.

It wasn't something he wanted, not for him. And he wouldn't want *anyone* to have to go through the experience of lying with someone just to have children, not if they didn't love the person. Charity would have to marry too, under the same rules. The thought was sickening.

And yet ... if his father had been willing to offer him such a marriage, what did he want in return?

Johan looked up, meeting his father's eyes. "And at what price?"

His father didn't try to deny that he wanted something. "I would like you not to testify against Jamal," he said, bluntly. "Your word could see him sent to the headsman."

Jolie gasped. "*You* testified against your brother? You ..."

He started to move his hand, casting a spell. Johan acted on instinct, freezing him to the spot.

"I'm not what I used to be," Johan said, addressing the table as a whole. "Please, remember that."

He turned away from Jolie, looking back at his father. "Why should I *not* testify?"

His father looked at him as though he'd never really *seen* him before. Johan could understand why his father didn't want him to speak – he was the only magician who could place Jamal at the palace during the riot, thus the only real witness – but it was harder to understand his father's shock. He'd even written a letter where he'd acknowledged that Johan had little reason to consider himself part of the family.

Or did he really believe that an offer of such a high marriage would change Johan's mind?

"I know that Jamal has been ... thoroughly unpleasant to you," his father said, finally. "And I understand that you may not think very highly of the rest of us. But we are still related by blood."

"In blood alone," Johan said.

Bitterness and frustration welled up inside him, breaking through his self-control. "You were disappointed in me from the start," he said. "You never even allowed me to explore what I could do without magic. You allowed Jamal and everyone else to treat me as a target for their spells. You ..."

He forced himself to keep his voice steady. "Where was your consideration when Jamal turned me into a birdbath and stuck me on the roof for hours? Where were you when Charity made me talk in rhyme for two days? What did you do when Chime turned me into a doll and played with me? Or when Jamal turned me into a mirror and snuck me into the maid's room? And who was it who got blamed for *that*?"

The memory drove him onwards. "Tell me," he snapped. "Why should I consider myself part of this family?"

"Because you are," his father said. His face was flushed, but his voice was under firm control. "I know – we were not the best family for someone like you. What I did ... I felt it had to be done."

"But you knew that it was pointless," Johan said. "I read the druid's file on me. Not a single spark of magic was found, until now. All those torments, all the times I was victimised that you justified by claiming that they might bring out my magic, were completely worthless. I never developed magic!"

"Until now," his father said. "And Charity and your other siblings *did* have their magic brought out by such ... *torments*, as you call them."

"But they clearly had the potential," Johan said. "I never did."

"And yet you finally developed magic," his father pointed out.

"Too late to have warm feelings towards *anyone* in this house," Johan said. "You were disappointed, mother" – he looked at his mother, who still seemed bored – "ignored me, my siblings tormented me ... even the maids were snide, when no one else was around. Why should I have any feelings for you that could even *remotely* be called warm?"

"I can have those maids sacked," his father said. "I ..."

"Don't you understand?" Johan demanded, feeling anger boiling up again. "You set the tone for everyone else. Sack all of the maids, send them begging on the streets or opening their legs for tourists and it won't even *begin* to make up for what everyone else did! Do you really believe that they would have been so unpleasant if you hadn't been effectively telling everyone that it was fine to treat me like that?"

He slapped the table. A crack appeared in it, heading towards Charity. She yelped and jumped backwards, falling over to the floor. A moment later, the cracks spread until the table shattered, dishes and plates falling to the floor. Johan stood up and stepped backwards, watching with sudden bitter amusement the terror on his family's face. No doubt they'd heard that even Inquisitors had been unable to reverse the spells he'd placed on the terrorists ... right now, they were actually *scared* of him.

And it felt good.

He waited for the final sounds to die away, then spoke into the appalled silence. "You called me here to make me an offer," he said. "An offer that would involve me refusing to testify against someone, my brother in blood alone, in exchange for a girl I don't want and marriage relationships I don't need. Tell me; why should I *not* testify against Jamal?

"I've known him since I was born," he added, daring his father to interrupt. "He has *always* picked on those weaker than him. His siblings ... even the ones with magic, but others. He picked on the maids, he picked on the cooks, he certainly picked on mundanes outside the house, even before he attacked the Levellers. Jamal has no political platform, no cause; he's just an unpleasant spoilt brat who has finally stepped well over the line. Nineteen people are *dead* because of him."

"Nineteen *mundanes*," his father said.

"*I* was mundane until then," Johan said. They stared at each other across a gulf of incomprehension. "And Jamal is what you made him."

But would Johan have been any different, he asked himself, if he had been born with magic?

It was a terrifying thought. He'd been powerless ... and it was *that* experience that made him empathise with the Levellers. The gods knew that he'd been humiliated just as badly as the mundanes who had been caught up in the riot, over and over again. But his father, who had been born with magic sparks dancing around his body, would never understand what it was like to be powerless. Magic was part of his father's life. He could never separate himself from it.

"There are decent magicians out there," he added, remembering Elaine. And Jayne. "They don't have to be assholes" – his father's face twitched at the word – "even when they're in charge. But Jamal *is* an asshole. You failed him as he grew up and it's now too late to save him from the consequences of his actions. So why are you even *bothering*?"

His father hesitated. "You are aware, of course, that the

family needs an heir," he said, finally. "I could not name *you* my heir, not until now. Jamal was indispensable until Jolie reached his maturity."

Johan sneered. "Are you sure Jamal ever did?"

"Your grandfather is dead," his father said, ignoring his sally. "If something were to happen to me, the family's patronage network would fragment without an heir, someone to take over and lead the family in my absence. Jamal was trained for that role from birth and I admit ... that might not have been good for him. But now ... I still need him."

"You can appoint Charity as your Prime Heir," Johan pointed out. "She is mature and responsible, which is more than you can say for Jamal."

"But that would also cripple her chances of making a good match," his father objected. He didn't even *look* at Charity. "No husband from one of the Great Houses is going to want to marry her when it means taking on a subordinate position ..."

"It's a fine time to start caring what someone *thinks*," Johan snapped, feeling his temper rising again. "You treated us all, even Jamal, as objects, people to be shaped into whatever pattern you felt appropriate. And when you thought I was useless, you just kept me a prisoner. But we twisted in your grasp. Jamal is a bully, I have no interest in returning to the family ..."

"I can appoint *you* my Prime Heir," his father said. "No one can deny that you have magic."

"*Don't you see?*" Johan shouted. "*I'm useful now and you're trying to use me!*"

He brought his anger under control, savagely. The table was one thing, but if he lost control again someone could get seriously hurt. He waved a hand at Jolie, releasing him from the enchantment, then turned to stare at his father.

"I've made up my mind," he snapped. "I will not be returning to the family, even as Prime Heir. You can bribe and bully and make deals and Jamal will no doubt survive his latest burst of stupidity. But you can do it without me. I *will* testify."

His father opened his mouth, but Johan spoke over him. "Don't even *think* of trying to pressure me," he warned.

"You *will* regret it."

He turned and strode out of the room. The door refused to open; he concentrated and it collapsed into a pile of sawdust. He marched out to the carriage, refusing to look back, and climbed inside. The driver cracked the whip, taking the carriage back towards the Great Library.

It wasn't until he was safely away that Johan let himself cry.

Chapter Twenty-Two

There was one entrance – officially – to the Great Library, but if you happened to control the wards there were three more, all carefully warded to keep them from sight. Elaine had given specific instructions to the driver to bring Johan back to one of them, knowing that he probably wouldn't want to be seen by anyone else as he came back to his rooms. But when he did return, he looked as if he had been crying. Feeling an odd flush of maternal instinct, she directed the library to show him into her room and ordered hot chocolate for both of them. She wasn't too surprised when he collapsed as soon as the door closed behind him.

"He wanted me not to testify," Johan said, as Elaine wrapped her arms around him. "And he even offered to make me Prime Heir."

He must be desperate, Elaine thought. Johan's testimony would be decisive ... at least if Jamal faced a free and independent jury. As it was, Johan's father would be trying his hardest to swing the Privy Council to his side. But getting his son to change his mind about testifying would be a shortcut to getting his eldest son out of jail.

She listened as Johan explained just what had happened at the dinner party. It didn't sound good; he'd lost control of his magic at least once, although no one had been seriously hurt when the table collapsed. But then, using magic in someone's house without permission was regarded as a breach of etiquette ... Elaine shook her head at the thought. The Conidian had probably been delighted when his son had used magic.

"I told him that I wasn't going to go back," Johan finished. "And that I *was* going to testify."

He paused. "He even offered to find me a bride."

"I think that won't be a problem," Elaine said dryly, although she could understand his concern about finding someone. "When the Great Houses realise just how powerful you are, you'll be beating offers of marriage away with a stick."

"I doubt it," Johan said. "Jayne ... Jayne is the only girl that showed any interest in me and I still don't know if she's serious. If she knew the truth ..."

He shook his head, bitterly. "I am so useless," he said. "I can't even do anything I want to do!"

"I thought you wanted to work magic," Elaine said, carefully. "And you *are*."

"I'm a freak even when I work magic," Johan said. "My family was *scared* of me."

"They'd be scared of me too," Elaine admitted. *She* had never been ambitious, but she'd found herself caught in the centre of a deadly plot that had almost shattered the Empire. "We both change the rules."

Johan's eyes narrowed as he looked up at her. "How do *you* change the rules?"

Elaine swallowed. "It's a long story," she said, as she stood up. The mugs of hot chocolate were sitting on the table, waiting for them. "Suffice it to say that I scared as many people as you."

Johan followed her. "I want to know," he said. "Please ... tell me what happened."

Elaine considered, briefly. She had always intended to tell him the truth, but she had no idea how he would react. And yet if she didn't tell him, he wouldn't trust her ... not entirely without reason. She knew too much about him, he knew far too little about *her*. It would become a barrier between them unless she was completely honest.

"Here," she said, waving one hand over her eyes. The glamour faded and vanished. "Try not to cry out."

Johan stared at her eyes, but seemed to take them in stride. "What ... what happened to you?"

"It's a long story," Elaine repeated, motioning for him to sit down facing her. "And, in truth, I don't know where to begin."

She knew she didn't dare mention the Witch-King, not until she was sure that Johan was untouched by him, but she could tell him the rest. "There was ... an accident in the library," she said, softly. "I ended up having the contents of every book within the library dumped into my head."

"I'm surprised it didn't explode," Johan commented, lightly. Did he see the darker implications? Elaine couldn't tell. "What happened then?"

"I learned more about how magic actually *works*," Elaine said. "My power levels were unchanged, but I could do a lot more with less. But the person behind the plot – who turned out to be my father – had planned everything; he took the knowledge and used it to attack the city, six months ago. I ... drained the Blight to stop him."

She had to smile at Johan's stunned expression. The Blight had been gone before the Conidian Family came to the city, but surely he would have heard *legends*. It had been impossible for anyone to clear, leaving a part of the city completely unusable ... until Elaine had drained it dry. But the price had been glowing eyes ... and she knew that she'd been lucky. Other magicians might have ended up badly mutilated or even killed.

"So you know everything," Johan said, thoughtfully. "There's no point in you reading your own books, is there?"

"Not the ones that were in the library at the time," Elaine agreed. The contents were burned into her skull, just waiting for her to look for them. "But thankfully that didn't include non-magical books ... or a handful of magical books that are effectively unique."

Johan looked down at his hands. "We're the same, aren't we?"

Elaine lifted an eyebrow, inviting him to continue.

"Both victims of magical accidents, both ... somewhat unique, both abandoned by our families and both desperate to prove ourselves," he said. "Isn't that correct?"

"Maybe not," Elaine said. "Ambition isn't really one of my attributes."

Johan surprised her by laughing. "You're a Privy Councillor," he said. "The only promotion you could possibly get is Grand Sorceress."

"Which would mean trying to fight one or more magicians with much more raw power than I," Elaine said. She'd improved her protections – even if they hadn't proved effective against Johan – but she had no illusions about how long they'd last against a skilled magician with power to spare. "And I'm not that stupid."

"I wanted to prove myself," Johan reminded her. "And now ... I don't even know where to begin!"

He frowned. "Did *you* have people who wanted you dead too?"

"Yes," Elaine said. "Quite a few."

There were people, she suspected, who would consider her time at the Great Library imprisonment, even if it was a gilded cage. But Light Spinner had had little choice; Elaine's knowledge made her a target for any magician who worked out what had happened to her. Given time, they could draw her knowledge out of her mind and then start using it to cast darker spells, spells that had been long-since forgotten by everyone. Apart from Elaine ...

"My father might want me dead," Johan said. "What do I do about *that*?"

"I've been giving it some thought," Elaine said, truthfully. "It may be some time before Jamal and his friends have to face trial for their crimes. Their lawyers are busy throwing up objection after objection and they all have to be knocked down, one by one. How would you like to leave the city for a few days?"

She had to smile at the eager expression on Johan's face. Elaine had never really wanted to travel – she was profoundly unadventurous; the only trip she'd made away from the Golden City hadn't been entirely of her own volition – but Johan clearly *loved* the idea. Not that she could blame him, she decided. She'd had the freedom of the city; he'd effectively been a prisoner in his father's house. He *wanted* to explore the world.

"I'd love to go," Johan said. "Where are we going?"

"I think you should have asked that first," Elaine said, lightly. She grinned at his expression, then leaned back in her chair. "There's a ... cabin used by the Inquisitors several days journey from here, up in the Western Hills. It's quite isolated, but also quite comfortable. Or so they say. We can go and use it, I think. It's isolated enough that we can continue experimenting with your powers without putting others in danger."

Johan made a face. "Am I really that bad?"

"You can lose control," Elaine reminded him. "And because your magic is unique, it's almost impossible for you to stop yourself until it starts to happen. I don't think you really *feel* that you're working magic."

She thought about reminding him about the damaged or destroyed wards, then decided he probably didn't need to hear it again. "You're also a target," she added. "If someone apart from your father realises that *your* testimony will help convict those terrorists, they will try to kill you. I think a few days or weeks spent away from the city will do us both good."

Johan winced. "*Can* my father kill me?"

Elaine hesitated, scanning her vast reserves of knowledge. The truth was that she simply wasn't sure. Unlike most magic, the subtle power holding families together didn't seem to rely on logical rules. Johan had told his father that he wouldn't be coming back, that he no longer thought of himself as part of the family. Would that be enough to allow the Conidian to have him killed without consequences? Could Johan have been safely killed while he'd been Powerless?

No one really wants to find out the hard way, she thought. *And there's no answer I can give him.*

There were hundreds of cautionary tales. Parents who turned on their children, children who murdered their parents ... all of whom came to bad ends. But sometimes there was no punishment ... and the only thing those tales had in common was the fact that the person who committed murder had been badly abused. Family magic could be very powerful – the gods knew that Kane had used it against her – but it could also be very subtle. The punishment might fall tomorrow, or it might fall so late that few would draw a line between cause and effect ...

A thought nagged at her mind, something important. But it refused to make itself clear.

"I do not know," she admitted. Most magicians – even sorcerers – turned up their nose at family magic. They called it female magic, even though it belonged to both sexes ... just like the high magic they worked in their lofty towers. But it was dangerously unpredictable and thus something to be avoided. "But he isn't your only enemy."

"No," Johan agreed. He looked down at his hands, wrapped around the mug of hot chocolate so tightly that she feared for the mug. "When can we leave?"

He glanced around, suddenly. "Is this place safe?"

"It's one of the most heavily warded buildings in the Empire," Elaine assured him. "And no one can get in here without my permission."

"Good," Johan said. "But I broke the wards ..."

"Only because what you did was unprecedented," Elaine said. "Someone else would have to break them down piece by piece and even *trying* would sound the alert."

She reached for a piece of paper and dashed off a quick note for Dread. He would have too much else to do, but he could provide them permission to find and use the cabin for a few weeks. Light Spinner probably wouldn't object either; if Johan was out of the city, threats against his life and demands for access to him would both decrease. She folded the paper, sent it out of the room via the library wards and then wrote a second note for Light Spinner. It would be well to keep the Grand Sorceress informed ...

Johan leaned forward. "When can we leave?" He asked again. "Will I have time to say goodbye to Jayne?"

"I think we'd be better to leave the day after tomorrow," Elaine said. It would give her time to get permission to leave the city too. There was an Iron Dragon line that ran near the Western Hills, passing through Falconine City, but she wasn't sure where they would have to go after that. "If nothing else, you will need time to pack."

"Oh," Johan said. He frowned. "What would I need?"

"Assume you can't get anything there," Elaine ordered. "And that we will be staying there for at least two weeks."

"Oh," Johan said, again. "That's a lot of clothes ..."

He scowled in sudden realisation. "Do you know cleaning charms?"

Elaine smiled at his expression. "Yes, I do," she said. They were normally taught to new students as exercises in control, but she had a feeling that Johan probably wouldn't be able to master them. "But we don't want to have to cast them every day ..."

She stopped as a black-edged envelope drifted into the room. Elaine tore it open, then muttered a curse as she saw the note. Dread was asking her to come at once.

"I have to go," she said. It was only ten minutes away on foot, but she knew Dread wanted her there as soon as possible. She would have to take the carriage. "You finish up here, then get some sleep."

"I will," Johan promised. "Ah ... can I ask Jayne out tomorrow night?"

"If you wish," Elaine said, "but let me arrange some protection for you both. If she agrees."

She pulled her long cloak over her robes, checked that her wand was in place, then strode out of the room to where the carriage was waiting. The driver nodded to her as soon as he saw her; he'd once told her that he preferred being on the night shift, even though it was rare for anything to actually happen. Elaine climbed into the carriage and sighed, running through a mental exercise to calm her thoughts. Whatever had happened – and it had to be urgent for Dread to send a message when she could have been safely in bed – would reveal itself soon enough.

Red Street was famous – or infamous – for its forbidden pleasures, both magical and mundane. Daria had often visited, telling Elaine of strange wines and spices from all over the Empire ... and sexual pleasures that had to be experienced to be believed. Elaine had never worked up the nerve to go, until now. The carriage came to a halt in front of a large apartment block, seemingly completely deserted. Indeed, the entire *street* was deserted.

An Inquisitor waved to her as she climbed out of the carriage, beckoning her to follow him. Elaine obeyed, walking through a door and into a long hallway. She glanced into one room and saw a handful of people sitting there, staring at a cluster of City Guardsmen nervously, then followed the Inquisitor up the stairs and into a small room. It was empty, apart from a gaslight, a bed ... and a dead body. Someone had dumped magician's robes on top of the corpse.

Dread looked up as she entered. "This is Graham, of

House Arndell," he said. "He was found dead an hour ago. The owner of this ... fine establishment dawdled before calling the Guard."

"House Arndell," Elaine muttered. "And we arrested Gavin, of House Arndell, only a few days ago."

"Indeed," Dread agreed. "What do you think the cause of death was?"

Elaine examined what she could see of the body. Someone had cut the magician's throat, presumably with an iron knife. Anything else might have provoked a magical reaction, even if the magician was too distracted to cast any spells. There didn't seem to be anything else that could have killed him.

"His throat was cut," she said, shortly. "Is there anything else?"

"Not as far as we have been able to determine," Dread said, "but the fact that this murder was committed by mundane means is highly significant. Don't you think?"

"It was a revenge attack," Elaine said, in understanding. "Someone wanted to strike back at the terrorists and decided to murder the brother of one of them."

"So it would seem," Dread agreed. "And here, it would be far too easy to get distracted."

Elaine nodded, remembering some of her classmates from the Peerless School. They'd gone out every night in search of pleasure and they hadn't always been subtle about what they'd done to get it. Paying a prostitute would have been one of the more decent things they'd done. If half of the rumours were true, she wouldn't have blamed the mundane portion of the city's population for hating every magician they saw.

"So they struck back," she said. "When is it going to end?"

"The Privy Council will want action," Dread said, heavily. "But we have nothing to go on, not here. By now, the knife will have been destroyed, along with any traces of this young idiot's" – he nodded to the body – "blood. Tracking down his killers will be a hard slow process."

"But you have wide authority," Elaine said. Inquisitors could use truth spells on mundanes at will, without any pesky legal impediments. After all, anyone who killed a magician was definitely beyond the pale. "Start with everyone here

...?"

"The owner has already confirmed that the victim came here with a girl," Dread explained, "so she has no idea who the killer was, merely ... that she came, she killed and left without impediment. By now, skin cells will be useless if we try to use them to track her down."

"I'd suggest informing the Grand Sorceress," Elaine said, wearily. "There's nothing else we can do now."

"They'll want the city turned upside down to find the killers," Dread said. They both knew who *they* were. "But that won't make life any easier for any of us."

Elaine scowled. "I'm taking Johan out of the city for a few days," she explained. Dread might not have received her letter yet. "Is that a good idea?"

"The best," Dread said. "Hopefully, this will be over by the time you get back."

Chapter Twenty-Three

Admitting mistakes did not come easily to Duncan Conidian.

He'd made a mistake when he'd allowed Johan to be bullied by the rest of his family. He'd made a mistake when he'd treated Jamal like a prince, despite his increasingly unpleasant behaviour. And he'd made another mistake by thinking that it would be easy to mend bridges between himself and his second son. For Duncan, blood was everything; for Johan, it was little more than an awkward relationship with a family of monsters.

The remains of the table lay in front of him. There were spells that could cause that much damage, but they had to be spoken aloud. Johan, on the other hand, seemed to have used *his* magic to destroy the table with nary a word. Somehow, he'd managed to develop control of his magic far quicker than even Jamal ... as also evidenced by how quickly and effectively he'd frozen Jolie. The younger boy was still in shock. His despised elder brother shouldn't have been able to just ... *stop* him. But Johan had.

Duncan had ordered the rest of the family to their bedrooms, leaving him alone. He had no time for his wife's perpetual unconcern, or his daughter's new habit of telling him the truth, no matter how hurtful, but for once he wasn't sure what to do next. Johan seemed utterly unwilling to meet him halfway – and, indeed, Duncan knew that he had a point. Why *should* he be loyal? And offering him Marina had been another mistake. Johan had *known* that he would never have a magical wife, if indeed he was permitted to have a wife at all. A born magician would have jumped at the chance, no matter what *Marina* thought about it. Johan, on the other hand, had refused her.

There has to be something he wants, Duncan thought, desperately. Deferens, damn him, had been right about one thing. Johan represented a whole new field of study and the people that controlled access would have a chance to make themselves rich and powerful. Who knew how much wealthy mundanes would pay for access to magic? *But what can I offer him?*

He turned the thought over and over in his mind, but came up with no answer. Johan might not take the vault Duncan had offered him, but if he chose to make use of his new powers he would never lack for money. What else did he even *want*? Duncan could withdraw his objections to his planned career, but those plans had already been derailed by his sudden development of magic. Johan wouldn't want to be a Civil Servant when he could be a Court Wizard ...

And if he chooses to enter the Peerless School he can apply for a scholarship if I refuse to pay. Duncan thought, grimly. *Or one of the family's enemies will offer to pay for him.*

He opened his mouth to call for Charity – perhaps she could go and talk some sense into her brother – and then closed it again as a maid ran into the room, carrying a black-edged envelope. Duncan took it, noting absently just how shocked the maid seemed by the mess on the floor, and opened it, skimming the letter rapidly. A magician was dead, seemingly killed by a mundane. And it had all the hallmarks, according to the Inquisitors, of a planned assassination.

Damn it, he thought, turning and walking towards the door. *Something else to worry about.*

He'd have to go to the Grand Sorceress. She'd be being bombarded with advice and demands for action and he would have to add his voice to them, or risk losing influence at the palace. The gods knew that Deferens or Lady Lakeside would be happy to edge him out, particularly in light of recent events. There were times, he privately admitted, when he wondered if his quest for wealth and power for his family was really worth the price.

"Summon my coachman," he ordered the maid. He scribbled a quick note to Charity, ordering her to remain inside tomorrow until he spoke to her, then passed it to the maid. "I'm going to the palace."

***

"They used magic to hide their tracks," the forensic sorcerer

226

said. "I can't even get a *hint* of their auras, let alone anything we can use to track them."

Elaine nodded, unsurprised. Anyone who killed a magician knew that the Inquisitors would come after them − and that they had the right to use truth spells and even torture to draw answers out of possible suspects. A drop of blood found at the scene of the crime would be enough to track them down and then prove their guilt; no matter how much magicians were hated, it was rare to see one murdered outside a duel. But *this* killer had put a great deal of forethought into the assassination.

It struck her as odd, a moment later. She'd assumed that it was a revenge killing, perhaps carried out by the Levellers, but why would *they* use magic? And how would they obtain it to use? The answer struck her a moment later and she scowled. There was no shortage of seedy magicians who might be prepared to work the spells for them, in exchange for gold and promises of future favour. Maybe some of them would be deterred by the thought of assisting in the murder of a fellow magician, but others merely wanted money and cared nothing for how it was earned.

"Probably," Dread said, when she asked him. "We will challenge the shadier magicians in the city, but I doubt we will find a lead. They would not have left him alive and free."

Elaine took one look back at the body, then nodded. "I don't think there's much more I can do here," she said. Whatever help she might have offered had been amply matched by the forensic sorcerer. "If you don't mind, I'm going back home."

"It should be fine," Dread said. "I have to go to the palace to provide the Grand Sorceress with a full report. I'll send you an update when I know what's happening."

Elaine scowled as she made her way out of the building, down towards where her carriage was waiting. The Grand Sorceress would come under immense pressure from the rest of the magical community, who would demand harsh action against the Levellers and anyone else who might be involved in the murder. At best, it would strain relationships between magical and mundane citizens still further; at worst, it would lead to all-out war. The mundanes couldn't win, but they did control much of the Empire's economy. A war, no matter how short, might be disastrous.

It also makes the Grand Sorceress look weak, she thought, remembering just how many kings and princes still held dreams of independence. *If they think that she is unable to keep the Golden City under control, they might start declaring themselves free of the Empire.*

It was a chilling thought. The Empire didn't have large armies to maintain its will; the near-monopoly on magic the first Grand Sorcerer and his followers had possessed had ensured that resistance would only end badly. But now, with so many magicians dead in the Golden City – and others influenced by the kings and princes they were supposed to watch – it would be harder for the Court Wizards to keep their rulers under control. And *that* would only lead to further chaos.

She climbed into the carriage and stared out of the window as the coachman took her back towards the Great Library. The streets were almost deserted, even away from the crime scene; the entire Golden City seemed to be holding its breath, waiting for *something* to happen to break the spell. It was said that the city never slept, but now it seemed to be frozen, not daring to move for fear that it would cause a disaster.

The Great Library was always quieter at night, although it never closed completely. It was a relief to see students flocking through the corridors, desperately trying to revise prior to their exams. Elaine remembered her own years as a student and scowled, recalling how hard she'd had to work to earn her grades. She felt a flicker of sympathy for four students who were being escorted out of the library for daring to eat in one of the reading rooms, which she ruthlessly quashed. No matter how hungry they became, they couldn't be allowed to drop food all over the books.

She walked into her quarters and stopped as she saw Johan lying on the sofa, a book in his hand. For a moment, she stared in horror, then recalled that she had left him there when she went to see Dread. Even so, it was still a fright. Shaking her head in annoyance, she rescued the book before it could fall from his hands and glanced at the title. *Sex Rites for the Young Magician.*

"Oh," Johan said, blearily. "I ..."

He blushed bright red as he saw that she was holding the book, then somehow managed to work up the nerve to ask a question. "Do those rites actually work?"

"Yes and no," Elaine said, feeling the knowledge shimmering through her brain. "The sorcerer who designed them merely added sex to the instructions because he rather liked having sex. You can strip out at least half of the instructions – including the sex – and they would still work."

She smiled at his embarrassment. "He *was* a typical teenage boy."

Johan couldn't have blushed any brighter if he'd tried "How do you *know* what's vital and what isn't?"

"Good question," Elaine said, in approval. "With most rites and rituals it's hard to see what is necessary and what can be left out ... and research into the subject rarely leads to a long life. But for me ... I see *all* of the known rituals, allowing me to cross-check. In this case, the sorcerer actually derived most of his rites from older rites; they're still there, just hidden between the sex."

She snorted. "And besides, for some of them, you would have to be an athlete to actually *perform* the rites as he specified," she added. "It isn't considered advisable to try."

Johan managed to stand upright, holding his hand in front of his face as if he were trying to hide his blush. Elaine had to admit that it looked endearing, although she knew better than to say *that* out loud. Daria had told her that men liked unstinted praise, but not being told that they were *cute*. She had never bothered to explain why.

"I'd stay away from sex magic if I were you," Elaine advised. "Even normal magicians tend to try to avoid it. The results can be unpredictable."

"I was just worried," Johan said. "What if the date goes really well and ... well, you know ..."

Elaine was tempted to let him embarrass himself a little more, but she was supposed to be his mentor, not his tormenter. "I think you have to ask her out first," she said, dryly. "And you really don't want to go to bed with her on the first date ..."

She stopped, crossly. He *was* a teenage boy; of *course* he wanted to go to bed with her on the first date. If he just wanted sex, he should have gone to Red Street ... not that Elaine would have allowed it, not now. And his father had kept him a virtual prisoner inside the house.

"You should give the relationship time to develop," she said, feeling a twinge of guilt at her hypocrisy. It hadn't taken *her* long to decide to sleep with Bee – but then, she'd expected to die. The new Grand Sorcerer might not have tolerated her existence, not with a head stuffed full of forbidden knowledge. Somehow, taking time to build up a relationship had no longer seemed to matter. "If she likes you, she will go out with you again and again. By the time the relationship becomes sexual, you'll have a solid foundation for future development."

"I'll do my best," Johan said. "But what if ..."

Elaine wanted to roll her eyes. Instead, she sighed. "There are contraceptive potions you can take that will ensure that she doesn't fall pregnant," she said. "Either one of you can take the potion, but I would advise *both* of you to take it. Most students learn to brew it in their first year."

Johan scowled. "Why isn't it sold?"

"It is," Elaine said. "But most students and qualified magicians prefer to brew their own. It tends to work better that way. For you ... if you *really* insist, I'll have some sent in for you."

"Please," Johan said.

"Very well," Elaine said, sending the order into the wards. There was no point in telling him that she'd kept a small supply for herself, at Daria's insistence. Without her friend, she rarely left the Great Library. "Tomorrow ... I want you to study your books."

Johan blinked. "Again?"

"I will probably be summoned back to the palace," Elaine said. She filled him in on what Dread had shown her. "Sleep in, if you like; eat breakfast, then read your books. I hope that we will have time to do more experiments tomorrow afternoon, but it will depend on what happens in the morning."

She watched him go, then undressed and headed into her

bedroom, where she threw herself down on the bed. There was no time for anything but sleep. Knowing her luck, Light Spinner would summon her at the earliest socially acceptable hour.

With that thought, she fell asleep.

***

When Johan opened his eyes, a note was lying on the bedside table addressed to him. He picked it up and saw that Elaine had indeed been summoned to the palace. It included a list of books he might like to read and suggested that he order them from the library staff, in addition to the ones he already had. It took him a moment to realise that she was trying to help, in her own way. Jayne would be bringing the books to his rooms.

He rolled out of bed, took a shower and dressed in comfortable clothes, then ate a leisurely breakfast. The broadsheet that the staff had placed on the breakfast tray included a detailed article on the death of a magician – they'd got the name wrong, Johan saw – that was long on hysterics and short on any actual information. There was no shortage of speculation about what the magician had been doing – there were even suggestions that he had been engaging in forbidden sex rites, which made him smirk – but nothing actually useful. The article concluded with a plea to the Grand Sorceress to catch the murderer or murderers as quickly as possible.

The next page reported in calm, matter-of-fact tones that Jamal and his accomplices were still in jail, something that made Johan let out a sigh in relief. Even now, he was still terrified of his elder brother, fearing what Jamal would have done if his father had died. After all, Jamal had actually suggested that Johan should be killed. But if Jamal broke free ...

I can fight, Johan thought, remembering what he'd done to the terrorists – and Jolie. The expression on his younger brother's face had made up for everything he'd suffered over the years. *He's never met anyone like me.*

But he knew that it wouldn't be that easy. Jamal could set protective wards up around himself that stayed in place,

Johan's only seemed to stay where he wanted them to stay when he was concentrating on them. He would need to practice much more before he was ready to face Jamal, if it did come down to a fight. Somehow, he doubted that his brother would face the headsman. He was just too good at getting out of trouble.

The thought depressed him until he ordered his next set of books – carefully *not* looking at the pile of books he still had to read – and Jayne entered the room, pushing a trolley in front of her. Johan nervously helped her unload, then pick up the books he had read.

And then he took the plunge. "Where would you like to go eat tonight?"

Jayne blinked in surprise – he felt his heart sink – and then smiled. "Somewhere *quiet*," she said. "And not somewhere *too* popular."

"My family only came here six months ago," Johan said. It wasn't entirely true – his siblings had been in the city for much longer – but it explained why he wasn't familiar with the city yet. "Can you pick a place?"

"I could pick somewhere expensive," Jayne said, with a wink. "How about Joan's Grill? It's not that large, but it is supposed to be good."

"Why not?" Johan said. She'd agreed ... and yet he still felt desperate. What if she changed her mind? Come to think of it, he didn't even know where the place *was*. "Where do you want to meet?"

"Outside the library will do," Jayne said, thoughtfully. "I have classes this afternoon, so I'll get dressed afterwards and meet you at sunset. Is that all right?"

"Yes," Johan said, who would have agreed to almost anything she asked. "I'll see you then."

He watched her leave the room, then sagged in relief. He had a *date*! Jamal and Charity had never had any trouble finding partners, but he had barely even laid eyes on a girl who wasn't a direct relative ... not until now. But fighting the terrorists had given his confidence a real boost ...

"Now I have to find something to wear," he told himself, as he walked over to the wardrobe and sighed. Jamal had hundreds of different outfits and Charity seemed to have thousands of dresses, but he'd never been allowed to develop taste. At least Elaine's staff had provided him with a handful of suits. "What do I wear tonight?"

Chapter Twenty-Four

"Congratulations on your date," Elaine said.

"Thank you," Johan said, nervously. He'd not managed to get much studying done, not after she'd said yes. He'd spent too much time fantasising about the date or, alternatively, about just how many things could go wrong. But his father had often told Charity that she couldn't go out until she had finished her work. What would *Elaine* say? "I know, I should have studied more ..."

"Probably not, in your case," Elaine said, eying the pile of books. "The problem is that much of the basic knowledge is useless to you. We can and we will work on exercises, but additional knowledge may hurt instead of help. And at least you got the packing done."

Johan nodded. They were supposed to be leaving tomorrow, unless something else came up to stop them from going. He'd packed carefully, but he couldn't avoid the feeling that he'd missed something. Elaine would have to inspect his work later.

Elaine scowled, her mind clearly elsewhere. "But there are more important matters to discuss," she added. "Where are you going?"

"Joan's Grill," Johan said. "Why ...?"

"I'll be there too," Elaine said. "And an Inquisitor or two, if I can swing it."

Johan blanched. "You can't be there," he started to protest. "I ..."

"I won't be sitting at the table with you," Elaine said. "But you *do* realise that you are a target? And you will become *more* of a target as the news continues to spread. Your protection is my first priority."

"That's why you attacked the terrorists," Johan mused. The thought left a warm feeling in his heart. No one had ever placed their life on the line to protect him before, not even

Charity. "But I should be fine."

"You don't *know* that," Elaine cautioned. "Your date won't know that you're not alone, I promise."

She stepped backwards and looked him up and down. "I went to Joan's Grill once with Daria," she said. "It isn't very pretentious, so you don't need a fancy suit or finest robes, but make sure you take a large napkin. You don't want to get food on your clothes."

"Thank you," Johan said.

Elaine picked a vial off the table and passed it to him. It was unmarked, but contained a greenish liquid. "That's the potion," she added. "It takes effect immediately and lasts for roughly two days. I'd take it just before you go, if I were you. But *don't* take her for granted."

"I understand," Johan said, fighting down his embarrassment. "Are there any *books* on dating?"

"Not in *this* library," Elaine said, ruefully. "I could have used them too."

Time went by faster than Johan had expected and, almost before he knew it, it was time to get ready. He pulled on a simple pair of black trousers and a white shirt, which – Elaine assured him – would be sufficient for where they were going. She gave him a pair of napkins, checked the bag of money she'd given him earlier and then watched as he drank the potion and passed her back the vial. Surprisingly, it tasted good.

"They don't want to discourage people from taking it," Elaine commented, when he asked. "If a mundane woman becomes pregnant, the pregnancy could be terminated with no ill effects, but a magician would suffer greatly if they killed their own child."

Johan nodded. He'd been looking up family magic in some of the older books and, while the authors never seemed to state anything for certain, they *had* been clear that intentionally harming or killing other members of the family tended to result in disastrous consequences. He wasn't sure how seriously to take it – Jamal never seemed to suffer for what he'd done to Johan – but killing a helpless unborn baby had to be far worse. Drinking the potion seemed a small price to ensure that the magician didn't have to abandon her studies or career to raise a child.

"You won't see *me*," Elaine said, ruefully. "I don't think Jayne will be happy to see her boss at the next table. But I will be there."

She passed him a small amulet. "Joan's Grill is on Westlake Street," she said. "If you speak the street name out loud, the amulet will guide you there. Do the same for the Great Library when you want to come home. I'd suggest walking her to her apartment block, but not going inside. You *will* be asked questions by her roommates."

Johan scowled, then nodded. "And I'll see you later this evening," he said. "Thank you for everything."

Surprisingly, Elaine flushed "You're welcome," she said. "Just be careful."

Johan was still mulling over what she'd said as he stepped out of the Great Library and looked around. Jayne was nowhere to be seen. An icy fist clutched his heart as he wondered if she'd been deliberately winding him up, then he felt a sensation of pure relief as he saw her walking towards him, wearing a white dress that fell to just above her knees. Her black hair seemed to fan out around her dress, drawing his attention to her face. It seemed paler than usual, almost perfect. And her smile was so warm that he felt himself melting.

"Thank you for coming," he said, as she clasped arms with him. They were on an actual *date*! "I hope you have a good time."

"I'm sure I shall," Jayne assured him. She felt very warm pressed against his body. He felt his heartbeat speeding up inside his chest, so loudly that he was surprised that she couldn't hear it. "Do you know the way?"

Johan shook his head. Before he could pull out the amulet, Jayne gently tugged him down the street, away from the Great Library. The massive halls of academia gave way rapidly to the streets of pleasure; she led him past bars, eateries and places that were completely unmarked, yet seemed to be heaving with customers. There were still fewer people on the streets than he remembered from his trip to the zoo, but at least they weren't completely alone. He wanted to show off a little ...

Idiot, he told himself, crossly. *Why do you think anyone would care?*

Joan's Grill wasn't bigger on the inside than on the outside. It seemed to have only thirty tables in all, about half of which were occupied by customers. Johan wondered just how many of them were magicians, before deciding that it hardly mattered. None of them seemed to be students, people who might know Jayne. It was rare, Charity had told him, for a magician to date a mundane. Such relationships were almost always mocked relentlessly by their peers. What would they think of *Johan*?

He felt a flash of the old resentment, for he knew what they would have thought of a Powerless. They would have pitied him or they would have mocked him; either way, Jayne would have been strongly discouraged from seeing him again. Who knew? The flaw in his body that had rendered him powerless might be passed down to his children.

Angrily, he pushed the thought aside as an olive-skinned woman showed them to a table in the corner. Instead, he looked around, wondering which of the customers was Elaine and her escorts ... if, of course, she hadn't been pulling his leg. But there was no way to be sure, not without being able to see glamours. And even if he *could* see them, he couldn't be sure what they were hiding. Charity had admitted that glamours were in common use by just about every magician in the world.

"So," Jayne said, as they inspected the menu, "tell me about yourself."

Johan hesitated, unsure of what to tell her. He didn't want to lie, but he also didn't want to admit that he had been a Powerless. The gods alone knew how she would react.

"My family used to be titled nobility outside the Golden City," he said, finally. They'd still been aristocrats, but they'd never been *high* aristocrats. "Now my father has ambitions to push himself to the very highest levels and dragged the family here."

"In the wake of all the chaos," Jayne said. She shivered. "I was out of the city at the time, but I heard tales ... terrible tales. They say that many of the injured will never recover completely."

She met his gaze. "Why didn't you go to the Peerless School?"

Johan swallowed. He'd anticipated *that* question, but he knew that his answer wouldn't hold up to careful scrutiny. And yet he really didn't want to tell her the full truth.

"My father insisted that I have private tuition," he said, finally. It was true enough, if one discounted the fact that his lessons hadn't included magic. "He didn't want to expose *everyone* to the Peerless School."

"My father felt the same way, but in the end he sent all of us to the school," Jayne commented. "Your father must have been very stubborn."

Johan nodded. It was true that some of the older families preferred to send only their eldest children to the Peerless School, knowing that the school taught loyalty to the Empire and the Grand Sorcerer as well as magic. When they came home, the children might no longer put the family's interests first. It was worse for the students who came from mundane households, he knew; they tended to have little in common with their families when they came home. They rarely stayed for long after knowing what life could be like.

It was easy to see why magicians looked down on mundanes. Healing spells could save lives; mundanes had to set bones and sew up wounds the old-fashioned way. Magical households were *clean*, even the poorer ones; mundane households were often dirty and smelly. Hot running water was easy to produce with magic; harder to produce without it. Why would anyone want to live in the filth if they could live in a clean home?

And the price was merely giving up their former families.

"He is the most stubborn person I know," Johan admitted. "But I don't feel I've missed out on much."

The waitress returned, took their orders and vanished back into the darkness behind the counter. Johan smiled after her, then looked back at Jayne. If she asked questions about his life, he could ask questions about hers.

"Tell me about *yourself*."

"Not much to tell," Jayne said. "I'm the fifth child and second daughter of House Rendang, which makes me effectively useless. Father just wants to maintain his current position, not try to rise higher, so I don't have to worry about an advantageous match. Instead, I want to be a Potions Mistress. I have the marks to seek an apprenticeship after I leave the school."

"I'm awful at potions," Johan confessed. "What about yourself?"

Jayne gave him a droll smile. "I was brewing at a third-year level when I was in first year," she said. "The Potions Master – a kindly old soul – put me in with the fourth years when I was in second year, then gave me private tutoring when I needed it. Right now, I'm three years ahead of the rest of my class in potions ... but not in anything else. I doubt they'll let me graduate early."

Johan considered it. "Can you become an apprentice while you're still in school?"

"Perhaps," Jayne said. "But most apprenticeships demand complete focus and concentration, not someone who is easily ... distracted. And I will be distracted by my other schoolwork."

"Good luck," Johan said, trying to remember what Jamal had said about potions. He'd been much ruder about the Potions Master, calling him a doddering old fool more than once. The tutor had committed the unforgivable sin – in Jamal's eyes – by being more concerned with ability than breeding. But Jamal had never had the patience to be good at potions. "I wish I could do something to help."

"Let me know if you know any masters who might take on an apprentice," Jayne said. "But if I can't get in before I complete my schooling, I will just have to brew on my own and wait."

She shook her head. "What do *you* want to do with your life?"

The food arrived, saving Johan from actually having to answer. It was strange to his eyes, a combination of meat, cheese, fried bread and raw vegetables, the sort of thing he would never have been allowed to eat at home. But it tasted very nice, he discovered, as he took a bite; the only downside was that they were expected to eat with their fingers, rather than knives and forks. Jayne dug in as though it didn't bother her; Johan hesitated, remembering his father's lessons.

Eating with one's fingers was not a good sign.

Hell with it, he told himself, and dived into the food.

"You never answered," Jayne said, as she took a break between bites. "What *do* you want to do with your life?"

Johan considered the question. As a child, he'd wanted to be a great magician; as a Powerless, he'd wanted to go into one of the careers that *didn't* involve magic. But now ... he just wanted to prove himself, if only *to* himself. He needed to know what he could do.

"I want to prove myself," he said, out loud. "I could be great."

Jayne smiled. "I'm sure you could be," she said, "but how do you intend to *become* great?"

"I wish I knew," Johan said, after a long moment. What *could* he do to become great? If he caught the remaining three terrorists ... assuming, of course, that there *were* only three of them left ... would that make him great? Or would it just make him more of a target? "I'll just see what happens."

"My father was fond of saying that *real* heroes go out and find opportunities to make themselves great," Jayne said. "They didn't just sit on their buttocks and wait for opportunity to come pass them by."

Elaine did, Johan thought. But Elaine hadn't *wanted* to be a heroine. Indeed, she'd managed to bury the truth behind a wall of mystery and a deliberately cultivated appearance of being nothing more than a simple librarian. Or was she really the mask and the heroine something she'd had to be, for a time, then discarded when it was no longer necessary?

"I'll just have to see what happens," he said, drolly. "But if I do become a great hero, you can be my Potions Mistress."

Jayne giggled. "I think I will be making the latest discoveries that will change the world far more than your heroism," she said, dryly. "You can kill a monster; I can come up with a potion that prolongs life. Which of us will change the world more?"

Johan smiled, then took another bite of his food while studying her. She was *gorgeous*; he wanted to take her in his arms and kiss her, then slip his hand into her shirt ... angrily, he pushed the thought aside as he felt a stirring in his loins. He didn't want to blow his chances by moving too far, too fast. Who knew *how* she would react to his touch?

They finished their dinner, paid – it was a very reasonable price – and then headed out of the door. Johan looked around, wondering who would follow them, then turned his attention back to Jayne as she led him back towards the Peerless School. The night seemed to have grown darker, with fewer people on the streets; even the streetlamps seemed to have dimmed, somehow. Or perhaps he was just imagining it.

"Thank you for being a gentleman," Jayne said. Johan felt a flicker of relief, suddenly realising that if he'd pushed her, the results would have been bad. Even if he didn't wind up being turned into a slug or an earthworm, he would certainly never have had another chance to go out with her. "I really appreciated it."

"I never go too far on the first date," Johan said, trying to sound experienced. By her smile, he suspected he hadn't succeeded. "And I had a lovely time too."

They stopped outside the apartment block. Before Johan had more than a few seconds to feel awkward, Jayne pulled him into a hug and pressed her lips against his. Johan froze, then somehow forced himself to kiss her back. The feeling moved rapidly from awkward to enjoyable and, again, he felt a stirring in his loins. She was pressing her breasts against his chest ...

She stepped backwards, breaking the embrace. "I'll see you again," she promised. Johan, who had been having wild visions of inviting her home to the Great Library, felt a mixture of relief and disappointment. "Tomorrow, in fact."

Johan watched her go, then turned to walk home. If anyone had seen him, he knew, the big grin on his face would tell them exactly what had happened.

***

Duncan hadn't expected much from the spies he'd placed in and around the Great Library. Johan was with the Head Librarian, which meant that he was under the protection of the most powerful set of wards in the city. But the gamble had paid off; one of his spies had spotted Johan leaving the building, accompanied by a young girl of roughly the same age. The spy, familiar with all of the Great Houses, had even identified her.

Interesting, Duncan told himself. House Rendang was fading fast, having lost most of its clients years before the previous Grand Sorcerer had died. Was this a power play on their part or was it a genuine relationship? Either way, it was something he could use to his own advantage.

Picking up a piece of paper, he wrote a note. It was time for him to start taking House Rendang seriously. And *that* was all they wanted from the Golden City.

Chapter Twenty-Five

"It went very well," Johan said, the following morning. "I had a wonderful time."

Elaine smiled. As promised, she'd followed Johan with Inquisitor Cass – Cass hadn't bothered to wear a glamour, which had resulted in them being interrupted by men intent on buying her a drink – but she hadn't eavesdropped on him. She *had* seen the kiss, however. It had suggested that Jayne was not adverse to the idea of a relationship after all.

"I'm glad to hear it," she said. "Are you ready for our trip?"

"I have to leave a note for her," Johan said, suddenly. "I didn't even tell her I was going!"

"An apprentice is at the whims of his master," Elaine pointed out. Johan might not be her apprentice in truth, but he was definitely working with her. "Jayne will understand ... but you can leave her a note if you like."

"I will," Johan said, reaching for a piece of paper. "Um ... what should I say?"

"The truth," Elaine said. "The Head Librarian is taking you out to the country for a few days, but you'll be back soon. And that you'll write."

Johan looked up, dismayed. "Write?"

"It lets her know that you're thinking of her," Elaine pointed out. "Girls like that, don't you know?"

She smiled again at his expression, then returned to her own thoughts. No matter how she looked at it, it would be good to be out of the city for a few days. The Inquisitors had turned up nothing to track down the killer, which meant that the whole city was on edge. Deferens and the Conidian were demanding action, Johan's father with the added suggestion that his son should be freed from captivity. After all, he'd pointed out yesterday, Johan might suffer consequences if he testified against his elder brother. Somehow, he'd managed to make it seem as though he was genuinely concerned for Johan.

He might well be, Elaine conceded, reluctantly. She *hated* people who could make black seem white, up seem down and right seem wrong – or vice versa. Johan's father might get his eldest son completely out of trouble; the gods knew he had even been pressing for a *visit*.

"Thank you," Johan said. He scowled down at the bag at his feet. "Did I pack enough?"

"Put a few more books in," Elaine said. "No, not ones from here; ones from bookstores. You will need something to read during the ride."

She watched him finish, then used a simple charm to render both bags effectively weightless. They couldn't take the carriage to the station, not if they wanted to remain unseen. No one without wealth and power would take a carriage in the Golden City. Hefting her own bag, containing a selection of books as well as clothes, she headed towards the door. Johan followed her a moment later.

"I meant to ask," he said, softly. "Is it *safe* for you to leave the Great Library?"

Elaine scowled. "The wards will work well enough for Vane," she said. She had a feeling that wasn't entirely what he'd *meant*. "Sadly, the library isn't my personal possession – or home. I just wear it until I retire."

Johan gave her a sharp look, but said nothing else. Elaine led him out of the library by one of the hidden exits, then started to walk down towards the station. They could pass a bookstore on the way.

***

Johan had never seen a bookstore before – or even a library, before Elaine had taken him into the Great Library. The bookstore awed him; there were thousands of books, many of them of dubious value. Charity had enjoyed reading romance before her father had found out and forbidden her to read any more; Johan had read a couple and decided that they were either utterly mushy or terrifyingly perverse. Who would have thought that magic could be used to enhance the sexual experience? Apart from teenage magicians, that was.

He found himself moving from shelf to shelf, examining the books. There were no books on magic, unsurprisingly, but there were books on everything else. One entire stack appeared to be devoted to Lady Light Spinner, with several different biographies written by different authors just waiting for his attention. Elaine snorted and pointed out that anything written while she was still alive was completely untrustworthy. Very few people would dare to disrespect the Grand Sorceress, certainly not in print. In the end, seeing that Elaine was getting impatient, he picked up a handful of history books and a pair of thrillers, then paid for them at the counter. They were surprisingly cheap.

"The inventor of the printing press has a lot to answer for," Elaine muttered, as they left. "I can't have the books students most want to see copied, for fear of losing track of them, but they can waste their money and material on trash."

Johan shrugged. "Why can't the older books be copied?"

"The ones we have are integrated with the wards," Elaine explained. "Stealing them would be impossible. But newer books ... they don't integrate so well. And besides, they'd have to be copied in the library itself."

She led him down the street at a brisk pace. "We don't have much time," she said, glancing at the sun. "The Iron Dragon leaves soon."

Johan had *loved* to hear tales of the Iron Dragons – giant locomotives that ran on rails, without magic – but he rapidly discovered that the sight outdid the tales. He went to look at it as Elaine bought tickets, drawn by a fascination he found almost impossible to put into words. The Iron Dragon was colossal, a giant machine crouching on the tracks, steaming smoke into the air. A faint stench of burning surrounded it, but he didn't take any notice as he peered into the cab. Inside, two men clad in the bare minimum of clothing were busy shovelling coal into the fire.

"There's no magic," he said. "None at all!"

"No," Elaine agreed. "I believe that some of the earlier models had spells to ensure that the boiler didn't burst, but as they grew more confident in their work they started refusing to allow magicians to help. Lucky, really; the shortage of magicians we have now would ensure that few could be spared, if they needed them."

A man in a fancy uniform blew a whistle; Elaine hurried Johan forward and into one of the coaches, ahead of the guard as he shut the doors one by one. Inside, it was cramped, but surprisingly cosy. Elaine found a pair of window seats, motioned for him to sit down and pulled a book out of her bag. Johan, his gaze riveted to the window, refused a book when she offered it to him. A moment later, the coach lurched and started to move.

Johan had never really realised just how *small* the Golden City was. Hemmed in as it was by the Four Peaks, there was little room for expansion save upwards. It seemed like moments before the Iron Dragon plunged into a tunnel – the entire coach fell into darkness – and came out the other end in open countryside. The Watchtower could be seen dominating the mountains, but there were few signs of civilisation. There didn't even seem to be any farms!

"They're some distance from the city," Elaine said. "The Emperors didn't have full control over their Empire, so some of their aristocrats used the poor geography to pressure the Emperor whenever they wanted something. Now, of course, food shipments are reliable and fairly cheap."

"And people enjoy hunting in the countryside," Johan said, remembering Jamal's boasts of happy hunting trips where he'd slaughtered hundreds of helpless animals. "They don't *want* it turned into farmland."

"No," Elaine agreed. "They don't."

She turned her attention back to her book, but Johan stayed at the window, drinking in the sheer immensity of the countryside. He'd never really seen it before, not even when the family had been moving to the Golden City. They'd insisted that he stay inside the carriage, even when they'd been completely alone. Now, he could see the wilderness with his own two eyes ... and felt something calling to him. Why would he stay in the city when he could explore the world?

The wilderness gave way to farmland, but he still stared, watching people working in the fields. A handful of pieces of machinery seemed to be working with them, technology that reminded him of the Iron Dragon. He waved at a pair of farm girls, but they either didn't see him or simply didn't bother to wave back. The Iron Dragon passed through a small settlement – it was nothing more than a handful of houses – and then raced back into farmland.

They crossed a bridge that seemed to be made completely of iron, then passed a small building where several different flags were flying outside. It took him a moment to realise that they'd crossed the line between the Golden City's jurisdiction and another part of the Empire, ruled by a client-king. But no matter how he stared, he couldn't see any difference in the landscape outside the window. None of the people he saw looked different either.

"The borders are not so precisely delineated," Elaine said, when he asked. She gave him a thin smile. "Most of the people who live here don't give two figs for the borderlands, or who is actually in charge. Their families blur across the borderlands; they try damn hard to avoid paying taxes to anyone. Every so often, the authorities try to do something about it."

Johan scowled. "And what happens?"

"The farmers play dumb," Elaine admitted. "Most of them are living hand-to-mouth as it is, so they just ... pretend they don't understand what the taxmen are saying."

She shrugged. "Besides, this place was part of the Empire for centuries," she added. "If you want to see somewhere truly different, you have to go much further from the Golden City."

"I will, one day," Johan said. "How many places have you seen?"

"Just Ida," Elaine said. "It was ... different."

They crossed another bridge, then the landscape changed. This time, the fields seemed to be awash with water, green plants growing up and out of it. Elaine identified it as a paddy field, where rice was grown, pointing out that rice was perhaps the cheapest staple food in the Empire. Those who couldn't afford bread often ate rice as a substitute. She happily started to explain how the Empire had spread crops and concepts from one part of the world to the others, helping to improve the lives of ordinary people, but Johan could barely follow the explanation. All that mattered was that he was away from the city and away from his family.

He caught sight of a girl picking her way through the paddy field and felt a flicker of envy, even though he knew that she would lead a very hard life. *She* would never know what it was like to grow up completely powerless in a world where power was all. Instead, her world would be restricted ... unless, of course, she developed magic. There were magicians who watched specifically for new-born magicians and recruited them before their magic – or their families – could kill them. Jamal had sneered at them at the Peerless School, but Johan couldn't help thinking that they had the best of both worlds. They certainly didn't have families to please ... or to sneer at them if they weren't magical enough.

Elaine looked pained for a long chilling moment. "The link with the library is fading," she said. "It isn't meant to be maintained at this distance."

Johan eyed her, nervously. "Are you going to be all right?"

"Yes," Elaine said, a little harshly. She rubbed the side of her head, then scowled. "It isn't as if I can do anything outside the library anyway."

Johan was unconvinced – she looked to be in pain – but held his peace.

"You might want to catch some sleep," Elaine said, as they entered another tunnel. She cast a series of protective wards around them. "It will be seven hours before we reach our destination. I'll key the wards to wake us then."

Johan shook his head, too engrossed with staring out of the window. Elaine leant back in her chair and fell asleep, her brown hair coming loose and falling down around her face. She was definitely more relaxed when she was sleeping, Johan decided, glancing at her for a long moment. It made her look years younger.

The Iron Dragon started to slow down as it approached a large city. Johan stared, drinking in the sight; it was very different from the Golden City. The city seemed to sprawl out for miles, but it was oddly uniform, with none of the variety of buildings in the Golden City. If there was a style, he decided, it was strictly functional. The only decoration he saw was a large statue of a man on a horse, carrying a sword which he held up in the air. It seemed strange to him; a single magician, even an untrained one, could kill the horseman long before he became a danger.

He watched as the vehicle came to a halt in the station. Unlike the Golden City, everyone he saw wore the same kind of clothing; the women wore long dresses, while the men wore trousers and veils that covered their faces. Johan stared, not even sure if they *were* men; his father had always said that someone who covered their face had something to hide. But there were no sign of any curves that might indicate breasts ... they had to be men. Why were they hiding themselves?

Elaine was still sleeping, so he left her alone as the Iron Dragon started to move again. Outside the station, he saw a temple dedicated to a god – he didn't recognise the writing – and then a series of smaller buildings that seemed like apartment blocks. But he couldn't tell what they actually were ... shaking his head, he watched as the Iron Dragon picked up speed, racing out of the city and back into the countryside ...

He must have dozed off, for the next thing he knew was Elaine shaking his shoulder and the Iron Dragon coming slowly to a stop. It still seemed like broad daylight – it struck him, suddenly, that they had been racing against the sun – but he felt tired. Picking himself to his feet, he took his bag and stumbled out of the carriage and into Falconine City. It smelt funny, he realised, and there were green-covered mountains in the distance, yet otherwise it wasn't that different from the Golden City. And the people thronging through the station looked much more diverse.

"This is the capital," Elaine said, when he asked. "The outer cities are always more uniform."

Johan blinked away sleep as they headed towards a grim-faced man in a carriage. Johan would have pegged him as an Inquisitor, he was sure, even without Elaine's introduction; his expression suggested, very strongly, that they should both be in handcuffs before they were helped into the carriage. He didn't say much to Elaine – he didn't say a word to Johan – merely cracked his whip and the horses stumbled into life. The city melted away behind them as they drove up towards the mountains.

"The cabin has been prepared for you," the inquisitor grunted. "You should be fine there for a few weeks, unless we need to use it urgently."

"Thank you," Elaine said, ignoring his tone. "What about food supplies?"

"There's enough, particularly if you hunt or fish too," the Inquisitor said. "Can you do either?"

Johan looked up, interested. He wasn't sure he *liked* the idea of hunting for fun, but hunting for food was a very different story. But he didn't know the first thing about hunting. Jamal had made it sound easy, yet Johan would have bet good money that he'd cheated. Magic often made it impossible for the animals to get away.

"No," Elaine said, tartly. Living in the Golden City her entire life wouldn't have trained her in how to fend for herself. "But we can come down here to buy food, if necessary."

"There are a handful of hermits who will probably appreciate the money," the Inquisitor said, brusquely. "They would hunt for you, if you asked."

Johan tuned him out, looking at the trees as they closed in on the muddy road. It was strange to realise that this was untamed beauty, a far cry from the gardens in the Golden City ... and yet, somehow, he felt *free* out here. The lingering sense of his father's constant oversight was gone completely. He could be happy ...

The vehicle turned a corner and he saw the valley laid out in front of him. There was a shimmering blue lake, surrounded by trees and bushes, hidden amongst the hills. He hoped that there would be time to go climbing, even if the sky was starting to look overcast. There was a peal of thunder in the distance and he smiled. He'd always liked rain.

"We have to walk from here," the Inquisitor said, pulling the carriage to a halt. "Get your bags while I talk to the horses."

The air smelled fresh and clean, Johan decided, as the Inquisitor led them up a pathway that seemed almost invisible. He wouldn't have seen it at all if it hadn't been pointed out to him, suggesting that there were hidden charms that kept it concealed from prying eyes. There was another rumble of thunder, closer this time, as they advanced up the path, then over a bog that threatened to suck them in if they stood still for too long. It looked as though someone had tried to build a makeshift bridge out of planks and then given up halfway through, he thought, as he saw the planks. By now, they were sodden and completely useless.

He smiled as the cabin came into view. It was small, made out of wood rather than stone ... but wood would be cheap here. Elaine didn't seem too impressed; Johan was delighted. It was a *long* way from his father, his brother and the rest of his family.

And, really, what else did he want?

Chapter Twenty-Six

Elaine had thought that she was used to roughing it – she'd lived in a roach-infested apartment before her promotion – but the Inquisition's cabin gave a whole new meaning to the word. It was larger than her former apartment, yet it was primitive; food was cooked over a fire, there was no such thing as hot running water and the toilet was unspeakable. If it wasn't for magic, she knew, she would have headed back to the city as quickly as possible, regardless of the risk. Even with it ...

Johan seemed delighted, she saw; it might not have been luxurious, but it was somewhere away from the city. The Inquisitor showed them the bedding – and the stockpile of food, held in stasis by a spell – and then headed back to the city, leaving them alone. Judging by the rapidly darkening sky, it was about to start raining at any moment. Elaine knew little about living in the countryside, but she was surprised that he hadn't wanted to stay the night. Driving back in the darkness would be terrifying ...

But he would have to put the horses somewhere, she thought, as she turned to look out of the window. The view was impressive, she had to admit; towering mountains, endless trees and – in the distance – the faint blue shimmer of another lake. But it wasn't the Golden City ... it seemed to stretch out as far as the eye could see.

"This place is wonderful," Johan said, coming back into the main room. "Which bedroom do you want?"

Elaine smiled. There were two bedrooms, one with a pair of bunk beds, the other with two separate beds. The Inquisitors wouldn't care if four of them were stuffed into the same room; Elaine would have found it unbearable. She'd had enough problems sharing an apartment with Daria, even though they'd had separate bedrooms. But it honestly didn't bother her which room she took for herself.

"Either one," she said, softly. She had to fight down a yawn. "Which one do you want?"

"The bunk beds, I think," Johan said. "You can have the other one."

Elaine nodded and went into her room to make the bed. She had to show Johan how to do it, something that reminded her of Millicent and the other high-born girls at the Peerless School; they hadn't known how to take care of themselves either. The orphanage had been far less kind to its inhabitants, teaching them everything from sewing to cooking. And girls who forgot to make their beds in the morning wound up with the worst chores.

"You'll have to change the sheets in a few days," she said, once she'd set up basic insect-repelling spells and a handful of other protections. "But until then, just make sure that you make the bed every morning."

"Yes, mother," Johan said. "I won't forget."

His tone was light, but Elaine could hear bitterness underneath it. Johan's mother had only taken a vague interest in her children at the best of times, particularly after discovering that Johan was powerless. Elaine had seen enough society dames to know that it was far from uncommon, but it still tore at her. *She* would have given her eye teeth for a mother.

Elaine nodded, blinking away tears, and walked back into the kitchen. The Inquisitor had explained that the cabin drew water from a mountain stream, then warned them to make sure that they always boiled the water before drinking it. Elaine filled a small kettle with water, then cast a spell to make the water boil before picking up two mugs, pouring powdered chocolate into them and adding the water. It wouldn't taste quite right, she knew, but it would suffice.

"Johan," she called, as she stirred the chocolate, "are you hungry?"

"Always," Johan said. "Is that normal for magicians?"

"It's also normal for teenagers," Elaine said, dryly. "I'm too tired to cook anything right now, so we'll have to make do with Inquisitor rations."

Thunder crashed, high overhead. Elaine glanced towards the windows, just in time to see the first raindrops falling from high overhead. They fell so rapidly that they seemed to fall in sheets, as though an angry god was tipping water over the mountains. Johan took his mug and walked over to the window, staring out at the rain. He would never have seen anything like it in the Golden City.

He might in the future, Elaine thought, as she created light balls to illuminate the room. *The weather-control spells were badly damaged by Kane ...*

She produced a ration bar and eyed it suspiciously, then broke it in half and passed one part to Johan. Her own half tasted of vegetable mush, a meal she was far too familiar with from the orphanage. Johan made a face as he chewed his bar, but he didn't ask what went into the recipe. Elaine knew that it included various potions designed to give energy to struggling Inquisitors. Few others ate potions in solid form.

"I'll cook something proper tomorrow," she promised, as she examined the stove. It *seemed* relatively simple, she decided, although she would have to gather firewood in the morning. "For now ..."

Johan yawned. A moment later, Elaine yawned too.

"Bed, I think," she said. She cancelled half of the light globes, realising that darkness had fallen completely outside the little hut. "Do you want a light in your room?"

"I could make one," Johan said. "If I didn't use the spell ..."

Elaine shook her head. "This building is made of wood," she reminded him. "And if you set fire to it, the Inquisitors will make you pay to rebuild it."

She hesitated, then dug a candle and matches out of one of the cupboards. "Use this if you need to go to the toilet in the middle of the night," she ordered. "Or knock on my door and I'll make you a light globe. Do *not* experiment on your own."

Johan looked rebellious, but nodded.

Elaine checked his room – noting with some pleasure that he'd already started to unpack and place everything neatly on the shelves – and then waved him goodnight, before walking into her own room. It felt oddly cramped, even though it was larger than the apartment she had shared with Daria.

Ruefully reflecting that she had grown too used to luxury, Elaine stripped down to her undergarments and climbed into bed. It was uncomfortable, even compared to the orphanage, but she was too tired to care. A moment later, she was asleep.

She was woken by the sound of a chiming bell. Elaine sat upright in bed, reaching desperately for her wand ... someone or something was *outside*. She pulled herself out of bed, clutching her wand, and slipped over to the window, drawing back the curtain to peer outside. A dozen sheep were milling around outside the hut, escorted by a large dog with disturbingly human eyes. Or was it a werewolf? Werewolves might have been rare in the Golden City – Daria had been an exception – but they were quite common in rural areas.

Feeling unaccountably grimy, Elaine pulled on her dressing gown and headed out into the main room. It was cold, cold enough to make her shiver; carefully, she cast a handful of heating charms and then started to look for the bath. As the Inquisitor had said, it was really a large metal tub and nothing else, barely large enough for her to kneel down in the water. Elaine filled it with water, then had to use magic to drag it back into her room, where she started to heat it. She had the feeling that the Inquisitors simply stripped off and washed in the main room, heedless of who might see. But Elaine had never been able to undress in front of Daria, let alone anyone else. She'd done quite enough of that in the orphanage.

When she finished, she dressed properly in trousers and a shirt – still feeling grimy – and took the tub back into the living room. Johan had awakened, she realised; he was standing on the porch, staring out across the countryside. After the rainstorm, the air was fresh and clear; in the distance, the mountains seemed to glow with light and magic. It reminded Elaine of stories about people who had encountered wild magic in the countryside, wild magic that had changed them – and not always for the better. She levitated the water up and tipped it down the drain, then walked out to stand beside Johan. He looked ... relaxed.

"Thank you for bringing me here," he said, softly.

"You're welcome," Elaine said. It was good to see him so relaxed. "I hope that you're ready to eat something?"

Johan nodded eagerly and followed her back into the main room. Elaine opened one of the cupboards and produced bread and cheese, followed by a large jug of milk. It was astonishingly creamy, she discovered, as she poured it into a pair of mugs. She honestly couldn't think why the milk in the Golden City wasn't so rich.

"So," Johan said, as he ate his bread and cheese. "What are we doing today?"

"More magic," Elaine said, reaching for her notebook. She was reluctant to risk experimenting with magic that required a human target – particularly after what had happened to Charity – but there were plenty of other experiments they could run. For one thing, she wanted to know the limits of Johan's endurance. "Incidentally, have you ever tried casting a spell on yourself?"

Johan blinked in surprise. "No," he said. "Is that ... I thought that was a bad idea."

"Depends on the spell," Elaine said. "Trying to heal yourself or to ... *improve* your body can have disastrous effects. But trying to fly isn't so difficult, if you have the power reserves."

"Improve one's body," Johan mused, a wicked grin on his face. "Do you think that Jamal ever tried to improve himself?"

"I doubt it," Elaine said, tartly. Everything she'd heard about Jamal suggested that he already considered himself perfect. "But others have done, over the years ..."

She shuddered at the memory. *She* had never felt the urge to try to improve herself, but some of the girls in her dorm had tried. One had warped her face, one had given herself breasts so large that they were bigger than her head and one had done something so terrible – Elaine had never been sure of the details – that she'd had to spend the rest of the term in hospital. After that, they'd all been given a stern lecture and threats of dire punishment if anyone tried again.

Not that it stopped the next generation, she thought. The Privy Council had debated the matter, once. In the end, they'd reluctantly conceded that they should make sure that glamours were taught to students at a very early age, perhaps helping them to realise that they didn't *need* to actually change their bodies. But the cynic in Elaine told her that it wouldn't work. Glamours weren't *real*, as she knew all too well.

She finished her breakfast and put the plates in the sink. Surprisingly, after Johan had finished *his* breakfast, he began to wash the plates. Elaine watched, with some amusement, as he wiped them clean; he hadn't been taught to do *that* by his family. But then, he *was* a good boy ... pushing the thought aside, she found her coat and shoes and waited for him to join her at the door. When he did, she led the way outside.

It was surprisingly warm as they walked away from the hut towards a muddy clearing. Elaine sucked in her breath sharply as her feet squelched their way through the mud, disliking it intensely ... and the sight of the bog, only a few metres away, did nothing to encourage her. It was a small bog, yet she knew that putting one foot wrong could result in her being trapped or worse. Could she actually sink to her death in the mire?

"Can we go walking later?" Johan asked. "I want to explore."

Elaine sighed, but nodded. "Let me set up a tracking spell first," she said. "This isn't the Golden City. It's far too easy to get lost out here."

Johan nodded.

They stopped in the middle of the clearing and looked around. According to Dread, the Inquisitors sometimes used it for practicing both spells and unarmed combat, but there was no trace of magic in the area as far as Elaine could sense. It had probably faded into the background over the years, she decided, as she located a large rock at one edge of the clearing. Beyond it, the trees closed in, casting a sinister shadow over the scene.

"You see that rock," Elaine said. "I want you to make it float in the air."

"Understood," Johan said. He concentrated ... and the rock rose up into the air. It was a far steadier movement than anything Elaine would have expected, particularly from such an inexperienced magician. Even if *she* had cast the spells, the rock would have wobbled badly as gravity fought to pull it back to the ground. "How long do you want me to hold it up?"

Elaine frowned. "Are you concentrating on it right now?"

"Yes," Johan said. "Should I stop ...?"

"Try and stop," Elaine said. A moment later, the rock fell to the ground and landed hard enough to send mud flying everywhere. Elaine wiped it off her shirt with a grimace, then looked over at Johan. A normal magician's spells would have left the rock in the air until they ran out of power. "Would you like to try something risky?"

Johan nodded, although his face was pale. "I want you to try to lift *yourself* up into the air," Elaine ordered. "Just imagine that you're floating about a metre above the ground."

There was a long pause. Nothing happened.

"It isn't working," Johan said, sourly. Like most youngsters – and all magicians - he'd dreamed of being able to fly. "Why isn't it working?"

"I'm not sure," Elaine said. If he had been a normal magician, she could have taught him the spells, but she had a nasty feeling that the results would be disastrous. "I want you to ..."

She broke off as she felt herself rising up into the air until she was about two metres over Johan's head. Her blood ran cold as she realised that Johan had not only tried something without warning her, he'd also endangered her life. What if he *couldn't* put her down safely and she broke a leg? The closest druid was miles away.

Good thing I didn't wear a skirt, the irrelevant part of her mind pointed out.

"Lower me down, gently," she ordered, fighting to keep her voice level. "You do *not* want to drop me."

Slowly, she felt herself being lowered to the ground. Gritting her teeth, she tried to sense the magic holding her, but felt almost nothing apart from the glow of her own wand. It was almost as if Johan's magic didn't really exist, which was impossible. There were a long string of near-disasters to prove that it *did* exist.

"If you had done that at the Peerless School," she said, once she was back on the ground, "you would have been sent to the Administrator for a caning. If you were lucky! You could have been expelled for *that* stunt."

Johan paled. "I just wanted to see if it worked," he said. "I ..."

"There were ways we could have prepared for it," Elaine snapped, more rattled than she wanted to admit. What if she'd been flung so high up that she could no longer breathe? "We could have done it over a lake, perhaps. What would you have done if I'd broken a leg?"

"I ... I don't know," Johan admitted. "I could have tried to heal it."

"That's not a good idea unless you happen to know what you are doing," Elaine said. "And you can't cast normal spells. We'd have to have a druid arrange for you to practice on a live patient and most of them would object, strongly. Healing is much more than just melding the bones together."

She took a look at his face and lowered her voice, slightly. "We will keep pushing the limits," she added, "but we have to be careful. We're all alone up here."

"Apart from the sheep," Johan said.

And a possible werewolf, Elaine added, in the privacy of her own mind. Most city-folk were terrified of werewolves, not without reason. There was no point in mentioning the possibility to him.

"Come on," she said, out loud. "Let's go make some sandwiches, then we can go on a walk."

Johan remained pensive until they walked back down the path and saw the lake in front of them. A boat was positioned on the shore, tipped upside down to ensure that the rain just cascaded over it and fell to the ground. Elaine had to smile as Johan discovered the sign that identified the boat as belonging to the Inquisitors, then promised that they'd find the paddles and take it out soon. The thought made her nervous – she had never been boating before – but it was worth it if it made Johan happy. They both needed to relax.

"Tell me," Johan said, when she said that out loud. "What do you *do* when you aren't actually working?"

"Read, mainly," Elaine admitted. "And I'm writing my

own spellbook. If it ever gets published ...”

Johan gave her an odd look. “Why ...?”

“I’ve been creating spells that have all of the unnecessary gibberish stripped from them, spells that require very little power to work,” Elaine said. “That means that we will end up with more low-power magicians.”

“And none of the high-power magicians like that thought,” Johan guessed. Elaine nodded. “Is that why they’re scared of me?”

“I’m afraid so,” Elaine admitted. “And that is why you have to be careful not to give them any other reason to be scared.”

Chapter Twenty-Seven

House Rendang, Duncan considered, was caught between a rock and a hard place.

They were one of the oldest families in the Empire, with a lineage that included at least one Grand Sorcerer, but they were *poor*. The rental on lands they owned were enough to maintain their position in the Golden City, yet not enough to allow them to consider themselves rich or diversify into more lucrative fields that would set their finances on steadier ground. In their place, he would have withdrawn from the Golden City entirely and spent a few decades saving money in a cheaper part of the Empire, but their pride wouldn't allow them to admit defeat.

It was a measure of how poor they were, he realised, that they only seemed to have a handful of servants. Their mansion was larger than the one he'd purchased six months ago, but there was something *faded* about it, as if it were slowly decaying into dust. It would take a small army of servants to repair the damage and they clearly didn't have the funds to hire them, even on a temporary basis. Duncan smiled to himself as the servant – clearly an old retainer – led him into the Rendang's study. They were desperate, giving him an advantage. He hoped.

The *real* question was just what was going on between Johan and Jayne. Jayne worked for the Head Librarian, which raised a red flag in Duncan's mind. Had *she* ordered Jayne to start a relationship with Duncan's son? It would hardly be unprecedented, not when the greater magical families would often try to court new-bloods to add their wild magic to the family's heritage. And it would help her attach more strings to Johan ...

Or was it the Grand Sorceress's idea? He barely knew the Head Librarian, but he'd spent enough time with Light Spinner to know that she didn't lack for courage or cunning, which was partly why she was still Grand Sorceress. It would be simple for her to quietly insist that Jayne spend time with Johan and then let nature take its course, or even offer the girl vast rewards if she cooperated. Apparently, Jayne was looking for a potions apprenticeship at a very early age. A word from Light Spinner could ensure that she had her choice of Potion Masters to teach her.

The Rendang rose to his feet as Duncan entered his study. He was a tall, powerfully-built man who somehow managed to look imposing, despite greying hair and a growing paunch. Duncan bowed – a gesture of respect, coming from someone who was nominally a social equal – and then stepped backwards. The Rendang stepped forward and held out a hand. Duncan shook it firmly, feeling a hint of triumph. He'd been acknowledged as an equal!

"Thank you for coming," the Rendang said, waving Duncan to a comfortable chair. "Can I offer you anything?"

Duncan's spies had told him that the Rendang Family was renowned for its wine cellar, but he knew he needed a clear head. "Kava would be sufficient," he said, briskly. It would be an insult to refuse altogether. "There are matters I would discuss with you."

The Rendang nodded. "I confess I am curious," he said, mildly. "What can I do for you?"

"I must speak bluntly," Duncan said. "Your youngest daughter appears to be courting my son. Is this happening on your orders?"

"I would not presume to tell Jayne who she could or could not court," the Rendang said. His face was set in an expressionless mask. "She is certainly not courting anyone on my orders."

Duncan nodded, believing him. The rumours about Johan might have reached the Rendang by now, but it would still be a gamble to have his daughter mingled up with a former Powerless. It could call the entire family line into question ... unfairly, of course, but what did *fair* have to do with malicious rumours?

"I wish to discuss a marriage contract between your family and mine," Duncan said. "I believe that Jayne has a great deal to offer my family and I have a great deal to offer you."

He watched the Rendang's mask crack, slightly. The Rendang Family was old, but poor. A large influx of cash from Duncan could turn their fortunes around. And he wouldn't think twice about using his daughter as a tool to get that cash, not when it benefited both sides. Johan, for all of his passion, had never realised that marriages were far more than just joining man and wife; they were a union between two families. On that scale, what did love matter?

But would the Rendang be willing to marry his daughter to Johan?

There was the question, Duncan knew. The Conidian Family was rich, but very new to the Golden City, no matter what they had been outside it. There would be whispers in High Society about the marriage, nastier than any he'd expected from marrying Jamal to Marina; there would be dark suggestions that it was all about the money. And they'd be right.

"I would certainly be prepared to open discussions," the Rendang said, finally. "What are you prepared to offer?"

Duncan knew he didn't dare stint, but at the same time he didn't want to look *too* eager. "I will offer ten thousand gold as her bride price," he said. "In addition, I will settle twenty thousand gold on the happy couple, as well as lands and properties outside the Golden City."

He couldn't help smiling at the Rendang's expression. It *was* a magnificent offer, enough to ensure that Johan and Jayne could enter High Society at the very highest levels. People who would have sneered at the Conidian Family would never dare to sneer at Jayne and *her* family, who were among the oldest blood in the city. And he had yet to finish.

"I will also buy out half of your debts," he added. "How does that sound?"

The Rendang licked his lips. "I have heard rumours that your son is a Powerless," he said. "He certainly did not attend the Peerless School. Is that true?"

"My son has magic," Duncan assured him, remembering the smashed table. "It merely developed later than expected."

"That is good to hear," the Rendang said. "Do I dare assume that you have a written proposal already drawn up?"

Duncan reached into the pocket of his robes and produced a scroll of paper. "This is the draft agreement," he said, passing it to the Rendang. "It covers all of the essential points."

"So it does," the Rendang agreed. He scanned it quickly. "I will have to consult with my lawyers – and Jayne, of course – but I dare say that it will prove acceptable."

"Thank you," Duncan said, as he rose to his feet. "And please assure her that she has my very best wishes."

He smiled as he was shown out the door, back onto the streets. A wife could not be forced to act against her husband, certainly not under the terms of the contract he intended to have both Jayne and Johan sign. Whatever orders she had from the Head Librarian would be negated by the marriage agreement. And she would have little choice, but to give her consent. She was too young to speak for herself.

And Johan? If his son wanted the girl, he wouldn't object either.

He was halfway home when a voice hailed him. "Duncan!"

Duncan turned and saw, much to his surprise, Deferens. The Privy Councillor had left his robes behind, instead donning an eye-catching red outfit that showed off his muscles to best advantage. He carried a long staff in one hand, complete with an iron ball on the end, and wore a sword on his belt. There was no sign of his wand, although it could easily have been hidden up his sleeves if necessary.

"Vlad," he said, crossly. He didn't really *like* Deferens – and the way he'd proposed the execution of his son chilled him to the bone. "What can I do for you?"

"Join me for a drink," Deferens said. He led the way into a bar, sat down in a booth and started to cast privacy charms into the air. "I need to talk to you."

Duncan sat down, cast his own charms, then looked Deferens in the eye. The man's unkempt hair had always annoyed him, as if he were *too* masculine to be real. He wasn't blind to the significance of the staff or the sword. But advertising it in public was rare, to say the least; it opened the magician to all kinds of rumours. Few would dare to mention them to his face.

"Well," he repeated. "What can I do for you?"

The waiter came over and bowed to them. Deferens ordered two drinks and sent the man away, then looked back at Duncan. "The Inquisitors have yet to track down the people responsible for the death of young Graham," he said. "They have arrested and interrogated the leaders of the Leveller movement – those your son didn't kill – but they were found innocent."

Duncan started. He hadn't heard that little titbit. "Innocent?"

"They were interrogated thoroughly," Deferens assured him. "Truth spells, mental probes, truth potions ... everything was tried. They were found innocent and released."

He smiled, briefly. It didn't touch his eyes. "What that means," he explained, "is that the *real* perpetrators have escaped justice. My source in the Watchtower tells me that there are no leads."

"I can work that out for myself," Duncan said. He allowed some of his irritation to slip into his voice. "What do you want from me?"

"This ... *Leveller* movement poses a threat to our way of life," Deferens said. He sounded as though he genuinely believed what he was saying, although Duncan knew better than to take anything for granted. Deferens was a practiced politician, after all, even if he *was* eccentric by normal standards. "I believe that it should be banned."

"The Grand Sorceress disagrees," Duncan pointed out.

"I am building a coalition of opinion that proposes that we ban it," Deferens said. "If a sufficient majority of the Privy Council agrees, she will fall in line."

Duncan considered it. The hell of it was that Deferens was right. Light Spinner might be the most powerful magician in the Empire – at least officially – but she wasn't all-powerful. The last Grand Sorcerer had had years to tighten his grip on the reins of power; Light Spinner had had barely six months. And there were question marks over her rise to power. If the Privy Council as a body voted against her, she would have to back down.

"And you want my support," he said, silently weighing up the votes. The Head Librarian was a cipher, perhaps Light

Spinner's puppet. That left eleven others ... how many others did Deferens have on his side? "What are you prepared to offer in exchange?"

"Your son is imprisoned," Deferens said. "I can arrange for him to be released into your custody."

Duncan felt a flash of hope. If he had Jamal back, he could at least *try* to knock some sense into his eldest son. And maybe he could marry Marina, which would make it harder for the Inquisitors to re-arrest him. There would be other powerful figures speaking in his support.

"I would like proof that you can arrange this," Duncan said, slowly. The Grand Sorceress had taken a personal interest in the case, which made it harder for things to slip by without being noticed. "What can you offer me?"

Deferens smiled. "Have you even been able to *visit* your son?"

Duncan shook his head, wordlessly. He hadn't – and nor had the lawyers he'd hired to defend Jamal when the case finally came to trial. As annoyed as he was with his eldest son, he still wanted to see him and make sure that he was safe.

"Here," Deferens said. He pulled a piece of paper out of his robes and passed it to Duncan. "A visiting permit. You can see him for up to an hour. And then ... you can join me in pressing for a quick trial."

Clever bastard, Duncan thought, sourly. He'd underestimated Deferens; the man might look like an overcompensating fool, but there was a sharp mind hiding under the ridiculous beard. Right now, with the magical community furious over Graham's death, there would be little enthusiasm for convicting Jamal's band of terrorists. They'd be seen as heroes ...

... Which would encourage the Privy Council not to send them to the headsman.

"Very well," he said. "If this permit works, you will have my support."

He stood up, ignoring the waiter, and marched out of the bar, heading up the long road towards the Watchtower. It was a longer walk than normal, but it allowed him time to clear his mind and *think*. Deferens seemed to have a workable plan, yet Duncan wasn't entirely sure that he trusted the younger man. There was something about the whole affair that bothered him.

The watchtower rose up in front of him and he paused, gasping for breath. Behind him, the Golden City lay within the hollow, surrounded by the Four Peaks. He turned to stare as he fought to calm his heartbeat, marvelling at how far he'd come. It still awed him to see the city's multitude of buildings, a strange jumble of designs that somehow worked together very well. But then, it *was* the capital of a planet-wide Empire. There were representatives from all over the world gathered in the city's embrace.

No wonder the best and brightest come here to learn, he told himself. *By the time they go home, they think of themselves as citizens of the Empire.*

There was no guard on the Watchtower's exterior door, but he felt the powerful wards as soon as he stepped inside. Any use of magic would draw an immediate response, he realised, as he walked slowly towards the desk. A bored-looking young man in grey robes sat there, dealing with a handful of people who were trying to file complaints. Normally, an Inquisitor would have taken the desk, but with the Inquisition so short-staffed they'd been forced to hire outsiders. They were nowhere near as honest as the full-fledged Inquisitors.

"I have a permit," he said, passing it to the young man. How had Deferens obtained it? "Where do I go?"

The receptionist waved to another man in grey robes, who took the permit, inspected it, then beckoned for Duncan to follow him through a solid stone door. It led to a stairwell that plunged down into the depths of the mountain, surrounded by dangerous flickers of magic. If someone tried to escape, Duncan realised, they might bring down the ceiling on top of them. After Hawthorne's escape, the Inquisitors were clearly not taking any chances. And Jamal was nowhere near as powerful – or insane – as the Dark Wizard.

They entered a darkened corridor and reached a series of doors, set into the rock. "You may speak to him for one hour," his escort said. "I must inform you that the interior of the room is constantly monitored. Should you attempt to draw your wand or any other weapon, you will face arrest and possible detention. If you are taken hostage, your life will not be considered a priority."

Duncan stared at the man, whose face was half-hidden in the gloom. "He's my son!"

"Everyone else in these cells is also someone's son," his escort said. "That does not make them *nice*. Or safe."

The door clicked open. Duncan braced himself, then stepped inside. The cell was tiny, illuminated only by a flickering lamp hanging from the ceiling. Jamal sat on a bunk, his hands chained together and one leg chained to the bed. Duncan saw the faint shape of a chamber pot under the bed and shuddered. His eldest son shouldn't have to live in a place like this.

"Father," Jamal said. His voice was a whisper, although Duncan couldn't tell if it was through disuse or through a reluctance to speak too loudly for fear it would be overhead. "You came."

"Finally," Duncan admitted. "How ... how are you?"

Jamal laughed, harshly. "I have been interrogated, at length," he said. "I told them I could tell them nothing and they *still* interrogated me ..."

Duncan felt his temper snap. "What in the name of all the gods were you *thinking*?"

He could understand the other idiots who had joined Jamal's gang. None of them could have expected to inherit much, beyond their family names and a sense of entitlement. But Jamal ... Jamal had been the Prime Heir. He would have inherited everything Duncan and his ancestors had built up over the years. And he'd risked everything just to lash out at the Levellers. How *could* he have been so stupid?

"It needed to be done, father," Jamal said. "*Someone* had to take the lead."

"And you fancied yourself a leader," Duncan finished.

He wanted to scream at his son. But memories intruded. He remembered the day when Jamal, barely three years old, had produced his first spark of magic. It had been fantastic to look at it and know that his eldest son would be powerful indeed. And he'd seen the exam results from the Peerless School ... whatever Johan might believe, Jamal had proved himself academically as well. Duncan was proud of him, even when he was angry. It had led him to be softer with his eldest son than, perhaps, he should have been.

"I'm sorry," he whispered, feeling tears welling up in his eyes. There would be time enough to convince Jamal to behave himself in future. For now, all that mattered was securing his release. He should have pushed harder, he told himself. The family's influence would have been enough to get Jamal moved to a better cell, at the very least. "I'll get you out of here. Whatever it takes, I'll get you out of here."

Chapter Twenty-Eight

"Is there anything better," Johan asked himself, "than messing around in boats?"

It had taken him several days to learn how to row properly, but once he had picked it up he'd discovered that it was surprisingly relaxing. The lake bordered a cliff that actually hid a handful of little caves and passageways, some of which he had even tried to explore, while the lake itself held dozens of fish which eyed the boat curiously. Sooner or later, Johan suspected, they would have to actually learn to *fish*, but until then he was content to merely watch them swimming under the water.

He looked over at Elaine, who was sitting on the shore reading a book. After one disastrous trip out on the water, she'd decided not to go out again. Johan hadn't given any thought to the dangers of drowning – he swam fairly well - but he hadn't realised that Elaine couldn't swim until it was almost too late. As it was, he was far too aware that if she'd been wearing her normal robes, she would have drowned before he could reach her.

Smiling to himself, he turned and rowed back towards where she was waiting. He *had* tried to use his magic to push the boat, but the results had been mixed. One experiment had tipped the boat over and flung him into the water, the other had pushed the boat into the rocky cliff face so hard that he was sure that he'd damaged the hull. It had taken him several hours of careful inspection to be sure that the boat hadn't sprung a leak.

"Hey," he called, as the boat neared shore. "A little help here?"

Elaine looked up, then raised her wand. An invisible force caught the boat and pulled it up onto the shore, allowing Johan to scramble out and pull it right out of the water. It was surprising just how heavy the boat was on dry land, even though it was light on the water, but Elaine had flatly refused to help him secure it the first time. If he couldn't do it for himself, she'd said, there was no point in doing it at all. Johan had felt like sulking, before reminding himself that he wasn't Jamal. He needed to know how to do things for himself.

"Thank you," he said, when he was done. Tipping the boat over, at least, was easier on dry land. "Do you think it's going to rain again?"

"Probably," Elaine said, looking up at the sky. It was the middle of the day, but it was already growing darker as clouds formed high overhead. "Make sure the boat is secure, then we will walk back to the cabin."

Johan smiled. In the last few days, he'd explored the area; sometimes with Elaine, sometimes on his own. Climbing the mountains had been trickier than he'd expected, but the views had been worth it ... and it was something Jamal had never done. The sense of being completely isolated had only grown stronger, even though he'd spotted a number of other cabins in the distance. If there were other people around they gave the Inquisitor's cabin a wide berth.

"Coming," he said, once he'd checked the boat again. "What are we having for dinner?"

Food seemed to taste better in the mountains. Elaine was an indifferent cook at best – Johan hadn't even been allowed to help the cooks at home – but it didn't seem to matter. It always tasted good after a long day of practicing magic, then walking or rowing to burn off energy.

"Bread, meat and cheese," Elaine said. She looked tired, even though she hadn't done anything more strenuous than sitting on a chair she'd dragged down from the cabin. "I think we both need to rest."

Johan scowled. Elaine could become exhausted by working magic, but *he* seemed to be largely immune to such problems. Walking, rowing and swimming made him tired; magic didn't seem to cost him anything at all. It was worrying, Elaine had told him; his magic was either *thoroughly* weird, because the energy had to be coming from somewhere, or he just had vast power reserves, well in excess of any other recorded magician.

Thunder rolled in the sky as they walked up the path, followed by the first splashes of rain. Elaine waved her wand in the air, trying to shield them, but her protective charm wasn't perfect. As the wind changed, it blew raindrops into their faces and sent streams of water gushing down their clothes. By the time they reached the cabin, they were both dripping wet and thoroughly miserable.

Elaine's shirt was so wet that it was clinging to her skin, revealing the shape of her breasts and nipples. Johan stared, then looked away, embarrassed. Elaine, thankfully, didn't seem to notice as she cast a warming charm, drying both Johan and herself. Johan kept his gaze fixed on the stove until they were both dry, then started to load it up with firewood and pinecones. It had been surprisingly fun to collect them, knowing that they were to be burnt.

"I'll light it," Elaine said, sharply. She pointed her wand at the stove; a moment later, the pinecones caught fire, burning brightly in the darkened stove. "I think we'll be staying in tonight."

Johan couldn't disagree, he decided as he looked out of the window. Visibility was down to a few metres at best, thanks to the rain – and he knew from experience that mist often followed a major rainstorm. Even if it was still technically daylight when the rain stopped, they might still get lost. Or run right into the bog.

"Agreed," he said, watching as the rain dripped down the window. "How safe is this cabin?"

"It's stood for hundreds of years, according to the Inquisitors," Elaine said. "I dare say that it will survive anything other than your magic."

Johan sighed. He hadn't meant to scare her when he'd picked her up, but it had clearly bothered her more than she wanted to admit. Charity had shown the same reaction to Jamal more than once ... and then she'd been weirdly subdued at the disastrous family meeting, after she'd been accidentally turned into a rat. He would have almost preferred a thrashing – his father's standard response to any misbehaviour from his younger children – than have her be worried about him. Or scared of him.

He watched as she laid bread, cheese and meat out on the

table, then sat down to eat beside her. For a long moment, he ate in silence, then Elaine started to talk, telling him stories of long-gone witches and wizards and how they'd changed the world. One story focused on the very first Grand Sorcerer, the one who had won the First Necromantic War, but there was an odd edge to her voice as she spoke. And Johan couldn't help feeling that the story was incomplete.

But it was something he'd never done with his family; he found himself enjoying it as she outlined several different stories. The King who had enchanted his Crown; the Prince who had walked away from the Throne; the Princess who lost her way ... they were all part of the Empire's heritage, a heritage that his father had tried to deny him. What good did it do to hide those stories? Even the mundanes knew them!

"Thank you," he said, when she had finished. "I wish ... I wish I'd heard more."

"There will be more," Elaine assured him. "Which one did you like best?"

"The Enchanted Crown," Johan said, after a moment. "Is it actually *real*?"

"It would be possible to make a crown that judges its wearer, I suppose," Elaine said, thoughtfully. "But what king would choose to favour a stranger over his own children?"

Johan nodded, sourly. Blood was the determining factor in families, after all; his blood still made him part of House Conidian, no matter how much he strove to deny it. He could barely imagine his father choosing to strip Jamal of his Prime Heir status; it was impossible to imagine that he would pass the family's collected wealth and patronage network to a stranger. His children were his only real hope of immortality ...

He stood up and walked over to the sofa. Elaine's books were sitting there; he picked one of them up and glanced at the title. *Hafiz's Protective Wards, Rituals, Rites and Spells.* The other book was far thinner, written in a purple liquid he suspected might be blood. *A Guide To The Various Venomous Sprites, Faye, Fallen Gods and Demons of the Netherworlds with particular attention to the Kings of Demons.* There was no author noted below the overlong title.

"Most of that book is nonsense," Elaine said, coming over

to see what he was holding. "You can generally tell the value of a book by its title. The longer and more pretentious it is, the less the practical value of whatever happens to be written inside. This writer took a few rumours, made others up out of whole cloth and wrote them down. But there are still people who take it seriously."

Johan smiled. "What are *you* doing with it?"

"I'm supposed to write a rebuttal we can slip into the library's copies," Elaine said, shrugging. "Something to tell people that trying the rituals in this book are a waste of time at best and a sure-fire murder charge at worst. The only ritual that actually works is one that ensures that only one person can read the book ... and that is actually a fairly common spell."

"Like Charity's diary," Johan said. "When I opened it, it was blank ... even though I knew that she had been writing in it."

Elaine lifted an eyebrow. "And when did *you* look in it?"

"I was *twelve*," Johan protested. "And I didn't get away with it either."

"Glad to hear it," Elaine mused. She grinned at him. "Girls do need a little privacy."

"I'll remember that if I ever have children," Johan said. He passed her the book, then picked up the other one. "Why this one?"

"You damaged my last set of wards," Elaine reminded him. "I wanted to try some of the other protections outlined in this book."

Johan frowned. "I thought that you had all of the knowledge stuffed into your head?"

"It sometimes helps to see the actual words and diagrams," Elaine admitted. She opened one page and held it out to him. "Although *this* is really too difficult for someone like me, no matter how much insight I have."

It took Johan several moments to work out what the instructions were telling the reader to do, then he had to swallow hard to keep from throwing up. The spells would remove a person's heart from his chest, then store it outside his body while maintaining a link to him that would keep him alive, no matter the distance between the heart and the magician. And, apparently, it would render the magician immortal, as long as the link was maintained. Johan had a vivid mental impression of a magician blown to tiny bits, but somehow remaining alive ...

He pushed the thought aside with a shudder. "Are there people who actually *try* this?"

"Some are reputed to have done it," Elaine said. "More try it and end up dead."

Johan gave her the second book, then went to find his own on family magic. It was heavy going; the writer had clearly been writing several centuries ago and a number of words were completely unfamiliar, but he thought he had the gist of it. As long as magic ran through the family, there would be consequences for deliberate betrayal, inter-family murder ... or even outright disobedience. But the writer didn't seem to know if they applied to Powerless.

"I should undergo an adoption rite," Johan muttered, sourly. Elaine had proposed apprenticing him, but an adoption rite would be permanent. "Wouldn't that provide me with a new family?"

"Perhaps," Elaine said. "But they can be dangerous if they are not entered into willingly."

She scowled. "And you would throw away *everything*," she added. "You would not stand to inherit *anything*; your father would not even be able to leave you a small token of his esteem."

"My father has no esteem for me," Johan said, bitterly. "He doesn't even *know* me. What was he thinking when he offered me Marina Clyburn as a bride?"

"There are few young magicians who would turn down such an offer," Elaine pointed out, mildly. "She is not only pretty, but intelligent, capable and very well connected."

"And my father has been mistreating me for sixteen years," Johan added, ignoring her comment. "Why are there no consequences for *him*?"

Elaine smiled. "Right now, his eldest son and Prime Heir is in jail," she said. "And his second son wants nothing to do with him. How do you know that *those* are not consequences."

Johan rubbed his temple. "If you turned someone into a

frog," he said, finally, "there would be cause and effect, wouldn't there? You'd cast the spell; someone would transform. But with this magic ... how do you tell if the magic is working against you or if it's just a wild coincidence?"

"You don't," Elaine said, simply.

"I hate this kind of magic," Johan said. "You can't tell" – he paused, looking up at her – "what's so funny?"

Elaine was chuckling. "Just about every classically-trained magician has the same reaction," she said. "The ones who don't are the ones who never go to the Peerless School."

Johan stared at her for a moment, then shook his head. "But why are there no consequences?"

"If your father genuinely believed that he was doing the right thing for you, or the family," Elaine said slowly, "it is unlikely that there would be any adverse consequences."

"But he *wasn't*," Johan protested. "He made a whole *series* of bad choices, including trying to marry me off. Or should I have accepted?"

"It might well have seemed the best thing to do," Elaine said. "As I said, Marina is pretty, rich and well-connected. Her marrying you would wipe away any stain on your reputation."

Johan snorted, rudely. "She wouldn't have wanted me when I was powerless."

"No," Elaine agreed, flatly. "She wouldn't."

"But her father and mine could have pushed us into it," Johan said. He looked down at the book. "It says that it is perfectly acceptable for the parents to arrange marriages for their children."

"As long as they pick well," Elaine reminded him. "And there is no good reason to believe that you and Marina would not mesh well together."

Except in bed, Johan thought. He wasn't stupid enough to say that out loud.

"Tell me," Johan said. "Apart from being formally disinherited, is there anything else I would risk by having myself adopted?"

"You would be better off apprenticing yourself," Elaine pointed out. She ticked off points on her finger. "You would not be part of your family; Charity and the rest of your siblings would be strangers to you. You would not be part of your family's patronage network; indeed, you could expect the family's network to work against you. Anything you think you own that is actually owned by your family would go back to them."

She took a breath. "Your family would not provide any support when you actually *did* choose to marry, nor would they support you when someone proposes that you are too dangerous to be allowed to live. You could not return to your family, no matter what happens. And you could not bear the family name."

Elaine looked up at him, her illusionary brown eyes meeting his. "You would separate yourself completely," she concluded. "The ties that bind would snap."

"Sounds perfect," Johan said.

"You might also end up in hot water," Elaine added. "For a start, you would disrupt House Conidian's line of succession. You could be sued on such grounds and I have no idea which way the case would go. Justice would not get a look-in when one side is a powerful patron and the other is a single young magician, no matter how remarkable. You might find yourself indentured to your own father. Except he wouldn't be your father, because you snapped the ties that bind you together.

"And then you might be in the same position with your new family ..."

Johan held up a hand. "My head hurts," he said. "Can I sleep on it?"

Elaine smiled. "If you like," she said. "But my *very* strong advice would be to go for the apprenticeship instead. It would force your father to loosen his grip on you, while not breaking *all* the ties you have with him."

"I understand," Johan said, standing upright. Outside, the rain was still pouring down from high overhead. "And thank you."

He walked into his bedroom, undressed and went to bed, dozing off to the sound of raindrops beating against the roof. In truth, he thought, he really *didn't* want to be part of the family any longer. But he needed an adopted family, at least until he was twenty-one. Somehow, he doubted his father would leave him alone long enough for him to secede from the family on his own. No, there would be an offer of becoming the Prime Heir ... and pressure to marry, and whatever else his father could devise to control him.

Being Elaine's apprentice would be better than enduring his father, he was sure. But it was still *limiting*. Elaine wasn't adventurous enough to leave the Golden City permanently and explore the world ... if, of course, she *could* leave the city permanently. Given her nature, it was possible that the Grand Sorceress would object to Elaine abandoning her post.

He scowled and went to sleep. His dreams were full of fire ...

And then he was awoken by a thunderous crash.

Chapter Twenty-Nine

Elaine had been half-asleep when she heard the explosion.

For a long moment, she wasn't quite sure whether she were dreaming or not. Few of her dreams had been pleasant since she'd picked up a pair of bright red eyes. But as she jerked awake, she heard another explosion, followed rapidly by a pulse of magic that shocked the last remnants of sleep out of her system. She grabbed her wand and sat upright, unsure of what was going on. Had Johan started to experiment with magic inside the cabin despite her orders?

She pulled herself out of bed and ran into the main room. Johan's room was quiet, seemingly undisturbed; the wards reported that he was still inside, half-asleep. Elaine stared at the closed door, then sensed another pulse of magic. Now she was awake, it was easier to tell that it came from outside the cabin. Running to the window, she looked out and saw a fireball rising into the air from the direction of the city. The smoke drifting into the sky suggested that the city was under attack.

Johan's door crashed open and he stumbled out, one hand raised in a gesture that suggested that he was about to start casting spells. Elaine turned and smiled when she saw it, the Peerless School tried to teach students not to telegraph their attacks like that, but teenagers – boys in particular – thought that it was an intimidating pose, But in Johan's case it was largely worthless. Gestures didn't seem to mean anything to his power.

"What ..." He stopped as he saw the fireball. "What's going on?"

"I don't know," Elaine said, grimly. "Did you sense the magic?"

Another ripple raced through the ether, followed rapidly by another fireball and explosion in the distance. Elaine gritted her teeth as Johan shook his head; he might not be able to sense the sudden shifts in the magical field, but *she* could. Someone was unleashing powerful magic in the heart of the city, magic powerful enough to do real damage. Part of her wanted to stay in the cabin and hide, part of her knew that it was her duty to assist the forces of law and order. And besides, she needed to know what was going on.

"Get dressed," she ordered, shortly. Getting down to the city would take at least an hour, if they were lucky and their neighbours agreed to allow them to borrow their horses. If not, the walk would take much longer. "We have to go down there."

She walked back into her room, pulled off her nightclothes and donned a pair of heavy trousers and a shirt. Her wand went into the belt, followed by a handful of potion vials she thought might come in handy. There were no weapons, apart from her wand; even if she could take the weapons the Inquisitors had stored in the cabin, she wouldn't have known how to use them. Johan's father, like most other aristocrats, had never felt the urge to teach his children how to use edged weapons. Magicians settled their disputes through magic and it was a poor magician who could be killed by a thug with a sword.

He should have taught Johan, Elaine thought, as she walked back into the main room. Johan, irritatingly, had already dressed himself; he carried a makeshift staff in one hand, as if he intended to use it as a club. *And I should have asked Dread for lessons myself.*

"Come on," she said, taking a pair of ration bars from the cupboard. "We'll eat on the way."

There was an unpleasant scent in the air, she discovered, as they hurried down the path to the road and then started walking towards their nearest neighbour. Magic danced through the air, sparkling uncomfortably whenever it encountered a shimmer of natural magic in the region. Elaine felt her hairs trying to stand on end and scowled, unable to escape the feeling that something was crawling over her body. The sheer level of magic unleashed in the city below was impressive – and terrifying. What was in Falconine City worthy of such attention?

Their closest neighbour was a small farm, probably the

owner of the flock of free-ranging sheep that had woken them on their first day. Elaine tapped on the door, then smiled at the young girl who opened it. She didn't *look* to be a werewolf, but not every werewolf had the canine features many shared. Pushing the thought aside, Elaine asked the girl to call her father. Moments later, a middle-aged man stamped out of a backroom and glared at them.

"We need to borrow your horses," she said, without preamble. "We can pay."

The man's glare only intensified. "How do we know that you will return them?"

Elaine could have pointed out that she was a Privy Councillor, but she doubted that he would believe her. Instead, she reached into her pocket and produced a handful of gold coins, enough to buy a dozen new horses. The man's eyes went wide, then he nodded and scooped up the coins. It was more money, Elaine realised to her annoyance, than he'd seen for his entire life.

"I'll take you down myself," he said, his glare fading away. "But I won't take you beyond the edge of the city."

"Understood," Elaine said, looking back towards the smoke rising up in the distance. "But get us there as quickly as you can."

The ride in the cart was worse, she decided moments later, than riding in the Inquisitor's carriage. In the carriage, she hadn't seen much of the outside world; in the cart, she could see the trees and cliffs all too clearly. The man whipped the horses into a frenzy and sent them running down the road, skimming the edge far too close for comfort. By the time they reached the bottom of the mountains, Elaine would have welcomed a fight with a Dark Wizard instead of another ride in the cart. Johan, irritatingly, seemed to have enjoyed the ride.

They passed hundreds of refugees as they headed down the road towards the city. Elaine looked at them, tempted to ask what they'd seen, but she knew it would be futile. There were still flames rising up from the centre of town; she scowled as the driver pulled to a halt, right on the edge of the city. If he could take them closer ...

"Thank you," she said testily, as she climbed down from

the cart. Johan jumped down beside her, looking rather pleased with himself. "And I hope you have fun with the money."

She couldn't sense any further twists in the magic field as they ran into the city, but as they drew closer to the flames they started to see dead bodies. Elaine stopped next to a young male body and cast a quick diagnostic charm, trying to find out what had killed him. The results were inconclusive, but it looked like he'd simply found himself unable to breathe. It looked bizarre for a long moment, until she realised that someone was using transfiguration as an area-effect weapon. Removing the oxygen from the air by transfiguring it into something else would take a vast amount of power – and it wouldn't last more than a few minutes, even for the most powerful of sorcerers – but it would kill everyone in the area while it lasted.

"If you find that you're having difficulty breathing," Elaine muttered to Johan, "run back the way you came."

There was no sign of whatever sorcerer had caused the devastation – Elaine hoped that meant that the Inquisitors had killed him – but the flames he'd unleashed were still burning their way through the town. Elaine swore inwardly as she recognised the odd reddish tint of the flames that marked them out as Hellfire, a magical fire that burned almost everything. The only way to quench it was to use the correct counter-spell and, judging by the fact that the flames were still spreading, the counter-spell was not easy to guess. She drew her wand and cast a standard cancelling charm anyway, just in case, but nothing happened.

"They'll destroy the entire city," she snapped, feeling the heat starting to press against her. It took a brave or foolish sorcerer to unleash Hellfire, if only because it was so hard to stop. "What was here that they hated so much?"

The thought puzzled her. Falconine City wasn't a great city; it was hardly the capital of an important kingdom, let alone the Empire. Attacking it made absolutely no sense at all, unless the objective had been random devastation, mass slaughter and terrorism. With Dark Wizards involved, it was quite possible that the attack *had* been random. And yet most of the devastation seemed to be concentrated in one place.

Johan caught her arm. "Up there," he snapped. "Look!"

Elaine turned and swore. The flames were licking around the lower levels of a five-story building ... and there were children on the top floor, screaming desperately for help. It was easy to tell that there was no way for them to get down; the Hellfire had the lower part of the building firmly in its grip. It wouldn't be long before it collapsed completely, throwing the children into the flames. She cast another counter-spell, but nothing happened; it would take hours to go through every counter-spell she knew and hitting the right one would be a matter of luck instead of judgement. Instead ...

"Stay back," she ordered. "I'm going to try to levitate the kids out."

Sweat poured down her back as she raised her wand, chanting the spell. Levitating was not her strongest subject at the best of times, particularly when she couldn't cast spells to reduce the weight of the object she was trying to levitate. A young girl let out a panicked scream as Elaine's magic caught her, hefting her up into the air and pulling her out over the fire and towards safety. The flames seemed to reach up towards her kicking legs – for a moment, Elaine almost believed the old superstition about Hellfire being alive and malicious – and then she was safe. Elaine sagged, then gritted her teeth and turned back to the next child, wondering how long her strength would hold out ...

... And where *was* everyone else? Where were the damn Inquisitors?

She almost collapsed when she put the third child on the ground, but somehow she managed to raise her wand and cast the spells to lift up the fourth child. Johan was pacing forwards and backwards beside her, clearly unsure of what to do; Elaine could only be grateful that he hadn't tried to help levitate the children. It was far too likely that his magic would go wrong and the children would be hurt ... she swore as she heard a creaking sound from inside the building and realised that the supports were about to collapse. Once they were gone, the entire building would tumble into the flames.

"I can't hold it," she gasped, barely able to breathe. For a terrible moment, she thought that the Dark Wizard had sucked all the air out of the area again. "It's not going to ..."

Johan stepped forward, clearly trying something. For a long moment, it seemed to work; the building still stood upright, despite its crumbling supports. But then there was a terrifying creaking sound and the entire side of the building fell into the flames. Elaine realised, to her horror, that he'd only made the situation worse. His magic had held up the supports at the cost of weakening the floors ...

Panic flared through her mind. "Stop that," she screamed. Up above, the children were screaming too as the flames licked at their feet. Hellfire would burn flesh, leaving them to die in horrific agony. There was a crash as one of the lower floors fell in, blowing flames and debris towards them. "Stop it now!"

Johan turned to face her. "I'm trying to help," he shouted back at her over the roar of the blaze. "I'm trying ..."

The building toppled inwards. Elaine saw the children, wrapped in flames, as they fell to their deaths. The fire seemed to roar in triumph as their screams cut off with a terrible sudden finality. She cast a sensing spell, but there was nothing apart from the fire. They were gone.

The gods take them, she thought, grimly.

"Don't try to help," she snapped, out loud. "Just ..."

Johan stared at her as if she'd slapped him, then stalked off. Elaine watched him go, too tired to care much, then turned back to the blaze. Counter-spell after counter-spell rose up in her mind and she cast them one by one, praying that she would find the right one eventually. A normal magician wouldn't know all of the spells ... all of the *known* spells, she corrected herself. Most magicians didn't bother to actually create spells for themselves – why would they bother when there were spells for all eventualities written down in grimoires? – but Dark Wizards loved the thought of creating spells that other magicians wouldn't be able to stop easily.

If you're actually casting the spells properly, she thought, grimly. The drain on her magic was so strong that she was honestly not sure if the spells were actually working. If they weren't, she might have missed the right spell and she would never know it. But she had to keep trying ...

It took nearly forty spells before the flames started to fade away as the magic powering them snapped. Elaine let out a sigh of relief and started casting the spell again and again, jabbing her wand towards the fires. The flames kept collapsing in on themselves and vanishing, although it didn't always help. They'd created enough heat to start mundane fires that would continue to spread chaos until they were put out.

She looked up as she saw steams of water hissing through the air and splashing down into the fires. A pair of male magicians, both seemingly much older than Elaine, were pulling the water out of the nearby river and using it as a makeshift fire hose. Elaine took a moment to admire their easy skill, then staggered over to face them. They weren't wearing robes or cloaks, but she would have bet good money that they weren't Inquisitors. For one thing, they seemed too old and doddering.

But that doesn't mean anything, she reminded herself. Age mattered not when magic was concerned, at least unless the magician went senile. *They might still be very dangerous.*

"Thank you," she said. She briefly outlined the counter-spell she'd used, then asked the question that had been bothering her since she'd heard the first explosion. "What happened here?"

"There was an attack," the first magician said. "A Dark Wizard."

"Came into the city," the second said, finishing the first one's sentence. They were life partners, Elaine realised, although she wasn't sure if it was sexual or not. At their age, it was hard to think that it mattered. "Attacked the factory, ripped it apart."

"Inquisitors tried to stop him," the first added. "Tore them apart, he did. Killed at least two, we think. Maybe more."

"Maybe much more," the second clarified. "Ignored us, of course. Too old for him."

Elaine scowled. "Why here?"

The first magician eyed her in surprise. "You don't know?"

"She doesn't know," the second magician confirmed. "She doesn't know what was born here."

"We do," the first magician said.

Elaine rubbed her forehead. Maybe it was just the intense drain on her magic, but her patience was on the edge of snapping. It was harder to get a straight answer out of the two ancient magicians than it was to get one out of students who weren't quite sure what book they were looking for, merely that it had something to do with potion ingredients, or something like that, but they were sure that the librarian could still find it for them.

"And what," she said, as calmly as she could, "was born here?"

"Iron Dragons," the second magician said. "The inventor made the first ones here; his heirs started to actually *sell* them. Their factories were right at the centre of the attack."

"Destroyed, of course," the first magician put in. "Ripped apart, along with all the workers."

"Very tragic," the second magician said.

"Keep putting out the fires," Elaine said. She heard someone barking orders in the distance and sighed in relief when she realised that it was an Inquisitor. "I'll do what I can to help."

The Inquisitor was wounded, but seemed unwilling to lie down and let others do the hard work. Elaine followed his orders, helping with the wounded even though most of her magic was gone and would take time to recover. As work parties were organised, the wounded were taken to makeshift hospitals and the dead bodies were stacked like wood in a park, where they would have to wait until they could be cremated. Somehow, Elaine knew that most of the dead would remain unaccounted for. The Hellfire would have burned them to dust and ash, leaving little behind.

Most of the mundanes – and even a handful of magicians – seemed stunned. None of them had seen sorcery on such a scale, even though they'd heard rumours from the Golden City. Elaine listened, without saying much, as the work parties chattered amongst themselves, trying to understand what had happened. The general theory seemed to be that a magician had been mortally offended by the Iron Dragons and other non-magical technology, a theory that Elaine suspected was actually accurate. If random terrorism had been the objective, surely much more damage could have been done.

As it was, the damage was localised, she thought, grimly. *The bastard wanted us to know what he was destroying. There could be no mistake.*

It was nearly forty minutes of backbreaking labour before she realised that she had lost track of Johan.

Chapter Thirty

Johan cursed his own mistake as he stumbled away from Elaine, unable to quite believe the scale of the disaster he'd caused. Jamal, for all of his faults, had never killed children; indeed, despite his boasts, Johan was sure that he had never killed *anyone* before the Leveller rally. Duelling at the Peerless School was heavily regulated and it was unlikely that any of the duels would be fought to the death. But Johan had killed ...

The screams of the dying children echoed in his head, mocking his failure. He hadn't been able to do nothing, yet all he'd done was help the fire bring down the building, killing the children before Elaine could save them. He should have tried to levitate them instead, despite his fears of accidentally hurting or scaring them; they would still be alive today if he hadn't failed them. Elaine had tried to save them, despite her limited power; *he* had killed them. It seemed impossible to avoid the guilt coursing though his mind. The kids had died and it was his fault.

He stumbled onwards, remembering the look of pure rage in Elaine's eyes. He'd failed her too, failed the girl who was his first true friend – who might no longer be his friend now that she'd seen him murder children. She had taken good care of him, helped him to learn how to use the magic he'd been gifted with ... and, in return, she'd watched helplessly as he butchered children right in front of her eyes. He could have put out the flames – surely, his magic would have sufficed for that – but no, he'd had to show off. And the results had been disastrous.

I don't deserve magic, he told himself, realising – finally – why the gods had denied him their power. Jamal wouldn't have killed children; Charity would have been horrified at the mere thought. But Johan had killed ... and through not thinking about what he was doing, instead of genuine malice.

It was no consolation to know that it had been an accident. He'd murdered the children as surely as if he'd strangled them all with his bare hands.

I should have stayed a Powerless, he thought. *I might have been a prisoner, but I wasn't a murderer.*

He stopped, looking around at the devastation. The houses seemed intact, but windows had shattered and several doors had been blown inwards. He couldn't tell if it had been random fire or the magicians breaking into homes, but it looked terrifying. The Golden City had been rebuilt with astonishing speed – and the Blight had been developed – after the incident that had marred the appointment of the Grand Sorceress; it was impossible to tell if someone would do the same for Falconine City. Maybe the ruined houses would be abandoned, left as a silent testimonial to the power of whoever had attacked the city.

A faint sound caught his ear and he stopped, trying to listen. Someone was crying ... Johan hesitated, then headed towards the house where the noise was coming from. The door had been blown open, leaving a pile of splinters on the floor just inside the house; the walls had been scorched with balefire, charring their surfaces. Johan paused at the door – the credo that one did not enter another person's house without an invitation was strong, even though it was clearly not a magician's house – and then stepped inside. The sound seemed to be coming from the kitchen.

"Um ... hi," he called, as he stepped into the room. "Where are you?"

A table had been shattered, several chairs seemed to have been smashed against the walls ... and a pair of dead bodies were lying on the ground. A young girl, barely more than three or four years old, was beating desperately at her dead mother while crying. Johan took one look and knew that the mother was far beyond saving. Her neck seemed intact, but it was bent at an angle that meant that it had been snapped. No magic, according to Elaine, could bring back the dead.

He stared at the girl, then reached out a hand. She shrank back from his touch, cuddling her dead mother as if she could still help her. The sight made everything suddenly *real* to Johan and he felt his stomach heave. He turned away, just in time to throw up everything he had in the corner. The girl stared at him, no longer crying, as he retched. Somehow, he managed to retain the presence of mind to find a bottle of water and take a gulp, enough to wash the taste out of his mouth.

"Come on," he said, reaching for the girl and picking her up. She felt light; none of *his* sisters had ever felt so light, but then he'd been younger when they'd been toddlers. "Let's see if we can find someone to help you."

He glanced into one of the other rooms and frowned. The devastation seemed much less focused in that room; a handful of pictures had been left on the walls. They all showed Iron Dragons, steaming madly as they made their way across the landscape. Johan felt an odd twinge of nostalgia – maybe he could run away and get a job on the tracks, well away from magic and magicians – which he pushed aside as the girl squirmed in his arms. Wearily, he carried her out of the building and looked around.

"So," he said, to the girl. "Where can I take you?"

The girl eyed him, then burst into tears again. Johan patted her back awkwardly, looking around for someone – anyone – who might be able to offer advice. He saw no one until he looked at the house on the other side of the road, where someone was peering out nervously behind a curtain. Johan lifted his free hand and waved, then smiled in relief as the door opened, revealing a middle-aged woman.

"Daisy," she said, looking at the girl in Johan's arms. "What are you doing out here?"

"Her parents are dead," Johan said, bluntly. The woman gave him an icy look, as if she hated to hear the word – or, more likely, didn't want him saying them in front of Daisy. "Where can I take her?"

"I'll take her, for now," the woman said. "What ... what happened?"

Johan frowned. "What did you see?"

"There were explosions and flames and ... I hid," the woman confessed. "I thought that we were all going to die."

Johan passed her Daisy, then stepped backwards. "Some of the houses were targeted specifically," he said, softly. Elaine might dismiss thrillers such as *The Great Inquisitor* as trashy fiction, but Jamal had enjoyed reading them – and Johan had borrowed his books, once or twice. The fact he hadn't bothered to ask permission first was only a minor detail in his opinion, at least at the time. "What did they all have in common?"

The woman looked up and down the street. "They all worked on the Iron Dragons," she said, finally. "Daisy's father was a foreman at the factory."

Johan nodded and walked away, leaving the woman to close her door and pray to all the gods that whoever was responsible for the devastation didn't come back. Part of Johan wanted to walk back to Elaine and beg her forgiveness, part of him knew that he could never look her in the eye again. He had killed children!

Guilt was not an emotion familiar to Johan. He'd certainly been ashamed that he couldn't live up to his father's expectations, but he'd never felt guilt for any of the attempts he'd made to pay Jamal back for the way he treated Johan. Besides, they were all minor pranks, nothing too onerous for a powerful magician to face. What did hiding an insect in someone's bed compare to turning someone into a pig for a day or two? But this was different. He would sooner have gone back to Jamal and offered to serve as his test subject, than kill children.

He fought down the urge to cry as he looked around. This part of the city seemed intact, but deserted; everyone was either hiding inside their homes or had fled to the mountains. Johan sat down on a rock in the middle of a crossroads and put his head in his hands. After the news reached the Golden City, they'd be demanding that he be hunted down like a dog. His father would probably lead the charge, frantic to wipe the stain of Johan's existence off the family name. The thought made him laugh, laughter that broke down into sobs. He'd wanted to be free of his family, but not like this.

In the end, not being able to go back made the decision easier.

Elaine had insisted that he carry a notebook and pencil around with him at all times, claiming that it would allow him to note down his ideas whenever he had them. Johan had thought that she was mocking him at the time, but he'd obeyed. Now, he pulled the pencil out of his pocket and placed it on his hand, holding it up in front of his face. Tracking spells were complex, particularly when the caster didn't know the person he was trying to track, but Johan knew that his magic was ... unprecedented. Maybe, just maybe, he could track down the person responsible for the devastation. If it cost him his life ...

... It was no more than he deserved.

And he wanted to prove himself. How better to do that than defeating a Dark Wizard.

"All right," he muttered, addressing the pencil. "Point me to the person responsible for this."

He closed his eyes, concentrating. When he opened them, the pencil was floating just above his hand and pointing to the south, towards the Golden City. There was nothing to show how *far* away the Dark Wizard was, but at least he had a direction. Johan smiled darkly and pulled himself to his feet, following the pencil as it led him out of town. If nothing else, he told himself, the Dark Wizard was in for one hell of a surprise.

***

"It was Hawthorne," the Inquisitor said. "The witnesses said that he just appeared in the middle of the factory and started throwing magic around."

Elaine shook her head, angrily. Right now, she didn't care about Hawthorne, no matter how dangerous he was. She cared about Johan. And Johan seemed to have vanished. Where had he gone?

Her imagination provided too many possibilities, all of them bad. If she hadn't lost her temper with him, he would have stayed with her. Instead ... Johan had fled her anger, determined never to return; Johan had been killed in the chaos or even committed suicide; Johan had been kidnapped by someone determined to duplicate his powers ... but, in the end, the precise details didn't matter. She had to find him before matters grew even further out of hand.

"There are too many missing people here," the Inquisitor reminded her. "I don't have the manpower to spare for a search."

Elaine gritted her teeth. She knew he was right. No one apart from Light Spinner and the Inquisitors themselves knew how many Inquisitors there actually were, but the Inquisition had taken a serious blow when Kane had devastated the Golden City. They simply didn't have the numbers to cope with all of their responsibilities. Right now, the surviving Inquisitors had to track down Hawthorne before he could do something worse, not help her find a missing boy. But the boy was vitally important.

"Thank you," she said, tartly. It wasn't fair of her to lash out, but she couldn't help herself. If she hadn't been so angry with him ... maybe he would not have run off. As it was, she couldn't see him anywhere. It wasn't like Johan *not* to try to help, which meant ...

Her blood ran cold. Johan wanted to prove himself. What was to stop him going after the Dark Wizard himself?

He wouldn't be that stupid, would he? Elaine asked herself. The thought was terrifying. An *Inquisitor* would hesitate to go after a Dark Wizard alone, no matter how powerful and skilled he was. Dark Wizards tended to have questionable grips on sanity, which gave them warped powers and a complete lack of scruples. But Johan was brave and determined to prove himself ... and, perhaps, blamed himself for the disaster.

He's a teenage boy, she told herself, angrily. *No teenage boy is ever stable*.

She turned back to look at the Inquisitor. "Do you have *any* idea where Hawthorne might be hiding?"

"No," the Inquisitor said, shortly. "We didn't even realise he was in the city until the attack began."

"Thank you," Elaine said.

She turned and walked rapidly towards the communications office. Crystal balls and other methods of sending messages instantly would cost money – she fumbled in her pocket to make sure that she had enough – but she needed to provide Light Spinner with an urgent report from the city. Post would take at least two days to reach the Golden City. She had the feeling that the Iron Dragons were going to be busy bringing in disaster relief supplies from all over the Empire.

The office was closed, but she saw one staff member cowering behind the desk. It wasn't a very good job of hiding, she noted, as she drew her wand; she could see him even when he stayed still. Tapping her wand against the door, she unlocked it and stepped inside, then lowered her wand in the hopes that she wouldn't look *too* threatening. The thought made her smile, ruefully. If there was one thing she *didn't* look, it was threatening. Very few people were scared of her.

"We're closed," a quavering voice said. "Come back tomorrow."

Elaine had to bite her lip to keep from snickering. "I need to establish a link to the Golden City, now," she said. She reached into her pocket and produced a handful of gold coins. "This is enough to pay for it, isn't it?"

The staffer stared at her, nervously. "I ... we're closed," he protested. "I ..."

What would Dread do? Elaine asked herself. The answer was obvious; he would bulldoze his way through any objections until he got what he wanted. But Dread was a trained Inquisitor, with a voice that could compel obedience from even the most hardened of criminals. He'd once told her that using the right tone was more effective than any charm. But Elaine didn't quite have the nerve ...

She put the coins on the table. "I would take it as a *personal* favour," she said, quietly. "Call the remainder of the coins your tip."

The young man staggered to his feet. "I can't," he said. For a moment, Elaine was surprised; a civil servant refusing a bribe? *That* was as unprecedented as Johan's powers. "The balls have been smashed."

Elaine blinked in surprise. "Someone has smashed your balls?"

"They shattered, just before the first big explosions began," the young man said. "I ... I can't put them back together."

"No, I suppose you can't," Elaine said. She searched her mind for options. "Do you have any inactive spares?"

The young man shook his head. Elaine glared down at the table, cursing under her breath. Crystal balls were fantastically complex pieces of art, each one produced by a trained enchanter; she knew the spells to make them work, but she couldn't hope to put one together herself, certainly not from destroyed balls. But what had happened to them? Had the first pulse she'd sensed disabled them or had someone managed to work out a spell to take them out? If so ... the results could be disastrous.

Magic communications held the Empire together. Light Spinner would hear, instantly, of a revolt on the other side of the world and be able to take corrective measures. Without magic, it would take months to get word from one side of the Empire to the other. If the network shattered, the Empire would shatter with it. At the very least, it would take years to put the network back together again.

And chaos suits the Witch-King, she thought. It would make it far harder for Light Spinner and her few allies who knew about the Witch-King to track him down if the Empire was coming apart around them. All of a sudden, she felt torn; she wanted to go after Johan, but at the same time she knew that she had to warn Light Spinner. They needed to put contingency plans in place for dealing with a mass communications breakdown.

"Right," she said, trying to sound like Dread. The look on the clerk's face suggested that he was not entirely convinced. "What other options are there?"

The clerk swallowed. "You can hire a horseman to carry dispatches, or you can put them on the Iron Dragon and have them taken to the city ..."

Elaine passed him twenty gold coins. "I am going to write a letter," she said. "You are going to take it to the Golden City, right to the Palace. I strongly advise you" – she tapped her wand meaningfully – "not to try to *open* the letter. The results would be unpleasant."

The clerk stared at the money, his eyes going wide. Like the farmer, it was probably more money than he'd ever seen in his life.

"I will," he said. He coughed. "I mean, I won't open the letter."

Elaine smiled. "Good," she said.

She picked up a piece of paper and an envelope, then scribbled out a quick explanation. Light Spinner – and Dread

– could extrapolate the rest, she suspected. The magic pulses she'd sensed might well have reached the Golden City. She sealed the letter, tapped it with her wand to make sure that no one could open it apart from the intended recipient, and passed it to him.

Once he took the letter – and the coins – Elaine strode out of the door. Whatever else happened, she had to track Johan down. The gods alone knew what he thought he was doing.

Chapter Thirty-One

Urgent summons to the Privy Council are becoming more common, Duncan thought, as he followed the others into the meeting room. One of his predecessors – who hadn't kept his seat under Light Spinner – had told him that the last Grand Sorcerer had summoned his council as rarely as possible, but then he'd been Grand Sorcerer long enough for everyone to have got into the habit of obedience. Light Spinner was just beginning her reign. Maybe, just maybe, some of her councillors believed that they could wrestle power from her while she was still finding her feet.

Of the twelve councillors, two seemed to be missing. The Head Librarian was away somewhere with Johan – Duncan's spies had been unable to locate either of them – but Lady Lakeside seemed to have absented herself too. Duncan puzzled over her absence, then looked over at Deferens and knew the answer. Lady Lakeside might not be willing to vote to liberate Jamal and the other terrorists, but if she wasn't there she couldn't vote *against* it.

Politics, Duncan thought, rolling his eyes as he took his seat. But politics had taken his family far and would take it still further, if they kept working away at it. Who knew? Jamal's child might even have a chance to become Grand Sorcerer. *We need politics to live and rule. That doesn't mean I have to like it.*

"As of now," Light Spinner said, without bothering with the formalities, "the murderer of Graham of House Arndell remains unknown. The Inquisitors have followed up every possible lead – they were far from *gentle* – but none of those they interrogated knew who was responsible for the killing. Nor have we been able to identify the magician or magicians who assisted them."

The table seemed to shiver with indignation. It was fiendishly difficult for a non-magician to escape magicians who were hunting him, at least without magical assistance of his own. The Privy Council would vote to hang the killer, when they caught him, but they would want the magician who had aided him tortured to death slowly and painfully. How *could* he turn against his own kind?

Money, probably, Duncan thought, ruefully. In his experience, principles only lasted so long; everyone had their price. A few thousand gold coins would tempt a magician to do anything, even kill a fellow magician. Or maybe there had been a grudge against House Arndell that had nothing to do with the young idiot currently locked up in the Watchtower. As far as he knew, the Inquisitors weren't following up *that* angle of approach. But it wasn't something he could mention at the table. The gods knew who that would offend.

"So we have a mundane who has killed a magician and got away with it," Deferens said, into the silence. "I fear that the Levellers are already moving on to the next stage of their campaign."

"There is no proof that the Levellers were behind the murder," Light Spinner pointed out, a hint of exasperation clear in her tone. "All of their leaders were interrogated, *thoroughly*. If one of them carried out the murder, they never informed their senior leadership."

"So we go through them all, one by one," Deferens said. "And then we send them all off to a penal colony somewhere, if they are no good as slaves."

Light Spinner's face was invisible, but Duncan was sure that he detected more than just irritation in the way she carried herself. Lady Lakeside would have argued with Deferens; Light Spinner couldn't, not without compromising her dignity. And, as perception was almost as important as reality, compromising her dignity would also compromise her position.

"That is not the issue here," Light Spinner said, finally. "There has been a petition" – she looked at Duncan – "filed for the release of Jamal Conidian and the other terrorists held within the Watchtower. We are, in fact, obliged to try them now."

"I move to dismiss all charges," Deferens said, quickly.

"Let them be released at once."

"Seconded," Lord Ahlstrom said. "We need such young men to maintain our society."

Light Spinner was unmoving for a long second – probably, Duncan reflected, regretting the absence of magicians who could present the opposing point of view. Lady Lakeside would not have agreed to let them go free without a fight; whatever Deferens had offered her to secure her absence, he decided, had been well worth it. And then there was the missing Head Librarian ... but as long as nine seats were filled, they had a quorum. They could vote ...

"The charges against them are serious," Lord Falcate said, flatly. He was known for being tough on everyone, including himself. "We should not just release them without some form of ... punishment. Maybe they should be publicly whipped."

"They are not mundanes," Duncan said, sharply. Public floggings were common for mundane criminals, particularly the ones not worth the effort of jailing or enslaving, but magicians were spared such indignities. "To have them whipped in public would suggest that we were desperate to prove that we took their crimes seriously."

"We *do* take their crimes seriously," Lord Falcate snapped. "They are responsible for the death of nineteen mundanes, vast amounts of pain and suffering and the appearance of a whole new kind of magician. Punishment is clearly indicated."

"For punishing mundanes who dared to suggest that our society be upended," Deferens reminded him, smoothly. "Do we really, after the death of young Graham, wish to buy the support of the mob?"

Duncan settled backwards, preparing himself. He suspected that six or seven of the ten Privy Councillors would definitely vote to free them, particularly if he proposed his compromise. The others ... might join them or abstain. Apart from Lord Falcate, there weren't any others who might vote against. That would leave Light Spinner effectively isolated at the table. If she vetoed their decision, she would face the combined opposition of the entire council.

He tapped the table as the argument grew louder. "I wish

to propose a compromise," he said, softly. "The prisoners come from good families, of decent stock."

There were nods, although he knew that some of them would definitely consider *his* family to be of lower stock than families who had spent their entire existence in the Golden City. But they would listen long enough to let him make his point.

"Let the families take responsibility for them," he said. "Whatever else can be said of my son, he has disgraced the family name. I will ensure that he cleans up his behaviour or goes straight back to the Watchtower. The families who wish their sons back can swear an oath to ensure that they no longer commit such crimes."

"But we may *require* them to commit such crimes," Deferens pointed out, as planned. "Who knows what the Levellers will do next?"

"There are ways to deal with the Levellers that do not require torture and humiliation," Lord Falcate said. "Let the oaths be such that those who break them will suffer terribly."

"I was going to propose that they no longer used magic on mundanes unless engaged in direct self-defence," Duncan said. "Such an oath would be sufficiently binding, without making it impossible to do their studies."

"So it would seem," Lord Falcate said. "But oaths have been broken before."

"The *prisoners* can swear oaths too," Light Spinner said. "Let them be enchained by oaths sworn on their magic."

Duncan winced. He had wanted to spare Jamal that, but Deferens had told him that it was unlikely that it could be avoided. An oath on his part was one thing; Jamal, if he remained Prime Heir, should be as unencumbered by oaths as possible. But there was no way to avoid it.

And it won't stop him from using magic altogether, he reminded himself. *It will just keep him out of trouble.*

"Agreed," he said.

"The oaths must be written carefully," Lord Falcate said, crossly. "Very carefully."

Light Spinner nodded. "All in favour?"

Eight hands rose into the air. Lord Falcate and Lady Erving had both abstained. Or perhaps they wanted to vote against ... not that it would matter. Eight votes was enough to force the issue, even against the Grand Sorceress.

"This is not a pardon," Light Spinner said, quietly. She knew it too. "This is not forgiveness, nor shall we forget what they did. If they act badly again, they will go back to the Watchtower, even if they don't break their oaths openly."

And if they do, Duncan thought, *it will kill them.*

He was torn between relief and fear for his eldest son as he walked up to the Watchtower, accompanied by Deferens. The younger man kept smirking, but said nothing, not even trying to demand a price for his help. Duncan was sure that there *would* be a price, sooner or later, yet he was too relieved to care. Maybe Deferens had his eye on the Grand Sorceress's position. It was against protocol to try to unseat one directly, but Deferens was ambitious enough to try.

The Inquisitors seemed to be out in force, he noted, as they entered the Watchtower and were shown into a single small room. They eyed the newcomers suspiciously, watching them as they waited for Jamal and his guards. Duncan almost felt his heart break when Jamal finally shuffled in, heavy iron chains attached to his feet and nasty-looking handcuffs binding his hands behind his back. Only a handful of magicians could cast spells while bound by iron, for reasons that escaped him; oddly, he found himself wondering if *Johan* could cast such spells. Duncan knew that *he* certainly couldn't.

"This is the text of an oath," an Inquisitor said. She was young, surprisingly so, with long blonde hair that dangled out of her hood. Definitely pretty enough to attract his attention ... but if she was an Inquisitor, she would be far too dangerous for him to toy with. "You will swear it upon your magic or you will not be allowed to leave the Watchtower. Do you understand the oath?"

She held the piece of paper up in front of Jamal's eyes. *Someone* had clearly been in touch from the palace; the oath was simple, direct, and covered all the points that had been discussed in the meeting. The charms on the parchment, he sensed, would provide a gentle reminder at first, followed by something more lethal. At worst, he knew, direct deliberate disobedience would mean death.

Forcing a magician to swear an oath was insulting, a cause for a duel. Every so often, someone suggested using oaths to bind the magic of newcomers to the Peerless School; equally often, such oaths were rejected. Magic was the gift of the gods; it was not for humans to bind ... or so he had been told. The real reason, he suspected, was that magicians simply didn't like bowing to authority, even their own.

"I understand," Jamal said, weakly.

The Inquisitor scowled. Somehow, she still managed to look beautiful. "And will you swear?"

Jamal bowed his head. "I will," he said. The Inquisitors unlocked the cuffs, allowing him to take the piece of paper in his hand. "I, Jamal of House Conidian, swear that I will not use my magic on mundanes except in direct self-defence. So it shall be."

The magic field altered, slightly, as the oath shimmered into existence. Jamal was bound now, by a force that was woven into his very soul. If he broke the oath, Duncan knew, he would die. But there was another oath that had to be sworn.

He took the piece of paper the Inquisitor offered him and scowled down at the words. Subtle magic crawled over the parchment, warning him of the dread consequences of swearing the oath. Jamal might have thought little of it, or had just been desperate to leave the Watchtower, but Duncan could not afford to be so blasé. He gathered up his resolve, forcing the words out of his mouth. It had to be done.

"I, Duncan, Patriarch of House Conidian, swear that I will take responsibility for my son, Jamal Conidian, and that I will ensure that his behaviour is free of all criminal activity," he said. "So it shall be."

The world seemed to grow dim around him for a long second as the magic took hold, binding him to his word. Duncan ground his teeth and waited for the sensation to fade. It wasn't the first oath he'd sworn, but it seemed to be harder than the one he'd sworn to always uphold the family's interests. Maybe, he told himself, as the world slowly returned to normal, it was a reflection of his doubts about Jamal. Oath or no oath, making a proper human being out of him would be a hard task.

"Very good," the Inquisitor said. Jamal was now Duncan's problem – in all ways. Failure would mean death. "You may take your son from the Watchtower."

Jamal waited until the chains were removed, then stumbled out of the room. Duncan followed him, after nodding goodbye to Deferens; the younger magician seemed inclined to stay and watch the other families as their children were released. It struck Duncan, suddenly, that Deferens had earned favours from seven other families, not just Duncan's family ... he would be very well rewarded for his work. Some of those families were among the most powerful in the city.

There were a handful of carriages waiting by the gates. Duncan motioned for Jamal to get into one, then followed him, passing the driver a coin and their address. The carriage rattled to life; Duncan tapped his lips when Jamal opened his mouth and started to speak; who knew who might be listening to their conversation? Besides, what he wanted to say could wait until they got back home.

Their family – minus Johan – met them at the door. Duncan felt his heart sink when he saw that Charity and the rest of Jamal's siblings seemed unenthusiastic about seeing him again, even after a long stay in prison. But then, it had only really been a week ... Jamal looked as though he had been in the Watchtower for months, if not years. He muttered orders to the menservants, telling them to wash Jamal, then dress him and escort him back down to Duncan's study. Jamal would not have a chance to get comfortable before Duncan laid down the law.

"Thank you," he said, when the menservants finally helped Jamal into the study. He had been washed and dressed in clean clothes, but he still looked subdued. Duncan could only hope that would last. "You may leave us."

He glared at his eldest son as Jamal slumped into a chair. "I owe you an apology," he said, simply. It was hard to keep the disgust out of his voice. "I really should have thrashed you more as a child. But I was so proud of how clever and powerful you are that I closed my eyes to a great many things. In hindsight, that was a dangerous mistake."

Jamal started, but said nothing.

"I covered for you," Duncan added. "I paid off the maids, or told everyone that they were lies. I ignored what you did to Johan and Charity and your other siblings. I told myself that they needed such treatment to help boost their powers ... well, the cost of my carelessness has been staggering. I will not be careless again.

"I have already altered the house wards," he snapped. "You will not leave without my permission. You will not use magic without my permission. You will not have your fun with the maids or anyone else. You will be kind and polite to your family, particularly Johan when he returns to us. And if you break any of those rules, the menservants I hired have my full permission to thrash you. If *that* proves too little to force you to change your ways, I will take other steps. Your status as Prime Heir hangs by a thread."

That produced a reaction. Jamal jerked upwards, staring at him.

"If Charity was a year or two older, or a boy, I would have made her Prime Heir," Duncan informed him, icily. "As it is, I cannot afford to remove you from the line of succession. Not *yet*. But if you are still unworthy of the position by the time Charity reaches the Age of Maturity, you will be removed and Charity will be Prime Heir. And I will *disinherit* you completely."

"You can't," Jamal protested. "I ..."

"The powers of a Patriarch are vast," Duncan snapped. "I cannot disinherit you if you are suitable for the position you would inherit, but it is my considered judgement that you are *not* suitable. If you do not shape up in two years, you will be removed from the family. Do you understand me?"

Jamal nodded, wordlessly.

Duncan scowled. He hated to berate his eldest son ... which, he knew now, had helped make Jamal the man he was today. He'd lost count of the number of times he'd punished the younger children, but Jamal had always been spared the worst of his fury. In hindsight, it had been a mistake. But it was one he was going to correct.

"You have done no end of damage to the family name," Duncan hissed. "I will see that corrected or you out. Go."

He pointed at the door. Jamal stared at him for a long moment, then stood up and slunk towards the door. Duncan knew better than to assume that the lesson had already sunk in, but it was a start. A few weeks of being treated like a child would hopefully make a man out of his eldest son. And if it didn't ...

Duncan sighed, reached into one of his locked drawers and pulled out the marriage contract. Once signed, Johan would be legally betrothed to Jayne. Even if the marriage was never consummated, it would make it harder for Jayne to spy on him ...if, of course, that was what she *was* doing.

And if they liked each other, he told himself, so much the better.

Chapter Thirty-Two

Johan was cursing his decision to walk within a mile, but somehow he forced himself to keep going, pushing through trees and climbing hills as he walked onwards. It had never really dawned on him, even after a week in the mountain cabin, just how far one might have to walk to catch up with someone else outside the city. The Golden City could be walked from one side to the other in less than an hour; outside the Four Peaks, the land sprawled on for hundreds of miles. Only stubborn pride kept him going – pride and a determination to show everyone what he could do. The pencil he'd charmed kept wavering slightly, but the direction never changed. It was nearly two hours before he saw the building.

It was hidden in the forest; he wouldn't have seen it at all, he realised, if he hadn't been following the pencil. It was a long low building, just like the warehouses on the edge of the Golden City; like them, it was probably larger on the inside than on the outside. He circled the structure, only to feel the pencil twisting in his hand. His target, he realised mutely, was *inside* the building. Johan hesitated, unsure of how best to proceed, then found the door. It was hanging off its hinges, as if someone had broken them to break into the building itself. Carefully, he stepped into the giant warehouse.

The interior was crammed with strange machinery, he saw, as he crept inside. None of it made any sense to him, even though he had always taken an interest in non-magical technology. One piece of machinery looked big enough to be part of an Iron Dragon, another seemed designed to be small enough to hold in one hand. A faint scent caught his nostrils and he looked around, seeing a body lying on the ground. Johan crouched down beside the body, but it was clearly far too late to save his life. The expression on his face suggested that he had died in screaming agony.

"That's the trouble with mundanes," a high-pitched voice said. "They die *so* easily."

Johan started, then looked around. The speaker was hidden behind the machinery, but his voice carried easily to where Johan was standing. There was something about the voice that chilled him to the bone, something that suggested that the speaker was more than a little insane. The pencil jerked in his hand as the Dark Wizard moved, then came into view. A chill ran down Johan's spine as he saw him for the first time.

"I am Hawthorne," the Dark Wizard said. The sneer on his face rivalled Jamal's at his worst. "Are you unhappy that your little friends are dead?"

Johan stared at him, then scowled inwardly. Hawthorne had clearly taken him for a mundane, something that was insulting .... but useful. *Let him think that*, his thoughts whispered, as he stared at Hawthorne. *It might be useful to have him underestimate you.*

Hawthorne was tall, almost painfully thin, with a long angular nose and unkempt dark hair that fell down over his shoulders. His eyes were black as night, with neither pupils nor irises; his hands showed the telltale signs of too many dark spells. They were long, thin and twisted, as if he had aged prematurely. Johan had no idea how old the wizard was, but he would have been surprised if he was any older than his father. But dark wizardry took its toll on a person's body and soul.

"I can see that you are," Hawthorne said, when Johan said nothing. "But I'm afraid they had to die."

He wants to gloat, Johan thought. He recognised the symptoms from Jamal, although Jamal had never killed ... at least before the riot in front of the palace. *Let him. See what he tells you.*

"It's really quite simple," Hawthorne continued, in a light and airy voice. "They thought they could challenge the gods. For this, they had to be punished."

He nodded towards one of the pieces of machinery. "They thought that this would make them the equals of the god-touched," he said, darkly. "I proved them wrong."

Johan shivered. The god-touched was a very old name for magicians, one that suggested that *they* were the only true humans living in the mortal world. Jamal had brought it up more than once to use as a weapon against Johan, calling him a soulless monster fit only to hew wood and draw water. The religion that sprouted such nonsense was very popular among magicians outside the Golden City, but utterly hated by non-magicians. It was easy to see why.

"When the gods made men, they made some of them out of clay," Hawthorne observed, darkly. "And they made others out of their own godly essence." He waved his hand in the air, causing a blaze of light to appear in the room. "How could the clay-men presume to match those who were made from the essence of the gods?"

He was insane, Johan realised. The cold chill running down his back grew worse. But there was also method in his madness. The attack on the city had been concentrated on where the Iron Dragons were produced, the people he'd killed specifically had worked on the Iron Dragons ... and this complex, whatever it was, was connected to them too. Hawthorne had targeted his attacks on places that most magicians doubted had the right to exist. If he hadn't killed so many people, there might have been little enthusiasm for giving chase.

"The god came to me at night and whispered that it was my duty to destroy the dreams of the soulless," Hawthorne informed him. His voice shone with conviction. "He told me that there would come a time when I could leave my imprisonment and escape – and he was right. I fled and came here, obeying the orders he sent me in dreams. I shall be rewarded beyond the dreams of even sorcerers!"

Definitely insane, Johan thought. There were people who claimed to have had visions from the gods, but their stories rarely stood up when they were tested under truth spells. Their believers claimed that the truth of their particular god was not for unbelievers; Johan suspected that most of them were just frauds, claiming to talk with the gods to collect worshippers. It was one of the very few points on which he ever agreed with Jamal.

"They were defenceless, of course," Hawthorne

proclaimed, turning away to walk down the stacks of machinery. "What could they do against me?"

Johan followed him ... and almost threw up again as the horrific sight came into view. Hawthorne had frozen his prey, then killed them one by one; one young man had been crucified, another seemed to have been flogged to death ... he couldn't even *look* at a young woman whose body had been ritualistically cut open. His gorge rose and he retched helplessly. If there had been something left in his stomach, he knew, it would have joined the blood in pooling on the floor.

"You people have no nerve," Hawthorne said. "They talked of beating magicians, of creating a kind of magic of their own, yet when I arrived they fell over themselves to beg for mercy from me. One of them even offered to be my servant, my slave, if only I would spare his life. How brave are those who never have to face those they scorn. All those papers suggesting that mundanes should consider themselves the equal of magicians ..."

He laughed, a low rumbling sound that rapidly became an insane cackle. Johan stared at his back as he turned away to look at one of the pieces of machinery, a long metal tube with a pair of metal balls sitting next to it. The purpose of the device, if device it was, baffled him; the balls might fit inside the tube, but then what?

"This," Hawthorne said, "is a weapon. Or so they say. But what good would it do them against *me*?"

"I do not know," Johan said, speaking for the first time. "But you didn't have to kill them all."

"He *speaks*!" Hawthorne proclaimed. "And there I was thinking that someone had accidentally torn out your tongue."

He turned back to face Johan, one hand twisting into a claw. "I could do that," he added, darkly. "Or I could ... oh, I could turn you into a mouse and set my cats on you. I did that to some of the people here."

Johan looked at one of the bodies, lying on the ground, and believed him. Someone who was killed while transfigured would return to normal upon the moment of their death, along with their wounds. A tiny cut for a mouse might leave a human ripped open from end to end. He couldn't even begin to imagine just how horrific their final moments must have been. For all of his faults, for all of his cruelty and the pranks he had played on Johan, Jamal was no dark wizard.

But he might be getting there, Johan thought. Or was he? Jamal could have wiped out the entire group of Levellers with his magic, if he'd thought of it. Instead, he'd tormented them ...

He looked up at Hawthorne and knew that, whatever else happened, he would never be scared of his brother again.

Hawthorne rubbed his clawed hands together, then smiled. "The god commands your death," he informed Johan. A wave of his hand had Johan's feet fixed firmly to the floor. "But how best to do it? There are so many ways you could die."

"Tell me something," Johan said, trying to buy time. Sheer terror was making it hard to think clearly. "If the clay-men are so worthless, why can we use their blood for magical rites?"

"We can use the blood of dumber animals in magical rites," Hawthorne pointed out, snidely. "The mere fact that their blood has ... uses does not mean that they are our equals, does it?"

Johan winced. He'd hoped that trying to undermine Hawthorne's faith in his crazy religion would work, but it hadn't. Hawthorne believed every word he said.

"And they can give birth to magical children," he said, desperately. "Why would that make them useless?"

"The gods sometimes choose to give us new blood," Hawthorne said. "They cause the child to appear in a clay-woman's womb, formed from their essence. Or are you not aware that there are spells that allow a human child to be brought to term inside a cow?"

His face twisted into a sneer. "I find your lack of faith disturbing," he announced. "All rationalisation by a clay-man unwilling to accept his place in the world. And you bore me."

He lifted his hand, holding it up in front of Johan's face. "Goodbye," he said. "Your death will be ..."

A streak of brilliant blue light struck him, sending him

flying backwards.

***

Elaine searched through her bag as soon as she left the office, hunting for the vial of Johan's blood. She'd never had the time to run any tests on it, but it would suffice for one thing; Johan couldn't hope to cut the link between it and himself. Blood called to blood, no matter the distance between them. Only the most powerful magicians could alter their blood to break the connection; she'd been careful not to even *mention* the possibility to Johan.

"All right," she muttered, as she felt the magic take hold. "Where *are* you?"

The vial seemed to be pulling her back towards the Golden City; the sense of distance suggested that Johan was still walking. Muttering curses under her breath, unsure of what was going through his mind, Elaine walked quickly to the nearest stable and passed the stable boy several gold coins. In return, she got a domesticated horse that had been enhanced by magic and trained by the best. She couldn't help eying the beast nervously as the boy brought him out onto the street – she'd never ridden a horse in her life, let alone a big black stallion that was taller than herself – but the beast gave her an oddly reassuring look.

"Arcane is trained and experienced," the stable boy assured her. "And your magic can help you to guide him."

He was right, Elaine discovered, when she finally managed to mount him. Once she was on the horse's back, it was surprisingly easy to guide him in the right direction, even if the horse seemed inclined to move faster than she would have preferred. She dug a ration bar out of her bag as they cantered out of the town, heading southwards. If Johan was on foot, she told herself, they would overtake him very quickly. Instead, the land grew rougher, harder for the horse to traverse. It didn't take too long for Elaine to realise that Johan was following a straight line rather than the roads.

"Now," she asked the horse, "why would he do that?"

There was no reply, of course. The stories of talking animals she'd read as a child had no basis in reality. Even a transfigured human couldn't talk in animal form, although

320

with the right sort of mental link they could still communicate. The best she could do with the horse was read its emotions and they were very basic, barely more than enough to tell her that *he* thought they could move faster.

Johan should have known better than to go off the roads, Elaine thought. They'd spent enough time exploring the hills and mountains to know that pathways and roads made it *much* easier to move faster. But Johan was definitely moving in a straight line ... why would he do that, even if he were trying to hide? It made no sense unless he was aiming directly for somewhere ... or someone. Her blood ran cold as she realised that Johan was actually following the Dark Wizard. Somehow – the gods alone knew how – he'd discovered a way to track him. And, instead of waiting for the Inquisitors, he'd gone off on his own.

Idiot, Elaine thought. Her thoughts communicated themselves to the horse, who whinnied uncomfortably. Elaine looked down at the vial of blood and concentrated, trying to get a fix on Johan's exact position. He didn't seem to be moving any longer. In fact ... the horse twisted, unwilling to go among the trees, then led her to a tiny road, half-hidden by a handful of aversion spells. She wouldn't have sensed it at all if the horse hadn't taken her right through the concealment spells.

But the spells didn't look powerful enough to be the work of a Dark Wizard ...

She slipped off the horse, wand in hand, as the building came into view. It didn't look special enough to be the lair of a Dark Wizard either, not when they normally took over castles or even built themselves homes amongst the clouds. Maybe Hawthorne was smarter than the average Dark Wizard ... but if he were smart, he wouldn't have attacked the city. Light Spinner couldn't let something like that go by; she'd have Hawthorne's head, even if she had to send a small army after him to get it. And Hawthorne had definitely been captured before and sentenced to death.

Elaine hesitated. The blood said that Johan was inside, but the gods alone knew what *else* was inside. Part of her wanted to summon the Inquisitors, part of her knew that she didn't dare wait for help. She cast a quick summoning charm in the air, calling the nearest Inquisitor, then headed towards the door. One look at the battered piece of wood told her that Hawthorne had broken his way into the building. Whatever this was, it wasn't his hideout. It was his next target. She cast a concealment charm over herself, then stepped inside.

She heard a high-pitched voice as she crept inside, speaking of a religion that many lower-level magicians embraced fervently. It made them feel superior to the mundanes, Elaine knew; somehow, she had never been tempted by such talk, even though she was a low-power magician. But then, she'd known mundanes in the orphanage. They had never been strange creatures to her, even if they had never fully been her friends either.

Careful, she warned herself, as she tiptoed around the pieces of machinery. *Your spells aren't perfect ...*

The sight of Hawthorne chilled her, even though she'd seen worse – much worse – in the books that had been crammed into her head. He actually looked surprisingly human, apart from the pale skin and very black eyes. At least they weren't red, she realised; red eyes were the mark of wild magic, suggesting that the person with them had been up to something *very* dangerous. Hawthorne had probably been experimenting on himself and wound up with ... what? She tensed as he seemed to look right at her, then past her. The spells were holding.

I hope, she thought, trying desperately to decide what to do. Hawthorne was dangerous, too dangerous for her; he'd killed several Inquisitors as well as other magicians. And Johan was a wild card, without any real training in fighting or duelling. His magic didn't really lend itself to proper duelling. She hoped he remembered how to protect himself, if nothing else. A reflected curse might be enough to kill Hawthorne ...

The Dark Wizard lifted his hand; Elaine knew that she could wait no longer. Lifting her wand, she cast the strongest stunner she could, blasting Hawthorne across the room and into a piece of machinery. It should have knocked him out, but his protections were stronger than that ... and her concealment spells would no longer work now that he was looking for her.

"Die," Hawthorne grated, staggering to his feet. "Die now!"

Elaine cast the counter-charm at Johan's feet, then jumped to one side as a flash of absolute blackness blasted past her. She didn't dare let that spell touch her, even with her enhanced protections. It would have killed her on the spot.

"Get out of here," she shouted at Johan. "Move!"

Chapter Thirty-Three

Hawthorne spoke a word that sounded like shattering glass. Elaine swore and ducked behind a table, just before a piece of machinery exploded into red-hot fragments. She lost sight of Johan and prayed that he was running, before she peeked out from cover and fired another spell towards the Dark Wizard. He raised one clawed hand and shot a burst of Balefire back at her, forcing her to jump back and duck behind another table.

"You need a wand," Hawthorne observed, as his magic advanced forward. Elaine felt a tingle as his power rippled through the air, trying to get a hold on her. She banished it with a counter-spell of her own invention, knowing that he would find it hard to stop. "You must be weak indeed."

Trying to get under my skin, Elaine thought, as she moved behind another table. A blast of fire that barely missed her indicated that her motion hadn't gone unspotted. *Millicent did it better.*

But Millicent hadn't been trying to kill her. The table she was crouching behind suddenly became hot, then melted into a puddle of molten liquid. Elaine lifted her wand, cast a handful of illusionary people in the air, then ran for the next piece of cover. Hawthorne fired at the wrong shapes, popping them out of existence. Elaine took advantage of his distraction to fire a curse at him that should have killed. Instead, it struck his protections and bounced.

"You're definitely weak," Hawthorne said, as he turned to face her. "Give up now and you will serve a useful purpose in the new world order."

Elaine scowled, rapidly channelling a spell through her wand. Hawthorne had been ranting about a god speaking to him; was it possible, she asked herself, that he hadn't been delusional at all? She wasn't sure if the gods existed, but she did know the *Witch-King* existed ... and an insane Dark

Wizard would make an excellent tool. Or it might just be a wild coincidence, except Johan had tracked Hawthorne down with ease. Could they *both* be touched by the Witch-King?

She cast the spell, throwing it at Hawthorne's face. It was a mark of his confidence that he didn't move, allowing the spell to latch on to his protections ... and start to drain them. Elaine had devised the spell to allow her to deal with more powerful enemies, knowing that most magicians would sooner cut off their own arms with blunt knives than try to cast spells on their own bodies. The slightest mistake could mean terrifying agony, not to mention the danger of inflicting permanent harm. Their magic was part of them, after all; whatever changes it made would be accepted by the body as natural.

Hawthorne's body was suddenly surrounded by a green and red glow as the spell started to work away at his protections, turning the magic that bound them together into harmless light. He let out a howl of rage, then threw a curse back at Elaine that slammed into her cover and blew it into fragments, the blast picking up Elaine and throwing her the whole length of the room. She grunted in pain as she slammed into the wall, then fell down and collapsed at the bottom. Her leg bent alarmingly, but thankfully it didn't seem to break. She tried to get to her feet, only to discover that she couldn't put any weight on her leg at all. Her wand ...

Her blood ran cold. Where was her wand?

"Here," Hawthorne said. She looked up, dazed. The glow was gone ... and Hawthorne was holding her wand in his hand, almost casually. "Looking for this?"

He leered down at her. "What a pathetic magician you really are," he sneered. "Without a wand, you are helpless. Your magic remains locked inside you, unable to seek release. What can you do that a mundane *cannot*, when you have no wand?"

There was a *snap*. Elaine stared in horror as he broke her wand. She knew that she didn't need it, at least for basic spells, but it had been with her from the day she'd gone to the shop with her tutor and bought it. It hadn't been special, or expensive, yet ... it had been *hers*. And now it was gone.

She had owned so little in her life before her promotion and now one of her few possessions was gone.

Hawthorne dropped the pieces to the floor, then lifted his hand, casting a spell. Elaine felt herself lifted into the air, her useless leg dangling down. Maybe she'd been wrong, she told herself, maybe it was broken after all. But Hawthorne wasn't likely to leave her alive long enough to decide between trying to heal herself or crawling back to the city. In hindsight, she should never have given chase without finding an Inquisitor or two to go with her.

"I would consider you for the mother of my child," Hawthorne said, drawing his attention back to her, "but you really are too weak. So weak you might as well be a mundane yourself."

Elaine braced herself, then hurled a spell right into his face, putting all of her remaining energy behind it. Hawthorne staggered backwards as blue-white light flared around him; the magic holding Elaine failed, sending her falling to the ground. There was a crack as her abused leg finally broke; Elaine screamed, unable to focus her mind enough to dampen the pain. Somehow, even being tortured seemed preferable.

"You ..." Hawthorne said. "You ..."

Not enough, Elaine realised, numbly. She'd tried to kill him, hoping that his protections were weak enough to allow her to burn though his skull, but he'd cancelled her earlier spell too quickly. He'd been hurt, and surprised by her ability to use magic without a wand, yet it hadn't been enough to give them a chance to escape.

"Maybe I was wrong," Hawthorne said. "Maybe you *would* be a good mother to my children. And the god says that you know something I ought to know."

Elaine collapsed into absolute despair. She'd failed; worse, she'd delivered everything she knew to a Dark Wizard. Light Spinner should have had her killed, the moment she realised just what had turned Elaine into a Bookworm. She was a colossal security risk even in the Golden City. Outside it, she might as well be a target ... and she knew, now, that Hawthorne's god was the Witch-King. Who else knew what she was?

It was hard to talk, but she had to try. "Tell me," she said.

"How do you know your god is telling the truth?"

Hawthorne slapped her, hard. Elaine fell back, stunned. Blood started to trickle down her cheek.

"My god is my lord and master," Hawthorne proclaimed. "He told me to smite the mundanes who dreamed of rivalling those infused with the essence of the gods ..."

Elaine put it together, too late. The Witch-King had manipulated Hawthorne, using him to attack the mundanes who were trying to find ways to develop non-magical technology. And it was possible that Jamal had been manipulated too ... it was impossible to be sure. The Witch-King's touch was difficult to detect; even in hindsight, it had proven impossible to trace the strings he had pulled to ensure Elaine's birth and abandonment at the orphanage. And yet it had all worked magnificently ...

But I stopped him, she told herself. And yet there was a quiet nagging doubt. *Or was what I did part of his plan*?

"On your feet," Hawthorne ordered. "You will be coming with me."

He reached out, grabbed Elaine's shirt and hauled her to her feet. Elaine gasped in pain as he forced her to put her weight on her leg, then staggered and fell against the wall. Hawthorne muttered a curse under his breath, then cast a spell; Elaine felt herself hefted up into the air, drifting helplessly behind him. This time she didn't even have the magic to cast another spell.

She tried to think through the crushing weight of despair, but it seemed hard to focus her mind on anything. Hawthorne would enslave her, then use potions to ensure that she became   pregnant ... all the time pulling spells and concepts out of her mind that had been buried for a very good reason. *He* wouldn't hesitate to use them ...

"Stop," a shaky voice said. "You'd ... you'd better put her down."

***

Johan had watched in horror as Elaine fought and lost, unsure of what to do. If he ran ... he couldn't leave her, not when she'd clearly tracked him to this place. Her capture was his fault, just like everything else. But he didn't know what to do ...

He stepped forward, concentrating on maintaining a protective bubble around himself. "Put her down," he repeated, trying to sound confident. His father would have sounded much more commanding, he was sure. "Now."

Hawthorne made a harsh noise. It took Johan a few moments to realise that he was laughing, unpleasantly. "You, little mundane, are demanding that I bow to your will?"

"Yes," Johan said, silently grateful that Hawthorne had never realised that he had magic. "If you let her go, you can walk away freely."

"I have a better idea," Hawthorne said. "Why don't you just kill yourself?"

He waved a hand in Johan's direction. There was a flash of light against the protective bubble, but nothing else happened. Hawthorne stopped, staring at Johan in surprise; he might have sensed the presence of a normal magician, but Johan was far from normal. His inability to make potions and sense magic had an upside.

"I said, stop," Johan said. He tried to sound like Jamal at his most arrogant, his most convinced that he was utterly unstoppable. "I won't ask again."

"You are using protective amulets," Hawthorne said, sardonically. "Do you think that they can stand up to a *real* magician?"

A corkscrew of light danced from his fingers, burning towards Johan ... and splintered into nothingness against the protective bubble. Johan took a step forward, concentrating on maintaining the bubble. He honestly wasn't sure if he could focus on two things at once, even if one of them involved killing Hawthorne. The bubble had to be maintained. It was unlikely that Hawthorne would mess around with freeze spells when he could use more lethal magic.

"I have no amulets," Johan said, quietly. His bubble flared with light again and again as Hawthorne blasted it with everything he had, to no avail. "All I have is myself."

"It's a trick," Hawthorne snapped. He turned to glare at Elaine. "What have you done?"

Johan looked at Elaine ... and felt a sudden flash of rage that overpowered his common sense. She was bleeding, one of her legs was clearly broken ... and Hawthorne had threatened to turn her into a brood mare. Sheer fury drove him forward, his magic lashing out at Hawthorne and sending the magician flying backwards. The magic holding Elaine in the air popped out of existence and she fell, Johan barely managing to catch her before she hit the ground for a second time.

"Keep ..." Elaine mumbled, blood dripping from her mouth. "Keep your eyes on him ..."

Johan looked up, then threw himself aside as a blast of fire crackled through the air. The Dark Wizard didn't even seem to be stunned; he threw fireball after fireball at Johan, forcing him to duck for cover. But that hadn't worked for Elaine ... he collected himself a moment later and told the fireballs, which were swooping down after him, to go out. They winked out of existence, leaving Hawthorne staring at him in disbelief. And then he threw a single white beam of light towards Johan. It struck the protective bubble and went right through, touching Johan's chest. But as far as Johan could tell, it didn't seem to do *anything*.

He's testing you, he told himself. *He wants to know what you can do. And what your bubble will stop.*

The beam of light grew brighter, wandering up towards Johan's eyes. Hawthorne wanted to *blind* him, he realised in mute horror; he squeezed his eyes shut, then concentrated on turning the bubble into a mirror. But it didn't seem to do anything, apart from stopping the light before it could reach him. A moment later, Johan told the light to go away and it did.

Hawthorne stared at him, his face twisted in horror. "What *are* you?"

Johan stared back at him, feeling rage boiling through his very soul. This man was the embodiment of the same ethos that had allowed Jamal and his other siblings to torment him, either in hopes of giving the Powerless magic or merely because those without magic deserved to serve as their betters willed. He had power; he thought it gave him the right to rape, burn and pillage at will, taking whatever he pleased because, in the end, he had power and those he tormented had none. He was despicable. He was a monster. He didn't deserve to have power.

"I am ... I am your punishment," Johan said. It was a line from a book he'd read, one of Charity's romantic novels about a dead man who came back to punish his killers while making love to his girlfriend, who had stayed faithful all along. The book had been dreadfully soppy, but it had given him a few ideas. "And you're not getting any more than you deserve."

Something seemed to *click* in his mind. The building was suddenly bathed in multicoloured light, light which seemed to surround Elaine and Hawthorne in particular. *Magic*, Johan realised, the magic that gave them their powers. There were other lights, fading away into nothingness, around the dead bodies, the last traces of the magic Hawthorne had used to kill them. But the light around him was different, as if it was not quite part of the living web. He closed his eyes, staggering ... and yet he could still see the light.

A thought blossomed and he took a step forward, concentrating on one very specific result. It was suddenly easy to reach out with his mind and sever Hawthorne's link to the web, to drain his magic and cut him off from the source. The magic seemed to *shimmer* in response, although he couldn't tell if it approved or disapproved ... or even if it were alive at all. And then the vision faded, just in time to allow him to see Hawthorne scream in pain and shock.

"You're not getting any more than you deserve," Johan said, concentrating. Hawthorne seemed to be getting older and older, his long dark hair shading rapidly to white, his body stooping into a hunch. "And this, too, is what you deserve."

Hawthorne shrank, just like Charity. But instead of becoming a rat, he became a tiny statue of himself. Johan stepped over to him and looked down, feeling oddly numb. He'd won, and yet ...

He turned and ran back towards Elaine, cursing himself. He should have thought of her *first*.

"I ... I can try to help with your leg," he gasped, kneeling down beside her. Blood had stained her shirt, leaving her looking as if she were on the verge of death. "Please, don't die."

"Don't try," Elaine mumbled. She sounded stunned and weak, but alive. "What did you do to him?"

"I took his magic," Johan said, bluntly. He tried to put everything he'd seen into words, but stopped when he realised that it just wasn't possible. "And then I turned him into a statue."

"You took his magic," Elaine repeated. Her voice was weak, but he could tell that she was astonished. "I ..."

She closed her eyes. For a long chilling moment, Johan was sure that she was dead. But then her heartbeat was still there, if weak. There was a crashing sound behind him and he turned, just in time to see a pair of Inquisitors charging into the building with drawn wands. Johan let out a gasp of relief and motioned for them to help Elaine. One of them bent down and cast a spell that wrapped her in a bubble of faint blue light. The other looked around, quietly noted the position of the bodies, then looked back at Johan.

"I'm going to need a statement," he said, quietly. He looked around the room again, searching – Johan realised suddenly – for Hawthorne. "And where is he?"

"There," Johan said, pointing to the statue. He was sure that Hawthorne couldn't free himself, not now his magic was gone, but he didn't really want to take chances. Even with his strange magic, Hawthorne had come far too close to killing him. And he'd beaten Elaine halfway to death. "Can you help her?"

"She will need some time, but she will recover," the first Inquisitor assured him. There was a confidence in his tone that made Johan relax, slightly. "We'll take her back to the druids. You can come with us."

"After you give your statement," the second Inquisitor added, "you may stay with her."

Johan scowled, but followed them and the floating Elaine out of the building. As far as he knew, there was no spell that would strip a person of their magic permanently; if there had been, he was sure the Inquisitors would have started using it when they took Dark Wizards prisoner. But he'd invented one ... somehow, he knew that would scare the magicians more than anything else he'd done. And who knew what would happen after that?

Never mind that now, he told himself, bitterly. There were more important things to worry about than his future. Or, for that matter, what would happen to Hawthorne once they turned him back to normal. *Elaine got hurt because she ran after you. You need to be there to look after her.*

Chapter Thirty-Four

"Welcome back to the world," a familiar voice said. Elaine opened her eyes to see Dread, standing at the foot of her bed. "How are you feeling?"

Elaine paused, considering. Apart from a handful of twinges from her leg, which wouldn't go away until she walked long enough to accustom herself to her repaired bones, she felt fine. The druids had to have kept her asleep after she fainted, taking their time to work on her so she didn't have to spend days recuperating. All in all, it was better than the treatment she'd had the last time she'd fallen into their clutches.

You weren't a Privy Councillor then, she reminded herself, tartly. A stab of guilt ran through her mind as she remembered the dead or dying in the city. *You're important now.*

"I've been better," she said, finally. She sat upright, realised that she was naked and grabbed at the sheet to cover herself. "What happened?"

Dread's eyes narrowed. "How much do you remember?"

Elaine concentrated. "Hawthorne," she said. She'd fought Hawthorne ... and lost. He'd snapped her wand right in front of her. If Johan hadn't done something, he would have taken her and raped her and used her to bear his children ... she shuddered suddenly with remembered fear. "What happened to him?"

"A very good question," Dread said. "He seems to have lost the ability to do magic altogether."

"... Shit," Elaine said, numbly. Johan had said that, just before she'd fainted, but she hadn't believed him. Not completely. Magic was resilient. There were ways to dampen it, or force someone to swear an oath not to use it, yet there was no way to actually remove it completely. Not until now. "How many people know?"

"It's meant to be a secret," Dread said. "But rumours have no doubt already started circulating."

"No doubt," Elaine agreed. She looked around, hunting for her clothes. "What happened to my clothes."

"They were stained in blood," Dread said. "The druids took the liberty of destroying them and provided you with a pair of spare robes in exchange. If you're sure you're fit to move, you can get up and put them on."

He pointed towards the wardrobe. Elaine scowled at him until he turned his back, then swung her legs over the side of the bed and stood upright. Her leg felt as if someone had stabbed it for a long moment, then the pain faded away into nothingness. Gritting her teeth, Elaine walked over to the wardrobe and found a pair of oversized robes. Casting the spells to resize them into something she could actually wear took a few moments – she made a mental note to get a new wand as quickly as possible - but eventually she was decent.

The effort brought back memories. There was a fund for poor students at the Peerless School, but it hardly stretched to new robes or anything else new apart from wands. She'd had more second-hand clothes than she cared to remember; she'd learned the spells that she needed to resize clothes very quickly, purely out of self-defence. Wearing something obviously unsuitable would have attracted mockery from the other students.

"They will do," she said, finally. A look in the side drawer revealed the pieces of her wand and her bag, which she opened and checked quickly. Thankfully, the protective charms had held; the vial of blood was still intact and sealed. "What happened to Johan?"

"After we took his statement, he insisted on remaining nearby," Dread said. He scowled down at the ground. "I'm afraid he blames himself for everything that happened. He was insisting that I should arrest him as a murderer. I ended up telling him to join a work gang and sweat it out."

He held up a hand. "I'd suggest you put your glamour back on," he added. "The people here have been scared enough."

Elaine flushed, but did as he said.

"Good," Dread said, examining her face. Thankfully, the

spell didn't need a wand to work, which was lucky. Wands were normally precise, but few magicians felt comfortable casting spells on themselves using them. The results could be unpleasant. "Follow me."

Elaine blinked as they stepped out into the sunlight. The druids had been busy; they'd taken over a number of buildings and turned them into makeshift hospitals. Hundreds of young women had been pressed into service as nurses, including some who would normally have been considered too young to work in a responsible job. Beyond them, there was a dozen Inquisitors and a small army of City Guardsmen. Elaine couldn't help wondering where the Guardsmen had been while Hawthorne had been attacking, but she knew better than to expect them to face a magician. It wasn't what they were paid to do.

The destroyed buildings were being cleared, piece by piece, by workers. Johan was one of them; stripped to the waist, his body shining with sweat as he moved debris by brute force rather than magic. Elaine wondered just how strong the temptation *was* to use magic; for someone who had been denied it all of his life, Johan didn't seem to *want* to use it now, even though it would have been helpful. But then, most of his spells went wrong one way or the other. He'd probably learned caution.

Johan saw her, dropped the piece of debris on the ground and raced towards her. Elaine barely had time to raise her arms before he wrapped her in a tight hug, almost lifting her off the ground. She hugged him back, then looked over at Dread, who was watching the whole affair with ill-concealed amusement.

"Tell me," he said. "Should I find you a room?"

Elaine flushed, brightly. "Yes, please," she said, once she trusted herself to speak. "We have a lot to talk about."

Dread led them to a building guarded by a pair of Inquisitors and pointed them into a small room. "There are privacy wards erected to protect your words," he said. Elaine, who knew perfectly well that those wards wouldn't stop the *Inquisitors* listening to them, was not impressed. "And you should get a bite to eat as soon as possible."

Elaine watched him go, then looked up at Johan. "It wasn't

your fault."

Johan sagged in front of her. "I killed those children," he said, bitterly. "And then I led you to your ... you were hurt because of me."

"No," Elaine said. She still remembered how guilty she'd felt after Kane had ripped through the Golden City, using knowledge he'd stolen from her mind. Family magic was *so* easy to misuse. At least Hawthorne would have needed years to draw *everything* from her. "That wasn't your fault.

"You tried to hold up the building," she continued, after a moment. It had been simple enough in hindsight to work out what had happened, although hindsight also showed several other possible ways to deal with the problem. "You did hold the walls in place, but that put additional pressure on the floors and they eventually collapsed."

"Plunging the children into the flames," Johan said. "It was my fault."

"It wasn't you who set the flames," Elaine pointed out, wondering just how Dread – who had explained to her that everything that happened hadn't really been *her* fault – had refrained from slapping her, or at least turning her into something that didn't talk. "Nor was it you who put their lives in danger. Hawthorne did that, purely to make it harder for people to chase him."

And perhaps to conceal what he was doing, she thought, although she doubted that it would have worked. He would have needed to flatten half the city and, even then, people would have wondered. Or maybe the Witch-King had other tools who could help ensure that the truth never got out.

"You are certainly not a murderer," she concluded. "Chasing after Hawthorne, on the other hand, was *dumb*."

"I know," Johan admitted. "I ... I just wanted to prove myself."

"I dare say you succeeded," Elaine snapped. She could understand the heroic impulse, as well as the desire to prove oneself; she just didn't share it. And yet she'd gone after Johan without waiting for the Inquisitors. "Are you now content or are you going to do something else stupid?"

Johan shook his head. "I won't run off again," he said. "But ... but they looked at me as though I was a monster."

"I'm not surprised," Elaine admitted, softening her tone. "If you took his magic permanently ..."

She shook her head. "Tell me," she ordered "Just *what* happened when you were facing him."

Johan did his best to describe his experience, but Elaine had to admit that it didn't quite make sense. Magicians – apart from Johan – could sense magic. But none of them had ever reported anything like a web of life, apart from a handful of magicians who had written books she had in her head, magicians who had seemed half-insane. It was impossible, even for her, to separate anything useful from their ravings. And there was absolutely nothing about removing a magician's magic. As far as she could tell, the only permanent way to make it work was to kill the magician.

"I'd prefer that not to get out," she concluded. "But it already has."

"I'm sorry," Johan said. "But I needed to tell them *something*."

"I know," Elaine agreed. She ran her hand through her hair, suddenly feeling very tired. "How long has it been?"

"Since you were knocked out?" Johan asked. "Three days."

Elaine scowled. Three days was more than long enough for the news to reach the Golden City. By now, the Privy Council would probably have met to debate the issue ... the gods alone knew what they would say. Johan's magic was strange enough, but if he had the ability to take magic away ... they'd want him dead.

A thought struck her. "Do you think you could *give* a person magic? Or boost their spells?"

"I don't know," Johan admitted. He looked at her for a long moment. "Do you want me to try?"

The temptation was overwhelming, Elaine had to admit. Most rituals to boost magic had a high cost, but she had a feeling that Johan's magic sat outside those rules. And what could she do if she combined her insights into how magic actually worked with additional power? There were spells she could never make work, no matter how much she broke them down ... but she could, if she had more power.

"No," she said, finally. There were dangers ... and not all of them were caused by the rituals. "But I think you should keep that possibility to yourself too."

Not that it will stop others from thinking of it, she thought. Johan had been important before; now, he would be wanted by every faction in the Golden City. Even the Levellers would want him, in the hopes that he could give them powers. *But would it be wrong of him to try*?

She shook her head, dismissing the thought. It was one that could be mulled over later, along with Hawthorne's connection to the Witch-King. Everything that had happened seemed to prove that Johan wasn't connected to the Witch-King himself ... unless Hawthorne had been sacrificed to convince her that was true. She scowled, feeling a headache coming on. The Witch-King was such an elusive enemy that it was impossible to be sure if he was involved or not. Much as she disliked duelling, she had to admit that it was simpler than matching wits with a wily immortal enemy who could lay plans over decades – or centuries. The amount of planning that had gone into producing Elaine alone was staggering.

I'll have to take a long look at Johan's family tree, she told herself, thoughtfully. *See what, if anything, pops out at me.*

But she knew that it was unlikely to be obvious. If indeed there was anything to find.

Johan was looking at her oddly. "Elaine?"

"Nothing," Elaine said, shaking her head. "Just woolgathering."

She looked down at the floor for a long moment, catching sight of a small spider scurrying back to its web, then looked back at Johan. "I think we should consider going back to the cabin," she said, slowly. In truth, she was unsure what to do. If they went back to the city, it would allow her to start limiting the damage as much as possible ... but it would also make them easier targets for everyone who wanted a piece of Johan. "But I need to take a look at Hawthorne first. And have a word with the Inquisitors."

"Understood," Johan said. "And I need to get back to work."

Elaine nodded. "Thank you for saving my life," she said,

softly. "He would have done far worse than kill me, if he took me prisoner."

"I endangered your life," Johan said. "I won't ever do that again."

Elaine smiled, led him outside, then turned to Dread as Johan hurried back to the work gang. "I need to see Hawthorne," she said. "What happened to him?"

"He's in the cells," Dread said, leading her towards a City Guard station. The exterior of the building had been scorched, but it was otherwise intact. "And seemingly powerless, as far as we can tell."

Elaine nodded as they reached the cell. The charm on the door allowed them to look inside without being seen, which let her study Hawthorne for a long moment. He looked *old*; the spells that had kept him youthful had snapped when his magic had been stolen. Judging by his bent form, he didn't have more than a few years left in him.

"He's been mumbling all day," the Guardsman on duty said. "I haven't been able to make out the words."

"Let me look at him," Elaine said. She hesitated, remembering her snapped wand. "Can I borrow your wand?"

Dread looked at her for a long moment, then reached into his robes and produced a simple wooden wand. His spare, Elaine realised; he carried more than one. But she wasn't too surprised that he was reluctant to give her his normal wand, not when it was important to him. Most male magicians took their wands very seriously, even if they didn't need them.

She took the wand and stepped into the cell, passing through a ward that kept Hawthorne firmly on the other side. The Dark Wizard – the *former* Dark Wizard – didn't even look up at her; she couldn't help noticing that they hadn't bothered to chain his hands and feet, as if he were a mundane. She wondered if the lack of care was a studied insult to the powerless man; once, there would have been iron chains, dampening potions and at least five Inquisitors guarding him at all times. Now, there was just a crippled old man.

This man would have raped you and forced you to bear his children, her thoughts reminded her. *You should not feel sorry for him.*

Lifting the wand, she cast the first diagnostic charm. The charm seemed confused; Hawthorne was thirty years old at most, yet his body was much older ... and damaged by magic. Elaine nodded, unsurprised, then cast the most subtle magic detection spell she knew, one used by druids when inspecting children for traces of magic. There was nothing, not even a tiny flicker. Hawthorne was not only completely powerless, he was effectively a mundane.

"What would happen," she mused aloud, "if you had children now?"

Hawthorne lifted his head to look at her. His eyes were blank, full of a bleak hopelessness that chilled her to the bone. He believed, he truly believed, that magic separated out the true humans from the clay-men who only *looked* human. And now he was nothing more than one of the clay-men. By his own lights, he was a subhuman monster, worthy only of servitude to the true humans. Elaine couldn't help feeling that Johan had been right. Hawthorne had only got what he deserved.

She cast the final charm and examined the results. Hawthorne had, at best, two years to live. Somehow, she doubted it would matter. His death sentence had been passed before his escape and, now that he had been recaptured, the sentence could be carried out. Dread could do it on the spot, if necessary. But she knew that they needed answers first.

"He's been touched," she told Dread, as soon as she stepped out of the cell. "*He* has his hooks in him – or had. Can you see what he can tell you?"

"I can try," Dread said. He sounded rather doubtful. "But his mind appears to have been damaged."

"Not really," Elaine assured him. The charms had made that clear. It was easy enough to tell when a person's mind had been damaged and Hawthorne's mind seemed intact. "He's just retreated into shock."

"You may as well keep the wand," Dread said, as she turned to leave. "There's nowhere here to get a proper one."

"Thank you," Elaine said. She wasn't blind to the significance of the offer – or the fact that, in some cultures, it was almost a marriage proposal. But Dread didn't mean it like that. If he'd ever been interested in anyone, with the possible exception of the Princess, he'd never shown it. "I'm going to take Johan back to the cabin, so please let us know if something happens."

She scowled as she walked out of the station, thinking hard. Something was *definitely* going to happen, that was a given. Johan had just turned the world upside down. And, once the factions realised the truth, they would react. They'd want him ... and they wouldn't want anyone else to have him. Her lips quirked into a bitter smile. Even Light Spinner would have her doubts about keeping him alive. They'd do something, all right ...

The only question was *what*?

Chapter Thirty-Five

"Lord Conidian," May said, as she slipped into his study. "Lord Deferens is here to see you."

Duncan lifted an eyebrow in surprise. Deferens had never visited him before – or anyone else, as far as his quiet enquiries had been able to prove. For all of his obvious power and connections, Deferens seemed to have little to do with his fellow Privy Councillors. It hadn't been until the Leveller incident that Deferens had even *spoken* to him outside the palace. And yet he clearly had the power to do him great good or great harm ...

"Send him in," he ordered, glancing around to make sure that nothing informative was in view. Deferens wasn't one of his children; Duncan knew that he might be a political ally now, but that could change within days. It was better not to tell him more than he actively needed to know. "And bring us both Kava."

Deferens was wearing another eye-catching red suit as he stepped into the room, matched with a kilt that hung down to just above his knees. Duncan watched, as emotionlessly as possible, as Deferens placed his staff carelessly against the wall and then sat down on the other side of Duncan's desk. His unkempt beard seemed to have grown longer, although his moustache was nicely trimmed. Duncan honestly wasn't sure if he was displaying a masculinity that was intended to shock or if he was overcompensating for something. Or perhaps he was just wearing his national dress.

Making a mental note to look it up, Duncan sat upright and looked Deferens in the eye. No doubt the younger magician had come to call in the debt Duncan owed him. It would be bad, after the sheer size of the favour Deferens had done *him*, but at least the debt would be cleared. Not to repay a debt had consequences both mundane and magical. Deferens would certainly try to make the latter as unpleasant as possible.

"So," he said. "What brings you to my abode at this early hour?"

Deferens smirked. "You haven't heard," he said. It wasn't a question. "Why not?"

Duncan felt a trickle of alarm running down the back of his neck. "Heard what?"

"About your son," Deferens said. There was an odd note of near-hysteria in his voice. "About what he did."

"Jamal?" Duncan asked, puzzled. Jamal had stayed inside since his release from the Watchtower; the changes Duncan had made to the wards had ensured it. "What did he do this time?"

"*Johan*," Deferens corrected. "Did you hear about what he did near the Western Hills?"

Duncan frowned, then shook his head. He hated not to hear anything at once, but if it were only rumour so far it might not have reached one of his clients yet. And Deferens clearly had very good sources, wherever they were. He'd certainly been able to help Duncan visit Jamal in his cell and then have him released, even conditionally.

"The Dark Wizard Hawthorne attacked Falconine City," Deferens said. "Your son was amongst those who rallied to stop him. He went after the Dark Wizard alone."

Duncan felt his heart sink. A Dark Wizard didn't earn his title by being rude to people or writing nasty letters to the broadsheets; he earned it through using dark magic to damage his mind, destroying whatever scruples he'd had left. Most of them self-destructed before too long, if the Inquisitors didn't get them, but before they died they often killed hundreds of people. Hawthorne had shown an unusual longevity, even before he'd been captured the first time around. It had only made him more dangerous.

And Johan ... if Johan had faced a Dark Wizard, Johan was almost certainly dead.

"Johan *won*," Deferens said.

Duncan stared at him in disbelief. A Dark Wizard was a formidable foe. Even Inquisitors hesitated to go after one alone. Normal procedure, as far as he knew, was to dispatch at least *three* Inquisitors in pursuit. Even a rumoured Dark

Wizard received the full treatment. For Johan, a magician who had only had his powers for two weeks, to fight one and *win* ...

"Strength is not everything," one of his tutors had said, years ago. *"A magician with vast amounts of raw power can still be tied in knots by a magician with less power, but knows what the hell he's doing. So be careful! And learn!"*

"He won," Duncan said, stunned. "How?"

"That is indeed the question," Deferens said. "The piece of information that is *not* yet widely known is this. Your son took his magic."

Duncan frowned. "*Hawthorne's* magic?"

"Yes," Deferens said, bluntly. "The Dark Wizard, according to my source, is no longer a magician at all. He's powerless, so powerless they haven't even bothered to chain him up."

"Impossible," Duncan said. He refused to believe it. "You can dampen a person's magic, you can force them not to use it, but you can't just *take* it! Even a necromantic rite wouldn't let you take a person's *magic*."

"And yet it happened," Deferens said. His voice was suddenly very serious. "I have verified the information as best I can. It is accurate. "

Duncan felt his mind reel, unable to process the implications. Magic separated the powerful from the powerless ... but what if the powerful could be stripped of their power? He couldn't imagine being without his magic; even as a child, he had played with his own magic and learned how to wield it. And without magic ...

He would no longer be the Patriarch of House Conidian.

Cold fear trickled down his spine. Just what had he and his wife brought into the world, then allowed Jamal to midwife?

"Tell me," Deferens said, breaking into his thoughts. "Could you live without magic?"

Duncan blanched. His entire *life* revolved around magic. Without it, he would no longer be a Privy Councillor, no longer Head of a Great House ... he wouldn't even be able to *live* in his own house. The building was saturated in magic, all keyed to the Head of the Household; without his magic, his power would be gone. He wouldn't even be able to open a door without Jamal's permission ... assuming, of course, that the house recognised Jamal as his heir. And it would be far worse for the families who had lived in their houses for generations. If they lost their magic, the houses would assume that they were intruders and evict them.

"So far," Deferens said, "only a few people know the truth."

Duncan scowled at him, his eyes narrowing. "You seem to be remarkably well informed," he said, darkly. "Just who is your source within the Inquisition?"

"Let's just say that their decision to bring in outsiders to make up the numbers was somewhat ill-judged," Deferens said. He made a show of stroking his beard, contemplatively. "Not all of them were as loyal as they could have been."

He winked at Duncan, then sobered. "But it won't be long before the news gets out," he added. "And there will be *panic* among the magical community."

Duncan could imagine it. If magic was all that separated them from the mundanes, what would happen to them if their magic was suddenly gone? They'd want to kill Johan before he could take magic from someone else ... and yet they'd also be terrified, if they believed that Johan was too powerful to challenge. Duncan could easily imagine them turning on his family, just because he'd birthed the monster. It wasn't rational, but panicking people were never rational.

"You need to decide what you intend to do about it," Deferens said, standing up. "Because this situation might just shatter the balance of power."

"I know," Duncan said.

The possibilities seemed endless – and terrifying. If Johan could take someone's magic at will, he might become Light Spinner's most feared enforcer. The fragile balance of power between the Grand Sorceress and the Great Houses would be shattered beyond repair. Or Johan might even take the seat of Grand Sorcerer for himself – or, perhaps, for the Head Librarian. It was becoming alarmingly clear, Duncan realised, that he had underestimated Elaine No-Kin. What if *she* intended to take advantage of her charge?

He watched the younger magician leave the room, then wrote a quick note to Jayne and her father. If Jayne was the only tool they had to influence Johan, they would have to use her ... because he doubted that there was anything else. He'd offered Johan everything from Marina – a bride who would allow him to enter High Society at the very highest levels – to becoming Prime Heir, but Johan had refused them all. All he'd wanted was to walk away from the family ...

I could disown him, Duncan thought, *or find him an apprenticeship ... but I'd still be blamed for his mere existence ...*

Cursing under his breath, he summoned Sergeant Brandish to his study. The Sergeant had been a City Guardsman before retirement and, as the elder brother of sisters who did private tuition, had plenty of experience keeping unruly young men in line. Jamal already hated him, Duncan had been amused to discover, but the Sergeant would continue to supervise him until he was ready to return to polite society. If, of course, that would ever happen. Duncan, looking at the sheer scale of the disaster Jamal had helped to create, had his doubts.

"Sir," the Sergeant said. He was short, but tough; the unmarked uniform he wore was tight enough to show off his muscles when he flexed. "Your son is currently working on his studies."

Duncan nodded, impatiently. He'd been reluctant to allow Jamal anywhere near the family books, but it was good training for the Prime Heir ... if, of course, he *remained* the Prime Heir. Charity had also been studying the same books, under a rather less gimlet eye. Her progress was slower than Jamal's, but she had much less experience. And, of course, she was also still studying. Duncan had seriously considered pulling her out of the Peerless School early so she could concentrate on preparing to become the Prime Heir, but he knew that she would never forgive him for it. One child hating him was too much.

"Good," he said. "And his conduct?"

"Improved after a dose of the stick," the Sergeant informed him, bluntly. "But he is still sullen and impolite whenever he thinks he can get away with it."

Duncan sighed. There were spells that could change a person's personality permanently, but using them on his own family would have been a breach of the family oaths he'd sworn when he'd taken over from his father. Besides, such spells often had unanticipated side effects that would make Jamal ineligible to take over when Duncan died. Not for the first time, Duncan cursed the poor timing. If Charity had been a few years older, he could have simply moved her into Jamal's place and disowned Jamal completely.

And if she hadn't been born a girl, he thought, sourly. *If she were Prime Heir, I would have to be far more careful about choosing her husband. He would have to understand that she would keep all the power.*

"I may wish to offer him the carrot in a few days," the Sergeant added. "There have been some traces of improvement."

"But how many of them," Duncan asked, "stem from something more fundamental than fear of punishment?"

He scowled. His own father had believed in using hexes and curses on his children, rather than his belt or a cane. Apparently, the old man had thought it was more humane to use magic; besides, it provided an incentive to learn how to block the spells. But Duncan had been taught, patiently, the importance of being firm, but fair; it had been a necessary lesson for when he'd taken over the helm of the family. Jamal, on the other hand ... would his behaviour remain changed when the fear of punishment was removed?

"It requires careful work over a year to ensure that his behaviour remains improved," the Sergeant admitted. "Indeed, he must come to understand *why* his prior conduct was so appalling and, sir, you gave him some awfully mixed messages. You never taught him the difference between right and wrong."

"I know," Duncan said, bitterly. "By all the gods, I know."

There was a tap on the door. May entered at his command.

"Sir, Lord Rendang and his daughter are here to see you," she said, holding out a card. "I believe that they are invited?"

"Show them into the sitting room," Duncan said, rising to his feet. The papers he needed were in one of his locked cabinets. "Sergeant, you may hand out rewards as you feel necessary, but there is to be no opportunity for backsliding."

"Yes, sir," the Sergeant said.

Duncan walked through the door, locking and warding his study once it was empty, then walked into the sitting room. It was intended to receive guests who came as equals – or members of the family. Meeting Lord Rendang there was a powerful message; Duncan already considered him part of the family.

Jayne didn't look *that* pretty to him, although it was clear that she would be a beauty as she grew older. Long dark hair framed a face that was angular, shaped by cheekbones that seemed too narrow to be classically beautiful. But her face was marred by a sulky expression that did nothing for her. Clearly, the news of her betrothal hadn't come as a welcome surprise; instead, she seemed furious. Duncan's own sister had looked the same way when their father had betrothed her, although she'd come to terms with it. And the marriage had been surprisingly happy.

"Lord Conidian," the Rendang said. "May I present my daughter Jayne?"

"Charmed," Duncan said. He bowed to the girl, who merely glared at him. "I believe that my son and yourself are already acquainted. That will make it easier."

"I do not wish to marry," Jayne said, in a low voice. "I have a career ahead of me."

"We have already discussed this," the Rendang said, sharply. "The choice isn't yours."

Duncan smiled. The Rendang thought he was getting the better part of the bargain – and he might well have been, although Johan was still a wild card. Jayne wasn't the Prime Heir, or even the eldest daughter; her marriage couldn't be expected to bring the family much in the way of wealth or influence. Having a match with Duncan's family would bring them all of that and more. And they got to keep their eldest children for other matches. Everyone won ... even Jayne. If she wanted to have a career, it was unlikely that Johan would stand in her way.

"You promised me that I could find a tutor," Jayne insisted, bitterly. Her voice was rising, becoming anger. "You promised ..."

"Times change," her father said. He'd had no reason to expect Jayne to become important, so making such promises had been easy. Now ... Jayne was suddenly wanted. What was the value of such promises when the family's fortunes could be saved by her sacrifice? "The family gave you everything. You will repay it."

Duncan sighed, inwardly. If Charity had made such a public scene, she would have had trouble sitting down for a week. Everyone born to the aristocracy knew that their marriages would be arranged by their families; it was just the way things were, the way things had been since the formation of the Empire. The marriages blended together magic, wealth and influence ... and if the couple didn't get along, all they really had to do was produce a handful of children and then their duty would be done. They could have as many outside relationships as they liked and, as long as they were careful, no one would care. It was just the way things were.

"I won't give up my future," Jayne insisted. There was a grim desperation in her tone that would have been shocking, if Duncan had been in the mood to care. "I *won't*."

"You will," her father said, with quiet menace. "Or I will disown you."

Jayne stared at her father, then glared at Duncan, magic crackling over her fingertips. The house wards shifted, ready to contain any magic she threw at him, but somehow she held herself back from casting a spell. Instead, she slumped, tears flowing down her cheeks. She knew, as well as everyone else, that she couldn't survive without her family's backing. What choice did she have, but to submit?

Duncan was largely unmoved. He'd been shocked when his father told him who he was going to marry, as had his siblings ... why should Jayne be spared from her duty merely because it upset her? She liked Johan, she knew him ... it was a far better basis for a relationship than the one Duncan had shared with his wife. Now ... he had his lovers and his wife had hers. It was the way things should be.

"Sign here," he said, holding out the papers. "Please."

The Rendang signed his name, then passed them to Jayne. She glared down at them, her fingers twitching as if she wanted to crumple them up in her hand, but didn't quite dare. Instead, she reluctantly took the pen and wrote her own name. Duncan signed below hers, asserting his authority as

Johan's father. The papers glowed with a brief golden line as the magic inside them came to life. Johan was now formally engaged to Jayne.

"Thank you," he said, to Jayne. He tried to gentle his voice, although it was apparent that it didn't have any real effect on her. Her sobbing only grew louder, her father awkwardly patting her back as if he thought it would make her feel better. "I look forward to welcoming you into the house."

And hope that you can help control Johan, he added silently. *If it fails, they're going to want to kill him.*

Chapter Thirty-Six

"Breathe in," Elaine instructed. "And then breathe out."

Johan, his eyes closed, did his best to obey. It was hard to quiet his mind, even just before sleep, but he had to try. After what had happened to Hawthorne, Elaine had suggested that he might be able to get in touch with his magic after all ...but, so far, all that had happened in three days of attempted meditation had been him falling asleep twice. Elaine had laughed and admitted that had happened to her too more than once.

"I can hear my heartbeat," he announced, after a moment. It was true; his heartbeat suddenly seemed to be pounding away. "But I can't feel anything else."

He opened his eyes. Elaine was facing him, sitting cross-legged with her own eyes closed. She looked oddly sweet and yet vulnerable in that pose, even though he knew that she had insisted they walk extensively until she was used to walking again on her rebuilt leg. And, for that matter, that she'd been casting spells with her new wand until she knew precisely how best to use it. She might have told him that wands were largely unnecessary, but she clearly hadn't been happy to lose the wand Hawthorne had snapped.

"No worries," Elaine said, opening her eyes. She hadn't bothered with the glamour; the red light that seemed to be burning inside her skull was as disconcerting as ever. Johan had wondered if he could get rid of it, but Elaine had flatly refused when he'd offered. Spells intended to repair eyesight might go spectacularly wrong when used by an untrained magician. "We can try again tomorrow."

Johan felt his eyes narrow as she stood up, smoothing down her shirt. "How long did it take you to master it?"

"Months," Elaine said. "But then, I was never a very powerful magician ..."

She broke off, glancing around as if she'd heard something.

"Someone is coming," she said, reaching for her wand. "A ward was just triggered, right by the bog."

Johan rose to his feet as she walked over to the window, wand in hand. They'd talked about what to do if the cabin was attacked, but in truth he knew that escape would be difficult, no matter how quickly they ran. If they stayed on the paths, they were likely to be tracked down with ease; if they went off the paths, they were quite likely to get lost. And if the enemy had werewolves or tracking spells, it would be very hard to break free.

"It's Dread," Elaine said, relaxing slightly. "And he's carrying a large bag."

Johan smiled as the Inquisitor stamped up to the cabin and stepped inside, after taking off his shoes. Dread still bothered him – he *was* an Inquisitor, after all – but he was clearly Elaine's friend, perhaps more than a friend. Elaine didn't seem to have a social life; Dread was the only person, apart from Light Spinner, she met on a regular basis. But he was still an Inquisitor.

"Hawthorne will be going back to the capital," Dread stated, as Elaine passed him a mug of hot Kava. "There are several druids who wish to take a look at him."

Elaine nodded, seemingly unsurprised. "You'd think they didn't trust the druids up here."

"They don't," Dread said. His tone was droll, almost sardonic. "The Golden City is the epitome of magical learning and research in the Empire. There is no possibility that anyone from outside the city can match the druids inside the city."

Johan smiled, remembering Charity's stories from the Golden City. There had been many social barriers between the students – and those who had come from outside the city often faced a hard task in being accepted by their peers. Jamal had never complained, but then Jamal had had the arrogance to brush his way through any mocking sneers. And besides, loath as Johan was to admit it, his brother was a powerful magician. He could have handled a few sneers.

"I have letters for you both," Dread added, opening his bag. Johan was impressed to note just how many protective spells there were on the leather, protecting the material inside from prying eyes. "Elaine, one of them is from the Grand Sorceress."

Elaine took a gold-edged letter and carried it over to the table to read. Johan watched her go, then took a letter Dread offered him. It seemed to have been enclosed in a white envelope that was expensive, but not as expensive as the ones his father used. And the hand that had addressed it was unfamiliar ... yet definitely feminine. He realised, with a thrill of delight, that it had to come from Jayne. It was suddenly hard to open it carefully, rather than tearing it open.

Inside, there was a single piece of paper. He read it ... and felt the bottom drop out of his world.

> *Johan.*
> *I thought you were a decent guy. I liked you. Now you've ruined my future. I had my life planned out, a life where I would accomplish something of my own. Now it has been taken from me by you. Your father made that quite clear to me.*
> *I will not marry you. I will not sleep with you. I will not have children with you.*
> *I swear to you that if we are forced to marry, I will make every day of our shared life a living hell.*
> *Burn in hell.*
> *Jayne, of no House.*

Johan stared down at the letter, unable to understand. What had happened? What the hell did she think he'd done? He hadn't cheated on her; they'd barely even started their relationship!

Elaine looked over at him. "Johan?" she asked. "What happened?"

"I don't know," Johan said. He was too shocked to be angry or sad, even though he knew he would be sooner or later. What had happened? "Jayne ... Jayne wrote me this letter."

He passed it to Elaine, then looked at the second letter Dread offered him. One look was enough to tell him that it came from his father; the envelope was expensive, the address written in his father's own hand. Feeling his shock gradually being replaced by anger, he tore the letter open and scanned it quickly. It was worse than he had dared fear.

Johan.
As a son of House Conidian, you are in need of a wife. I have taken the liberty of arranging for your betrothal to Jayne, of House Rendang. She is a younger daughter, but it is clear to me that you like her and care for her. The wedding will take place as soon as reasonably possible ...

Johan crumpled up the rest of the letter, wondering just how his father thought he would react to such a suggestion. There were so many subtle insults in the handful of paragraphs that it was hard to imagine that his father didn't know that they were there. Calling Jayne a younger daughter was a snide reminder that she wouldn't inherit much from her family – and thus she might not be a suitable wife for the Conidian's second son – but if Johan liked her, it might not matter. And besides, it would make them more dependent on Johan's father.

Someone must have been spying on us, he realised. Someone had seen them when they were eating and taken the news to his father. His father, not one to miss an opportunity to get his hooks in someone, had made a deal with Jayne's father, effectively *buying* the man's daughter for Johan. But *Jayne* hadn't consented ...

She wouldn't have had to consent, Johan recalled, remembering the marriage laws he'd looked up when the first suitor had come looking for Charity's hand. The suitor had been over twice her age, but that hadn't stopped their father taking it seriously. Charity had been deeply worried until the offer had finally been rejected. *She could only legally object after she turned twenty-one ... and if she reached that age, unmarried, few people would want her because they would suspect that there was something wrong with her. If her parents couldn't marry her off ...*

"I won't," he said, savagely. "What was he thinking?"

Elaine took the second letter from his hand, unfolded it and read it, quickly. "Is he out of his mind?"

"He must be," Johan said. "Why ...?"

"He's desperate," Dread said, very quietly. "You were important before you did ... your trick to Hawthorne; now, you're the most valuable and yet dangerous person in the Empire. If someone manages to get control of you, they'd have a good chance to become the next Grand Sorcerer."

"I am not a tool," Johan snapped. Bitterness and rage billowed up within him. Darkness seemed to fall over his vision. "I am not ..."

"Careful," Elaine said. Her voice seemed to come from a far distance. "*Johan*!"

Johan opened his eyes, unsure of when he'd closed them. The room was shaking, the tremors slowly fading away to nothingness. Dread was standing in front of him, one hand raised as if he were about to slap Johan hard. Johan hadn't realised just how close he had come to losing control completely. He sagged and had to be caught by the Inquisitor before he hit the floor.

"I can't ... she hates me," Johan said, desperately. "What have I *done* to her?"

"You've done nothing to her," Elaine said, sharply. "And it speaks well of you that you care enough to be angry."

Johan stared down at his hands. Part of his body was hinting that it really wouldn't mind being married to Jayne, the sooner the better. His mind told that part of his body to shut up; Jayne had had her ambitions, ambitions she could no longer realise ... just because he'd taken her out on a date. What had she done to deserve it? As the wife of a Conidian, she would be expected to be nothing more than a brood mare. At the very least, she would have to put off her studies until after she'd had several children.

What is the difference, he asked himself numbly, *between what Hawthorne planned to do to Elaine and this*?

It would be rape, plain and simple. He couldn't go through with the wedding.

"He can't force me into this," he said. "Can he?"

"I confess that your case is unique," Dread said. "But if you were prepared to reject the family altogether ..."

"Then I will," Johan said. "Or ..."

"There may be other problems," Elaine said. "Your

brother has been released."

Johan stared at her, too stunned by the first letters to be angry at this new piece of news. But then, it really *wasn't* a shock. He knew Jamal's skill at getting out of trouble too well to be surprised. If his father was unwilling to forget custom and tradition and promote Charity to be Prime Heir, he had to move the heavens and earth to free Jamal before it was too late. There would be no other candidate for Prime Heir until the younger kids reached eighteen years old.

"Why?" he snarled, finally. "How much did he have to pay?"

"There were oaths made," Dread said, simply. "Your father pledged his life that Jamal would behave himself."

"I'd better start looking for suitable clothes to wear for the funeral," Johan said, grimly. He knew that he would miss his father, but after the two pieces of bad news he found it hard to care if something happened to him. "A purple serge suit, a yellow and black polka-dot tie, green and mauve-striped shirt, gold monogrammed boots and a white bowler hat."

Elaine snorted, as if she were trying to hide a giggle. Dread merely scowled at the pair of them.

"I'm serious," Johan said, forcing himself to hold down a giggle himself. "Jamal cannot behave himself – and some idiot has just handed him a sure-fire way to kill his own father!"

"Your father does have excellent incentive to ensure that Jamal behaves himself," Dread observed. "His own life is at stake."

"Jamal is still Prime Heir," Johan snapped. Maybe he should have accepted his father's offer and become Prime Heir himself, even though it would have tied him to the family he wanted to escape. "What's to stop him breaking the oath and killing my father? What blasted idiot thought that *this* was a good idea?"

"The Privy Council," Elaine said, tartly. "And wouldn't there be consequences if your brother killed his father deliberately?"

"I *know* him," Johan insisted. "Jamal is not even remotely capable of not acting badly."

"Your father will handle it or die," Dread said, before

Johan could continue. "I assume that you wish to head back to the Golden City?"

"I think so," Elaine said. She smiled, then pocketed the gold-edged letter. "You'd think there would be a crystal ball here."

"The Inquisitors who normally come here are expected to recuperate," Dread pointed out. "If they knew what was going on, they'd feel compelled to do something, even if they were at death's door. We are not taught how to relax or to give up."

Johan smiled, remembering the *Grand High Inquisitor* books Charity had been fond of reading. They'd been trash; the hero of the book alternatively catching Dark Wizards with effortless ease or bedding his way through the planet's population. It was a minor miracle, Johan remembered thinking, that he hadn't also left thousands of children in his wake. But then, he would probably have known how to prevent his conquests from becoming pregnant.

The thought made his smile grow wider. There had been a note in the back of the book, where the author had claimed that she had known hundreds of Inquisitors *very* intimately and her stories were based firmly in reality. After meeting some Inquisitors for himself – and a Dark Wizard – Johan was fairly sure that she'd made them all up from whole cloth. It was a bigger miracle that the Inquisition hadn't sued.

"We'll go down after lunch and catch an Iron Dragon, if they're running normally now," Elaine said. "And, once we're back at the library, we will try to sort out this ghastly mess."

***

This time, Elaine couldn't help noticing, Johan was not so fascinated by the Iron Dragon, or the countryside as they headed back to the Golden City. He alternated between rage and frustration – and a bitterness that his relationship with Jayne had been so easily destroyed. Elaine was no expert in relationships, but she understood how the girl had felt – and, no doubt, she had believed that Johan had asked his father to arrange the match. There were girls who would be delighted at the arrangement. Jayne, clearly, wasn't one of them.

Johan's father had sent the marriage contracts in a separate envelope. Elaine examined them carefully – she'd had to talk Johan out of destroying them – looking for loopholes. But there was nothing that suggested itself to her; Johan's father and Jayne's father had given their approval and both children were too young to legally object. If she'd been more powerful, Elaine suspected, her own Guardian would probably have sold her off to the highest bidder. Or maybe he had tried and the Witch-King had interfered. It would have taken Elaine away from the Great Library, ruining one of his plans.

"They can't force us into bed together," Johan said. "Can they?"

"There *are* potions that can do just that," Elaine commented, still reading the documents. "I don't think Jayne would miss them trying to use such potions if you were locked in the same room together."

It was interesting just how few clauses there actually were. Stripped of legalese, Johan's father had promised to give Jayne's father a lot of money – and not much else. It was odd to see a daughter sold so blatantly, which made her wonder if she was missing something. Normally, the true nature of the deal would be concealed behind a tissue of nonsense; here, it was blunt and almost shockingly honest. But then, Jayne *was* a younger child. Perhaps they'd just decided that the niceties weren't important.

Poor girl, Elaine thought, grimly. She looked over at Johan. *Poor boy.*

"I think there's only one loophole we can use, short of you severing all ties with your family," Elaine said. That would have been tricky even before Johan had stripped Hawthorne of his power. Now ... he would need at least one Great House obliged to defend him. "I want to take you on as my apprentice."

Johan hesitated. "Is that wise?"

"You would need my consent to get married in that case, as long as you were my apprentice," Elaine said, simply. "I would obviously not grant consent, so you wouldn't have to honour the marriage contract. Your father might claim that you can't take on an apprenticeship without his permission, but the Grand Sorceress already gave her consent, which automatically overrides your father's opinion."

"And, as you offered me the apprenticeship before the contract was signed," Johan said, "father can't claim that you took me on just to help evade the marriage."

But that was what we are doing, Elaine thought. Johan was right, though. The apprenticeship had been offered before the marriage contract.

"I will," Johan said. "Will you take me as your apprentice?"

"I will be a hard taskmaster," Elaine warned. There were still too many question marks over Johan's powers – and how they would respond to an apprenticeship oath. But she knew that she dared not let Johan become a pawn in the power struggle she knew was threatening to sweep over the Golden City. "You have been warned."

"You already have been a hard taskmaster," Johan grumbled.

Beside him, Dread barked a laugh.

Johan scowled at him, then held out a hand. "Tell me," he said. "How do we do it?"

"Once you have spoken to Jayne," Elaine said, firmly. "You need to patch things up or cut them neatly first, or your feelings will interfere with the bond."

Chapter Thirty-Seven

The Waving Wand was neutral territory, as everyone knew. It was a single bar, in the heart of the city, owned and operated by an incredibly powerful sorcerer who seemed disinclined to take part in the constant struggle for supremacy among the different factions. Instead, he just served drinks and excellent food, and chatted to his customers, while remaining strictly uninvolved in politics. The one time a faction had tried to pressure him was still legendary amongst the city's population, most of whom liked the idea of a place where the factions could meet without automatic hostility.

Johan stepped into the bar, glancing around in astonishment. It was large, divided up into a number of booths that allowed the inhabitants to have private conversations without being overheard; a stern message warned newcomers that troublesome customers would be transfigured into pigs and fed to better-behaved visitors. That would be murder, Johan knew, as well as cannibalism, but the warning seemed to have been taken to heart. There were plenty of people in the bar, yet there was no fighting. They weren't even waving their wands at one another.

He caught sight of Jayne, swallowed hard, and walked over to where she was sitting. She looked miserable, wearing her Peerless School robes rather than the library uniform or the dress she'd worn on their first date. Her black hair had been tied into pigtails, making her look younger than she actually was; her face had been scrubbed clean of makeup. Johan had no way of sensing a glamour under normal circumstances, but he was sure she wasn't using one. She truly was as miserable as she looked.

"Hi," he said. "I ..."

Jayne raised a hand, as if she were going to slap him, then lowered it slowly. "You *bastard*," she said. "I ..."

"It wasn't my decision," Johan said, quietly. Elaine had

told him that Jayne would rant and scream at him, but he was not to lose his temper. She wasn't to blame for the situation either. "My father ... my father wants to control me."

"He's already got his hooks in me," Jayne snapped, bitterly. "What Potions Master will take me on now?"

Johan scowled. It was rare for a husband – rarer still for a wife – to take on an apprenticeship; the relationship between master and student was very close, often too close for comfort. In theory it wasn't actually supposed to become sexual, but all the books he'd read had brought up the possibility. It was quite easy for intimacy in one field to drift into another. Even if Johan didn't object, people would talk ... particularly if Jayne hadn't given him children.

"I intend to break the contract," he said, simply. "You will not be forced into marrying me."

Jayne looked at him, sharply. "My father has already taken money from your father," she said. "I was ordered ... I was told ..."

"Don't worry about it," Johan said. He could guess. Sleeping together before marriage would hardly seal anything, not when it was common among young magicians, but their parents might expect it to bind them closer together. "And you won't lose your job at the library either."

Jayne looked up, tears in her eyes. "Are you *sure*?"

"Positive," Johan said. Elaine had assured him that she didn't care about whatever pressure Johan's father could bring to bear. The Great Library was neutral too, at least in theory. It would be hard for Johan's father to influence Elaine's staffing decisions. "As long as you don't resign, the job is yours."

"My father has been pressing me to resign," Jayne said. "What will become of us?"

"You will not be blamed," Johan said, carefully. "I think you can just resume your life."

But he had a feeling that it wouldn't be that simple. His father might just keep pressuring Jayne, in the hopes that it would force Johan to concede and go back to the family. It would be cruel, but Johan knew that his father's determination to make the family wealthy and powerful often pushed him into doing cruel things. But surely they had wealth and power enough already?

I'll be Elaine's apprentice, he told himself. *There would be no point in pushing at Jayne once I take the oaths.*

"I would understand," he said, "if you didn't want to see me again."

The thought was a bitter one. He'd liked Jayne – and seeing the glances some of the younger staff threw at him when they thought he wasn't looking had chilled him to the bone. *They* believed that it was his fault that Jayne's life had been damaged, perhaps ruined. And how could he really blame them, when dating him had been enough to turn Jayne's life into a nightmare? And it hadn't even been his fault!

"I don't know," Jayne said. She reached out and squeezed his shoulder, then stood up. "I'll let you know."

She walked away despondently. Johan watched her go, realising that she wasn't swinging her hips or doing anything even remotely seductive. She just wanted to leave.

He heard someone clearing his throat and looked up, into the eyes of a man dressed in black robes. "There is someone who would like to meet with you," he said. Johan saw the wand at his belt and knew that he was dealing with the owner personally. "Would you wish to talk with him?"

"Depends," Johan said. He looked past the owner and froze. *Jamal* was standing there. For a moment, he was tempted to say no, then he changed his mind. "Why not?"

Jamal didn't look very good, Johan realised, as his elder brother sat down facing him. He looked thinner, almost gaunt; his face was pale and worn. But his eyes still had traces of the old arrogance Johan had come to hate ...

.... And yet he didn't hate him so much now. When he'd been younger, Jamal had seemed all-powerful, but now he'd faced a Dark Wizard ... and won. Whatever else happened, he told himself, he would never be scared of his brother again.

"I have been told to apologise to you," Jamal said. There was nothing in his voice to convince Johan that he actually *meant* it. "Father says that I acted badly."

"The understatement of the year," Johan answered, flatly.

"And you tattled on me," Jamal added. "Why did you do

that?"

Johan sighed. "You haven't learned anything, have you?"

Jamal reached for his wand. "I can ..."

"Nothing," Johan said. "You can do nothing. Not here and not elsewhere."

"Not here," Jamal agreed. "But why?"

It was strange, Johan realised. He had his memories of Jamal as a terrifying figure, always ready to cast a spell to humiliate his younger powerless brother. But now ... he had the oddly-reduced person sitting in front of him, still with traces of arrogance, yet weaker than Johan remembered. And Johan had magic too ...

"You have always had power," Johan said, quietly. Maybe it was worth an attempt to teach his elder brother where he'd gone wrong. "You never had to earn it, you never had to do anything to prove yourself worthy of it; you just had it. Birth gave you advantages that many magicians couldn't match. You never really realised that those advantages came from sheer luck, rather than anything else.

"And when you discovered that others didn't have those advantages, you looked down on them," he added. "You looked down on your fellow magicians who came from poorer backgrounds, you looked down on people without magic ... you even looked down on your younger siblings, just because they weren't *you*. And you treated me very badly.

"Did it never occur to you that what you were doing was wrong? Did you never think that the people you tormented might have had thoughts and feelings of their own? Did you never realise that you were just becoming a pointless bully, rather than the worthy heir to a Great House? Or were you so consumed with the thought that you were unthinkingly superior that you never even *wondered* about your actions?"

"I am strong," Jamal said. He didn't meet Johan's eyes. "The strong rule the weak. That is the way of the universe."

Johan smiled. "Really? Ask Hawthorne what he thinks of that *now*."

He sighed, tightly. "But you never even questioned your own doctrine," he said. "You just *did* it. And, when you finally got into trouble, you were more outraged at being arrested than you were at your own actions."

Jamal gave him a long look. "Is it true? Did you really render a Dark Wizard powerless?"

"I did," Johan said, calmly. He looked into his brother's face and smiled. "I will never be scared of you again."

"No, clearly so," Jamal said. "Father ... father wishes you to take my place."

"Father can wait until the skies fall and the heavens open," Johan snapped, remembering the one story that most of the religions shared. One day, there would be a final conflict between the gods and their chosen followers. The winner would be the sole god of the next universe. "I have no interest in returning home."

Cold rage burned through his mind. He could lash out at Jamal, he could force him to endure everything that Johan had endured, he could even take his magic ... and yet it seemed pointless. After Hawthorne, his brother was just a nuisance. It would be fitting, part of Johan's mind whispered, to rid him of his magic. Let him see what life as a Powerless was like. But somehow it didn't seem worth the effort.

"You can tell him, furthermore, that I am going to apprentice myself to the Head Librarian," he added. "I will no longer be under his control. And he can take his plans and shove them ..."

Jamal let out an incredulous bark of laughter. "You're going to apprentice yourself to the *Head Librarian*?" he asked. "What is she going to teach you? Shelving books? How to chase down people who don't return their books on time and turn them into books themselves? How to ..."

"How to be someone who isn't part of a Great House," Johan said, quietly. He wanted to punish the insults Jamal had aimed at Elaine, but he had something more fitting in mind. "I think, *brother*, that you will not be Prime Heir much longer. Charity is far more suited to the role than yourself. Our father has finally realised just what sort of person you are. If you don't manage to improve yourself ... you might find yourself being kicked out of the family."

He twisted his face into a sneer, an expression he'd learned from Jamal himself.

"And what will *you* do, without the family? You are powerful, but unfocused; you have no magicians lining up to offer you an apprenticeship of your own. Father will not offer any reward for taking you on, not if you are disowned. You will sink into the gutter or go work outside the city ..."

"*Enough*," Jamal barked. His fingers were clutching his wand. "You have said enough and more than enough. I should ..."

"Go right ahead," Johan taunted. "But just remember what happened to *Hawthorne*."

Jamal's fingers slipped away from the wand. "I ... I'll make you pay, somehow," Jamal promised, as he stood up. But there was a flash of fear in his eyes that ruined the effect, somehow. "Be seeing you, *brother*."

Johan watched him leave, then blinked as the owner came over to his table again. "There is one more person who wishes to speak with you," the owner said. "Can he join you?"

"Of course," Johan said, as grandly as he could. Inside, he was puzzled. Who *else* would come to speak with him? "Please, invite him to sit down."

The newcomer wasn't dressed in robes, merely a suit that suggested that he was a prosperous merchant. There was no wand, no trace of anything that could be considered magic apart from a protective amulet around his neck. Johan had seen plenty of similar artefacts in various books, back when he'd been trying to convince his family that he would be safe outside, away from the house's wards. His father had never been convinced.

Johan studied him, thoughtfully. He looked young, about twenty-five, with sandy-blonde hair and a faint smile flickering over his face. In some ways, there was a diffidence about him that reminded Johan of Elaine, but there was also a sharpness in the man's eyes that reminded him of his father. This man might have no magic, yet he was clearly not a man to cross.

"My name is Hawke," the man said, as he sat down. "And I wish to discuss politics."

Johan took a wild guess. "Leveller?"

Hawke nodded. "Among other things," he said. "I

understand that we have you to thank for the capture of some of the terrorists?"

"Yes," Johan said, unsure of what to say. As a Powerless, he would have been devoted to the Leveller cause, but now ... he shook his head, angrily. Did he think that his sudden power meant that Jamal had been right all along? "But they were released ..."

"Under strict conditions," Hawke said. He smiled, rather sadly. "To tell you the truth, I was expecting that they would be released without charge."

"Me too," Johan said.

Hawke placed his fingertips together. "I shall come right to the point," he said. "We have heard rumours that you stripped a Dark Wizard of his powers. Is that actually true?"

Johan hesitated, then nodded.

"We also heard rumours that you were a Powerless," Hawke added. "Is that true too?"

"Yes," Johan said, flatly.

"Which leads us to the all-important question," Hawke said. "Can you give other people powers as well as take them away?"

"I do not know," Johan said. Elaine had refused when he'd offered to try, pointing out that power-enhancing rituals often came with a cost. So far, he seemed to have escaped madness ... but Elaine was a more normal magician. Who knew what would happen to her if he tried? "Dare I assume that you want me to try?"

"Among other things," Hawke said. "We no longer wish to be subordinate to the magicians who rule the world. There are ... threads we can follow that may give us a surprise, but we need magic too."

"If you had magic," Johan pointed out, "you would no longer be *mundane*." He scowled. "And what would that make you?"

Hawke met his eyes. "And what has it made *you*?"

"I wish I knew," Johan said. Part of him was tempted to try, just to see if it could be done; the experiment would definitely settle the question. But Elaine had warned him not to experiment without her and he intended to do as she said. Besides, he needed to be her apprentice. It was the only way to get Jayne out of trouble. "The experiment would have to be carefully planned."

"Do it now," Hawke said, bowing his head. There was a naked desperation in his voice that surprised and worried Johan. "Make me a magician!"

"Not now," Johan said. He didn't dare do anything in public, not when there were so many rumours flying around. "Why ...?"

Hawke reached into his pocket and produced a small frog, tinier than his hand. "This is my daughter," he said, softly. "There were two groups of magicians who searched our houses after that young idiot was knifed to death. The Inquisitors were polite, the others ... the others turned Mildred into this and said that if I didn't find the murderer, she would be stuck this way forever. I ... none of the magicians I spoke to were prepared to break the spell! She's only *nine*!"

Johan felt a cold shiver of horror running down his spine. He'd been transfigured more times than he cared to count, often into something worse than a frog. But Mildred would never have faced a magician, certainly not on a regular basis. Johan had reluctantly become used to being turned into something as a joke; Mildred had to be finding the whole experience nightmarish. She was so small that someone could squash her accidentally.

"Give her to me," Johan said. He took the frog and looked down at it – *her*. The frog was trembling against his hand. "I ..."

He closed his eyes and concentrated, willing Mildred back into human form. His hand was suddenly dashed against the table as the frog expanded outwards, back into a small girl with long pigtails. She was so much like a younger version of Jayne that she made his heart stop for a long moment. Mildred rolled over and hugged her father, tightly. She was sobbing so loudly that she was attracting attention from the other customers, despite the privacy wards.

"I'll do what I can to help," Johan promised. If he'd known who was responsible, he would have gone to wherever they lived and stripped their magic away before anyone could stop him. "And I will talk to the Inquisitors.

The person responsible for this will pay."

Taking one last look at the restored girl, he walked out of the bar and headed back towards the library, already composing what he wanted to say to Dread. It was clear that *someone* apart from the Inquisitors had been trying to catch the murderer ... and equally clear that the Leveller leadership had had nothing to do with it. To torment a young girl like that was torture – and the fact that it was pointless only made it worse. Dread, he was sure, would take a very dim view of it. If nothing else, the vigilantes would probably get in the way of the official investigation.

And, now that he had spoken to Jayne, he could take up the apprenticeship.

And his father could take his worthless marriage contracts and rip them into very little pieces.

Chapter Thirty-Eight

"He said *what?*"

"He said that he was going to take on an apprenticeship," Jamal said. "He said it was going to be with the Head Librarian."

Duncan stared at him in absolute disbelief. The Head Librarian? What could *she* possibly teach anyone? It wasn't as though operating a library was actually *difficult*. And why would Johan want to be a librarian anyway? He wanted to travel the world and prove himself, not be tied down in one building for the rest of his life. Rumour had it that the Head Librarian was stuck there for the remainder of the Grand Sorceress's term. The previous one had certainly been trapped until the Grand Sorcerer had died.

But she'd definitely left the city at least once ...

He pushed the thought aside and looked up at his son. "What else did he say?"

"Not much," Jamal said, softly. "He ... he just said that he didn't want to be part of the family any longer. And that the Grand Sorceress had already given her approval."

"Thank you," Duncan said, crossly. He'd hoped that Jamal and Johan would patch together their differences if Jamal apologised, but it was clear that it hadn't gone the way he had hoped. An *apprenticeship*? No matter who took him on as a pupil, Duncan knew, the ties binding Johan to his family would fray to the point where Duncan could no longer hope to influence him. "You may go."

Jamal stood up and left the room. Duncan stared down at the table, thinking hard. Was Johan so determined to escape the family that he was prepared to apprentice himself to the Head Librarian – or was there something else going on? On the face of it, the very thought was absurd; students apprenticed themselves to Potions Masters or Alchemists or even Charmers, not librarians. Besides, there were plenty of openings in the Great Library that didn't require an apprenticeship. For the poorer students, it was the easiest way to earn some spending money.

In theory, Johan would need his father's approval to take on an apprenticeship, but if the Grand Sorceress had already given her approval Duncan knew that it was far too late to object, at least openly. And besides, Johan could take the oaths and then ... it would be hard to free him from the apprenticeship, even if he had taken the oaths without his father's permission. It was illegal to force someone to break a magically-binding oath, even for the Head of a Great House. If Johan took the oaths ...

There was a knock at the door. "My Lord," May began, "Lord ..."

Duncan sighed. "It's Deferens, isn't it?"

"Yes," May said, showing no sign of surprise. For all she knew, he monitored the wards at the door constantly, although that would have left him no time for doing anything else. "He wishes to speak with you urgently."

"Show him in," Duncan said, with another sigh. He was far too aware of just how indebted he had become to the younger wizard – and of Deferens' access to places and information he really shouldn't have been able to reach. Duncan liked being in control, but he had a feeling that it was Deferens who was really in command. "And then bring us both a stiff drink."

Deferens looked deeply worried, he realised, as May showed him into the room. His outfit was as neat as ever, but his face was pale. He plonked his staff down, leaning it against the wall, and then sat down without an invitation. It was such a breach of etiquette that Duncan realised that Deferens was on the verge of absolute panic.

"Do you know," he said, without bothering with any small talk, "just who your son met after your other son left him alone?"

"No," Duncan said, feeling a sinking sensation in his chest. At this point, he wouldn't have been surprised to hear that it had been the Grand Sorceress herself. Or, alternatively, the leaders of the opposing factions in the Golden City. "Who did he meet?"

"Hawke," Deferens informed him. The name was unfamiliar to Duncan. "The Leveller leader."

Duncan stared at him. "My son met a *Leveller*?"

"Indeed," Deferens said, grimly. "Hawke is a prosperous merchant who pays his taxes on time, which is more than can be said for most of them. This somehow gives him the impression that, despite being mundane, he should have a say in how his taxes are spent. He is one of the leaders of the Leveller Movement and, perhaps, its biggest funder. And, despite being interrogated by the Inquisitors, he managed to hide his involvement in the death of young Graham."

Duncan's eyes narrowed. "How do you know he was to blame if he managed to fool the Inquisitors?"

"There are ways to fool truth potions or spells that even a mundane can use," Deferens said, softly. "They can wipe their own memories, or ingest a counter-potion, or even ... well, there are dozens of potential methods. But who else would have a motive for killing Graham?"

He cleared his throat. "The problem is that he spent quite a bit of time talking to Johan," he concluded. "And what, I wonder, did they talk about?"

Duncan considered it. He wouldn't have blamed Johan, back when everyone had thought him powerless, for being attracted to the Levellers. Now, though, Johan had come into his powers ... and, clearly, had the power to make himself a very important and feared person indeed. Why would he *still* want to talk with the Levellers? And what might they have talked about?

"I wish I knew," he said, slowly. "First an apprenticeship with the Head Librarian, now this ..."

Deferens used a word in a language Duncan didn't recognise. It didn't sound pleasant.

"The Grand Sorceress is making a power bid," he snapped. "*That's* what's going on!"

Duncan stared at him. "How do you know?"

"What sort of apprenticeship could he get," Deferens demanded, "if he works under the Head Librarian?"

He snorted, rudely. "But the Head Librarian is Light Spinner's closest ally on the Privy Council," he added. "If Johan swears to obey her, and that is part of the apprenticeship oaths, he will effectively be Light Spinner's tool. What will happen when some magician decides that he disagrees with her? *Your son* will be sent to strip him of his magic!"

Duncan blanched. Power was everything to a magician; it was what separated them from the teeming masses of powerless mundanes, all of whom were helpless before a magician. The thought of losing his power was a magician's worst nightmare. What Johan had done had made the entire community uneasy, even if it had only been a Dark Wizard who had been stripped of his powers. But Hawthorne had never posed such a fundamental threat to the entire social order.

Johan might not want to do what Light Spinner said. But the oaths of apprenticeship would force him to obey.

"Or what if she decides that someone *deserves* magic?" Deferens asked. "Could your son give it to him?"

"I ..." Duncan broke off, remembering the yearly tests the druid had run. All of them had agreed; Johan had no magic, nor had he any prospect of getting it. By the time Johan had turned seven, Duncan had known that the tests were useless ... which hadn't stopped him from clinging to the last tiny flickers of hope. "He had no magic."

Deferens lifted his eyebrows, quizzically.

"Johan had no magic," Duncan said. "All the tests agreed that he had nothing, not even a spark that could be fanned into a flame. And now he has strange powers and ..."

"And an ability to take magic from someone," Deferens said. "If he had no magic, yet somehow developed it, what's to stop someone else doing the same?"

Duncan hesitated. He wanted to argue that it was something in his family's bloodline that had produced Johan, but he had seen all of the test results. There had been nothing there; even the handful of procedures he'd pushed the druid into running, ignoring the man's advice, had produced nothing. And yet Johan had developed powers.

"Nothing," he said, finally. "Nothing at all."

Deferens stood up and started to pace. "We have to act now," he said, shortly. "As Patriarch of House Conidian, it is your duty to rein in your wayward son."

"Johan isn't listening to me," Duncan said. "And how can I blame him?"

He'd failed. He'd failed all of his elder children. Jamal had become a bully, Charity had withdrawn into herself ... and Johan, who had suffered the worst, wanted nothing more to do with the family. The family magic prodded at him, reminding him of his failure; somehow, he would have to do better for the younger children. But he wasn't even sure where to begin.

"Then you need to stop him, now," Deferens said. "You have to have him killed."

Duncan's head snapped up, staring at him. "I can't ..."

"You must," Deferens insisted. "What will happen to House Conidian if your son becomes Light Spinner's most feared enforcer? How will the other Great Houses react to this development? And what would happen if Johan decided to avenge himself on you?"

"No," Duncan said. But Deferens was right. If the balance of power shifted so badly, the other Great Houses would start looking for someone to blame ... and House Conidian was vulnerable. Everything that Duncan and his father and his grandfather had worked for would be destroyed under the concentrated malice of the older Great Houses. "I can't kill my son."

"Some would say that you should have killed him long ago," Deferens said, quietly. "And they will blame you for that too."

Duncan shuddered. A Powerless in the family suggested weakness in the blood. When one appeared, they were often killed after it became clear that they would never develop magic – or expelled from the family and, if they were lucky, given to a mundane family to raise. But he had never been able to bear the thought of giving up his son, even though it might have been better for him. And yet ... Johan's presence, even though it was largely unknown, had damaged the family's prospects even before he developed his powers.

A Family Patriarch had ultimate authority over his children, at least until they reached the age of maturity. He could arrange marriage contracts, steer their education, even select their friends ... and discipline them if they were naughty. And, if they were too disgraceful for the family to tolerate, he could disown them or even kill them. But it was a dangerous line to cross. It had been bad enough contemplating removing Jamal as Prime Heir. Killing one of his children was worse.

And if you're wrong, he thought numbly, *the magic that binds the family together will turn on you.*

"There's no choice," Deferens said. "Act now or be forever lost."

Duncan knew what he had to do. He just didn't want to do it.

It wouldn't be *criminal*, he knew. It wouldn't break his oath. But it was still a terrifying and appalling thought.

"Damn you," he muttered.

***

"You need to spend this evening in silent contemplation," Elaine said, softly.

"I want to contemplate tearing the person who did *that* into very little pieces," Johan said. He'd told her and Dread about the stunt someone had pulled with Hawke's daughter as soon as he got back to the Great Library. Dread had been predictably furious and set out to find the person responsible. "To do that to a kid ..."

"You're *meant* to contemplate why you want to be an apprentice," Elaine said. She didn't sound offended, merely understanding. "And if you want to back out, you can."

Johan frowned, giving her a long look. "Are you ... are *you* having second thoughts?"

"My offer of an apprenticeship was genuine," Elaine assured him. "But you do understand that you will be binding yourself to me for at least five years? If you want to back out, the time is *before* you take the oaths."

"If I can," Johan said. He wasn't blind to the risks Elaine was taking. If, for some reason, his magic refused to allow him to uphold his share of the oaths, Elaine would be binding herself to him without him being bound to her. "But I have already made up my mind."

Elaine smirked. "I will be a very hard taskmaster," she said. She'd said the same thing every time the subject had

380

been brought up. "And there will be a great deal of hard work."

She smiled, more openly. "And research into your powers," she added. "If we could find out a way to duplicate them ..."

Johan shrugged. The druids who had examined Hawthorne had all agreed that he was a mundane; indeed, if they hadn't *known* that he'd been a Dark Wizard, they might have assumed that he'd been a victim rather than a victimiser. There was no trace of magic left in his body; Dread had noted that the side-effects of his experiments might well kill him before the former Dark Wizard could face the headsman. Johan was honestly not sure why they hadn't simply killed him at once.

"If you can," he said, remembering Hawke's desperate plea for powers. Elaine had been disturbed by the request; Dread, thankfully, hadn't stayed around long enough to hear *that* part of the story. It was hardly criminal to pray for powers – Johan had done it himself, more than once – but if it were possible ... it would turn society upside down. "But I want to learn more than I want to be studied. And I want to explore."

Elaine made a face. Johan had already discovered that she didn't like travelling, let alone roughing it in a primitive cabin, even if they *did* have magic to help with the hard work. But he had convinced her to agree that they could travel ... maybe next time they'd stay in an inn with proper room service. It would be expensive, but Elaine seemed to have plenty of money, even discounting her salary as a member of the Privy Council. And Johan still had the money his father had given him. He'd checked with the bank and apparently there were no obvious strings attached.

"We can try," Elaine said. "But not for long."

Johan smiled. Elaine had been raised in an orphanage, where there had been dozens of kids, and she'd gone to the Peerless School ... and yet she was scared of crowds. Put her at a table with twelve others and she would barely say a word. But Johan, who had been a virtual prisoner inside his home, had no trouble blending into the crowd. He could have happily gone to one of the parties Jamal had taken such pleasure in describing, although he might have skipped the entertainments. Drunken students were bad enough, but when they started to use magic ...

"Of course not," he assured her. He looked around her room, noting that she'd somehow managed to bring in even more books. Most of them looked to be on apprenticeship oaths; one of them which she was skimming through, discussed applying such oaths to mundanes, who could not normally swear oaths. "Did you write the oath?"

Elaine nodded. "It should be upheld," she said. She passed him a piece of paper. "But you have to be careful. Your magic is so ... strange."

Johan nodded. Part of the reason magicians ruled – apart from godlike power – was because they could swear oaths that would be magically-binding. A magician who gave his word, bound up in his magic, would *keep* it or risk the consequences. And those consequences could be anything from a nasty scar to the loss of their magic or even death. But writing an oath for mundanes ... *that* was hard. The magic simply didn't lock onto them properly.

He looked down at the sheet of paper, careful not to even mouth the words as he read them. It was simple enough; he swore himself to be a good, faithful and true apprentice, to listen to his mistress and learn from her to the best of his ability. Elaine's side of the oath was even simpler; she pledged herself to serve as his tutor and do her best for him, unless he broke his side of the oath.

"It's almost like a marriage," he said, in surprise. "Love, honour and obey ..."

"The oaths for apprenticeships are more binding," Elaine said. "Most married partners are faithful only until they have produced their first children, then they tend to start finding lovers while remaining married in name only."

Johan shuddered. He knew more than he wanted to know about his father's affairs – it was astonishing what one could hear if one was quiet – but his imagination couldn't cope with the idea of his mother doing anything of the sort. She must have done it with his father, at least long enough to produce her brood, yet afterwards ... the very thought was impossible. He pushed it aside, then scowled. His mother had never paid much attention to any of her children.

If I have kids, he told himself, *I will treat them better.*

"We should take the oaths now," he said. "Tradition be buggered. We can do it here and now."

"We need to do it in the Garden of Apprenticeships," Elaine said. "Or someone will raise a legal challenge."

Johan rolled his eyes. What sort of person would raise a legal challenge to a simple apprenticeship? But *his* apprenticeship would hardly be *simple*. Like it or not, he was sacrificing his family ties, but giving Elaine a great deal of power over him. The slightest irregularity could be used as an excuse to try to pry them apart.

"Fine," he said. A thought occurred to him and he smiled. "But I refuse to have a stag night."

Elaine snorted, rudely.

Chapter Thirty-Nine

When she'd been living in the apartment with Daria, Elaine had been woken at dawn by the sound of the temple singers calling the faithful to prayer. In the Great Library, wrapped in spells that muffled all sound within the building, she needed to use a spell to snap herself awake at the appointed time. Coming awake, she swung her legs over and out of bed, then stood up and glanced at the clock. It was just before dawn.

She touched the wards and sent an order – wake Johan, gently – then headed into the bathroom, where she stripped and washed every last inch of her body. The rituals of accepting an apprentice were set in stone; Johan might have been correct that all they really had to do was say the oaths together, but Elaine knew that the rituals existed for reasons that were separate from the legal niceties. They gave their practitioners time to reflect on what they were doing, why they were doing it and if they *really* wanted to do it. Once she was clean, Elaine used a spell to dry herself and reached for the white robe.

The wards quivered a message to her – Johan was awake and washing too – then fell silent. Elaine nodded to herself, then tied her hair back into a long ponytail. Magic made grooming so much easier, although she remembered a girl from the Peerless School who would take hours to set her hair without magic. She'd been teased regularly until she'd mastered spells to silence her tormentors, but Elaine thought she understood. There was a certain comfort, sometimes, in doing things the mundane way. Besides, magic should be treated with respect, not used as a toy. No one knew better than her just how dangerous magic could be.

Once she was ready, she picked up the wand she'd borrowed and cast a simple light spell into the air, then cancelled it and placed the wand at her belt. She knew that she should practice casting spells without a wand – it had shocked her just how hard it had been to throw that spell at Hawthorne – but there had been no time. There might not be time in the future too, she knew; tutoring Johan while studying his magic was likely to take up much of her time, to the point where she might have to pass most of her duties to Vane permanently. Her deputy probably deserved her title too.

It was a bitter thought. Elaine loved books; they had been her friends and companions since she'd learned to read, taking her places she knew she would never have the nerve to visit in real life. Becoming a librarian had seemed the natural career choice; spending the rest of her life in the Great Library had seemed a worthwhile use of her time. And she'd gratefully accepted the promotion because, if she was being honest with herself, most of the work that involved interacting with customers could be passed on to Vane. But now ...

Maybe I should claim Howarth Hall, she told herself, and smiled. There were so many creditors that it *still* remained empty, despite the vast number of people who wanted to own a house in the Golden City. Maintaining it would still be beyond her, but perhaps she could rent rooms to visitors and only keep one floor for Johan and herself. But she still didn't want anything from the young gambler who had largely ignored her and then sold her out. Besides, his creditors might just start pressuring Elaine instead ...

Bracing herself, Elaine strode out of her room and down into Johan's suite. She tapped once, then opened the door; Johan was standing in front of the mirror, admiring himself. The white robe he'd been given made him look like a druid, although there was no belt of herbs or sickle hanging down to mark his rank. And, of course, the robe was of a different sheen; he couldn't pass for a druid at close range. But then, falsely claiming to be a magician or a healer was a criminal offence.

"You look good," she assured him, as he turned to face her. The white robe would be worn once and then placed in storage, at least until Johan's eldest son decided to take on an apprenticeship. His family didn't have any robes in storage and probably wouldn't have let Johan use them if they had. "But you also look tired."

"I couldn't sleep," Johan confessed. "Is that normal?"

"I was never an apprentice," Elaine admitted. "I have no idea if it is normal or not."

Johan smoothed down his robes, then sighed. "Do we get something to eat before we go?"

"I'm afraid not," Elaine said. "Once we swear the oaths, we will go eat at the temple and then come back here."

"It *does* sound like a marriage," Johan remarked. "What else do we do together?"

Elaine flushed, then rubbed her cheek in some annoyance. They *would* be living together, but as master and apprentice rather than husband and wife. She would give him a room in her suite, maybe even reconfigure parts of the library to grant them more space. Maybe they *did* need to find a house they could use ... hell, maybe she should swallow her pride and go outside the city. It was cheaper there, with fewer prying eyes.

"We work together," she said, sternly. She saw him trying to fight back a giggle and rolled her eyes. "And you learn from me. I have a ton of books you have to read before you get a morsel of breakfast."

Johan scowled, then realised that she was joking. He knew how to read – his tutors had been good, even if they hadn't been magicians – but she knew that he didn't share her fascination with books. For her, they had been an escape; for him, they had just been part of the prison walls holding him in. Still, there were quite a few books he ought to read – and not all of them were on magic. His father, for some reason, had never bothered to teach him more than a little etiquette.

Probably thought that his powerless son would forever remain a secret, Elaine thought. *And now it's too late to rebuild his relationship with Johan.*

"We should get a great breakfast," Johan said. He made a show of rubbing his tummy. "What do they serve at the temple?"

"The kind of food they think that all apprentices should be served," Elaine said, dryly. In truth, she had no idea. There were ritual meals, but they weren't part of the apprenticeship ceremony. "Are you ready to go?"

"I should have a wand," Johan said, softly. "Even if I can't use it, I should have one."

"We can buy you one if you like," Elaine said. She wasn't too keen on the idea – her problems with casting spells without a wand still nagged at her – but it could be done. "There is a more important question to be asked now."

She took a breath. "This is your last chance to change your mind," she said, forcing her voice to remain calm. The prospect of taking on an apprentice scared her, but it was also something she needed to do. "If you want to back out, you can do it now."

Johan hesitated, then shook his head. "I need this," he said. "I need to be free of my family, Jayne needs to be free of *her* family ... I have to do this."

Elaine scowled, angrily. She didn't have the clout to convince a Potions Master to take Jayne, certainly not now. Light Spinner, on the other hand, could probably talk one into it, certainly after Johan had sworn himself to Elaine. The gods alone knew where Johan and Jayne's relationship would go, if his father hadn't managed to kill it, but it would be at least five years before they could marry. But then, she doubted they would want to marry at all.

"Not the best of reasons," she said, reluctantly. "An apprenticeship exists to help the student develop. If you feel that this is best for you ..."

"I do," Johan said. "And ... I know this won't be easy for you, but I really appreciate it."

Elaine felt herself melt. How many others had told her that? No one, apart from Daria once or twice. Bee, for all the attentions he'd lavished upon her, had never truly *needed* her. But Johan needed her ... she pushed the emotion aside and stood upright, then looked him up and down. Her mouth was suddenly very dry.

"It's time to go," she said, quietly.

The Great Library never slept. Even when most students were tucked up in bed, there was always a handful of students trying frantically to study. Elaine would have preferred to leave through the hidden exits, but tradition couldn't be ignored, not on this day. She led Johan through the winding corridors and out through the main entrance, ignoring the stares and sidelong glances from the students and a couple of her staff members. There was no sign of Jayne, thankfully. The girl had taken a week off to hide in her room in the boarding apartment, according to Vane. Elaine could only pray that she was all right.

She won't be, her thoughts mocked her. *How would you feel if your life was suddenly upended so brutally that there was no hope of recovery?*

Elaine's life *had* been, she knew, but she'd been offered the post in the Great Library and started to rebuild her life. Or had she merely walked into a gilded cage? But she had at least enjoyed being in her prison, while Jayne would have hated every last moment of *hers*, even if she did like Johan. Johan's father, she told herself, had a lot to answer for.

Outside, the first shimmers of light were beginning to rise above the Four Peaks. Elaine motioned for Johan to climb into the carriage, then turned and took one final look at the Great Library. When she returned, she knew, the library would no longer be her first priority. She would have an apprentice, someone to whom she owed her full attention. Vane would need a promotion, or at least a raise. Once Johan was inside, she joined him and pulled the door closed. The driver, already briefed on his duties, cracked his whip and set the horses into motion.

Elaine closed her eyes, silently praying that they would reach the Garden of Apprenticeships before the sun rose fully above the Watchtower. Long-standing tradition insisted that apprenticeship oaths were spoken as soon as the first rays of sunlight reached the garden, symbolically linking the oaths with the magic of the dawn. Elaine knew that it didn't make a difference if the oaths were spoken at dawn or in the dead of night – or the middle of the day, for that matter – but it was important to honour tradition. Or, as Light Spinner had once cynically pointed out, to be seen to do so.

She reached out and squeezed Johan's hand, sensing his nervousness. He had good reason to worry, she knew; no one really understood how his magic would react to the oaths. Even Elaine, for all the knowledge in her head, had been stumped. It might behave normally and bind him to her, or it might do nothing, or ... it might do something completely unprecedented. Elaine would have bet money, if she'd been asked to bet, on the latter. When Johan became emotional, he started to lose control of his magic and surprises happened. It was almost the only normal thing about his powers.

The carriage rattled to a halt. Elaine jumped out, noting with relief that the sun hadn't yet risen high enough to cast light into the grove, and then motioned for him to join her. Johan hopped down, then followed her towards the line of trees. The Garden of Apprenticeships was surrounded by trees – and a number of spells – intended to keep prying eyes out, although they weren't truly effective. How could they be when so many people needed to use the garden?

Inside, the grove was hidden in darkness. Elaine muttered a spell that gave her basic night vision and looked around, silently admiring the effort the monks had put into creating their garden. There was a single pond of bubbling water, a series of paths that wrapped around the garden in a pattern that invoked the blessing of the gods ... and a flat patch of stone where they were meant to take their oaths. Statues of the gods were everywhere; Elaine could have sworn that they moved whenever she took her eyes off them. A chill ran down her spine as she looked into the statue of a winged human, its motionless face cast in an expression of profound sadness. There was something about it that terrified her, something oddly familiar ...

Johan coughed; the spell was broken. "Here we are," he said, very quietly. "What do we do now? And where are the monks?"

"This is a private moment between us and any witnesses we choose to invite," Elaine said. Unlike a wedding, where it was considered bad form not to invite everyone who was anyone, an apprenticeship ceremony was meant to be private. She had thought about inviting Dread, Light Spinner or Jayne, but in the end she had chosen to keep it completely private. No one knew what would happen when Johan spoke the oaths. "Do you have your oath?"

Johan reached into his pocket and produced the piece of paper – and a silver knife. "I do," he said, his voice barely above a whisper. Elaine checked, out of habit; it was the right piece of paper. "And I have the knife."

"Good," Elaine said. She reached into her own robes and pulled out her own knife. The oath was already memorised, ready to be spoken. When the time came, they would cut their palms and clasp hands, allowing their blood to mingle. It would seal the magic between them, binding mistress and apprentice together. Even after the five years were over, there would still be a link. "Come with me."

The garden seemed to grow colder as she led the way up towards the patch of stone. Magic crackled around the plinth, an echo of all the oaths that had been sworn since the Golden City had been founded. The first Grand Sorcerer had intended to keep a record of such oaths, Elaine knew, but it hadn't stopped the monks from creating somewhere truly holy. Even those who doubted the existence of the gods didn't doubt the power of magic – or of oaths, sworn by two magicians. And even if they had, it was oaths that bound the Empire together.

She looked up to see the first rays of sunlight sweeping down towards the garden. The trees shielded where they were standing, but that would change in a few minutes. She drew her wand, cast a numbing charm on her right hand, then cast a second charm on Johan's hand. It wasn't, strictly speaking, part of the ceremony, but the last thing they needed was pain to distract them when there was so little time. Blood-based rituals had to be completed very quickly or they would have to be started again, if the caster was lucky. There were plenty of horror stories about what happened to people who cast rituals that went wrong.

"All right," she said, as she lowered her wand. Her hand already felt useless, barely responsive to her thoughts. It was never easy to use such spells on one's own body. "When I give the order, cut your palm and clasp hands with me, then speak your oath."

Johan nodded, lifting his knife. "I'm ready ..."

The magic surrounding them spiked, suddenly. Elaine threw herself aside as a blast of red light came out of the darkness, aimed directly at her. There were *figures* there, emerging from the trees; Elaine stared in horror as she realised that someone had decided to profane the ceremony. Desperately, she lifted her wand and threw a spell at one of them, blowing him backwards to land amongst the trees. Two of his compatriots threw spells back at her, propelled with such power that all she could do was dodge.

"Get back," she snapped at Johan. He wasn't ready to duel with anyone, even if he had managed to beat a Dark Wizard. She had no idea how bad it could become if he tried to fight. "*Go!*"

She swore as she darted back, looking around. The sunlight was already streaming down into the grove; the ceremony was ruined, utterly. They would have to do it again tomorrow, right down to the smallest detail. She cast an emergency charm, summoning Dread and the Inquisitors, then raised her wand just in time to block another curse. Blue-green balefire flared in front of her, then crackled out of existence. Johan's bubble-shield stopped two more curses; his hands were raised, but he looked unsure of what to do. One of the magicians just crumbled to the ground; the others jumped back, then started hurling spells at Johan. One of them even animated the statues and sent them running at him. Elaine was almost impressed.

That moment of inattention killed her. She barely noticed the magic surge before it struck her, slicing through her protections and right into her flesh. Her body went rigid, as if she could no longer move; she tried to muster a counter-spell that didn't involve her wand or hand gestures, but it was already too late. She was glass, she realised numbly; she'd felt the spell before, back at the Peerless School. A second spell sent her falling over backwards ...

... And her body and thoughts shattered into a million pieces.

Chapter Forty

"No!"

Johan had been unsure of what to do as the newcomers attacked. All he'd been able to think of was self-protection, using his magic to shield himself from their attacks. But then a curse had stuck Elaine and she'd turned to glass and ...

She'd shattered.

He didn't know what would happen to someone who was transfigured into an inanimate object, which was then destroyed. A person who died in an animal form returned to human upon death, he knew, but what about a shattered form? Should she be spread across the ground in a thousand bloody pieces or was she merely trapped, eternally suffering? There was no way to know, merely ... she was dead. His one friend, the one person who had cared for him and taught him and had been willing to give up her job to offer him an apprenticeship was dead ...

Brilliant magic crackled over his protective bubble, seeking a way in. Johan gritted his teeth, feeling cold anger burning through his body, then concentrated on precisely what he wanted to happen. A magician, waving his wand frantically as he threw curse after curse, exploded into a shower of rats, which scattered in all directions. Another vanished with a pop, so completely that air rushed in to fill the space where he had been. A third caught fire and screamed, held alive and aware as the flames burned his body to ash; Johan ignored the screams, hunting for the remaining magicians. The fourth was tossed into the air and thrown far from the city. A fifth magician, trying to run, collapsed as every bone in his body shattered into dust.

Johan took a step forward, then stopped. A sixth magician was cowering on the ground, shaking madly. Johan gestured, willing the wizard to float up into the air and spun him around; somehow, he was unsurprised to discover that he recognised him. Jamal might have shorn his hair, but there was no mistaking the face or eyes. Or maybe he had finally just mastered the art of seeing through glamours.

"Well," he said, bitterly. "Look who *I* found."

Jamal stared at him, his eyes shocked and uncomprehending. Johan stared back at his brother, cursing himself for a fool. He should have killed Jamal at the Waving Wand, even though the owner would have tried to curse him into next week. If he had, Elaine would still be alive. If he had ... he fought down the urge to scream. She'd given him everything and he'd turned her into a target. Jamal and his gang of thugs had killed her as surely as they'd killed the mundanes, back when the whole affair had begun. Had it really only been three weeks ago? It felt like years.

"You swore that you would not hurt anyone else," he snapped, glaring at his brother. "Why didn't you die?"

Jamal cackled, blood pouring from his mouth as he spoke. "You're not a mundane any longer," he said, between gasps. "You're a *freak*."

Johan felt the urge to just rip Jamal apart with his bare hands starting to rise up within him. Somehow, he managed to force it aside. Jamal was right; his oath had only protected mundanes, not magicians ... it might not even protect a Powerless. But Johan was no longer powerless. And he'd let his brother live.

"You'll kill our father," he protested, as the implications dawned on him. "You killed Elaine. That's *murder*."

Jamal laughed, bitterly. "Killing traitors is not murder," he said. "And you are still a *freak*."

Johan stared at him in shock. Killing Elaine wouldn't break Jamal's oath, but it would definitely break their father's oath to keep his son from engaging in criminal activity. Their father would die, leaving Jamal – who was still the Prime Heir – Head of House Conidian, his position unchallengeable. Had Jamal calculated that he could still come out ahead, Johan asked himself, or had he merely escaped justice one final time? It would be far harder to send the Head of a Great House to the headsman than even a firstborn son.

"Why?" He hissed. "Why did you do this?"

"Had to be done, you *freak*," Jamal said. "You ..."

Johan reached out and gripped his neck. "Tell me," he demanded. Jamal's eyes went blank, as if someone had cast a hypnotic curse on him. Johan *had*, he realised. His need to know the truth had led him to accidentally enslave Jamal's mind. "Why did you come after us? Why did you kill Elaine?"

"Father ordered me to kill you," Jamal said, his voice dazed. There was no possibility of deceit. "You're a danger to everyone now. For the good of the house, you have to die."

"No," Johan said. The very thought was staggering. "He couldn't ..."

But he knew his father too well. Everything he did was for the good of the family, everything from keeping Johan a prisoner to indulging Jamal, making sure that the former stayed out of sight and the latter was ready to step into his father's shoes at a moment's notice. There had been dangerously powerful magicians before, but none of them had ever offered the prospect of turning the entire world upside down, not like Johan.

"You talked to the Leveller scum," Jamal said. "What would happen if you allied with them?"

"What indeed?" Johan asked. "And you ... why did I let you live?"

He stared down at his brother, broken and humiliated, and felt cold rage driving him forward. The web of life shimmered in front of him, showing him precisely how Jamal drew on magic and shaped it into spells. No longer caring if he hurt Jamal – or himself – Johan reached out and snapped Jamal's connection to the web. His brother howled, the shock snapping him out of his near-trance; Johan let go of him and watched, dispassionately, as he fell to the ground, hands scrabbling at the stone.

"No power," he said, softly. "You're a *Powerless*."

Jamal pulled himself to his feet – somehow – and hurled himself at Johan, who stepped to one side. His elder brother had always been too dependent on magic for everything from protection to fighting; Johan had had to learn to be quick on his feet, just to avoid the first few hexes cast by his siblings.

It was easy to step aside and stick out a foot, tripping Jamal over and sending him falling back to the ground.

"No more respect," Johan sneered. "No more fear. No more prospect of taking over from father. Nothing, but a lifetime spent as a prisoner – if indeed you last long enough to return home. I dare say that there are thousands of people who want a little revenge on you now."

He kicked Jamal, then turned to look at where Elaine had fallen. She deserved a proper grave, but there was no time. If his father had been prepared to send Jamal out to kill him, risking his own death if the oath *bit*, he would have something else prepared in case Jamal failed. Johan took one last look, silently promising his dead friend bloody vengeance, then turned and started to walk towards the family house. Like so many other places in the Golden City, it was only a few minutes' walk away.

There were few people on the streets; most of them barely noticed him, even though his face was twisted by fury. His magic was somehow pushing their attention away, he realised numbly; he was glad of it as he walked up the street towards the family's house. The Inquisitors would certainly try to stop him if they knew what he had become and he didn't want to be stopped, or be forced to fight Dread and his compatriots. Or perhaps he did; despite their own oaths, the Inquisitors had allowed Jamal and his friends to go free. If Johan had killed five of them and broken Jamal, that left four …

Assuming that there were only ever ten of them, a voice whispered, at the back of his mind. *Do you really think that Jamal was the only one with such extreme views? Or that his friends were the only ones who looked to inherit nothing, but their names and their magic?*

The voice was right, he realised. There *would* be others, others who thought that their power gave them the right to prey on people who couldn't defend themselves. And they would no doubt cheer Elaine's death, because she had been a low-power magician. They were in for a shock, he told himself, as he kept walking forward. *Johan* would deal with them. *Johan* would judge them. And, if they were unworthy of their magic, *Johan* would strip it from them. They would no longer be able to use their magic to earn honours and awards they did not deserve.

He stopped in front of the door and paused, then pushed himself forward. The wards didn't rise up to try to stop him, although he was unsure if they simply thought he was allowed to enter or if he'd knocked them down without *meaning* to knock them down. He felt a pang of grief as he remembered talking to Elaine about how frustrating his powers were – he was never truly sure if he was doing something – and all the experiments they'd planned to try to test the limits. But now she was dead ...

No one will die like that again, he promised her, as he twisted the door knob. Unsurprisingly, it opened; he decided that the wards had merely been configured to allow him to return, if he saw fit. His father's attempts to force him back wouldn't have worked if he couldn't get back into the house. The thought made him snort as he stepped inside, then closed the door behind him. Once, he would have scurried back to his room as quickly as possible, hoping to escape the unwanted attentions of his father or siblings. Now ... now he could take his time and enjoy himself.

"Master Johan," a voice said, in surprise. "You're back!"

Johan turned to see May standing there. She had never been the worst of the maids, but she'd always looked down on him, even though he was her master's child. And why not, he knew, when she picked up her attitude from the way his family treated him. Jamal had had his fun with May, Johan knew, but nothing could ever have enticed the girl into *his* bed. What had the powerless Johan to offer her?

"Yes," he said. He concentrated; her clothes ripped as they were torn away from her body by an invisible force. Her breasts, the ones she had used to taunt him, sprang free, bobbling in front of his eyes. "I'm back."

May stared at him, then turned to flee. Johan stuck her feet to the floor, sending her flying forward to crash to the ground. Magic surged through her, blurring the boundary between her body and the floor. She let out a screech of pain that almost made him think better of what he had done, then cold rage pushed him onwards. Leaving her behind – naked, trapped and helpless – he walked onwards to his father's study. This time, the door was firmly locked. Johan closed his eyes and concentrated again, focusing on an image of the door crumbling to dust. When he opened them, the door was nothing more than falling sawdust. The wards had shattered at the merest touch of his magic.

Dimly, he remembered the children who'd died because of his mistake and wondered what would happen to the house. But it was hard to care.

His father looked up, his eyes widening in horror as Johan stepped into the room. One hand reached for the wand at his belt; Johan ignored it, even though he kept part of his mind focused on the protective bubble surrounding him. As far as he knew, he was no more invulnerable than Elaine or anyone else. A knife dipped in fast-acting poison would kill him as surely as any curse or spell.

"Elaine is dead," Johan said, flatly. "The Head Librarian, a person who was also a Privy Councillor, is dead. Your son killed her on your orders."

It wasn't entirely true – Johan had no idea who had fired the fatal curse, although he certainly couldn't think of any good reason not to blame Jamal – but as long as his father believed it ...

"No," his father said. Sweat was pouring down his brow as he fought to stave off the consequences of his oath. "I gave no such orders."

"But you ordered them to kill me, *father*," Johan said. His rage was gone, replaced by a cold dispassionate calm that was worse than anger. He could do *anything* now and feel absolutely nothing. "You broke the most important rule of the family. We do not turn on each other."

"There was nothing else I could do," his father said. "Where are they?"

"Jamal has lost his magic," Johan sneered. His father recoiled backwards, as if he'd been slapped. "The others ... they died. I killed them."

Once, the thought would have bothered him. He'd wracked himself with guilt when he'd blamed himself for the death of innocent children – and nearly losing Elaine to Hawthorne. Now ... it didn't bother him at all.

"You sent your eldest son to a fate I'm sure he considers

worse than death," Johan snapped, when his father didn't react. "You could have lost your ties to whatever other families helped produce that gang of thugs. And you broke your oath! Why? Was it really so important to have me back in your clutches?"

"I was so *scared* when I realised that you were powerless," his father said. "But I couldn't bear to lose you. I kept you close, fearing for your life and the family's safety. You rebelled against me because you didn't understand that it was all for your own good."

"I spent a week as a doll before someone could be bothered to free me," Johan said, with deadly menace. "And there were some things Jamal did that I refuse to mention, some jokes that were never funny to anyone with a decent mind. How was *that* for my own good?"

He allowed his voice to harden. "You allowed me to be tortured because you thought I deserved it for failing you," he added. "You felt that I was to blame for my own condition, even though I am your child; the gods know you spent enough money on paternity tests when I was found to be powerless. I think you hated me because you thought I proved that your blood was weak. You were *ashamed* of me."

His father was starting to gasp in pain. No matter his struggles, his oath was slowly killing him, drawing on his magic to rip the life out of his body. The magic Duncan Conidian had mastered and used as a tool to rise to the highest levels of society was turning on him, like a tame animal that had finally had enough of being beaten and kicked. It was strange, Johan realised, as he peered into the web of life; piece by piece, the magic was turning venomous. And yet it was still part of his father's mind.

"There is an option, father," Johan said, very calmly. "I can take your magic. Your oath will not kill you if there is no magic to drive it. But you would never be able to cast a spell again."

His father shuddered, convulsing. For a moment, Johan thought that he was too late for his father, then somehow he managed to open his eyes. It was hard to tell, Johan realised, just which way he would jump. To abandon his magic would mean abandoning his place in society, leaving Charity or Johan himself to take over House Conidian. But to keep it would mean certain death. The longer he struggled, the more pain he would be in before the oath finally overwhelmed him.

"You would live as I did," Johan added. "You would be powerless."

"No," his father gasped. "I won't ..."

"Yes, you will," Johan said. It was easy now to snip his father free of the web of life. The oath vanished at the same instant, along with his father's magic. "Killing you would be *so* easy, but you can serve as an object lesson instead."

He felt a keening echoing through the house as the wards started to react to his father's sudden absence. They were no longer linked to him – and they couldn't seek out the Prime Heir. He had no magic either. Johan smiled as his father stared at him in horror, then lifted a finger. His father floated up into the air and drifted over towards the door.

Years ago, Jamal had dared the younger Johan to sit in his father's chair. A security spell had frozen him the moment he'd sat down, then his father – alerted by the wards – had thrashed him soundly for entering his study without permission. Jamal, of course, had gotten away with it completely. Now ... Johan moved around the desk, cancelling the wards as he went, and sat down at his father's desk. It might as well be his now. The wards fizzled around him, then slipped back into neutral mode. They'd probably accept Charity, but no one else.

"Stand up," he ordered, once he had lowered his father to the ground. By now, the Inquisitors would probably have found Elaine's remains – and Jamal, if he hadn't crawled away to die somewhere. It wouldn't take a genius detective to tell where he'd gone. "I want you to take a message to the Inquisitors."

His father was moaning in shock. Johan snorted, disgusted; *this* was how his father dealt with only a tiny taste of Johan's life? No, he had never truly realised what being powerless *meant* in a magical household. How could he have? It was completely outside his experience.

Until now, Johan told himself.

He shaped his thoughts, casting a compulsion charm.

"This is what I want you to tell them," he said. Elaine *would* be avenged — and so would all the others who had been hurt and humiliated by magicians. "Listen carefully."

Chapter Forty-One

Her thoughts were ... shattered.

One of the protections must have worked, Elaine thought, through a wave of ... pain that wasn't really pain. Her memories seemed dull, almost as if they belonged to someone else; her thoughts keep breaking up and reforming in her mind. Something had happened to push her right to the brink of death, but what? Her thoughts slipped together, blurring into one ...

Elaine sat upright, glancing around urgently. The sun was rising; her memory shuddered, then spat out a reminder. She'd been with Johan, on the verge of taking him as her apprentice, when they'd been attacked. And then there had been a spell ... her mind shied away from what had happened afterwards. Instead, she looked around for Johan, but the only person she saw was Dread.

Her mouth felt dry, but somehow she managed to speak. "What ... what happened?"

"I was hoping you could answer that question," Dread said, as Elaine sat upright. At least the protections had managed to repair her clothes as well as her body. "You were shattered glass ... and now you're human again."

Elaine shuddered. If the protective spell hadn't worked – or hadn't worked perfectly – she would have been eternally trapped between life and death, unable to do anything other than to go mad. Suddenly, she thought she understood the Witch-King perfectly. He'd been so afraid of death that he'd bound himself to a decaying body that would never, no matter how much magic he used, be human again. And maybe one of his spells had also prevented him from taking refuge in madness.

She heard a sobbing sound and glanced over towards one of the trees. A young man who could almost pass for an older version of Johan was sitting there, crying. His hands were cuffed behind his back. Elaine frowned, then realised that it had to be Jamal, Johan's elder brother. The oaths he'd been forced to offer the Inquisitors hadn't been enough to keep him from returning to crime and terrorism.

"There is no magic in him," Dread said, quietly. He held out a hand, helping Elaine to stand up. Her legs felt oddly fragile, as if she'd broken them again. "And I haven't been able to get any sense out of him at all."

Elaine leaned on Dread and stared over at Jamal. He looked broken, as if everything had finally proven too much for him. It was clear that he had soiled himself. Elaine shuddered again at the vacant look on his face, then turned away. Jamal wasn't her problem, as unpleasant as he was; Johan was her problem. And where the hell *was* he?

"We don't know," Dread said. "Where do you think he might be?"

He thinks I'm dead, Elaine thought. She'd wondered if Johan would have tried something to restore her, but no magic could bring back the dead. Every time it was tried, the results were always bad. Speaking to the ghost of someone long gone was about the best magic could do. *Where would he go if he thought I was dead?*

"He's gone home," she said, in sudden horrified realisation. "He'll think that his father authorised this attack."

"He might well have done," Dread pointed out, as they started to walk towards the edge of the garden. "The oath would have forced him to ensure that Jamal did nothing *criminal*."

Elaine gritted her teeth. The oath might not have been violated, not if Jamal had been *ordered* to kill his brother. Johan had still been under his father's authority; if he believed that his son had transgressed too far, the Conidian would have been within his rights to order his son killed. It wouldn't have been criminal if Jamal had been acting under orders. She turned to look at the sobbing youth, then decided that it was unlikely that they would get any sense out of him. He could just wait there for the Inquisitors to pick him up.

"Send a warning to the Grand Sorceress," she said. There were more people in the street now, all of them glancing at her in surprise. Inquisitors were not known for helping people, at least unless they were truly important. Elaine silently bid goodbye to her anonymity; before now, hardly anyone outside the Privy Council and library staff had known who she was. The broadsheets would probably follow her with as much interest as they showed to the other senior aristocracy. "Tell her that we might be looking at another Kane."

Dread muttered a curse under his breath. "Lord Conidian has a great deal to answer for," he said. "I shall so advise the Grand Sorceress."

Elaine suspected that it was already too late. They should have moved to make Johan her apprentice the moment they realised just what he could do, rather than leave him hanging until the tree finally came crashing down. The Conidian had been too persistent in his efforts to regain control of his son for them to assume that he would stop, once Jamal had been released. Perhaps they should have bargained, gained Johan's freedom from his family in exchange for Jamal's release from jail. But it was too late now.

He thinks I'm dead, Elaine thought, numbly. Johan had shown himself willing to blame himself for incidents that were outside his control. What would he do now that he thought his only real friend was dead – and that his father was responsible for her death? He had power enough to do real damage to the city and the established order. *What is he thinking now*?

They turned the corner – and ran straight into a roadblock. A pair of Inquisitors were driving people out of the street, warning them to stay away from the houses. Elaine sensed that many of the occupants had raised their wards, sealing themselves inside their homes; she wondered if they had an inkling of what was going on or if they merely had a guilty conscience. The men and women who lived here, in the heart of the Golden City, had committed many crimes to reach their lofty stations. They had just been lucky enough to avoid being caught before it was too late, before they couldn't be arrested and charged.

Dread let go of her arm – she could stand straight now, thankfully – and walked over to his brethren. Elaine watched him go, then concentrated on extending her magic perceptions as much as possible. House Conidian was wrapped in its wards, keeping the outside world from breaking in ... and anyone inside from getting out. Elaine wondered briefly if Johan had finally learned to manipulate wards or if it was their typical setting, before deciding that it didn't matter. Johan had to be inside.

"You'll need to hear this," Dread called. He waved to her, beckoning her to follow him past the roadblock and up to a tent someone had erected just inside the secure zone. "It isn't good news."

The tent was surprisingly small on the inside, but there was still enough room for an Inquisitor and Duncan Conidian. One look told Elaine that something was very wrong with Johan's father; he talked like a stuttering parrot, rather than the man she recalled from Privy Council meetings. She met his eyes and shuddered when she saw absolutely no life in them at all. Johan, she realised, had used a compulsion charm to make him obey – and, as always when he tried to cast standard spells, the results had been unexpected. Duncan Conidian no longer had a mind of his own.

"You are to bring the magicians before him for justice," the Conidian said. "He will judge them all to see who prove worthy. Those who are not worthy will be stripped of their magic and forced to live as mundanes."

Elaine stared at him for a long moment, then started to cast diagnostic charms. The Conidian had no magic any longer, she discovered; his son had stripped him of it, perhaps in a genuine attempt to save his father's life. A magical oath couldn't bite if the oath-breaker had no magic, she deduced. It wasn't as if people had often lost their magic before Johan had appeared on the scene. And his mind had definitely been destroyed.

"So it would seem," Dread said, when she outlined her conclusions. "Did he do that on purpose?"

Elaine shrugged. There was no way to know.

"Which leads to a more important question," Dread said. "*Can* he be killed?"

Elaine swallowed. She *liked* Johan; she didn't like the thought of trying to kill him. But she understood what Dread meant; if Johan had gone mad with power, he had to be stopped before he could do significant damage to the city. If Kane had made the Empire shake on its foundations, what could Johan do?

"Yes," she said, bitterly. She had barely given the matter much thought, but there were several definite possibilities. Johan was strong, but his strength was matched by weaknesses. "Set up a killing ward; he won't sense it until he walks right into it. And then make sure it kills instantly."

She scowled. "He can protect himself as long as he focuses on protection," she added. "So you have to distract him if it comes down to a straight fight."

"He isn't invincible," one of the Inquisitors said. "He can be killed."

"He might also be our best hope with the ... *other* problem," Elaine pointed out, addressing Dread. Was the Witch-King behind everything that had happened? If so, killing Johan might be the only way to stop him. But if he wasn't, Johan might be their best weapon against the damned lich. "We need to try to talk him down."

"I think he's gone mad," Dread observed. "And who can really blame him?"

Elaine eyed him, surprised. That was unusually understanding for an Inquisitor. They were normally more concerned about punishing breaches of magical law than understanding why they had taken place. But then, she knew, Johan might merely be the first in a whole new breed of magician. The other Powerless might have had power all along, only to be killed by their families before it emerged. Johan might be needed in the future for more than just the Witch-King.

"But he is making demands," the other Inquisitor pointed out. "What happens when those demands are refused?"

And they would be, Elaine knew. Even the Grand Sorceress couldn't force magicians into a position where they might lose their powers − and the ones Johan would definitely want to face, the Heads of the Great Houses, would definitely refuse to enter House Conidian. No, it was far more likely that the Grand Sorceress would open some of the forbidden tomes from the Black Vault and unleash dark magic on the house, Johan might not be able to survive some of the darker spells, no matter how carefully he protected himself. There would be consequences if the spells were used – if the city's population saw them, magicians would start trying to duplicate their effects – but that might not matter.

It wouldn't, Elaine realised, bitterly. *Johan is threatening to shatter the very foundations of our society.*

She looked up at the other Inquisitor. "What about the rest of the family?"

"Still inside the house, we assume," the Inquisitor said. He seemed doubtful about answering Elaine's questions, but Dread nodded impatiently, convincing him to talk. "The only person to emerge was this ... puppet."

He indicated Duncan Conidian. Elaine shivered, remembering just how badly Johan had been treated by his siblings. In hindsight, it was a miracle that he hadn't gone completely mad with power the moment he'd realised he had it. Now ... with his friend presumed dead, he could torture his family in any way that pleased him. It was possible, she told herself, that the remainder of the family had been out of the house, but she knew it was unlikely. Most students wouldn't have climbed out of bed until the sun was higher in the sky.

She reached into her pocket and touched the vial of blood. She'd planned to destroy it, once they'd sworn their oaths; the handful of charms she'd cast on the blood had revealed nothing of any significance. But it did suggest something else ...

Elaine closed her eyes, thinking it through. Johan's magic was very good at dealing with direct threats. He could just imagine himself surrounded by an unbreakable barrier and he would be, at least until his concentration slipped. But there were more subtle forms of magic ... she considered the spells, one by one, then dismissed them. Johan deserved better from her than to be struck down by a cowardly spell. She needed to try to talk him down.

"I'm going to get in there," she said, shortly. "Someone has to talk sense into his head."

Dread gave her a long considering look. "You do realise that he may think that you're someone *pretending* to be you?"

The other Inquisitor had a different objection. "The house is heavily warded," he said. "We would need hours to break through the wards."

Elaine wasn't so sure. She might not be a powerful magician, but she had knowledge and precision – more of the former than any normal ward-maker or curse-breaker. Every ward had weaknesses, particularly the ones that had to allow multiple people to step through them without impediment. And she had a vial of Johan's blood.

And she had his father. There were options. She just had to pluck up the nerve to use them.

"I think I can get in," she said, willing Dread to believe her. "But I don't know if I can take anyone else with me!"

Dread stepped away from her, pulling a tiny bracelet out of his pocket and putting it on. It was so unlike him to wear any form of jewellery that Elaine stared at it in surprise, but it still took her a moment to realise that a crystal ball was hidden amidst the gold. Dread started to mutter into it, too low for her to hear; his brother gave Elaine a long considering look, then stepped back and strode out of the tent.

"Very well," Dread said, finally. He returned the bracelet to his pocket, then gave her a smile that was barely noticeable. "You'll have your chance. But you won't have long."

Elaine nodded. Light Spinner was probably looking at the forbidden tomes right now, trying to find something that would allow her to end the crisis with a minimum of bloodshed – or anything so revealing that sorcerers would start work on trying to duplicate it. Elaine could have found her something, but she knew that she had to get to Johan first. The gods alone knew how much time she would be given before Light Spinner attacked.

"I'll need him," she said, indicating Duncan Conidian. "Can you help me get him outside."

The wards felt ... strange, she realised, as they walked up to stand in front of the door. They crawled with magic, linked to aversion charms, jinxes and finally curses to deal with anyone persistent enough to brush aside the other effects, but there was something about them that was almost *alive*. She scowled as she reached out with her magic, wondering if the Conidian had broken the laws on creating magical artefacts that could actually *think*; there were too many horror stories about such devices for any breach of those laws to be taken lightly.

Or maybe they're just confused, she thought, as she probed them gently. *Their master isn't dead, but he can no longer operate them; his Prime Heir isn't any better. Who would be their master if both of them no longer have magic?*

There was no way to know. Instead, she lifted her wand and cast the first spell, careful to keep one hand on Duncan Conidian at all times. He shuffled after her as she undid the first piece of the wards, then stepped through to challenge the second piece. Magic crackled around her as she pushed onwards; a single mistake, no matter how innocent, would see her revealed as an unwanted intruder. Sweat trickled down her back; she cast the next set of spells, closing her eyes to focus on the magic running all around her. The final ward rose up in front of her and she braced herself, then pushed Duncan Conidian forward. As she had hoped, the wards recognised their master's blood and allowed them both to reach the door.

Inside, the magical energy died away to almost nothing. Elaine hadn't been in many magical households, but she had expected more than *this*. She was almost disappointed; there should have been magic everywhere, blended into the stone, responsive only to the members of the family. But then, the Conidian Family was new to the city. It took years for a family home to become *theirs*. Carefully, she positioned Duncan Conidian somewhere where she hoped he would be safe – or at least stay out of the way – then started to advance down the corridor.

Elaine had barely gone any distance when she stumbled over the maid. She was naked, her feet clearly stuck to the floor; Elaine tapped her lips hastily when the maid stared at her, then knelt down beside her and tried to break the spell. Unsurprisingly, it didn't work. Her body had melded itself to the floor. It would require very precise magic to free her. If Johan died, Elaine realised grimly, the maid might be stuck there for the rest of her life. Most magic didn't last that long without renewal; Johan, on the other hand, had ensured that more than magic held the maid prisoner.

"I'll be back as soon as I can," she muttered. She wasn't sure she dared try to use his blood as a guide when the wards might react – harshly – to such magic. "Do you know where he is?"

The maid pointed down the corridor towards a heavy wooden door. It was ajar, as if he were inviting her in ... or, more likely, that he simply hadn't bothered to close it. Elaine could hear a low whimpering sound from inside, as if someone had been broken so completely they couldn't even cry. A cold shudder ran through her body, but she forced herself to stand upright.

"Thank you," she said.

Wand in hand, she advanced slowly towards the door.

Chapter Forty-Two

Mariah Conidian was a society beauty as well as a powerful magician. Everyone said so. She moved through the world with a smile on her face and time for everyone, apart from her children. Even Jamal, Johan knew, had had very little attention from their mother. The best that could be said of her was that she had never tormented Johan or sought to make him something he wasn't. But then, she had spent most of her time just being beautiful.

Johan stared at her, feeling numb. His mother had used the most powerful cosmetic magic in the world to make herself almost inhumanly beautiful. There wasn't a single mark on her face, nor was there anything to show that she had given birth to seven children. She could easily have passed for Charity's sister rather than her mother, if Charity had spent half as much effort trying to make herself look pretty. It struck Johan, as he studied his mother, that Charity had been just as desperate to escape as Johan himself.

Of course she would, he thought. *She knew what life awaited her if she stayed.*

"You never did anything," he hissed, pushing the thought aside. "Why didn't you say a word to your husband about the way he treated me?"

His mother gave him a vapid smile that sent a shiver running down his spine. "Because I didn't care," she said. Clearly, willing her to tell the truth had its own dangers. "I didn't care about *any* of you. All I wanted was to be a society queen. That was the bargain I made with your father, when we were married."

Johan stared at her. He'd never given serious thought to having children – his life before he'd discovered his powers had suggested that he would never have the chance – but surely he would have cared more for them than *that*! How could a woman who had spent nine months carrying a child to term just abandon him to the tender mercies of his siblings? And it hadn't just been the lone Powerless either. Even Jamal had been abandoned by his mother.

"A worthless bargain," Johan hissed.

His mother, for a moment, looked surprisingly serious. "Everyone has different ambitions in life," she said. "Your father wishes to be a powerful sorcerer, a man who merely has to snap his fingers and everyone jumps to obey. Just because those ambitions are different doesn't make them *wrong*."

Johan stared at her in disbelief. "You abandoned your children because you wanted to be *popular*?"

"Power comes in many forms," his mother said, sternly. "Don't you, of all people, know that?"

"You'll get your wish," Johan said, feeling cold rage bubbling up within him. "You will be popular, all right, and even *pretty*."

His mother's form hardened, becoming stone. Johan examined the statue thoughtfully for a long moment, shaking his head wearily. His mother could be placed at the heart of the city, where everyone would admire her features, eternally preserved in stone. He had no idea if she was still aware, despite being stone, but if she were he knew she would appreciate what he'd done. There would be people coming from all over the world to see her.

The door opened. Johan turned in surprise; he'd thought he'd dealt with the rest of his siblings already. Charity hadn't been too bad – he was inclined to release her, once the world had allowed him to judge the magicians – but the others would definitely be punished. And, once their punishments were over, they would have to earn back their powers. If they had picked on him as a child, they couldn't be trusted with magic.

He stared as Elaine stepped into the room, wand clasped in her hand. For a moment, he froze in absolute disbelief; Elaine was dead, he'd seen her shatter into a million pieces. It had seemed utterly beyond even his powers to try to restore her; he'd read enough horror stories to know that he shouldn't try to bring the dead back to life. She had to be an illusion, cast by a sorcerer who wanted to kill him. After what he'd done to his father, there would be no shortage of those.

"Johan," Elaine said. The voice sounded right, he had to admit, but it *would*. There would be glamours built into the illusion to fool him into accepting it, despite any small discrepancies. "You have to stop this."

***

Elaine hadn't known what to expect when she entered the small office. Johan might be foaming at the mouth or coldly, calculatingly, plotting his takeover of the world. There was precedent for both of them, she knew; a magician whose magic was suddenly boosted was at grave risk of going mad. And she knew that Johan might well go the same way, even though he hadn't even *been* a magician until recently.

But instead, he just looked sad. Sad, broken and determined.

"You're not Elaine," he snarled, glaring at her. If looks could kill – which was quite possible in his case – she would have been incinerated on the spot. "Whoever you are, you are not my friend."

"Your brother's spell didn't kill me," Elaine said, keeping her voice level with an effort. He'd seen her shatter. He had to have assumed that she was dead. The gods knew it had taken hours before she'd even regained the slightest ability to *think*. "Do you remember the book of protective wards I was looking at? One of them saved my life."

"Which is precisely what I want to hear," Johan sneered. "Who *are* you?"

"Elaine," Elaine said. Her temper couldn't be allowed to flare, not now. She had to remain calm. "Do you remember the hot water I gave you?"

Johan nodded, surprise clearly visible on his face. He'd insisted on washing in his room, so Elaine had used magic to heat the water for him. But he'd forgotten to put in cool water before dipping his toe into the tub, scalding himself. Who would have known about that, but Johan himself – and Elaine? She had certainly never mentioned it to anyone else.

"You're plucking things out of my mind," Johan said. "I ... you're *dead*."

415

***

Johan couldn't help feeling a quiet nagging doubt. He didn't know just how far a glamour, combined with deceptive spells, could go; could they really pull thoughts out of his head? Or were they simply using magic to tell him something he wanted to hear? It wouldn't be hard to think of memories Elaine and he shared that no one else would ... he stared at the form of his friend, feeling his heart harden in cold determination. The person who was wearing his friend's form would *pay*.

"And you have stripped both your brother and father of their magic," Elaine – or the person who was pretending to be Elaine – said. She turned to look at the statue of Johan's mother – the statue that *was* Johan's magic. "How many more are you going to hurt before you realise that you've gone off the right path?"

"And who are you," Johan demanded, "to tell me which is the *right* path?"

"I'm your friend," Elaine said. "Haven't you done enough?"

"It isn't enough," Johan said. "The world is full of magicians who abuse their powers, who hurt and humiliate and kill those they deem beneath them. I was created to stop them."

Elaine gave him a long considering look. "Is that what you really believe?"

"Why else," Johan demanded, "would I even exist?"

"There may be a greater purpose for you," Elaine pointed out. "Or you may be being misled by a voice in the back of your head."

Johan felt a flare of anger. He couldn't be angry at Elaine, no matter what she said, but the person wearing her form ... he'd kill him. But he also wanted to win the argument.

"If I hadn't been there to testify against Jamal," he said, coldly, "he would have gone free."

"Perhaps," Elaine said.

"There's no doubt about it," Johan snapped. "Do you think that the testimony of a group of *mundanes* would have stood up against magicians? That was why my father worked so desperately to bring me back under his control! I could be forced to recant my testimony and Jamal would go *free*! And he *did* go free."

"He swore an oath," Elaine said, quietly.

"Which he didn't actually break," Johan thundered. He stood up, leaning on the table like his father had done when he'd been yelling at his children. "And he was able to use my father's oath to kill him!"

The thought was staggering. If Jamal hadn't lost his own powers, he would have taken over House Conidian despite being in disgrace. Who would put the head of a Great House in the dock? Somehow, he doubted that Lady Light Spinner would have taken the risk. Jamal would not only have control over the family's money, he would also have controlled the family's patronage network. There could have been a very real risk of civil war.

"My brother will not be able to threaten the stability of the city again," he finished. "And nor will anyone else!"

"Apart from you, it seems," Elaine said, waspishly. "Or don't you realise just how much trouble you've already caused?"

"Now they care," Johan observed. "Where was their *concern* when I was being treated like an object?"

He stood up, lifting his hand. "You are not Elaine," he snapped. "I saw Elaine *die*. And I will make you *pay* for impersonating her."

***

Elaine almost panicked as Johan raised his hand. Despite Dread's warning, it had honestly not seemed possible to her that Johan might not think that she was the *real* Elaine, even though hindsight suggested that it was at least a possibility. Part of her wanted to run, but she knew it would be futile; unlike most normal magicians, Johan didn't seem to need line-of-sight to cast antipersonnel spells. Instead, she braced herself and jabbed her hand into her pocket, breaking the vial of Johan's blood. The glass cut her hand – she hissed in pain – allowing their blood to mingle.

"I take you as my apprentice," she said, out loud. The magic – subtle magic, but none the less powerful – crackled around her, forming the mental link. Johan had already given his consent when he had accepted her offer; he'd never thought to rescind it. "I choose to link my mind and magic to yours ..."

She closed her eyes, suddenly very aware of his presence. His magic didn't seem to react at all to the oath, but his soul did; she felt her mind extend until it was touching the very edge of his mind. And, beyond, she could see the web of life he'd tried – so inadequately – to describe to her. It was strange and beautiful ... and *magic*. For the first time in her life, despite becoming a Bookworm, she really understood what magic truly was.

We manipulate it when we cast spells, she thought, *but Johan is directly linked to the magic ...*

But there was no time to admire it, not now. Their memories clashed together, flashing through their minds. Johan would see everything, she knew, from her first memories of the orphanage to the terrible moment when she'd turned to glass and shattered ... and slowly pulled herself back together. A stab of guilt passed through her mind as Johan saw it, their thoughts so close that his guilt was hers; he'd never even *tried* to restore her. But how could he have known that she would have survived?

Not your fault, she thought, knowing that he would pick up her message – and the truth behind it. *Stop blaming yourself for problems that are not your fault.*

Her memories grew stronger, a blur that only seemed to reveal flickering images that made up the essence of *her*. Her first day at the Peerless School; her graduation, with few honours; the pain and shock of discovering that she was a Bookworm. Millicent's stunned face as she realised that Elaine was capable of much more than she thought, Bee leaning over her the first night they'd made love ... she couldn't help smiling at the shockwave of embarrassment and lust from Johan as he saw *those* memories. And the Witch-King's looming presence as she threw the Blight's wild magic at Kane, hoping to bring him down.

"I am who I am," she said, out loud. Johan could no longer dispute it. Nothing could have created so complex an illusion. "Do you see me now?"

Johan's memories opened up in front of her. His first set of magic tests, blurring into dozens of others; his father's eagerness to prove his son's magic turning to disappointment and shame that his son was so weak. Endless torments and humiliations, each one a reminder that he couldn't protect himself from his own siblings, let alone outsiders. An isolated existence, broken only by the few times he'd managed to sneak outside and explore his hometown – and then the Golden City, when his family had *still* kept him prisoner. And, always, the threat of being murdered by his own family, just to conceal the fact that they had birthed a Powerless.

He isn't touched by the Witch-King, she thought, feeling a wave of relief that almost stunned her. Johan might have been touched by madness, grief and guilt, but he wasn't under the Witch-King's control. And that opened up all sorts of new options. If, of course, she could talk him out of imposing his rule on the city.

"I see you," Johan said. She felt another stab of guilt, mingled with a set of thoughts of just what he had intended to do to the person he thought was impersonating his friend. "You're alive!"

Her eyes snapped open as she felt him wrap his arms around her and hug her, tightly. "You're alive!"

"Not if you crush me," Elaine said, unsure if she actually spoke or thought the words. From what she'd read in books, the mind-merge would eventually recede, leaving them with a link that would be unbreakable, but nowhere near as intimate. All of a sudden, it was easy to see why so many apprenticeships became sexual relationships. "Or if you kill me."

"I wouldn't have killed you," Johan protested. "I thought that you were ... someone pretending to be you."

She knew that he was telling the truth, although he would not have hesitated to kill the person he thought was impersonating his friend. His only real friend, she knew now. Johan's life had been so limited that he'd clung to Elaine as soon as she'd shown him kindness, kindness she hadn't had to show. And she cared deeply about him, more than she'd ever realised. He reminded her far too much of herself.

"It's all right," she said, wrapping her arms around him. "But you have to stop this madness."

Johan looked at her, a trace of betrayal in his eyes – and more, much more, in his thoughts.

"You've seen it too," he said. "You *know* just how badly magicians treat mundanes. Surely I shouldn't let them get away with it."

Elaine hesitated. The hell of it was that she didn't disagree, not completely. And she knew that he would see that doubt in her mind. If there was a way to strip magicians of their power, forcing them to live a normal life, the threat of using it might keep them in line. But it could also become the weapon of a tyrant, forcing magicians to serve him ...

"I think we have a more important problem right now," she said, instead. "You caused a panic – and this house is likely to be destroyed. If I could get through the wards, the Inquisitors could also break through – and you would be killed. I won't let that happen."

Johan stared at her, bleakly. "So ... what do we do?"

"You come with me," Elaine said. "We leave the Golden City for good."

The thought was terrifying. She would have to sever her ties to the Great Library – and, even if she returned, it would never be the same. And she hated the thought of going outside the Golden City for longer than a few days, even though it was the only way to keep Johan alive. And if she failed to talk Light Spinner into supporting her, their life expectancy wouldn't be very long at all.

Risky, she knew. There was the knowledge in her head – and the sheer power Johan possessed, both valuable prizes for anyone with the nerve to try to take them. But she could see no alternative. Now that they were bonded, there was a good chance that Johan's death would take her with him. And she couldn't knowingly lead him to his death.

But the Witch-King was still out there ... and, now that she had seen the web of life, she suspected she knew where to start looking for him. If they could find and destroy him, they could return home as heroes ... or, at the very least, build lives that would remain stable.

"Come with me," she said. She cast a spell that incinerated

much of the study. The effort tired her, but it had to be done. "We'll let everyone think that you died here."

Johan followed her without arguing, although she could sense the questions drifting through his mind. She cast an illusion over him, rendering his body invisible, then sent a silent command to him to release the maid. Johan obeyed, undoing his spell as soon as Elaine waved her wand. The maid climbed to her feet and fled towards the servants quarters. Elaine watched her go, feeling a strange mixture of emotions. Half of them were from Johan.

"Dread can help us smuggle you away," she started, then stopped. Dread *wouldn't*; his oaths would force him to take Johan into custody or simply to kill him outright. Given the danger, Elaine suspected the latter. "No, concentrate on remaining completely invisible and just keep following me. And *don't* touch anyone."

"I won't," Johan promised. "And thank you."

"We shall see," Elaine said. "We shall see."

Chapter Forty-Three

"Perhaps you would care to explain to me," Light Spinner said, "precisely why you decided to hide Johan from the Inquisitors and then bring him to *my palace*?"

Elaine winced at the Grand Sorceress's tone. Light Spinner had good reason to be angry, not least because of the Privy Council's divisions and increasingly strident attempts to insist that Johan be killed or brought under firm control. At least, now that he was officially dead, such demands were being abandoned.

But several Family Heads are dead, killed by their oaths, she thought. *The chaos has only just begun.*

"Because he represents a weapon we can use against the Witch-King," she said. She'd filled Johan in on the missing part of her story during their walk to the palace, although he had picked up most of it from her mind. At least those memories weren't embarrassing. "And because he doesn't deserve to die."

"An interesting argument," Light Spinner observed, caustically. "Stripping someone of their magic isn't a crime?"

"It isn't actually against the law," Elaine pointed out. It hadn't been thought to be even theoretically possible, she knew. There were ways to prevent someone from using their magic, but not to actually take it from them. "And besides, he was well and truly provoked."

Light Spinner's eyes seemed to glare at her for a long moment, then she settled back in her chair. "Maybe," she said, finally. "But you know that most of the world won't see it that way."

Elaine nodded. "Hence my decision to convince everyone that he was dead," she said. "And that will ensure that the secret remains a secret."

"Let us hope so," Light Spinner said. "And what do you

intend to do with your secret apprentice?"

"Go hunting for the Witch-King," Elaine said, simply.

Light Spinner snorted. "*You* will leave the city for months – or years – searching for him?"

"Yes," Elaine said, although she had to admit that Light Spinner was right to have doubts. Leaving the city would hurt, even if they went to another city – and she knew better than to think that it would be that easy. They'd have to go into territory damaged by the wars and still largely uninhabited, hundreds of years later. "Whoever goes has to have the knowledge I have and the power Johan has."

"If you're sure," Light Spinner said. "But there is the question of ensuring that Johan does not go on another rampage."

Her brown eyes seemed to tighten for a long moment. "Can you stop him through the apprenticeship bond?"

"I believe so," Elaine said, not entirely truthfully. She could have, if it was a normal bond, but it wasn't settling in properly. Or maybe it was just taking its time. "But I think he's learned his lesson."

"I wish that were true of the rest of his family," Light Spinner said. "House Conidian will be moribund until Charity reaches her majority ... and by then the patronage network Duncan ruled may have fragmented."

Elaine grimaced. It had been simple enough to convince Johan to undo most of the spells he'd cast on his family – although she had no idea why he had transformed his younger sisters into dolls – and it had helped create the illusion that Johan was dead, but it would be a long time before House Conidian recovered. There was at least one seat on the Privy Council up for grabs – two, if her resignation from the Great Library was accepted – and the power balance would shift. The deaths of other family heads would only make matters worse.

Perhaps she should stay and help, she thought. But there was little she could do. Politics was hardly her forte. Either Light Spinner held it together or a new Grand Sorcerer unseated her and took her place.

And the Levellers were still out there, waiting for their chance to challenge the established order.

"And I wonder just who benefited from all of this," Light Spinner mused. "Duncan overplayed his hand quite badly, badly enough to make me wonder if someone else was involved. But who?"

Elaine shrugged. "I do not know," she admitted. "But I'm sure you will deal with them."

"Let us hope so," Light Spinner said. She rose to her feet, signalling the end of the interview. "Go back to your library, pack your stuff and go. And may the gods go with you."

Elaine bowed her head, then turned and left the room, leaving Light Spinner alone.

***

"She thinks I'm dead," Johan said.

"I'm afraid so," Elaine said, as she checked his packing. This time, there would be two suitcases of clothes each. They would travel on the Iron Dragons to the closest settlement to the remnants of the Necromantic Wars, then move from there. "You can't go talk to her."

Johan nodded. Somehow, the thought of losing Jayne wasn't so painful now. He wasn't sure if it was something he had picked up from Elaine's mind or a side-effect of growing up, but he knew that they'd had very little, if they'd had anything at all. Jayne would go on to apprentice herself to a Potions Master – Elaine had promised that one of her friends would see to it – and she would become a great Potions Mistress herself. Or so Johan hoped.

It didn't really matter, he told himself. He would never see her again.

He stared down at his hands, wonderingly. Jamal was powerless, his father was a broken man and his other siblings had been shocked into decent behaviour for the first time in their lives. Well, apart from Charity, he reluctantly concluded. *She* had deserved better, at the last. He'd exacted revenge for years of mistreatment, yet ... there was a part of him that knew that it had brought him nothing. All he had was the certain knowledge that if the city's population knew him to be alive, they would all turn on him.

"I know," he muttered. "And I can't speak to Charity either."

"No," Elaine said. "Let her assume the title without knowing that she isn't the first in line. It will make it much easier for her in the long run."

"Yeah," Johan muttered.

It was strange facing Elaine ... and seeing himself from her point of view. And seeing her memories; most of them had faded, but a number of the most vivid had remained in his mind. She'd seen the Witch-King's influence reaching out over the land, she'd seen death staring her in the face, even performed a forbidden rite to bring back the souls of the dead ... but those hadn't been her most vivid memories. But he tried to avoid thinking about the ones that truly stood out. It was not *right* for him to dwell on them.

"Your packing seems good," Elaine said. There were fewer books this time; they were leaving for months, perhaps permanently. They couldn't take books from the library this time. "We leave tomorrow, early in the morning."

Johan nodded, wondering why he couldn't summon up the enthusiasm for the ride on the Iron Dragons. He should have been excited ...

"You won," Elaine said, quietly. She sat down next to him and put an arm around his shoulders. "You escaped your family, you accomplished your goal ... and now you don't know what to do next."

"Thank you," Johan said. She was right. "What did *you* do?"

"I walked straight into the Great Library," Elaine admitted. "You ... may find it a little harder. But I will be there for you."

"Thank you," Johan said, again. "You're the only one who ever was."

***

In his study, behind a set of the most powerful blood wards known to magicians, Vlad Deferens raised a glass in silent salute. It had all worked out better than he had dared hope. The freakish magician was dead, House Conidian was in tatters and several other Great Houses were tottering as they came to terms with the loss of their Heads. And Lady Light Spinner's weaknesses had been exposed for all to see. The only wild card had been the Levellers, but even *they* had been no real problem.

He smirked to himself as he took a sip of his wine. It was astonishing just how easy it had been to create an aura of fear, one that had affected even those born with the power to warp reality at will. The sight of several magicians stripped of their powers had helped, of course; it would have been kinder to threaten to castrate them. For a magician, there could be no worse threat than that of losing their powers. Even ancient magicians, doddering on their last legs, clung to their magic.

The pieces were in place. Soon, very soon, he would move. And then the world would be his.

He picked up the dark-covered book and opened it to a random page. There was power within the covers, spells long lost and forgotten ... just waiting for him to use them. The weak would call some of them *dark*, perhaps even *evil*, but Deferens knew better. All that mattered was taking power and *wielding* it. Light Spinner had taken power, even he had to concede, yet she knew nothing about its usage.

Looking into the mirror, he took a moment to smooth out his long moustache.

And he never even saw the Witch-King looking back.

The End

The Series Will Continue In:
The Best Laid Plans
Coming Soon!

Elsewhen Press

delivering outstanding new talents in speculative fiction

Visit the Elsewhen Press website at elsewhen.press for the latest information on all of our titles, authors and events; to read our blog; find out where to buy our books and ebooks; or to place an order.

Sign up for the Elsewhen Press InFlight Newsletter at elsewhen.press/newsletter

Elsewhen Press
an independent publisher specialising in Speculative Fiction

Bookworm
Christopher G. Nuttall

Book I of the Bookworm series

Elaine is an orphan girl who has grown up in a world where magical ability brings power. Her limited talent was enough to ensure a magical training but she's very inexperienced and was lucky to get a position working in the Great Library. Now, the Grand Sorcerer – the most powerful magician of them all – is dying, although initially that makes little difference to Elaine; she certainly doesn't have the power to compete for higher status in the Golden City. But all that changes when she triggers a magical trap and ends up with all the knowledge from the Great Library – including forbidden magic that no one is supposed to know – stuffed inside her head. This unwanted gift doesn't give her greater power, but it does give her a better understanding of magic, allowing her to accomplish far more than ever before.

It's also terribly dangerous. If the senior wizards find out what has happened to her, they will almost certainly have her killed. The knowledge locked away in the Great Library was meant to remain permanently sealed and letting it out could mean a repeat of the catastrophic Necromantic Wars of five hundred years earlier. Elaine is forced to struggle with the terrors and temptations represented by her newfound knowledge, all the while trying to stay out of sight of those she fears, embodied by the sinister Inquisitor Dread.

But a darkly powerful figure has been drawing up a plan to take the power of the Grand Sorcerer for himself; and Elaine, unknowingly, is vital to his scheme. Unless she can unlock the mysteries behind her new knowledge, divine the unfolding plan, and discover the truth about her own origins, there is no hope for those she loves, the Golden City or her entire world.

ISBN: 9781908168320 (epub, kindle)
ISBN: 9781908168221 (368pp, paperback)

For more information visit bit.ly/Bookworm-Nuttall

Elsewhen Press
an independent publisher specialising in Speculative Fiction
Also by Christopher G. Nuttall

THE ROYAL SORCERESS
Book I of the Royal Sorceress series

It's 1830, in an alternate Britain where the 'scientific' principles of magic were discovered sixty years previously, allowing the British to win the American War of Independence. Although Britain is now supreme among the Great Powers, the gulf between rich and poor in the Empire has widened and unrest is growing every day. Master Thomas, the King's Royal Sorcerer, is ageing and must find a successor to lead the Royal Sorcerers Corps. Most magicians can possess only one of the panoply of known magical powers, but Thomas needs to find a new Master of all the powers. There is only one candidate, one person who has displayed such a talent from an early age, but has been neither trained nor officially acknowledged. A perfect candidate to be Master Thomas' apprentice in all ways but one: the Royal College of Sorcerers has never admitted a girl before.

But even before Lady Gwendolyn Crichton can begin her training, London is plunged into chaos by a campaign of terrorist attacks co-ordinated by Jack, a powerful and rebellious magician.

ISBN: 9781908168184 (epub, kindle)
ISBN: 9781908168085 (400pp, paperback)
For more information visit bit.ly/TheRoyalSorceress

THE GREAT GAME
Book II of the Royal Sorceress series

After the uprising in London, Lady Gwendolyn Crichton is settling into her new position as Royal Sorceress and fighting the prejudice against her gender and age that seeks to prevent her from fulfilling her responsibilities. But when a senior magician is murdered in a locked room and Gwen is charged with finding the culprit, her inquiries lead her into a web of intrigue that combines international politics, widespread aristocratic blackmail, gambling dens and personal vendettas... and some of her discoveries hit dangerously close to home.

Continuing on from the end of *The Royal Sorceress*, *The Great Game* follows Gwen's unfolding story as she assumes the role formerly held by Master Thomas. A satisfying blend of whodunit and magical fantasy, it is set against a backdrop of international political unrest in a believable yet simultaneously fantastic alternate history.

ISBN: 9781908168375 (epub, kindle)
ISBN: 9781908168276 (400pp, paperback)
For more information visit bit.ly/TheGreatGame

Christopher G. Nuttall

Elsewhen Press

an independent publisher specialising in Speculative Fiction
Also by Christopher G. Nuttall

A Life Less Ordinary

There is magic in the world, hiding in plain sight. If you search for it, you will find it, or it will find you. Welcome to the magical world.

Having lived all her life in Edinburgh, the last thing 25-year old Dizzy expected was to see a man with a real (if tiny) dragon on his shoulder. Following him, she discovered that she had stumbled from her mundane world into a parallel magical world, an alternate reality where dragons flew through the sky and the Great Powers watched over the world. Convinced that she had nothing to lose, she became apprenticed to the man with the dragon. He turned out to be one of the most powerful magicians in all of reality.

But powerful dark forces had their eye on this young and inexperienced magician, intending to use her for the ultimate act of evil – the apocalyptic destruction of all reality. If Dizzy does not realise what is happening to her and the worlds around her, she won't be able to stop their plan. A plan that will ravage both the magical and mundane worlds, consuming everything and everyone in fire.

ISBN: 9781908168337 (epub, kindle)
ISBN: 9781908168238 (336pp, paperback)
For more information visit bit.ly/ALLO-Nuttall

THE FIRST BOOK IN THE
INVERSE SHADOWS UNIVERSE

SUFFICIENTLY ADVANCED TECHNOLOGY

For the post-singularity Confederation, manipulating the quantum foam – the ability to alter the base code of the universe itself and achieve transcendence – is the holy grail of science. But it seems an impossible dream until their scouts encounter Darius, a lost colony world whose inhabitants have apparently discarded the technology that brought them to the planet in order to adopt a virtually feudal culture. On Darius, the ruling elite exhibits abilities that defy the accepted laws of physics. They can manipulate the quantum foam!

Desperate to understand what is happening on Darius, the Confederation dispatches a stealth team to infiltrate the planet's society and discover the truth behind their strange abilities. But they will soon realise that the people on Darius are not all the simple folk that they seem – and they are sitting on a secret that threatens the entire universe ...

ISBN: 9781908168344 (epub, kindle)
ISBN: 9781908168245 (336pp, paperback)
Visit bit.ly/SAT-Nuttall

About the Author

Christopher G. Nuttall has been planning sci-fi books since he learned to read. Born and raised in Edinburgh, Chris created an alternate history website and eventually graduated to writing full-sized novels. Studying history independently allowed him to develop worlds that hung together and provided a base for storytelling. After graduating from university, Chris started writing full-time. As an indie author he has self-published a number of novels, but this is his fifth fantasy to be published by Elsewhen Press. Following on from the success of the bestselling *Bookworm*, Elaine's story continues in *Bookworm II: The Very Ugly Duckling*. Chris is currently living in Borneo with his wife, muse, and critic Aisha.